Free yourself from pain,

free yourself from fear,

free yourself from death,

free yourself from evil,

free yourself from all your human
limitations and become as a god.

All you have to do is accept without
questioning the supreme wisdom of—

THE KARMA MACHINE
THE KARMA MACHINE
THE KARMA MACHINE
THE KARMA MACHINE
THE KARMA MACHINE
(repeat for all eternity)

THE KARMA MACHINE

BY MICHAEL DAVIDSON

POPULAR LIBRARY · TORONTO

POPULAR LIBRARY EDITION
April, 1977

Copyright © 1975 by Michael Davidson

ISBN: 0-445-03202-2

To my parents, my wife, and J. L.
(who provoked me into writing this book).

Printed in Canada

CHAPTER I

A Newly-Aware

Yeshua stirred.

"Glide in, my son, glide in," Amitabha whispered as he hovered over Yeshua's air bed. With a wave of his hand, he dismissed the half-dozen white-robed technicians who had been assisting him. He wanted this first moment with Yeshua, alone.

"Aware yourself, Yeshua, but gently, gently. Do not strain to be. Your 'to be' is a constitutional right with us, you know," he smiled, more to himself than to Yeshua.

A naked male frame, a bit under two meters long, well-proportioned, though somewhat lacking in muscle tone, the as yet unpurposed timeship of Yeshua Nabi, began to struggle to sit upright on his air bed.

Amitabha maneuvered the pressure dials so that the rose-colored columns of air supporting Yeshua eased him into a sitting position. He brought the temperature up ten more degrees as well. The room temperature was almost normal.

Yeshua's eyes were now wide open. Wide open! Like a hand in a glove, terror informed the consciousness now probing hungrily into every cranny of his brain!

"Am I?" he was at last able to gasp. These were Yeshua's first words as a Newly-Aware.

"You are, my son!"

Yeshua, now completely conscious, devoured the countenance of Amitabha.

5

"Friendly?" he asked, after several moments of tremulous contemplation.

"Friendly."

And without question, Amitabha, with just a speck of gray in his beard and a trace of extra flesh on his bones, smiling quietly down at him, was comfortable to behold. Not unimposing, however. Calm, like a great cool stone, lay just behind his sharp blue eyes.

"Am *I*?"

It was not a strange question to Amitabha. "It is indeed you, my son. You are to be called Yeshua. The significance of this will become clear to you when we purpose you a year from this day. Actually, you are a very important person to us, Yeshua."

"Purpose me? Important person?"

"You will learn all, my son. But not by gulps. Aware yourself gently."

"Who are you?"

"I am your era-guardian, Amitabha. Your father and teacher, Yeshua. Fear nothing at all."

"Where am I?"

"You are in Sukhavati-Entopia. A strange name, but a good place."

"What has happened to me? Where have I come from? Why is my mind so blank?"

"You have been on psychic leave, a period of total sabbatical. And today is the day of your conscious return. You are what we call a Newly-Aware. Your mind, my son, is not totally blank. You know how to speak, do you not? You will gradually remember all that you need—and want—to remember. You have forgotten only what you have contracted to forget."

"And now I want you to look about you, Yeshua, to familiarize yourself with this chamber and with all the objects in it. After half an hour—there is a clock on the wall—I want you to arise, draw aside the drapes from the large window on your left, and look at the world outside. You must slowly orient yourself to what is presently for you a new environment.

"In one hour from now, my aide, Ananda, will be in to bring you some light nourishment, and to talk with you further. I promise you this, my son: in just three days time

6

you will be horizoned, and you will possess a firm grasp on your present sequence of reality. I will see you again tomorrow. Until then, *Vita tecum!*"

"*Et cum spiritu tuo,*" Yeshua found himself replying, he knew not why—although he somehow understood the Latin formula, "Life be with you," and "With your spirit also."

When Amitabha had departed, Yeshua scanned the room. He knew with certainty that the room was clinical: white and clean, containing various pieces of apparatus made of stainless steel and black rubber tubing. Besides these, the room contained his air bed, two chairs, a table and a small bureau. Its dimensions were ordinary: about four by five meters, with a large window in the wall to his left. The bed which supported him with such tender rigor was more tangible than visible: a pure column of faintly rose-colored air, precisely pressured to give him perfect support without the slightest irritation to skin, muscle, or nerve. One could have reposed on such sculptured pressure for weeks, months—perhaps, years—without incurring bedsores or nerve deterioration.

One picture hung on the wall: a man, clean-shaven, in military uniform. (He suddenly realized, by contrast, how luxuriant were his own beard and hair.) Underneath the picture was a small brass plaque. Yeshua got off the air bed to walk over and read what was on the plaque, and immediately fell to his hands and knees! Weak as water! He found his legs totally unable to support him.

Awkward and unsteady as a babe, he reached for the chair by the side of the bed and pulled himself into it. How icy it was! He realized that the farther he got from his air bed, the colder the room became. But it was warming up. He could feel that, too. A blue woolen robe lay neatly draped over the back of the chair. He unfolded it and finally managed to get into it, amazed at the sprawling uncertainty of his bodily movement.

Warmer now, he sat for some minutes in the chair, trying to piece together a universe out of twenty minutes' jagged shards of experience.

He was alive. He was someone called Yeshua. Indeed, he was a man, supposedly, of some importance. He was

7

being cared for by this kindly though imposing man, Amitabha. His situation seemed to be under control. He understood words and could use them. He knew, in a general way, the nature of the various objects in the room, although he certainly could not divine the functions of some of the complicated pieces of equipment.

Although he now began to feel safe, he could not yet fully define him*self*. Who was he, really? He wanted to look into a mirror, but there was none in the room. "Then how," it occurred to him to ask himself, "do I know what a mirror is?" He did not know.

The room was now warming rapidly. Feeling a bit of strength returning to his legs, Yeshua cautiously arose and, leaning against the wall, made his way around the room to where the picture hung. The name below was not printed in his own language; it was in Russian. "How do I know that?" he mused, as he laboriously spelled it out. "Mikhail Strastnik." The face had nobility. Wide brows; dark sunken eyes, solemn but kindly; a firm, clean angle of cheek and jaw. Intelligence and command were stamped into every feature. By no means did Yeshua feel the cool serenity in this portrait that he found in the countenance of Amitabha. Strastnik's face was marked "Express!"

Had he found a mirror in the room, Yeshua would have noted that his own image projected a personality wavelength somewhere between Strastnik's and Amitabha's. A pool of dreaminess lay behind his own eyes—it was not the same as the cold calm behind Amitabha's, but perhaps closer to that than to the fitful summer lightning in the skull of Strastnik. Yet his own lighter, aquiline features were much more mobile than Amitabha's—closer to the energetic contours of Strastnik, though not so massive, so Slavic.

By now, Yeshua's attention had focused on the window. When he was able to pull the drapes aside, he would for the first time be able to see the world to which he had come, he knew not how. "*Tathagata:* the 'thus-come-one'." The Sanskrit word rose like a gull, unbidden, from the depths of his own mind.

But as he edged along the wall toward the window, still not trusting his legs to carry him directly across the room,

8

there were three soft knocks on the door. Still too surprised by everything that was happening to have patterned a response, Yeshua said nothing. The knock was repeated. He waited. The door opened a few inches. A quiet, cheerful voice spoke through the gap.

"May I come in, sir?"

A man entered the room. He was considerably shorter than Amitabha; his close-cropped black hair contrasted with his light gray clothes. Then Yeshua remembered that Amitabha had told him he was sending his aide.

"You are Ananda?"

"Yes, Yeshua, and I have come to bring you some nourishment. Are you now aware?"

"Aware? I'm *awake,* no question about that. But my mind seems to be burning off a fog ten kilometers thick. Do you know, I never did get to the window. I haven't seen the outside world yet."

"If I may make a suggestion, Yeshua, I think it would be best if you took some nourishment first. We can look out together—even walk a bit later, if you feel up to it. But I should imagine that just now, you still feel rather weak and cold."

"Yes, I still do feel weak, and still a little cold, although I believe the room is getting warmer. Tell me, why has the room been so cold?"

Ananda laughed heartily. "Oh, you've been a good deal colder than this for quite a while, sir! Here, let me help you to your chair, and then I will bring in some nourishment."

As Yeshua settled comfortably in the chair, his legs completely done in from their first effort, Ananda disappeared through the door for a few moments. Yeshua thought of nothing whatsoever. His head was in a condition not dissimilar to that of his legs. He let time flow through him like some kind of spirit-blood. It was good.

Ananda returned, wheeling a cart which supported a steaming covered dish and several pieces of apparatus, the nature of which was completely unknown to Yeshua.

"I think, sir, we should begin with this," Ananda announced, as he fastened a set of white earphones on Yeshua and plugged them into a black box about 20 centimeters square, bejeweled with a complex array of gleaming knobs and dials. Yeshua noted that Ananda, though friendly and informal, was distinctly deferential to him—which added to his curiosity about his own identity.

"Are you ready, sir?"

Yeshua heard him indistinctly through the earphones, and nodded. Gently, the rich black germ of earth, the live salt of sea, the green and gold of light, entered his psycho-chemical organism, entered his brain through his audio nerves in wavelengths of musical form, and then resonated off his brain throughout his entire metabolic system. His body became an orchestra played upon by the music. No doubt of it: he was growing definitely warmer, definitely stronger in his limbs.

Ananda removed the phones. In reality, the music had lasted only five or six minutes, but Yeshua would not have been able to guess whether the experience had been a matter of minutes or hours.

"By this era, sir, your system has been so refined, and is so efficient, that you need only a minimum of organic molecules to sustain full health and vigor. But you have now been without any nourishment at all for so long a period that I thought you needed a dose of, well—putting aside the technical name—psychic vitamins." Ananda chuckled quietly. "How did you like the experience, sir?"

"It was delightful. It was . . . I would gladly have gone on listening."

"Oh, you were not merely listening, Yeshua. You were taking nourishment. And now, sir, we have some broth for you. It is highly concentrated, and it is to be thinned out with *time*. In fact, it is wholesome and palatable only when mixed with duration—queen solvent of all that is rich and complex." (He pronounced this last phrase grandly, without poking for the words; it sounded like some much-used ritual formula.)

"I am going to leave you for a while now, Yeshua. I want you to take each consecutive spoonful only after you feel your center calling for it."

Yeshua lifted a spoon of broth to his lips. It was comfortably hot, thick, and marrowy, the very heart of protein. It left him drifting on a long roller of energy which, some minutes (?) later, subsided into a lull of ruminating

10

surf. Duration was indeed a solvent, mused Yeshua. Then there was undertow, and he knew it was time for another spoon.

An indeterminate but considerable length of time elapsed in consuming the small bowl of broth. But he now felt exquisitely satiated and strangely happy. He rested a while. Then Ananda returned.

"Just a small dessert to conclude your repast, sir. We by no means wish to overtax you, but it is your rebirthday."

Walking over to the cart, Ananda uncovered a projector of some kind, turned off the lights in the room, and focused a picture on the opposite wall—not a steady image, but a vibrating, pulsing composition with shifting rhythms of color and proportion. "Relax, Yeshua, and let the icon-mobile penetrate."

After a while, Yeshua felt himself in light trance. The polychromatic sequences were amazingly witty. Yeshua found it peppermint, ice and sherbet as it echoed biochemically through his system.

Ananda flicked it off. Yeshua laughed out loud and sat there, shaking his head like a dog shaking off a cold bath. "That tickled and sparkled as it went through me, Ananda!"

"Ah, that was a very good brand, sir. Visual no. 37, Catalogue 14. We have more overwhelming ones, but this is what was called for on your first day. And now, tell me, please, how do your legs feel?"

Yeshua, tentatively at first and then with assurance, put his full weight on them. "Much stronger, Ananda. I feel very well."

"Good. Now, would you prefer to step outside with me and look around, or shall we just draw the drapes and see what we can see from here?"

"I'd definitely prefer to go outside and see everything directly."

"Excellent! Why don't you lean on my arm a bit, sir, just till your leg muscles remember their former wit."

Yeshua took his arm and Ananda swung open the door to a long corridor, about 50 meters in length. There were several other doors leading off the corridor, one of which looked like the entrance to a vault. The whole door was really nothing more than a massive timing mechanism imbedded in some unbreakable transparent plastic, almost 50 centimeters thick. Ice and frost had congealed over some areas of the huge portal.

"What is in there?" Yeshua asked as they walked by.

"You will learn all about it eventually, Yeshua. Pay it no mind for now. You have a tremendous experiential quota to fill today as it is."

They had come to an exit. "Well, Yeshua," Ananda announced, "here we are. Beyond that door lies Sukhavati —Sukhavati Entopia, to be more ceremonious.

"A strange name," said Yeshua.

"But a good place," Ananda smiled.

CHAPTER II

Sukhavati Entopia

The first thing that struck Yeshua as he stepped outside the door was the purity and intensity of color. Expressing it to himself mathematically, he was stunned by what seemed to be blue^2, green^3, red^2, yellow^3, etc.

The second thing he noticed was that the air filled him with a kind of effervescent buoyancy. Whether it was higher in oxygen or ozone properties, he did not know. What he did know was that, weak though he had been just a short time ago, his legs were now almost begging to dance, jump and prance about.

Yeshua found himself on the balcony of a white two-story building—an official building of some kind, he thought, because it was capped by a dome. The dome itself was inset with a large clock and topped with a symbol that Yeshua instantly recognized as an Egyptian ankh (☥).

12

In one panoramic sweep of his eyes, Yeshua took in the fact that he was on an island of about 10 to 15 kilometers in radius. The view of the island and the sea beyond was scintillating. His own position was only about a kilometer from the very center of the island, where he noted a whole complex of buildings, some of them similar to the one he had just left, but much taller and more imposing. The terrain rose irregularly from the sea to the island's center, although there was an equally high point to the northwest. Roughly speaking, the inner 5-kilometer circle was intensely urban; the outer 5 to 10 kilometers were lush with farmlands, groves and pastures.

"Ouch!" Yeshua slapped his hand to his neck! He could still hear the bee droning away, though he could not actually see it in flight. It really stung!

"A bee?" Ananda asked solicitously. "Oh my, we do have a lot of gardens and small parks in this part of Sukhavati. We are simply overflowing with flowers and bees. You are not allergic to their sting, I trust."

"I don't know."

"Oh, excuse me sir," Ananda laughed. "Of course you wouldn't know. Even we won't know until we consult our files."

"Wait! What's that, Ananda?"

Yeshua's eye had caught the almost imperceptible trace of something in the sky: some kind of nearly transparent film below the deep cumulo-nimbus cloud banks.

"You've caught it, Yeshua! Very keen of you. Most Newly-Awares don't really notice it until the second or third day. That's our barrier, our IMOB—our Inadmissible MicroOrganism Barrier, to be precise. Its function will be fully explained to you when you are horizoned. Even now, from the name, you can guess what it pertains to. It covers the whole of Sukhavati like a canopy. Not a mean engineering feat, sir, as you will be studying shortly."

Off to the west, about ten kilometers out to sea, lay another promontory much smaller than Sukhavati and, to judge by its colors, predominantly browns and black, not nearly so fertile.

Yeshua could not make out any buildings on it, although a few rectangular land patterns suggested that at least part of it was under cultivation. Here and there, a

13

thin winding line up a hill suggested a road. The island lay outside the barrier—the IMOB, as Ananda had called it.

"I gather that that small island to the west is also inhabited, Ananda," Yeshua said tentatively.

"In a way it is, and in another way it isn't. That's a matter that's going to concern you personally, Yeshua. After you are purposed, you will have much to do with that island. But wouldn't you like to take a short stroll through the streets of Sukhavati, sir?"

"Yes, I'd like that very much."

Ananda first led him back to his room, where a kind of toga of white linen with crimson piping around the neck had been laid out for him. Simple, but really quite handsome, thought Yeshua. A pair of sandals, exactly molded to the curve of his arch, had also been left for him. His feet felt married to them as he stepped into them.

For the first time, really, Yeshua took note of the clothes Ananda was wearing. Not at all like his own robe. More pajama-like. A loose-fitting top of gray linen, short sleeved, with a broken line of purple piping around the neck, and shorts of the same gray material, down to just above the knees.

They walked out into the corridor but turned right this time, and descended a stairway to the ground floor. The street-level entrance was covered by a wickerwork wooden arch interwoven with flowers and vines of every kind. It was literally heavy with sweetness. Yeshua breathed in deeply and relished it in his lungs. A stone walk, not straight, but meandering meditatively for some 20 meters, led to an outer hedge and the street.

As they were about to step out past the hedge to the sidewalk, it suddenly began to cloud over. In less than 30 seconds, the sky was completely shadowy and gloomy! Yeshua was startled, even frightened a little, until he was reassured by the utter calm of his companion. Ananda took out his pocket watch, which, Yeshua couldn't help but notice, was of pure gold with a jeweled ankh on its cover. It was the only ornate item that Ananda possessed.

"Three thirty-seven," Ananda said at last. "Right to the tick." Noting Yeshua's inquiring look, he responded, "We cloud over once in the morning at 10:48, and once again

14

in the afternoon at 3:37. They used to come exactly at 12 hour intervals, but the technology of the dark continents got more sophisticated. This will all be explained to you in due time."

"It got dark so fast!" exclaimed Yeshua. "I was frightened."

"You must not try to aware yourself by gulps, Yeshua. Time is the queen solvent for all that is rich and complex, you know. You must mix your experiences with duration, sir, if you wish to digest the maximum meaning out of them."

The tone in which Ananda had delivered this last bit of advice was schoolmasterish and plodding—as if he had gone through the same routine many times before. Yeshua glanced at him sharply, obviously annoyed. Ananda caught it.

"I mean no insult, Yeshua, but you *are* only a Newly-Aware. You must try to avoid all upset."

In five or six minutes, the gloom, like that of a total eclipse, passed away. The multitude of birds, which had also muted their extravaganza, switched on again, almost electronically. The sun, in full Aztec splendor, assumed his royal duties. High above, the thick but mobile banks of cumulo-nimbus drifted off to the west, whence they had come in the first place.

The two strollers turned left on the sidewalk and leisurely sauntered down what was apparently a little-frequented, quiet side street. Most of the edifices here were one-story residences, each with a profusion of flowers, ivy, hedges and shrubbery. The sidewalks, too, were set at irregular but somehow rhythmic intervals, with broad trees in full leaf.

They approached an intersection where, for the first time, traffic appeared. Several people walked by them, and Yeshua almost gasped at their striking physical bearing. Ananda seemed healthy and vigorous; Amitabha, even imposing. But these people in the street, lean and bronzed, seemed—every one of them, male and female—to be professional athletes or dancers, graceful and awesome as stalking lions. Men and women of every race: brown men and black, caucasion and oriental.

A few virtually noiseless vehicles shaped like shiny

15

aluminum teardrops skimmed the streets. Literally skimmed the streets: they hovered a few centimeters above the concrete roads, held up by a hard whisper of air pressure. Yeshua remembered his bed.

On the third or fourth corner, after they had been walking for about 15 minutes, there was suddenly a high whistle of air brakes, and a crash. The crash was not very loud; it sounded more like a lot of pans and kettles colliding than anything else. The vehicles were considerably whacked out of shape, but the two drivers did not appear to be more than badly shaken up. They were, however, much annoyed with each other. Their gesticulations and verbal abuse grew more enthusiastic by the minute. While Ananda and Yeshua stood there spellbound, two persons, obviously officials, one male and the other female, came on the scene. They were both dressed in light khaki outfits, cut like Ananda's, but with black piping around the neck and on the sleeves. The officials attempted to pacify the antagonists. They were successful with one but not the other. The woman official abruptly took the wrist of the more intractable combatant and examined a gauge that was strapped around it like a wrist watch. Shaking her head in displeasure, she immediately produced a syringe from a leather kit on her belt and plunged it into the jerking arm of her subject. Yeshua would have sworn the victim's calm was simultaneous.

A few minutes more, and the officials had taken down names, facts, witnesses, and had succeeded in restoring total equilibrium. As their wrecked vehicles were being towed away, the two former antagonists were seen to shake hands, and to accept rides offered by sympathetic onlookers. The entire episode had not taken more than 15 minutes.

"What was that thing strapped to his wrist?" Yeshua asked—and as he asked, he noticed for the first time that Ananda had one also. It was probably not a watch, since he had already seen Ananda consult a heavy gold pocket watch. As a matter of fact, glancing around quickly, it seemed to him that *everybody* wore one.

Ananda smiled. "It's a Psychosomatic Stress Indicator, sir—PSI, pronounced 'sigh.' As you see, all of us wear one. You will be issued one directly after you are hori-

16

zoned. You don't really need one till then, because you will be under my immediate supervision practically every minute these next few days."

Not only was Ananda's general behavior toward him deferential, but even the people passing by, Yeshua realized, if they came close enough to see him clearly, bowed their heads in friendly but rather formal courtesy. They did not so greet one another.

"The people smile at one another when they meet, but they *bow* to me. Why is that, Ananda?"

"You are, Yeshua, as I believe Amitabha informed you, a person of considerable importance to Sukhavati. Even if they did not recognize your face (and most of them already do), your station would be evident to them by the crimson markings on your robe. Your special role and responsibilities will shortly be explained to you———"

"I know, I know!" interrupted Yeshua impatiently. "When I am horizoned, in three days time!"

"Please don't be put out, sir. You are, as yet, despite the high rank to which you are destined, only a Newly-Aware. There are definite limits to the experiential shocks your central nervous system can absorb. But eventually, nothing on heaven or earth will be hidden from you. That I promise."

Their stroll had brought them to another section of town where, Yeshua perceived, the houses were closer together, less roomy, and interspersed with other buildings given over to small manufacturing. At least this was Yeshua's surmise, given the audible burr of machine drills and the metallic odor. The noise level was by no means high, and there were still flowers and trees in the area, but clearly this was a less attractive residential zone than the one from which they had first set out.

Ananda appeared to hesitate for a moment. He smiled, then coughed a little, nervously. "I have brought you here, Yeshua, at the express wish of Amitabha. I'll be frank to say that I, myself, thought this particular excursion would have been more appropriate a little later on. But Amitabha wished you to make it almost im-

17

mediately. He has great confidence in your native balance and powers of judgement.

"Sukhavati is not perfect, Yeshua. Here, as you can see, the citizens do not live as graciously as in some of the other residential areas. Not that they are wretched; quite the contrary is the case. But . . . you had best look for yourself. . . ."

Yeshua turned to enter one of the buildings, a workshop of some sort, when Ananda caught him by the arm, startling him. It was the first sudden gesture this gentle guide had made.

"Just remember one thing, if you please, sir. We are *starting* with the imperfections. You have not yet seen our glories. Form no precipitate conclusions! You are only a Newly-Aware."

Yeshua entered the workshop. Men and women in dark bronze linen outfits, cut short like Ananda's, were busy over a variety of cutting and drilling machinery that apparently worked by laser. Intense peaks of light, followed immediately by short puffs of smoke where the laser bit through steel, fitfully lit up the barracks-like workshop.

A foreman, dressed similarly to the others but with yellow piping around his sleeves, approached them. Ananda took the foreman aside and spoke to him privately for a few moments.

"Welcome to Fabrication Unit No. 6, sir," the foreman said at last to Yeshua. "We are honored to have been the fabrication unit chosen for your inspection. Mingle freely, sir, and please ask whatever questions you like."

Strong and stocky, not so graceful as the strollers Yeshua had encountered in the streets, the foreman nevertheless exuded health and cheerfulness. So did they all, in this workshop. If anything, they displayed more basic animal vigor than the others Yeshua had seen. The women, in their light linen tunics, hinted a voluptuousness that increased the depth of his inhalations. Certainly there was no proletarian sullenness evident in the men and women working in this unit, Yeshua mused. The workers smiled at him when they met his glance and tendered him the same courteous head-bow that he had received on the streets.

One of the women operatives caught Yeshua's special

attention. Her gorgeous red hair was superb against her bronze-colored tunic. While dressed in the same simple and modest style as the others, she pulsed with an erotic energy that echoed up and down his spine. Feeling his glance at last, she looked up, smiled at him, and bowed her head courteously. Yeshua walked over to her. She had just risen from her bench to reach for some supplies from a shelf on the wall behind her.

"What do you make here?" Yeshua asked, more to speak to her, and because he had been instructed to ask questions, than out of any real curiosity as to the fact.

"We fabricate precision parts for our radio-telescopes, sir. *These* parts," she asserted with evident pride, "cannot be produced by automation. They have to be made by hand—by very skilled hands!" She laughed a little and held up her own hands, as if to offer evidence. Her hands were both quite feminine and quite strong, Yeshua discerned.

"How much do you make?" He was still taking in the environment, as much through his pores as with his eyes and ears.

The girl glanced at Ananda with a puzzled expression.

"Remember," Ananda quickly interjected, "he is just a Newly-Aware."

"Oh yes," she murmured, smiling gently at Yeshua. "Sir, we don't get paid in money or anything like that. We are paid in awareness."

"In what?"

"Awareness, sir. Duration is like a mine. There are levels after levels to descend. And the most precious ore always seems to lie the furthest down. You can't really enjoy duration, any more than sex or wine, if you are not something of an artist. You must be knowledgeable. It takes instruction."

Turning to Ananda, she asked softly, "He hasn't been horizoned yet, has he?"

"This is his *very first day!*" Ananda whispered it, but with such emphasis that Yeshua caught the last three words.

She turned once more to Yeshua and gazed at him

musingly. A look of tenderness not unmixed with amusement, yet still somehow deferential.

Yeshua groaned in response. "I know. I must aware myself gently."

She laughed.

"But do you have any grievances, any complaints?" Yeshua broke out a little impatiently. "Ananda said I would be seeing the seamier side of Sukhavati here, and I certainly haven't seen much amiss."

Again the worker glanced at Ananda.

"Tell him, Sudraheen, it's all right," he said resignedly.

"Sir," she began with an air of determination, "four hours of fabrication is a bit much. We believe we could achieve the same productivity in a three-and-a-half or even three-hour working day. Because, you see, we would be that much fresher and energetic in our efforts. But even more important than that, we would like more instruction time with the Leonardos and the Archimedes personnel. We are truly appreciative of the efforts of the Rothschilds, but we feel able to immerse ourselves more deeply into the mysteries of duration than we do at present!"

Yeshua was totally unable to resist the opportunity: "Aware yourself gently, my child!" he admonished pompously.

The Sudraheen, Ananda, and even the foreman, who happened to overhear, burst into laughter.

"Please," said Yeshua, when their laughter had subsided, "if this tour is supposed to be for my general education, and especially if I'm supposed to be seeing some of the problems of Sukhavati, can you not tell me anything I can understand? This business of being paid in awareness is beyond me, as you surely realize."

"There is another thing," said the Sudraheen, her whole body now pertly indignant. "Women do not receive a proportionate number of managerial positions in the fabrication units! Oh, a few of the more brilliant ones get appointed, but you have to be much more able than a man to get an equal position."

Yeshua nodded. This, at least, was within his comprehension.

Ananda shuffled his feet uncomfortably on the cork

floor. "I do believe, Yeshua," he mumbled at last, "that Amitabha's intentions have been carried out. You must be getting tired now, and we should probably be on our way."

But Yeshua was quite attracted to the Sudraheen. "Won't I see you again?" he asked.

Now it was her turn to be ill at ease. "Well, yes . . . I guess you could if you liked. But you will see, sir, that there is so much for you to do, and so many interesting people you will be meeting—it *would* be a bit out of the ordinary for *you* to be seeing a Sudraheen, sir."

"Yeshua, we must go now," Ananda broke in abruptly, taking him by the arm. "You have too much to do before you are horizoned to expand your social life now. Later, perhaps."

Before they went out through the door, Yeshua turned for a last survey of the scene. He found the Sudraheen still staring after him, tenderly and wonderingly. As their eyes met, she smiled and, somewhat shyly, waved goodbye.

The foreman accompanied them out the door to the street. "I hope it's been informative, sir."

"Ananda thinks it has, and I'll defer to his more mature judgement." Ananda and the foreman laughed again.

Ananda shook hands with the supervisor. "We thank you for your kindness," he said simply. "Come Yeshua, we are going back to your room. You have earned—and you require—a long rest."

Back in his room, Yeshua stretched out in sybaritic ease on his air bed, completely naked as before. Ananda had instructed him in the manipulation of the various temperature and pressure controls. As he tuned these to his exact demands, he also flipped the switch for a light massage. "Delicious," he thought, as he ebbed into trance.

"No!" He caught himself! "That comes later," he remembered. Ananda had warned him. Experiential duration analysis was a tricky process, beyond the ken of a Newly-Aware. For the time being, he was bidden to reflect on the day's experiences and to begin to construct some kind of personal world out of them. Horizoning, he knew, would complete the task.

21

CHAPTER III

Preparation

It was not Ananda's voice, but the deeper voice of Amitabha which awakened him. Three or four separate perceptions flashed through his mind at the same moment. First, he had fallen asleep and slept pretty much around the clock. Second, he was being awakened by intercom rather than by personal visitation. Third, none of this bothered him. He found himself much less fearful than he had been on his first day. "They must sense this in me," Yeshua mused, "since they used the intercom to wake me, rather than come themselves."

"Yeshua," said the deep, pleasant voice on the intercom, "will you please arise now and get dressed. Ananda will be in in a few minutes, to take you to my residence."

It took him but a minute to jump—literally jump, he felt so refreshed—out of the air bed and put on his linen robe. He wondered: ought he to wash, to bathe? There was no facility for it in his room and, to tell the truth, he felt no need for it at all; no film on his teeth, no crust in the corners of his eyes, no oiliness of skin—even his linen toga seemed spotless.

Nor did it occur to him to wonder about his breakfast, although in the previous 24 hours he had consumed nothing more than a small bowl of broth. He felt no hunger at all.

There was a knock on the door.

"Come in, Ananda."

"Good morning, sir. We are going to Amitabha's residence today. As a matter of fact, you will be staying there for most of the coming year, until the day you are purposed."

Ananda paused for a moment, looking him over with some amusement. "You really did sleep, Yeshua. I came in just after the afternoon eclipse, and you were far away. I didn't have the heart to disturb you. Amitabha wasn't surprised. I checked with him about it, and he said you have a very high experiential threshold, so that your perceptions participate in you at a very deep level. Naturally, you would get very tired your first few days in Sukhavati.

"But you know, sir," he continued, "later on you will probably need only an hour or two of sleep a night. Amitabha takes none at all."

One of the air-cushioned teardrop vehicles Yeshua had observed the previous day was waiting for them in the quiet side street. A chauffeur opened the door for them, bowing his head courteously as he did so.

It was quite early in the morning, and even the main thoroughfare, which had been busy enough the day before, was practically deserted. The windows of the car were open, and the morning breeze, cool, but redolent of flowers and the sea, was . . . was paradisaical. No other word for it.

Neither passenger had the esthetic effrontery to break silence. Yeshua sank back in the rich leather unholstery of the skimmer, as Ananda called it, and took in the broad, peaceful avenue lined with trees, bright shops and smartly designed office buildings on both sides.

"Aah!" Breathing deeply, Yeshua almost moaned his pleasure. "Sukhavati *is* a good place," he said at last.

Their skimmer turned off the avenue at—Yeshua was able to make out the sign—Ferme Street, and then, two blocks later, turned left again on Sidhartha Drive. Here the homes were even more spacious, more imposing, than in the residential area from which they had come.

The driver drew up in front of the largest of the villas, distinct from those around it in that it boasted a small dome. The same arrangement of clock and Egyptian ankh that Yeshua had noted previously was set into the dome, but so covered with ivy that Yeshua though it could have very little functional value. The dome, along with the formal garden and pool at the rear of the building, sug-

23

gested that the residence had some kind of official status.

The skimmer whispered to a halt and the chauffeur got out and opened the door for them. A chest-high stone wall overflowing with roses marked off the grounds. A man in a uniform similar to the driver's opened the front gate for them. They were ushered into a hall, where still another servant met them and led them into a shadowy book-lined studio. It was a large, comfortable room, two or three times the size of Yeshua's room back at the clinic—or wherever it was he had been staying. The servant bid them be seated. Amitabha would be with them presently.

Yeshua settled down in a big, overstuffed, dark green leather club affair. He could hear voices in a room nearby, probably above them, but he could not make out what was being said.

Amitabha, almost unexpectedly, appeared at the door of the study and strode in briskly. Nodding a greeting to Ananda, he stepped directly over to Yeshua, who rose to his feet instinctively. Amitabha took both of Yeshua's hands firmly.

"Vita tecum, Yeshua."

"Et cum spiritu tuo," Yeshua found himself responding.

"How are you, Yeshua?"

The man certainly possessed dignity of bearing, Yeshua reflected. The calm baritone of his voice completely filled the large room. His robes, too, were resplendent: violet, with purple piping around the neck and sleeves. He was looking Yeshua up and down with an intensity that indicated he would not depend on any answer that Yeshua might make to his question.

"I am very well, sir," Yeshua finally replied. The "sir" came of itself.

"Yes. I can see that is so. Please sit down. Ananda, we must unfortunately excuse you. Something came up at the observatory—I had a call about twenty minutes ago—and I would like you to check it out with the head Kepler. Thank you, Ananda, for taking such excellent care of our Newly-Aware."

"It was my very real pleasure, sir," replied Ananda, rising to leave. "He was, as you said he'd be, perceptive."

"Oh, don't get up, Yeshua," he added hurriedly. "I'll be

24

seeing you again, and frequently, never fear—unless you object, and would prefer another guide." He smiled.

"No, no," Yeshua responded. "You were very patient with me. I hope I will be assigned to you, or you to me, however these things are arranged. I still don't know what's going on, of course, and . . ." his voice trailed off and his shoulders rose quizzically.

Amitabha smiled and placed his hand squarely and firmly on Yeshua's left shoulder. "Your infancy is almost at an end, Yeshua; your adolescence is about to begin."

Ananda shook hands with his charge, bid them both good-bye, and departed for the observatory.

"You have eaten," Amitabha glanced down at a memo on his desk, "once, I believe. Some protein broth, a few audio-energizers, and a visual. Do you feel hungry yet?"

"No, I do not, as a matter of fact," Yeshua answered reflectively. "I don't feel hungry at all." He knew, somehow, that he had gone rather a long time not to feel hunger.

Amitabha smiled. "Ananda may have explained to you that in your present . . . ah . . . sequence of reality, you need a minimum of organic molecules to sustain life. You will find, by the way, that you will have no need to evacuate bodily wastes more than once or twice a month.

"But let me get you a quick ole-up," he added abruptly. He pressed a button on a console on his desk, and a servant appeared. "Light vapors, please," ordered Amitabha.

The servant returned in a moment with two small crystalline flasks crowned with ruby-red stoppers.

"Just put the flask to your nostrils, so," explained his host, demonstrating as he talked. "When you remove the stopper, inhale once, deeply. It's an olefactory invigorator."

Yeshua followed instructions, inhaling, so it seemed to him, down to his ankles. The vapor went through him, sharp and aromatic as a liqueur, strong and bracing as a brandy.

"Rrumph!" he muttered involuntarily. Amitabha laughed. "Feel ole-upped?" he asked.

"I hadn't realized I was down, but my angle of elevation is certainly 30 degrees higher than it was a minute ago."

25

Amitabha stood there, smiling at him silently for several moments. "Now to business," he said at last. "I want you to tell me simply and directly what you have so far experienced in Sukhavati, and what you have intuited or concluded from those experiences. Think before you speak. Gather your perceptions together, and distill the essential truths out of them."

After some minutes of concentrated thought, Yeshua answered: "I seem to have been neither fully dead nor fully alive, up until yesterday morning. You or Ananda said something to me about my having been on a psychic sabbatical. I came to, or was brought to consciousness, yesterday morning; and my mind, presently, is a mixture of sunlight and shadow. I can speak, for example, but I cannot remember anything of my own past. I must *have* a past—I am not a child—but I can't remember my past or my childhood.

"Speaking of childhood, I want to mention that I have been struck by the fact that there appear to be no children on the island—nor any aged, for that matter! Everyone appears to be between 25 and 40 years old."

"There are just a few children here," said Amitabha. "They are the children of our returned Prodigals. You'll hear more about that later. But you are correct: we have no aged. I want you to continue, however, with your report."

"I was afraid when I first became conscious," Yeshua continued. "But the few people I have so far met on Sukhavati have been friendly to me, and have allayed my fears. Everything—no, *nearly* everything I experience seems perfect and beautiful, yet strange. For example, it seems strange to me that I should not be hungry after having eaten but once in 24 hours. But I don't know why that seems strange. I . . . I am confused."

Amitabha moved the discussion forward, as if there were a designated point he wanted to reach. "You said that *nearly* everything you experienced had seemed perfect. Why did you say 'nearly'?"

Again, Yeshua paused to reflect. "Well, in 24 hours I have been stung by a bee, I have witnessed the collision of two skimmers, and I've heard a Sudraheen, whatever

26

that means, complain about her working conditions and the position of women in Sukhavati society."

"Yet you like it here?"

"I have found such troubles very bearable. I am amazed at the colors, entranced by the odors, and overwhelmed by the beauty and general friendliness of the people around me. Sukhavati seems like a very good place, even if not a perfect one."

"Sukhavati Entopia! Exactly so!" Ambitabha exclaimed.

"It is time now, my son, to begin the general instructions, in preparation for your horizoning tomorrow. Some of what I am going to say is very close to your conscious mind—almost within your reach. To use the Platonic expression for it, you are going to recollect the truth of much of what you are about to hear.

"Does the name Sukhavati mean anything to you, Yeshua? Think. What *kind* of a name is it? English? German? Russian?"

"It . . . it sounds like an ancient word . . . like Sanskrit, somehow. I can't tell why."

"You are correct! It *is* Sanskrit—or, at least, Pali, a derivative dialect. It means 'The Happy Land,' and it was a famous term in Mahayana Buddhist literature. Now, does *that* term, Buddhism, mean anything to you? It was one of the great world religions, Yeshua—although some of its more knowledgeable devotees objected to calling it a religion.

"Can you recall any of the major doctrines of Buddhism?"

Yeshua was getting excited. "It's as if you were massaging numb areas in my brain and bringing them back to life. As soon as you mention something, it seems to be an old and familiar fact. But until you speak of it, I can't formulate it. It's a lump of idea in my brain; it's there, but formless!"

"Yes," Amitabha smiled, "I understand. All right. I will describe the religion, but briefly and even simplistically, because to try to put it into words is already simplistic, and because it will spark a fuller and more subtle understanding in you as I proceed.

"According to Buddhism, Yeshua, men live and die,

and are then reborn in accordance with the principle of karma—which is to say, in the words of another world religion, Christianity, 'As ye sow, so shall ye reap.' If a man, Yeshua, were greedy as a pig, ate like a pig, wallowed in filth like a pig, dealt with others as a pig deals with others, his appropriate form of rebirth would be that of a pig. And, conversely, as the ancient Hindus taught, if a low-born laborer, a Sudra, an outcast assigned to clean latrines—if such a man were to perform his duties conscientiously, his heart set on doing his duty, his dharma, rather than on acquiring wealth, he would be reborn into an upper caste, the Kshatriya, or even the Brahman. Such is the principle of karma.

"It was the hope, of course, of both the Hindus and the Buddhists, to escape the cycle of rebirth altogether—to be so free of earthly desire that upon death one could rise free, free of the gravity of lust and ambition, to be absorbed in Brahman, the cosmic soul of the Hindus, or in Nirvana, the ineffable absolute of the Buddhists.

"The latter concept, Nirvana, is an especially interesting one. Its literal meaning is, 'blowing out,' and Europeans first interpreted this as pure annihilation—a death-wish on the part of Asiatics, for whom life was generally burdensome anyway. Widespread hunger, disease, the early death of loved ones, etc.

"But as the Eastern religions came to be better understood in the West, educated people began to realize that Buddha was *not* preaching annihilation. Indeed, that interpretation of Nirvana is considered one of the grosser heresies by Buddhists. By the term 'blowing out,' Buddha was simply referring to an experience so exalted, so disproportionate to our space-time world, that there were no human words for it. Most mystics have felt this in their approach to the absolute. St. Paul, a Christian, says, 'Eye has not seen, ear has not heard; neither has it entered into the heart of man to *conceive,* what good things God has prepared for those who love him.'

"Yeshua, you are nodding your head. Does any of this begin to come back to you?"

"Yes! Yes! I remember a story now about the Buddha. One of his monks comes up to him and threatens to leave the order, unless Buddha will explain Nirvana more explicitly. He insists on knowing whether he will exist or not exist in Nirvana. Buddha replies that he never promised the monk to teach him theology, but rather to free him from suffering. And then he gives the monk a parable. He says, 'Tell me, when a fire burns out, in which direction have the flames gone: north, south, east or west?' The monk replies, 'I can't answer that, master. When fire goes out, it does not go a *place*. The question is inappropriate.' 'Then,' says the Buddha, 'neither can I answer a question put to me in human words about Nirvana.' Do I have the story right?"

"Essentially, correct, Yeshua! Do you see how whole islands and continents of mind are coming back into focus for you?

"But you know, my son, this concept of Nirvana proved too elusive a doctrine, too icy and distant a goal to warm the hearts of the masses—or even some of the scholars. It belongs to early classical Buddhism. A later development, Mahayana Buddhism, while it did not contradict the final end of Nirvana, put the emphasis on reaching a kind of heaven, an abode of happiness ruled by a benevolent Bodhisattva—one who vows to save all creatures from the world of suffering before entering Nirvana himself. Sukhavati . . ."

"Sukhavati!" Yeshua interrupted excitedly. "That was the name of the Buddhist 'Pure-land,' the heaven ruled by the merciful Bodhisattva, *Amitabha!*"

Amitabha smiled. "You have it, Yeshua. And of course, I have been named after him. To be more precise, however, Amitabha is actually my *rank,* not my name. But since there is only one of that rank on the island, it serves as my name as well. The same holds true of you, also. You hold the rank of Yeshua, but there can be but one of that high rank in Sukhavati. There are several Anandas, though, and many Rothschilds and Archimedes, and even more Sudraheens. The Ananda you know is really Ananda Randall. He was originally an Englishman.

"I am Amitabha Djilov; my cultural base-frame of reference was, and is, Yugoslavian. You, my son, are Yeshua Nabi. Your ground-conscious level was, and remains, Israeli. And so the title of Yeshua fits in nicely with your cultural aura—but that is a mere coincidence. Many who have held the title had markedly different backgrounds. Oh, there is so much to tell you that I am losing track of my original point.

"You recall, then, that Sukhavati was a Mahayana Buddhist heaven which partially displaced the earlier Buddhist concept of Nirvana. I say partially displaced it because, even in Mahayana Buddhism, the aim, after thousands of eons of Sukhavati bliss, was to move on to Nirvana. But, as you know, no one hurried!"

Amitabha got up and walked over to one of the many bookcases lining the walls of the study. "Here it is," he said, selecting an old leather-bound volume with gold lettering. He opened it to the bookmark. "Here, read the underlined passages, Yeshua. It will save a lot of verbal explanation."

Yeshua took the book. It was a volume of Buddhist scriptures, and the place marked was: Sukhāvativyūha, Chapter 15. He read the following passage to himself:

This world Sukhavati, Ananda, which is the world system of the Lord Amitabha, is rich and prosperous, comfortable, fertile, delightful, and crowded with many Gods and men. And in this world system, Ananda, there are no hells, no animals, no ghosts, no Asuras (devils), and none of the inauspicious places of rebirth . . .

And that world system, Sukhavati, Ananda, emits many fragrant odours, it is rich in a great variety of flowers and fruits, adorned with jewel trees, which are frequented by flocks of various birds with sweet voices, which the Tathagata's miraculous power has conjured up . . .

And all the beings who have been born, who are born, who will be born in this Buddha-field, they all are fixed on the right method of salvation until they have won Nirvana. And why? Because there is here no place for, and no conception of, the two other groups, i.e., of those who are not fixed at all, and those who are fixed on wrong ways. For this reason also, that world system is called the "Happy Land."

"Yes, Yeshua," Amitabha asserted in a strong voice, "there is no place here for those who are not fixed in their views, or for those who are fixed on wrong ways. Everyone here—I should say *almost* everyone here—is fixed in the way of salvation, and will ultimately experience Nirvana. We call it 'the blissful cloud of unknowing,' though all other knowledge, even Sukhavati knowledge, pales in comparison. Yes, we will all, or nearly all of us, be zenithed!

"But *not* all. And that concerns you, Yeshua. It concerns your role in Sukhavati. You will understand these things after you have been purposed, a year from now."

"Would you explain?"

"If it's anything pertaining to Nirvana, or to being purposed, I will not explain! Not at this time, Yeshua. There is a tremendous amount of ground we must cover merely for your being properly horizoned."

A red light flashed on the ivory console on Amitabha's desk.

"Excuse me, my son. That's an urgent signal, and I must respond." He flicked a switch and said, "Go ahead, please."

A voice came into the room. Yeshua could not see either microphone or speaker anywhere around him. "Two Prodigals departing through Sluice Gate No. 4, sir. What restraint tactics are we to employ, priority, moderate, or low?"

Amitabha's face came closer to anger than Yeshua had yet seen it. "Never, I repeat, never, under any circumstances, are you to employ high restraint tactics on Prodigals! Not during my era, anyway! I thought I had made that amply clear. If you encounter a situation that seems to involve Sukhavati security, use moderate restraint. Otherwise use low—and I expect low to be customary. Understood?"

"Understood," replied the official at the other end. "Thank you, sir."

"Excuse the interruption, Yeshua. It is extremely important to our community that you be soundly instructed.

31

Nothing but a red alert can intrude upon us, and I don't think we'll have another one of those for a while.

"Now, what is your reaction to the Buddhist world-view we have been discussing, particularly with regard to karma, rebirth, and Nirvana? You were, as I told you a moment ago, originally an Israeli, and your ground-consciousness is western, not oriental. Does Buddhism make any sense to you?"

"It makes some sense, surely. All the teachings of the major world religions are flooding back into my memory. It seems to me that among the religions of the West, the Catholic faith had some very interesting points in common with the Hindus and Buddhists. Yes, it's becoming clearer to me now. Neither the Protestants nor the Jews entertained the idea, but Catholics came close to the karma-rebirth cycle in their doctrine of purgatory. At least, the old-time Catholics did. Later on, as I recall, the more sophisticated of them let the doctrine lapse."

"This is interesting," Amitabha interrupted. You are saying something new to *me*. I never thought that one of the western religions had anything like the doctrine of karma-rebirth."

"Oh yes, I'm quite convinced of it, sir. See what the Roman Catholics were saying. Unlike Protestants and Orthodox Jews, who both maintained that after death, each person found himself in basic friendship or enmity with God—that is, in heaven or in hell—Catholics maintained there was a third state. In fact, if I am recalling this thing properly, they expected that very few were actually so heroically good, or so heroically vicious, as to end up in heaven or hell. They seemed to believe that the vast majority of the human race 'muddled through' in ambiguous mediocrity—not so devoid of love that they warranted damnation, and not so free from gross selfishness that they deserved instant union with God. What the vast majority of poor human beings needed, they taught, was *further* illumination, further growth in love, further purification: in short, purgatory!

"And they needed more or less illumination of mind, stretching of will, purification of appetite, according to the life they had previously lived. No action is ever really lost. It's all buried somewhere in the memory, and can be

32

brought to light. Or, putting it another way, we are each of us, at birth, an uncarved block. (The Chinese Taoists used to like that image.) We are each sculptors, shaping our own basic characters. Every act of ours whittles, chips, chisels off a bit of the original block. We end with various degrees of beauty and deformation. But few are so beautiful that they do not need some touching up at the hands of a master, and few are so hideously marred as to defy reclamation. Really, there is much in common between the doctrines of purgatory and karma-rebirth. Life continues, and we must pick up where we left off in our struggle to reach the absolute. Buddhists and Catholics are both saying that a single life-experience may not be enough to fit a person to embrace the infinite. Most of us die, not really old and ripe, but still green, selfish, and adolescent. To go from birth to the beatific absolute in one life-experience is quite a leap."

Amitabha laughed out loud. "Very good, Yeshua! You are really warming up to your subject. Believe me, your selection as Yeshua was no accident!"

Yeshua blushed a little—but not enough to deter him from pursuing his theme. "I now remember a vision of a medieval saint—Catherine of Genoa, I believe. After death, she said, souls were not dragged down to hell or pulled up to heaven by an intruding God. On the contrary, she asserted, it had been given to her to understand that each soul found its own place—the spot most natural for it in the whole universe. It was as if every creature had its own specific gravity of soul. You couldn't *drag* a soul into the beatific union, if it felt radically unsuited!"

"Yeshua, Plato would be proud of you! You recollect well!"

Now Yeshua was a little embarrassed. It dawned on him that he had waxed eloquent in the presence of someone who probably knew far more about the subject than himself. "If I recollect so well," he finally asked, "how is it that I cannot recall even a detail about my own previous life?"

"You will in all likelihood never remember that, my son. In several crucial areas, your brain has been unwrinkled. Oh, a faint neural imprint is probably still there—we don't dare erase too drastically until our

Freuds amass more data. But take it on faith for the moment (after tomorrow you'll have hard evidence for it): you, yourself, along with the entire society of Sukhavati Entopia, have freely willed it so. You have asked to be selectively unwrinkled. You do not really want to remember the *personal* dimension of your past. Ideas, yes. These are still useful to you, and you will find yourself remembering more and more pertinent information. But personalities, subjective experiences and human relationships? No. Of these, you have willed to remember nothing. When you are horizoned tomorrow, you will understand why."

The red light on Amitabha's console flashed again. Amitabha jumped up with real impatience and flicked a switch. "Yes," he said, quietly and coldly.

"Sir, it's the Alexander at Sluice 4 again. I do evaluate a security risk. I repeat, a security risk. Your presence here appears to be necessary."

"Very well, I'll take a skimmer and be down—Sluice 4, did you say?—in six minutes.

"Yeshua, I'm sorry. I must go. We are by no means finished, but I really must go. What I must attend to right now will, one day, comprise one of your own duties —one of the most important of them. I am presently serving in a dual capacity, until your era-maturity commences.

"I suggest that you take a book while you are waiting for me—or better yet, why don't you go up to the meditation garden on the roof. You will have a magnificent view of the whole island up there, and it will help you get oriented. I should be back within the hour. The entire staff is at your service, if you need anything. You don't know them, but they all know who *you* are, and why you are here." And with that, Amitabha shot out of the room.

Yeshua sat where he was for a moment, reflecting on the past hour's conversation. It thrilled him to feel his mind erupt as it just had on the subject of the world religions. What other geysers of knowledge and emotion lay just the other side of numbness? He had been able to recollect, as Amitabha put it, a good deal about Buddhism. But what did all that have to do with him personally? On this question, he drew a blank. "No, why be a hypocrite?" he reproached himself. Some connections and inferences were stirring at the bottom of his consciousness. But they were too fantastic to entertain. He allowed the sparkling hints to subside, awaiting further conversation with his "era-guardian."

The volume of Buddhist scriptures was still in his hands. He put it down. Enough religious speculation for now, he thought. His eye took in the other books lining the study. "No, no more reading for now," he said aloud. Yeshua stood up abruptly and walked out of the room.

It was a spacious residence, indeed. Corridors seemed to run all over the place. As he stood by the door in indecision, an official in khaki, with navy blue piping, came down the hall in his direction.

"Sir?" His courtesy and deference could not obscure the intense curiosity he obviously felt toward Yeshua. "May I be of service?"

"Yes. Could you direct me to the meditation garden, please? Amitabha said I might wait for him there."

"Certainly, sir." He smiled and bowed his head. "Just follow me." They turned right at the next corridor and, after a rather long walk, came to a flight of stairs. "It's three flights to the roof, sir. Would you like to take the lift instead?"

"No, thank you. I'd like to stretch my legs, to tell you the truth."

"Very good, sir. Oh, wait just a moment, if you will. I've a very fine pair of binoculars in my office, and if you really want to see the city, you should use them. Let me fetch them. Only take a minute." He dashed around the corridor and returned with a leather case.

"Very kind of you," said Yeshua. "How will I get them back to you?"

"Oh, I'll hear you coming down the stairs, and I'll stick my head out. I'm just in office I D, down the hall." Yeshua nodded. The official smiled and returned down the corridor.

The three flights did not cost Yeshua an extra breath. "Quite an improvement," he mused, "over the day before."

On the roof, on every side of the thrusting dome, there lay before him another of Sukhavati's sumptuous gardens, interspersed with pathways of whitewashed pebbles and set with oases of chairs, tables, and shade trees. More unusual, a central fountain not only provided a liquid musical background, but issued forth in little irrigation streams radiating through the garden. Unseen pipes evidently collected the flow and returned it to the fountain.

Yeshua strolled over to the outer wall of the garden, about one and a half meters high. Resting his elbows on the wall, he gazed out at the serene city spread out below. "Marvelous!" The whites and pinks and yellows of the buildings blended in perfectly with the soft blue sky and the many green parks throughout the island. He wondered where Sluice Gate 4 might be. The IMOB—what was it again? The Inadmissible MicroOrganism Barrier?—extended beyond Sukhavati, a full kilometer out to sea. Transparent though it was, he could make out the IMOB to the north, away from the sun, but he could not see where it touched the sea. Too misty.

Once again, his eyes traversed the tranquil city. He used the binoculars now, picking out first one scene and then another. Something caught his eye on another rooftop in the southeast part of the city. Judging from the low, barrack-like buildings in that area, it must have been the Sudraheen section, the manufacturing district he had visited on his first day.

Interested because he had been there and had conversed with some of the workers, Yeshua focused his glasses more carefully. Two Sudraheen—he could make out that one was a woman, the other a man—were spreading sheets up on a clothesline. Apparently they were convinced that they had secured their privacy, for there was no doubting the amorous nature of the play that ensued. And they *did* have privacy—with the single exception of the garden atop Amitabha's official residence, it was unquestionably the highest point in the whole area.

Yeshua laughed, and meant to turn away. And eventually did turn away—but not so quickly that he did not see one of the loveliest, most voluptuous female forms he could ever have imagined. The story of David and Bathsheba now came to his mind, and he remembered long sections of Old Testament narrative.

Yeshua walked away to another part of the garden

36

and, for a while, watched the noiseless skimmers make their way along the wide tree-lined avenues. There was plenty to hold his attention—including the 10:48 cloud eclipse. Even though he had already experienced it, he was startled by the sudden darkness. "That will take some getting used to," he thought.

A building to the east also attracted his attention. It supported a great shining bowl: a mirror, it finally dawned on him, collecting the sun's rays. For what purpose he did not know. But he passed the better part of an hour in this way, scanning first one part of the town, then another.

Deciding it was time to return to Amitabha's study, he strode over to the stairway. Turning his binoculars for one last scan of the city, he picked up the Sudraheen suburb again. He found the roof. "One hour later!" he exclaimed aloud. He quickly returned the binoculars to their case. Somehow, he knew that what he had seen was extraordinary.

As Yeshua turned to go down the stairs, he practically bumped into Amitabha.

"Careful, Yeshua, don't fall! They told me you had come up to the meditation garden to wait for me. Yeshua! What is it? You're face is flushed. Has anything upset you?"

Yeshua told him straight out. "Isn't an hour rather remarkable?"

Amitabha laughed. "Not for the Sudraheen, Yeshua. Frankly, that is one of the principal arts they practice. I use the word art with some precision. For you or me, surely, an hour would be remarkable—also unthinkable! Never fear, we will eventually get around to that subject, as well as all others pertaining to your life on Sukhavati.

"But now, let us go back to my study. I believe it won't hurt to order some broth for you (I, myself, have eaten this week), and then we will discuss the significance of the second part of the name of this island: Entopia. Sukhavati Entopia. It's a queer name, I know, but it says a great deal in brief—which is a habit we try to cultivate around here."

Back in the study, the broth having been peacefully

and meditatively consumed, Amitabha picked up the thread of his instructions.

"What, if anything, my son, does the word Entopia mean to you?"

"Nothing."

"Does it remind you of anything?"

"It reminds me of another 'topia word—Utopia."

"Meaning?" Amitabha was flipping through an old dictionary.

"Meaning perfection. A perfect society."

"Correct, Yeshua. It's traditionally defined as 'an imaginary and indefinitely remote place'; also, 'a place of ideal perfection, especially in laws, government, and social conditions.' The word comes from two Greek words, you know: *ou,* meaning no, and *topos,* meaning place—the literal meaning of Utopia being Noplace—unreal, imaginary. It was coined by the English Renaissance scholar, St. Thomas More."

"Stop, Amitabha, stop! Give me a minute! Every time you introduce a new topic, it sets off a thousand little firecrackers in my brain. I begin to remember different attempts at Utopian communities. I remember bits and pieces of Renaissance history . . . it's all rushing to the surface of my mind."

"Yes, yes," sighed Amitabha, looking at his gold watch, "I know." It was magnificently jeweled—the only ornate item that he had on his person. "But tell me, Yeshua, what are your reactions to Utopia?"

There was a moment of silence. Then Yeshua answered. "Negative. No, partly negative."

"Explain yourself."

"My first reaction was negative, because men in the past, if my present recollections are all accurate, were never able to achieve Utopian goals. Worse, they were frequently subject to terrible disillusionment when they failed. The case of Russia comes to my mind. There was a leader there—Sta . . . Stalin, I believe—who played havoc with their movement. Several such movements have ended in despair, in reigns of terror."

"But you said, Yeshua, that your reaction was only *partly* negative. Where is the positive side?"

"This is very precipitate judgement on my part, sir.

38

You are not giving me much time to sort things out. But my feeling is, that while Utopian goals were false *historically,* (i.e., they couldn't be achieved), they were somehow true *psychologically,* meaning that men couldn't live without them—couldn't even be *men* without them."

"Say on, my son. You're warming up to it now."

"Well, suppose the human race had ever become reconciled to the status quo, had abandoned all Utopian dreams. Isn't it the case that the shark reached a remarkably functional structure at a very early point in the history of life on this planet, and thereafter ceased to evolve? The analogy just came to my mind. It's a very efficient creature, but it's still a shark! Man is not nearly so efficient, I suppose, but he transcends himself. That is his nature. For this species, evolution, progress, demands a dream, a splendid motivation."

"Excellent analysis, Yeshua." Amitabha was smiling again, as he had smiled during their duscussion of Buddhism. Our expectations of you will not be disappointed, I think. But to return to the point at hand. If a Utopian society *could* be achieved, what then? Would you elect to live in one?"

A long pause ensued. Amitabha began to rephrase the question.

"No, I understood the question well enough, sir," Yeshua interrupted. "It's the answer that's giving me trouble." Again there was silence. Finally, he spoke. "I'd probably like to live in such a society for a while. But I don't know for how long."

"Why not?"

"Frankly, it would probably get very boring. It seems that man *needs* difficulties, problems, imperfections to overcome. Oh yes, I've got it now! There is something I had been trying to remember in this connection: 'challenge and response.' It was the thesis of a 20th century historian, Toynbee, that great civilizations did not spring up, as was popularly believed, in secure, favored spots, free of danger, but rather, when and where men made a full human response to the dangers confronting them. I think I believe that. Utopias are not altogether human. Put it another way: they're dull!"

"Yeshua, I thought this would take much longer than

it has. You do have a knack of cutting to the heart of a question. It is a pleasure to be your instructor.

"Now all that remains for me to tell you today is to emphasize that Sukhavati Entopia is not Sukhavati Utopia. We're not some imaginary perfect society in Noplace, in Dreamland. We are the most advanced human society yet achieved, and we're very much 'in place.' We are a happy community, I believe, but by no means a perfect one— as you have observed for yourself, and as I have been perfectly willing for you to observe . . . although I understand you made Ananda a little nervous in the process." Amitabha chuckled.

"Here, come over to the wall map. I want to show you just where we are."

Yeshua followed his instructor over to the wall, where a large map of the world, hitherto unintelligible to him, was displayed.

"Here we are, Yeshua, right down in the chain of the old Ross Dependency Islands, at 174 degrees of longitude, west; and 61 degrees latitude, south."

"But . . . but doesn't that put us very close to the frigid region . . . what is it called? There it is on the map: Antarctica! We ought to be freezing!" Yeshua almost shouted.

"Gently, gently, my Newly-Aware," Amitabha scolded. You have seen some of our defects; you have by no means seen all of our glories."

"Yes, that is what Ananda kept repeating to me."

"If you look out to sea on a clear day, Yeshua, you will occasionally spot an iceberg drifting by. But we have achieved perfect climatic control within the IMOB—the technical details will all be explained to you later."

Yeshua stood looking at the map. How is it that it does not say Sukhavati Entopia on the map, sir?"

"It won't for a long time to come, if we can help it," Amitabha smiled back at him. "This was only a scraggly, barren island when we arrived here. The world had no interest in it. The world has no interest in it now. They are not aware that any significant change has occurred here."

"I realize that we are outside the usual sea routes, but can't we be seen from the air?" Yeshua asked.

"Cloud eclipse, my son. Two of them, remember? One

in the morning, at 10:48, and one in the afternoon, at 3:37. We have electro-magnetic control over those cloud formations you can see to the west. They continually hover nearby, and we rotate them overhead just long enough to block out the two daily photo-satellites that are sent out by the Federations."

"The what?"

"The Three Federations. You have some world history to catch up on in the next few months, Yeshua. We will want you to be well informed on these matters. But in brief, the earth is now politically organized into three giant federations: The Western, the Central, and the Eastern. Theoretically, they all belong to the World Federation. But except for a few joint scientific projects, the World Federation accomplished little more than the old United Nations or the older League of Nations ever did."

"Sir, how many people live on the island?"

"About 140,000, Yeshua—144,000, to be more precise. Oh, but look at the hour! I want you to relax the rest of this afternoon, and to retire early, my son. To-morrow, you know, will be one of the biggest days of your whole era. And many more questions will be answered for you then, though not all."

"I know, but——"

"No, Yeshua, nothing more today! The rule for the first few days is, as you know, 'Aware yourself gently.' Tomorrow, my son, your awareness will take an exponential leap. It will not be so gentle. You need your rest, Yeshua. Take my word for it." Amitabha buzzed for the servant.

"Please conduct Yeshua to his room now, and see to his needs. *Vita tecum*, Yeshua."

"*Et cum spiritu tuo*, Sir."

CHAPTER IV

Yeshua Horizoned

A Helen awakened him. Her high rank he learned only later. There was still no more than a glimmer of light in the sky. He looked at the clock—5:30. No wonder Amitabha wished him to retire so early.

"Arise, Yeshua. I will help you prepare." She showed no trace of surprise or embarrassment at his nakedness. "I am your Helen." This she announced simply, but with a kind of piercing tenderness. It produced in Yeshua a quiet, joyous awe.

She had brought in a tray with a small flask, a basin and a sponge. "This will be a little cool, Yeshua." And she began to sponge him lightly with the liquid in the flask. It was cold, like ether, but it evaporated immediately, so that he needed no drying. She sponged him delicately but thoroughly. It aroused no urgent desire in him, although she was a beautiful woman. "Too early in the morning, perhaps," he mused, "and too cold." But the explanation did not really satisfy him, and he was left mildly disturbed. Perhaps it was the solemnity in the still morning air. He knew that this was, for him, a sacred day.

"And now, these vapors, Yeshua," she said softly, handing him a vial. "They are stronger than any you have had, but breathe them deeply. This day will be taxing." He removed the stopper and breathed. A current of wakefulness and strength passed through him.

Helen took the vial from him and brought over a linen garment to his air bed. Like his previous robe, it was white with crimson piping. But rich gold threads were woven into this one, and a golden sunburst design with a crimson ankh in the center was stitched over the heart. Though still light in weight, it was an exceedingly rich garment.

Helen now took both his hands in hers and gently pulled him to his feet. Having helped him into the ceremonial robe, she placed her hands on his cheeks and lightly kissed him. First his forehead, then his eyes, then his mouth. "Welcome, Yeshua, welcome," she whispered.

In the early morning light, Yeshua caught the mysterious aura of her long blonde hair. Her figure, slighter than the Sudraheen's, was somehow more noble, more delicate. Her chin, her throat, her breasts were girl-like; yet her bearing was queenly. He could find no word to say in reply, but he was glad in every fiber of his body. It was good to be there with her.

"Come," she said softly, and took him by the hand. She led him out into the totally still corridor. "We must be the only ones up," he thought to himself. Down a half-flight of stairs, they came to a lift. They entered, and descended several more levels. Yeshua was surprised by the extent of the building; there appeared to be even more levels below than there were above the surface.

The doors of the lift slid open and she ushered him out into another long corridor. The carpeting was especially thick and rich on this level. Their footsteps were noiseless. At the end of the corridor, Yeshua found himself standing before heavy portals of bronze and leather; no other doors in the residence approached these for weight and grandeur. Helen pressed a switch on the wall and the heavy doors swung slowly open. She took him by the arm and conducted him in.

Yeshua found himself in a large, dimly-lit auditorium —or was it a court, or a chapel? Several hundred people were seated, waiting for his arrival! (And he had thought that no one else would be up at such an early hour!) But they were not seated facing the front of the huge hall; rather, half were seated to the left, half to the right, facing one another. Through their midst, Helen shepherded him down the center aisle.

Near the end of the aisle, almost lost in shadow, stood

a dais, and on it sat a figure in flowing ceremonial robes. As Helen brought him closer, he realized it was Amitabha. When the two of them were directly in front of the dais, Amitabha stood erect and, on that signal, the whole assembly rose to their feet.

"Citizens of Sukhavati," Amitabha began in a strong, clear voice. "We are assembled here, representatives of all ranks, functions and sub-functions: Sudraheens and Rothschilds, Alexanders and Leonardos, Freuds and Durkheims, Archimedes and Heisenbergs, Lao-Tzu's and Yajnavalkyas. We are gathered here on the 3rd of August, the day fixed by the Sophia. We are here, as all of you know, to horizon Yeshua Nabi.

"Let us observe tradition, and pause in veneration and thanksgiving to Sidhartha, the Founder." So saying, Amitabha turned round and faced a kind of crypt at the end of the hall. The Sukhavati representatives turned with him. An officer in light khaki dress—an Alexander, Yeshua later learned—approached the crypt and pressed a pattern of buttons on a side panel. The doors of the crypt slid open. Dimly lit though the whole scene was (almost an apparition, Yeshua thought), he could see within the crypt a robed figure lying outstretched on an air bed. A crown was suspended from the ceiling so that it hung just a meter over the head of the Founder. Whether he was dead or alive, conscious or unconscious, Yeshua could not make out—only that he lay still, arms folded across his breast majestically, on the rose-colored columns of his air bed. All bowed their heads. After some moments, Amitabha signaled and the doors to the crypt slid shut, and the assembly took their seats.

A chair had been placed for Yeshua directly below the dais, facing Amitabha. Helen sat him down there and took a seat, evidently reserved for her, in the row just across from him, on the left.

"Will the judgment engineers now initiate the Sophia." Amitabha's voice boomed out through the cavernous hall. Four men—he learned later they were a Freud, a Durkheim, a Yajnavalkya and a Heisenberg—went to the console of a large metallic box about two meters high, two meters wide and five meters long. The whole apparatus, despite its great weight and mass, was evidently on rollers, for the four men guided it electronically from the side wall of the auditorium into the central aisle, just in back of Yeshua.

One of the four men whom Amitabha had called judgment engineers, flipped a switch, and there was a low whirring hum in the apparatus. Then a voice was heard from a tape within this large box called the Sophia.

"Name?"

"Yajnavalkya Nabi."

Yeshua recognized his own voice! Yet the first name did not correspond to his own; only the last name was correct. The tape continued:

"Era-age?"

"One hundred and twenty-three."

Yeshua's mind was spinning. One hundred and twenty-three! He turned perplexedly to Helen who smiled back at him reassuringly.

"Reason for request for psychic sabbatical?"

"Awareness satiety. Urgent need for horizon modulation."

While Yeshua could not recognize the official, even bureaucratic, voice of the one putting the questions to him on the tape, the answering voice was authentically his own—though he had not one neural wisp of memory to confirm it. But there was no time to spend on logical analysis; the tape rolled on:

"Do you now willingly submit to judgmental probing of your unconscious?"

"I do."

"And do you willingly accept in advance the psycho-socio decree to be handed down by the Sophia on the basis of judgmental probing—including both your interim-of-suspension, and your future status in Sukhavati?"

Here there was a pause.

"Yes! I do!"

"One last question: do you now authorize selective memory-euthanasia, discretionary unwrinkling?"

"I do."

"Please sign this document."

There was a momentary pause on the tape. Then the bureaucratic voice resumed:

"Are you Helen Yuan, Era-Helen to Yajnavalkya Nabi?"

"I am."

The voice on the tape was not at all similar to the voice of the woman seated near him. Yeshua was certain of it.

"Please sign here as official witness." There was another pause in the tape recording.

"Yajnavalkya Nabi," the official voice announced, loud and clear. "I speak for all citizens of Sukhavati. We wish you—here the voice grew quieter, and even a little tremulous—"that is, we wish to thank you for this long era of dedicated service. May you enjoy ever new awareness on your sequential pilgrimage. And may you one day abide at the peak of the universe!"

Another halt in the recording. Then:

"Helen . . ."

"Yajna . . ."

"It's time," interrupted the official voice again. "Apply electrodes. Middle-sleep range: 18 amps. At 8:04, switch to deep-sleep, 24 amps. Ready . . . now!"

Yeshua heard a hum and then, a minute or so later, a deeper hum. Then a new voice came over the tape.

"Yajnavalkya Nabi," said this new voice, less officious and more businesslike than the first, "we are now going to take the judgmental criteria-input for the Sophia. Please allow your responses to flow automatically. By that I mean, do not try to *help*—it is impossible to hinder. Do not attempt to clarify, embroider or emphasize. Do you understand my instructions?"

"I understand," said a far-off voice (Yeshua's).

"Very well, let us begin judgmental probing of your unconscious mind. First question: Do you enjoy public esteem, Yajnavalkya Nabi?"

"I do."

"Is it a serious matter for you?"

"I enjoy it less than I did at era-origin."

"Can you do without it entirely?"

"No."

"What are your needs, Nabi, regarding women? Do you wish to be solaced?"

There was no immediate answer.

"Let me be more specific. Do you wish a return of Sudraheen vitality?"

"No."

"Then what relationship with women do you now require?"

"Era-bonding, one-to-one."

"Do you crave the satisfactions and privileges of holding power?"

"Not much."

"Are you willing to accept a condition without power?"

"I am unwilling."

"Very good, Nabi. Now, you will make no verbal response to the next set of questions. Simply relax your mind and your emotions, and yield your thought currents to the electronic probe.

"What degree of awareness fulfillment did you obtain this era in your rank of Yajnavalkya?"

A medley of voices, those of the four judgment engineers, sometimes clear, sometimes confused, now came over the tape.

Low voice: "Write this down. Ready?"

Someone in the background, barely audible, answered, "Yes sir." Then there was a whirr on the Sophia, and the sound of papers being shuffled.

Low voice: "89.6 median; crest 96.1. Unusual. Very high degree of awareness fulfillment, even for a Yajnavalkya."

Normal voice: "Second question, Nabi. What degree of emotional fruition did you experience? We want your personal satisfaction quotient."

Low voice: "Get ready to take this reading now." (Another whirr on the machine.) "Here it comes. 85.2 median; 91 even, crest. Not bad here, either!"

Background voice: "I have it, sir."

Low voice: "Now we have to get his doubt quotient. Raise the amperage to 28."

Background voice: "Don't you think that's too high, sir?"

Low voice: "Not for a Yajna. An accurate reading of the doubt quotient is absolutely essential for the Sophia's psycho-socio decree. In the lower ranks it is not quite so crucial. Do you have the amperage up? Good."

Normal voice: Nabi, this is your last question, a very important one. Do you have any doubts as to the supreme value of the Sukhavati Entopia venture?"

The whirr of the machine was prolonged for fifteen or twenty seconds.

Low voice: "Here it comes! Read it very carefully."

Background voice: "7.5. That's bad! And it seems disproportionate, both to this degree of awareness fulfillment and to his personal satisfaction quotient."

Low voice: "Wait, you're forgetting something! You must subtract a 2.3 Jewish reluctance factor from his doubt quotient!"

Background voice: "What are you saying? Are you claiming that the computer is anti-Semitic?"

Normal voice: "Not at all. The Sophia recognizes the authenticity of whatever ethnic tendencies can be passed on genetically. Nabi was a Jew. Given their unique history of persecution and suffering, survival required of the Jews the development of their capacity for suspicion. A highly critical and suspicious stance can be passed along genetically, if only the suspicious members of a given group survive. We subtract 2.3 from his doubt quotient in the interests of bio-socio accuracy—not anti-Semitic prejudice."

Background voice: "That brings the doubt quotient down to 5.2, sir."

Low voice: "And that's tolerable."

Normal voice: "Yajnavalkya Nabi, the Sophia now has the necessary information. Judgmental probing of your unconscious is hereby terminated. Farewell and sleep well, until the time of your recall."

With that, the tape clicked off.

Amitabha and the assembly rose from their seats. Helen leaned over and touched Yeshua on the arm, and he arose also, facing Amitabha.

"Citizens of Sukhavati," Amitabha began in his sonorous clear baritone. "Seventy years have passed since Yajnavalkya Nabi departed on psychic sabbatical—the circumstances of which you have all just heard. And a few months ago, as you know, Sukhavati lost her Era-Yeshua, who similarly departed. Immediately upon receiving input of the latter's departure, the Sophia came up with a name to fill that position. I am now going to ask the judgment engineers to play back the psycho-socio decree of the Sophia.

The Sophia once again began to whirr. A mechanical bass voice, evidently the voice of the Sophia, itself, proclaimed without emotion: "A computed synthesis of the contemporary social needs of the community of Sukhavati Entopia, together with the combined aptitudes and desires of the available candidates, indicates the selection of Nabi, previously Yajnavalkya, as Era-Yeshua. He is, moreover, a possible future candidate for the office of Amitabha. His powers are to be thoroughly tried and tested; his responsibilities, within the scope of his present office, unlimited." The hum of the Sophia faded into the enveloping silence of the auditorium.

Then Amitabha pronounced in a firm voice: "Be it confirmed this day throughout the community of Sukhavati Entopia that Nabi, previously Yajnavalkya, has been restored to us by the Sophia, *Yeshua* Nabi! I now call on all here assembled to raise their right hands and to recite with me the traditional oath of allegiance to an Era-Yeshua."

The hall rang out with the glad words:

Envy, there is none.
We acknowledge thy origin,
Born of mathematics and truth,
Thy Mother, the inviolate Sophia.
Shepherd us, teach us, guide us
Through the era unrolling, Yeshua Nabi!

"Step forward to the dais, Yeshua Nabi," commanded Amitabha.

At the pressure of Helen's hand on his arm, Yeshua stepped up to the platform.

"Receive and wear this crimson thread of your rank," announced Amitabha, placing the thread over his left shoulder and under his right arm.

"Receive this jeweled watch, functional sacrament of Sukhavati, land of the living, land of uncoiling time, time without end!" Amitabha placed a golden necklace over

49

his head and inserted the attached watch in a breast pocket of his robe.

"Receive this wooden staff, the shepherd's crook, sign of your sacred office."

Yeshua, his mind outracing even his heart, received all these symbols.

"It is done!" proclaimed Amitabha.

"It is done!" the assembly chorused in unison.

"Enter it into the Sophia," ordered Amitabha. "Yeshua Nabi: Office commenced August 3rd, in the 125th year of Era A.D., Amitabha Djilov!"

"It is entered!" one of the judgment engineers responded.

"*Vita vobiscum!*" Amitabha cried out in jubilation.

"*Et cum spiritu tuo!*" roared the assembly.

With that, the lights in the hall, hitherto subdued, were turned on to their full intensity. And the representatives of all the ranks of Sukhavati society milled around the newly-horizoned Yeshua, congratulating him, applauding him, embracing him, and welcoming his return.

CHAPTER V

Realization: Helen

But it was too much for Yeshua. Too many surmises, inferences and conjectures had linked arms in his mind and were reeling around in drunken frolic. Helen knew it intuitively and, in short order, she had maneuvered him out of the happy throng of well-wishers. "Yes, yes," she fended off his congratulators, "thank you very much, but Yeshua must retire now. As you know, he begins his month of realization almost immediately."

She had him out a side door of the assembly hall in about five minutes, while the Sukhavati citizens stayed on to discuss the new event and to enjoy the festive holiday. As the two emerged into the quiet corridor, Yeshua was still without speech. He looked at Helen imploringly.

"I'm taking you to my own room," she whispered to him. "Yours will be besieged all day by function representatives from every district of Sukhavati."

They passed through a maze of corridors and descended still another level. "In here," she murmured, as she pulled him by the arm and took him into a quiet room facing an inner courtyard and garden. "No one comes very much to the old courtyard, now that the library has been moved to the second level."

The room was cool and shadowy, blinds down against the bright glare in the garden. She sat him down on the air bed and gently pushed his shoulders down. "Close your eyes," she urged with soft authority. He did as he was bid, but he was taut as a wire. Quickly she adjusted a pair of earphones over his head. "Think nothing at all for now. Just listen."

He allowed the music to melt into the rigidity of his spinal column. His tissues and nerves soaked in the melodic irrigation. After some time, his mind unlocked and he heaved a great sigh. "Now," she said, sitting beside him, stroking his head, "you can talk if you like," and she removed the earphones.

Yeshua half sat up in bed. "There is no dying here!"

"There is no dying here," she affirmed quietly.

He looked straight into her eyes for a long time. Then the tears came. He buried his face in her breast and clasped her to him hard. Now he wept uncontrollably. "I won't die, I won't die!" he kept gasping. "I will live forever!"

She allowed him to go on for a long time, stroking his head, soothing him. Finally he subsided, and she pressed him gently back till he lay prone. *"Vita tecum,"* she murmured. *"Et cum spiritu tuo,"* he whispered back. He understood now the full import of the Latin formula.

"I lived here previously," Yeshua mused dreamily, "and I can't remember it."

51

"You lived here many times, in many different eras, Yeshua, performing many different functions."

"On the tape, I said I willingly accepted selective memory-euthanasia. I wish now that I had not. Why would I have agreed to such mental crippling, do you know?"

"You'll know why in another 70 or 100 years. Even though Sukhavati is the greatest society the human race has yet achieved, we all eventually tire of our particular function, of our awareness level—and, I suppose, even of one another, Yeshua. We're all finite, after all. And so, we move on. But we don't want to carry that burden of finite memories and relationships with us to our new horizon. For one thing, after two or three era sequences, it would get to be too complicated. And imagine what it would be like after twenty or thirty rebirths! So we willingly submit to selective erasure. Parts of our brains are carefully unwrinkled by micro-electronic techniques."

"But," Yeshua persisted, "how is it that I *half* remember things? Here, I'll give you an example. On my second day here, I think, it occurred to me that to eat but once a day or less, and not to be hungry, was very strange. But why did I think it strange? What basis of comparison did I have?"

She took his hands in hers. "Your base level of consciousness, Yeshua, is pre-Sukhavati. You were not born here—none of us was, by the way. We all, like yourself, came here from the dark continents." She smiled. "That's what we call the outside world, still subject to disease and death. What is happening is that you automatically tend to compare everything you experience here with the deepest behavioral patterns you have—those of your first existence."

Yeshua now sat up abruptly. "How do we do it?" he asked.

"Do what?"

"Go on living and living. How is it we don't age, get ill and die?"

"Oh, you'll soon be having long sessions, I assure you, with our Pasteurs, our Harveys, and so on. They'll give you a thorough technical explanation for it. The IMOB, of course, is crucial."

Yeshua sat silently for awhile, lost in thought. When he did speak, he brought up another subject entirely.

"This new function of mine, Helen, which seems to be associated with my name—why is it so important to Sukhavati? Is the ceremony I experienced today held every time someone gets horizoned?"

She laughed and then grew serious. "The judgment-criteria input for the Sophia, together with the judgment-decree, are always publicly announced, certainly. But seldom in such a solemn setting as you witnessed today. The public hearing assures each of us, as well the community, that perfect justice has been done. If a lower function has been decreed for us, it is because we not only *deserved,* but even needed and *wanted* that particular era-experience; if not consciously, then unconsciously. And, if a higher function is decreed for us, it is both because we are ready for it and because the contemporary community needs us in that particular role.

"The whole thing boils down to this, Yeshua—and I want you to listen closely: we now possess the technological capacity to actualize the karma-rebirth theme of the Asiatic world religions! The citizens of Sukhavati, Yeshua, are happily meshed in the processes of electronic Buddhism."

She had to smile again at his wide-eyed, half incredulous wonder. "You see—or I should say, you *will* see—that is why there is practically no social unrest on the island. Everyone acknowledges the justice of the Sophia. I realize you don't have a very sound idea as yet about the nature of the Sophia. That will come, never fear. But be sure of this: there is no envy of your high position. Because, as the public oath testified, 'We acknowledge thy origin, born of mathematics and truth, thy Mother, the inviolate Sophia.' Oh, there is a *little* unrest. You'll learn about that later."

"But you haven't told me what is so important about my particular function," Yeshua persisted.

"Yours is an extremely vital role, Yeshua. You are second, really, only to Amitabha. That, by the way, is why *I* have been chosen, of all the Helens of Sukhavati, to solace you," she said with a tender smile.

"But I mustn't get off the subject. Yes, yours is the priestly role!"

"Priestly?" he asked wonderingly.

"Have you any idea, Yeshua, how much motivation it takes *to live forever?*" She looked him in the eye for a long, solemn moment, and then she sighed. "No, you have not; you've only just been horizoned. But after you have been purposed, you will know; and you will be continually sustaining the purpose of the rest of us. That's part of your function as Yeshua.

"And then, too, you'll be dealing with the problem of the Prodigals—those who unpurpose themselves, those who first commit thought-suicide and then, indirectly, body-suicide. Believe me, Yeshua, you will need to be purposed to the marrow of your bones to deal with them. They form a kind of underground suicide cult. The problem is becoming more and more serious."

She was lost in serious thought for a while. When she recovered herself she abruptly changed the subject. "Yeshua, that's enough for one morning. You need more music now, and perhaps a visual. Lie quietly while I arrange these things. Later this afternoon we may take a walk and talk some more."

But about an hour before afternoon eclipse there was a knock on the door and Yeshua, drowsy on the air bed, heard Helen greeting Ananda. He sat up as Ananda came bursting into the room.

"Congratulations, sir! What a joyous day! Very auspicious! I thought you might like to take a little stroll with me, just for relaxation's sake."

"Yes, yes I would," Yeshua shot back, almost leaping out of bed. There were a few things he thought he would rather check out with Ananda than with Helen, much as he now felt drawn to her.

Helen laughed at his haste, as though she had already intuited the topic of their conversation. "All right Yeshua, go with Ananda." She kissed him lightly on the forehead.

"Do have him back early, Ananda. You know what kind of a day this is for him."

As they emerged from the imposing front entrance of Amitabha's residence, Ananda remarked, "Actually, I've brought my own private skimmer with me, sir. Everyone in the community is talking about you today—it's been declared a holiday, you know—and we'll get no peace if we walk in town. But we can be out to the sea in about ten minutes if we take my skimmer, and no one will bother us there. Shall we go?"

"By all means, Ananda."

Neither man broke silence during the short drive. The skimmer soon turned off the wide avenue onto a much narrower and less trafficked road. A few minutes later, Ananda turned onto a gravel road that had no skimmers on it at all.

"The ride here will be a bit bumpy, but we'll be alone on this part of the island," said Ananda.

Now Yeshua could see the ocean. It was, in fact, his first close observation of it since his conscious return. As they skimmed closer, the sounding majesty of the surf nearly overwhelmed him. The slow swells of azure blue and the crashing cascades of green and white set up a tide in his own blood. There, in the distance, more plainly than he had ever yet seen it, stretching from sea to sky, stood the transparent shield and crown of Sukhavati, the immense IMOB.

"Dug right into the ocean bed?" Yeshua asked, motioning with his head toward the huge dome, some two or three kilometers out to sea.

"Yes," Ananda replied. "It was the single most difficult piece of construction ever undertaken in Sukhavati. Our chief Archimedes will be filling you in on that shortly. You'll be spending a lot of time with our technical people this entire first year, you know, until you are purposed."

There was a long pause.

"Ananda, tell me: Helen knew what I wanted to talk to you about, didn't she?"

Ananda laughed unrestrainedly. "I dare say so, sir."

"And *you're* laughing, so *you* know. Am I correct?"

"I can guess what it is, Yeshua. And it's quite natural, too. I should be puzzling about the same thing, in your place."

"She . . . she has been assigned to solace me?"

"Yes."

"Assigned by the Sophia?"

55

"That is correct, sir, by the Sophia. Do you not find her congenial?"

"Helen is . . . is breathtaking, Ananda. That's not the problem. The problem lies in another direction altogether: she was *assigned* to me! It feels strange to have her as an involuntary pawn. It feels strange to have her love when I have done absolutely nothing to merit it. I haven't *won* her affection; Sukhavati has donated it to me!"

"Oh, that's your base-level consciousness, sir—strictly from the dark continents, pre-Sukhavati. For those in the higher functions, the Sophia is always called on to help achieve really satisfactory solacing. We can't risk failure at the highest levels, sir. With the lower ranks, the Sudraheen for instance, it's different. But they are not even involved in era-bonding, you know."

"Ananda, this solacing business—does it mean she sleeps with me?"

"That, of course, is between the two of you, sir. There is certainly no law against it, and it is even the usual, though not invariable, arrangement. But there's ever so much more to it than that, Yeshua. You can barely imagine the process at your present—if you'll pardon me—adolescent stage of awareness."

"Is Amitabha, too, solaced in this way?"

"No. Amitabha needs no solace. No one needing to be solaced gets to be an Amitabha. One of the questions, you may recall, specifically put to you by the judgment engineers was, 'Do you need to be solaced?' "

"I remember. My answer on the tape was yes. They also asked me if I wanted a restoration of Sudraheen vitality. I said no. But tell me, please, what was it exactly that I refused?"

"The Sudraheen, Yeshua, live on the first level of awareness. The physical well-being they experience on this island, free of disease and old age—though we do age somewhat, you know: say ten years or so in any given era, until restored in the next—this physical well-being is what chiefly preoccupies and delights the Sudraheen. Needless to say, sexuality is one of the major arts for them—and I use the word 'art' advisedly. At least two or three hours every day is given over to the exploration of every kind of sensual awareness. Their proficiency and endurance in the pursuit of this art is beyond the non-Sukhavati imagination.

"So great is our mere physical exuberance on this island, that it's not easy for a Sudraheen to break away to the next level of awareness. They not infrequently experience many consecutive eras as Sudraheen, before being advanced by the Sophia to the next rank."

"What is the next rank, Ananda?"

"The rank of Rothschild."

"And what do they do?"

"Well, sir, the Rothschilds explore the awareness that comes of certain kinds of practical achievement—of making money and spending it, of being successful in the world. Actually, it tends to be a transitional type of function, leading easily to that of Leonardo or Archimedes, who direct their whole era to the pursuit of the specialized awareness derived from esthetic or scientific experience."

"You're getting just a little ahead of me, Ananda. Could we return to the Sudraheen for a moment? You said there is no era-bonding among them. I take it that means they do not practice monogamy."

"Nor polygamy, either, sir. With the Sudraheen, there is neither marriage nor the giving in marriage. No limitation on the possible numbers of sexual relationships exists in that rank, except the population of Sukhavati itself."

"And what if I were to choose one of them for solacing?" Yeshua asked, thinking immediately of the striking redhead he had met the first day, on his visit to Fabrication Unit Number Six.

Ananda roared, "Oh you are quite incapable of that kind of existence, sir!"

"You mean . . . ?"

"It's not for the reason you think, Yeshua. You are physically equipped for it—never fear about that. Physically, you have the same basic constitution that the Sudraheen men do. But you have had so many era-experiences since your Sudraheen days! You have been psycho-socially refined so many times over. While you retain no memory of particular sexual experiences, you have just about exhausted all the possibilities of the sex

57

act. To put it bluntly, Yeshua, whether you know it yet or not, mere ejaculation bores you! It has to be so. There's no other way to become even a Yajnavalkya—a professional contemplative, a meditator. And that was your *previous* era-function. For a Yeshua, sir, life with a Sudraheen would be quite impossible, quite out of the question. The Sophia, as you will learn, can neither deceive nor be deceived."

"But I still feel attracted to women," argued Yeshua, who didn't at all like the future that Ananda was painting for him. "I was attracted to that Sudraheen girl I met down in the Fabrication Unit, and I am physically attracted to Helen now."

"No question about it, sir; you are not a neuter! You haven't really got my drift yet, Yeshua. What I am trying to say is this: in your present state of psychosomatic refinement, the exultation-increment you would receive from the sex act would keep you in euphoria for months. But by the same token, it would take you months to build up to it. One curve of Helen's left forearm, one elliptical line of her right thigh, would hold you rapt for hours! You are now, moreover, incapable of making physical love until complete emotional and intellectual rapport has been established. But when all these dimensions of the act come together . . . well Yeshua, let me say this: mere ejacualtion compares to solacing, as a flashlight to the sun!"

He paused to give Yeshua time to reflect on this new revelation.

"Yes, I could see you were attracted to the Sudraheen on our recent visit, Yeshua," Ananda continued. "Do you know what would have happened if I had left you alone with her? Nothing! You'd have been of no use to her, I warrant you that. You'd still have been enchanted by the flex of her wrist or by her left ear-lobe, long after she had given you up for lost. And you wouldn't even have been able to to do justice to her ear-lobe, if she could not look at the sea the way you look at it.

"No, Yeshua, you are not ready to be the island's celibate, her Amitabha; but neither are you able to revert to the Sudraheen lifestyle. It would take you many eras of psychic devolution to go back that far. Mind you, the

Rothschilds or the Alexanders—those are our security forces—can revert, and frequently do. Occasionally, even a Leonardo or an Archimedes regresses on his strenuous pilgrimage. But you, sir? Impossible! It is you who will purpose us all one day."

So long had they been in deep conversation that the afternoon cloud eclipse took them by surprise. Ananda pulled out his watch and checked it out of force of habit. They were silent a while, watching the quilted cumulus roll over them.

"What," queried Yeshua, changing the subject, "would happen if, one day, cloud-control were to malfunction, and we were discovered by the Federations?"

"The Alexanders are going to have a lot to say to you about that very question—and about other matters pertaining to our security."

The clouds began to shift back now, and the sea again unsheathed her swords of light.

"Well, you have explained many things to me, Ananda, and I am grateful to you for it. But you know, coming back to Helen and myself, I still wonder how I can possibly be attractive to her, when I have virtually been forced upon her by an impersonal computer."

"An impersonal computer!" Ananda echoed, his face flushed. Yeshua noted his anger—the first he had displayed since the two had met.

"Really, sir, I think you would do well to withhold judgment for a few decades on some of the more complicated facets of Sukhavati life. We shouldn't have given the name Sophia—which as you know means wisdom in the Greek—to a mere logic-box. The Sophia, Yeshua, is no impersonal computer. She exercises our *communal free will*, and is deeply insightful! You know nothing about her yet. But I guarantee you this: she made the choice that you and Helen would have made under optimal conditions!

"The problem with human decisions is that they are so frequently made under duress, under restraint, in the fog and smoke of mood. The Sophia, Yeshua, represents us at our *best!*"

His pupil sighed. "I'm going to need time to digest all this. I'm going to need time."

"Our chief commodity," Ananda laughed, taking out his watch. "Well, we had best be getting along. Helen will be wondering if I've turned Prodigal and kidnapped you."

They talked very little on the return drive, and that little was deliberately inconsequential. Ananda wished to avoid force-feeding Yeshua's still delicate psyche. As their skimmer whispered to a stop in front of Amitabha's residence, Ananda said, "This is called Dharma House, Yeshua—just so you'll know, if the phrase comes up in conversation.

"I won't be seeing you for a month or so," he continued. "You'll be undergoing realization hot and heavy. Those Archimedes people don't live at my leisurely pace. They won't give you a minute. But you get a few days off at the end of each instruction sequence, and I'll be checking with you at those times."

Helen was running down the stairs to meet them. "In the meantime," Ananda added, looking in her direction, "you'll be in good hands."

When the two of them were back, alone in her room, Helen seemed to avoid meeting his eyes. For the first time, he saw her nervous and anxious toward him. And this is what did it for Yeshua—more than all her previous calm and good humor. When he saw her now, unsure of herself in her relationship to him, he took her by the hands and soothed her eyes with his own. "You really do want me, don't you Helen. I was not imposed on you?"

"You were *found* for me, Yeshua! Out of all eras, out of all Sukhavati, you were found for me—and I for you!"

CHAPTER VI

Realization: Archimedes

"Queen-solvent for all that is rich and complex," was the description of time that Ananda had given him on his first day. And though time was unending in Sukhavati, there seemed never enough of it for Yeshua, so diverse and so fascinating were the experiences he now had to digest. Days and weeks rolled by without his taking count. Mornings and evenings, there was Helen. And it was as Ananda had predicted: every intonation of her voice, every plane of her face, held a mystery for him; and he for her. Together: body, mood, and mind, they made a universe—a universe which they explored with a gentle intensity that was astonishing.

And during the day, he was taken in tow by teams of highly trained Archimedes, Heisenbergs, Lavoisiers, etc. Yeshua had, of course, gone through those scientific era-experiences himself, and he was able to recollect a good deal, once his instructors began to massage his mind with problems and experiments.

It was enough for them, sometimes, to merely state a hypothesis in physics, or draw up a mathematical equation, and he would often call to mind the conclusions, the derivatives, and the alternative possibilities. Even though they expected much, they were awed by his quickness and penetration.

Yet, there were areas where he really needed solid instruction. He had been on psychic-sabbatical for—how long did Amitabha say it was?—about 70 years. Time had not stood still, nor had science, during those years.

It was the basic principles that delighted him the most, particularly in the field of biotheology, where the great breakthroughs, the human victories over aging, disease and death, had occurred. Here his favorite instructors were a team of brash adolescents, only twenty to thirty years into their present era.

Hans was a Lavoisier, originally from the Netherlands; Mobutu, a Heisenberg, from Tanzania; and Li, a Darwin from Szechwan, China: all members of the sprawling Archimedes class—larger in this era, Yeshua was told, than in any previous one.

Their discussions with him seemed at times (to Helen, at least) interminable; yet they never fell flat for Yeshua. For one thing, in the privacy of their lab, they treated him with an informality he found refreshing. His ration of respect in the rest of Sukhavati was so adequate, that he positively enjoyed becoming the butt of their occasional teasing and joking. But no matter what the topic of discussion might be, Yeshua invariably brought it around to "life," or "life over death." (Helen told him he sometimes discoursed on these themes in his sleep. His dreams, of course, like the dreams of everyone else in Sukhavati, were electronically fed into home-tapes, which were picked up weekly by the Freuds, for analysis by the Sophia.)

"We may define a living organism," Hans began one afternoon, in customary put-on pomposity, "as a highly specialized, enclosed chemical environment, in selective interaction with its ambience"—here he coughed twice, as if to call attention to the grandeur of his phrasing—"by whose instrumentation, the special features that give the organism its character are constantly being renewed. It thus tends to be self-perpetuating and exists in a state of labile equilibrium." He coughed once again, while Mobutu and Li groaned audibly.

"The elementary unit of life," Hans continued, eyeing his associates as he would a couple of impertinent schoolboys, "is, of course, the cell. In protozoa, the cell constitutes the entire organism; metazoa, by contrast, are composed of a large multiplicity of cells, which are frequently highly differentiated and united by a higher or lower degree of symbiosis—the mysterious relationship defining their mutual dependence."

Li groaned again. "You are not instructing Sudraheens or Rothschilds, you know!" Mobutu almost shouted at him. "Yeshua recollects his elementary biology; don't forget, he was once an Archimedes himself—before he defaulted. So will you kindly get to the point?" Yeshua caught the "defaulted," and laughed.

With great nonchalance, Hans picked up Mobutu's wrist and commenced to read his PSI. "Your psychosomatic stress reading," he said calmly, "indicates that you ought to lie down on your air bed for twenty-three minutes and listen to phase-three music."

"Listen to me, the two of you," Li interrupted in a more serious tone. You know that Yeshua comes before Amitabha for a realization progress report in three weeks. Don't you think we've fooled around long enough?"

"All right," Hans capitulated. "I'll get to the point—if the two of you will stop interrupting.

"Now, Yeshua, you know that a single protozoan, which multiplies by mitosis—by dividing its single cell into two—is theoretically immortal, barring accidents. It is only the metazoan, the multicellular organism, which is alloted a finite span of life. It becomes, as you know, progressively disorganized, and terminates in death—a mere inorganic system.

"But *why*, Yeshua, *why*? There doesn't seem to be any theoretical bilogical inevitability about this sequence of events. After all, organic systems utilize atoms of matter —carbon, oxygen, hydrogen, nitrogen, etc.—which themselves undergo no disintegration. It is the collapse of organization, design, form, which leads to the death of living things. But tell me, Yeshua, since nothing is without purpose, what is the purpose of death? Is death useful?"

"In pre-Sukhavati times, and even now, in the dark continents," answered Yeshua, "yes. Death was and is useful!"

"Explain why," Mobutu challenged him.

"Because metazoan disorganization is actually an expedient for furthering evolution. Prior to Sukhavati, immortal creatures would have disadvantaged their own species in its struggle for survival against other, relatively short-lived, quickly-mutating species, which would have enjoyed opportunities for adaptation and improvement.

So nature herself established the control mechanisms for aging and death.

"But this isn't the part I like!" Yeshua blurted out, interrupting his own discourse.

"Not the part you *like*," echoed Hans in a stern voice. "You were too long a Yajnavalkya, my boy, and all your Archimedes discipline has deserted you! Since when is science a matter of liking and disliking?"

"Let him alone, will you," Li commanded. "The part you like, I know, Yeshua, is the story of the breakthrough, the discovery of the fundamental principles of biotheology. Can you state these principles? Never mind the technical details—only we Archimedes people need be burdened with those—just give me the basic principles."

"Could I have them presented to me one more time, Li? I think I have them, but to make it all indelible, I'd like to hear Hans go over it. He gives it a certain grandeur."

"A privilege," said Hans, with a triumphant glance at his colleagues.

"The breakthrough occurred, not with the construction of the IMOB, as many of our Sudraheen and Rothschilds seem to believe, but with the application by Sukhavati metascientists of the insights of Freud and Dante to the field of biotheology. More particularly, to the problem of life-stabilization.

"To be sure, we took pains to rid ourselves of all harmful microorganisms by means of the IMOB and appropriate radiation; but that was only the groundwork. The really thrilling discovery occurred when we realized that much of what the twentieth century genius Freud had written was *biology* as well as psychology. He may even have guessed it himself. He had written of a kind of death instinct, in unconscious conflict with the will to life that healthy human beings experience: *thanatos* versus *eros*. Sukhavati scientists discovered that death instinct on the level of metazoic cell life. Cells *want* to die!"

"Yes, but get on to Dante—where does Dante fit in?"

"Well, it was Dante who first intuited—the poets are always a step ahead of the scientists, I have to admit it—that the primal force of the universe was not earth, air, fire or water, nor the ideal forms of Plato, nor the atoms of Lucretius, but *love*. 'The love that moves the sun and stars,' as Dante intuited, is the primal force of the universe. Newton knew that every single particle of matter in the universe attracts every other particle, and he even knitted together some mathematics to clothe the insight, but it was Dante who put his ear to the heart of the universe and heard it beat.

"Now. Listen closely, Yeshua. The two insights come together in a way that you already know. In all anticipatory stages of evolution, death issues out of love. Immortal living things in those early stages would have frozen the species at elementary levels of development. The death of individuals, allowing for new mutations and adaptations, is a biological act of love for the species— for the advancement of life itself.

"One example: there is a gaudy, bright-colored moth which, after reproductoin, deliberately exposes himself to his natural predators. Why? He has a very nasty taste, and his enemies won't soon forget eating him! His self-sacrifice, therefore, adds an increment of safety for his offspring. Love, you see, even on this primitive, instinctual level, lies *behind* the death instinct, and is written into the very genes and chromosomes. Dante was right!

"And even after the advent of man, the process had perforce to go on. If we had frozen the human race to the generation of early Babylonians and Egyptians, we'd have gotten the pyramids and the calendar, but not the fugues of Bach or the physics of Einstein.

"However, as early as the 20th century, there were indications that the human race was peaking—was throwing off individuals like Gandhi, Tolstoi, Buber, Pope John the XXIII, all wedded to non-violence and to compassion.

"Then came our founder, Strastnik, whom we call Siddhartha, the Founder; and after him the first Newly-Awares: a collection of men and women in whom *the death instinct was no longer needed by nature, no longer useful to the species and, therefore, no longer in the service of love*. Such a generation does not need to die to make room for other individuals, to allow further mutations and adaptations. *Individual immortality is no longer a detriment to evolution; it is the point of evolution!*

"The biotheological breakthrough occurred first in them; their very cell-life was permeated by spirit——"

Yeshua's eyes were dancing with excitement. "But weren't there individuals before this time, men like Buddha and Jesus and Yainavalkya, who had already reached this point? Why shouldn't they have lived?"

Hans eyed him shrewdly. "And do you know for a fact that they are dead?" he asked finally.

"Hans! No fairy tales, please," admonished Li. "Granted, Yeshua," he continued, "that evolution had already reached its culmination point in a few gifted historical personages such as Jesus and Buddha; nevertheless the groundwork for immortality had not yet been prepared. Human beings, as you know, are 'body-souls,' and *both* dimensions of personality have to be taken into account if a man is to escape aging, disease and death.

"No doubt the death instinct, even on the cellular level, had been overcome in the extraordinary individuals you mention; but there was as yet no *community* sufficiently organized, sufficiently wealthy and technologically trained, to construct a project like the IMOB, to insure proper radiation, to guarantee central surveillance of each individual's psychosomatic stress. In short, there was as yet no Sophia! The Sophia, unfortunately, is eternal in only one direction: the future. It had, unlike the mythical Yahweh, a beginning."

"Well, Yeshua," Hans broke in, eager to resume his role as mentor, "have you followed the reasoning so far? The important thing is to see how the pieces of the puzzle all come together. First, there is the biotheological triumph over what we call the Freud factor, that is, the death instinct on the cellular level. This occurs at the precious moment of Evolution-Conversion, when the basic decision to live for others is made. Operative here, of course, is the Dante factor, the cosmic primal force of love. Understood so far, Yeshua? Good.

"You are now ready for Strastnik's Law, the metascientific statement of the victory of life over death: *What is absolutely and freely self-donating, cannot not-be.* I'm going to write the mathematical equation for this on the board—you've seen it many times on Sukhavati flags and emblems. Now you're in a position to understand it."

Hans rose and picked up a piece of chalk. He wrote the following equation: $\infty\lambda\approx=\female$. The first symbol, ∞, means 'infinite.'

"The next symbol, Yeshua, is the Chinese character for altruism and reciprocity. It is composed of the symbols for man (λ) and the number two ($\approx$). 'Man-One.' you understand, would signify self-centered, unloving man. But 'Man-Two' indicates self-donation and love. The last symbol ($\female$), as you know, is the Egyptian hieroglyphic for immortality. So Strastnik's law can be stated: $\infty\lambda\approx=\female$. Infinite self-donation equals immortality.

"The potentiality of immortality is thus present from the first moment of Evolution-Conversion. And Jesus, Buddha, Yajnavalkya and others had this potentiality. But the potentiality cannot be actualized until the planetary—or at least, the local—life-support system has been suitably altered. You need the IMOB, which is inordinately difficult and expensive to erect, along with the appropriate radiation. Both dimensions of the human being flesh and spirit, must be provided for."

"And that is why," Mobutu added quietly, "it would do the gentiles—the inhabitants of the three Federations—little good to discover our technological secrets. Their detection of our life-support system would not be enough to save them, but it would be more than enough to destroy us. You must understand this much now about the problem of Sukhavati security. Later, the Alexanders will go into more detail with you.

"If they ever found out about our existence here—about our *unending* existence here—they might perhaps desist long enough from war, rapine and commercial rivalry to construct their own IMOB, or a series of IMOBS. But not having undergone Evolution-Conversion, the death wish on the cellular level would still be dominant. Continuing, therefore, to die as before, they would conclude that we were hiding from them the more crucial technological secrets of immortality. They would certainly attack—and you know that we are committed to non-violence. They would overwhelm us, imprison us and torture us till we died—and we would die outside the IMOB—in the vain hope that we would finally blurt out some formula or other for the elixir of life. For all these reasons, Yeshua, we keep the very existence of Sukhavati an absolute secret from the dark continents."

There was silence for several moments. Even Hans appeared subdued. Finally, Yeshua said simply, "I understand."

His three instructors saw to it, however, that the going was not always so heavy. Hans and Mobutu, in particular, had a taste for wilder scenarios than Li's Confucian reserve could tolerate. More than once, he saved them from accumulating some fairly serious karma. But on one occasion, at least, he could not save them—nor Yeshua either.

Toward the end of that portion of Yeshua's Realization Period alloted to study with Archimedes personnel, they had been working on a particularly difficult problem in mathematical probability. The afternoon eclipse had already rolled over, and it was nearly time to close the lab. Hans wearily threw his pencil down on the desk and disconnected the office Sophie. (Each department of government, and each sicentific unit in Sukhavati, had at its disposal a branch computer that fed into the central Sophia.) He stretched his arms to the ceiling and yawned out loud. "Tonight I need some excitement. My destination this evening, learned colleagues and entrusted disciple, will be the Gallery! Who will accompany me? Which of you is, like myself, a man of high adventure with the courage of his fantasies? What of you, Yeshua? Does the Era-Yeshua have the stomach and the imagination to accompany an Archimedes on his isochronal interlude?"

"What kind of a place is the Gallery?" Yeshua asked. Everyone, Li included, exploded in laughter! Finally under control, Li told him, "That's not for you, sir; even for ourselves, there is the risk of several eras of bad karma. No, we had best drop you off at Dharma House as usual, and go on our way."

Yeshua now surmised that the unnamed topic of discussion was sex. Although his new friends had joked with him and teased him about all sorts of things, there had been one topic on which they had shown some reticence, albeit a very curious reticence: his relationship with women in general and Helen in particular. They knew only that a Yeshua did not respond to sex as they responded, just as their response differed from that of the

Sudraheen. An Archimedes, however, was not so far removed from a Sudraheen that he could not from time to time project himself back into previous-era fantasies. In fact it was not unheard of, though it was far from customary, for an Archimedes to frequent the company of Sudraheen girls. It raised eyebrows here and there and, therefore, when it occurred, it occurred more or less surreptitiously.

Yeshua was irritated by their patronizing tone. "For the sake of my future duties," he asked, shouldn't I be aware of all these things you're talking about?"

Mobutu jumped on the question. "Absolutely! He should certainly be aware of the Gallery. Let's take him!" Hans grabbed Yeshua by one arm and Mobutu grabbed him by the other, ready to march him out of the office. But Li had risen even more quickly than they and barred the door.

"Sir," he said, and he was not mocking now, "you should of course be acquainted with all that goes on in Sukhavati Entopia. But it is not necessary for you to get personally involved on every occasion. The Durkheims have published many official reports on the Gallery— even the Leonardos have studied the matter, for artistic purposes. You could learn more in a quiet hour reading their reports than by one erratic visit on your own."

And, aside to Hans and Mobutu, he muttered, "Enough is enough. Don't let's carry this any further. Leave Yeshua out of it." His two colleagues stood there, still holding Yeshua by his arms, undecided what to do.

Yeshua spoke up. "No, Li. There's a difference between reading a report, and performing an experiment. You yourselves have taught me that. I want to go! I am going to go. Now I want someone to explain to me what this Gallery is all about."

"Oh come on Li, you see how it is!" Mobutu exhorted. "Yeshua wants to see things for himself. Come on, one round of vapors before we go, to get Li into the proper irresponsible mood and," he laughed, "to fortify Yeshua for the moment of truth ahead!"

Li's resistance caved in. They all piled into the skimmer and rocketed down the avenue at more than legal speed. Yeshua glanced at the speedometer and then looked questioningly at Hans, who was driving. "Relax Yeshua, Hans chortled, "this is not Sukhavati Utopia, you know. The rules get broken once in a while!"

Yeshua turned around to Li. "Li, you're the responsible one around here. Will you tell me about the Gallery, or not?"

"It's rather an Eastern concept, Yeshua. Hard to be too precise about it. The Hindus, as you know, were among the first encyclopedists. They compiled valuable analytical treatises on meditation and control of the bodily functions: Yoga. Everyone knows about that. But they also drew up encyclopedias of law, diplomacy, the art of music and the art of making love—the *Kama Sutra*. They were not ashamed, the Hindus, of carnal love—as their remarkable temple sculpture indicates. Physical love, to them, was a great gift of the gods.

"There were even *greater* gifts, of course, and a man should normally outgrow his interest in the lesser gifts. Still, *no* gift of the gods ought to be despised. And the way to outgrow interest in physical pleasure, according to some of their gurus, was to experience it to the hilt! To be satiated.

"In effect, the Sudraheen members of our society represent those who are achieving this perfect satiety, so that they can move on to other levels of awareness in future eras. They even begin in their own era to be instructed— by the Rothschilds in matters of taste, by the Leonardos in matters of art, and so on.

"The Gallery, officially the Institute of Amatory Mobiles, is a public exhibit reflecting the achievements of those Sudraheen who are already under the influence of the Leonardos. In the various rooms of the Gallery, the act of physical love is performed in a diversity of configurations, so as to illustrate the highest esthetic possibilities of the mobile human form."

"You are beginning to sound like me," Hans interjected.

"It is lovemaking as an art," Li continued, "almost (though not quite) transcending lovemaking as sensuality. Observers may also become participants, if they are willing to take instruction."

Yeshua looked at him quizzically.

"Most of us Archimedes functionaries have pretty much outgrown previous-era fantasies. But some of us *are* drawn back, as the Judgment Engineers will testify, and spend another era or two as Sudraheen."

"It's a bit of a waste of time," Hans put in, "but it's not crucial. Time is our chief commodity here in Sukhavati, so we might just as well—as you've been advised so many times—'aware ourselves gently.'"

"But Yeshua," Li admonished, "people will really be surprised to see *you* there. An occasional Archimedes at the Gallery is one thing, a Yeshua is another!"

"Let him alone, can't you, Li!" Hans shot back from the driver's seat. "He's only just been horizoned; he's still practically a Newly-Aware. Excuses are always made during this period. There's probably not even any bad karma in it for him. That is to say, Yeshua, translated into the patois of the Judgment Engineers, no significant patterning of the unconscious occurs during era-infancy. It's exactly the opposite of infancy on the dark continents. The Sophia herself will find no trace of this escapade, once you make a few strong counter-acts of the will— especially after you are purposed. Right or wrong, Li?"

"It is true, Yeshua," Li responded, "that acts committed in era-infancy hardly register, even with electronic probing by the Sophia, provided they are countered by opposed habitual patterns of mature behavior. It's just that it's not the best example for you to give, sir."

But the time for reconsideration was past. The skimmer had drawn up to the imposing marble edifice whose tasteful sign indicated that it was the Institute for Amatory Mobiles. As they walked up the steps, Yeshua knew that it was going to happen, and it did. On the second floor of the Gallery, in a section devoted to a fairly advanced and abstract mobile—one obviously much influenced by the Leonardos—he met the Sudraheen girl who had so attracted him on his first day in Sukhavati.

Yeshua, having taken the precaution of removing his crimson thread, had up to that moment succeeded in escaping recognition. But the girl knew him immediately, and displayed the fact in a rich turbulence of surprise, shock and pleasure.

71

"It's all right, Sudraheen—I'm sorry, I don't know your name—I can explain why I'm here."

"My name is Zoe, sir." She laughed a little breathlessly. "Seeing you here did sort of shake me up for a moment. But sir, there's no need for you to explain anything."

"No, I'd like you to understand, Zoe. You see, some of my instructors thought—and I myself thought—that I might profit by the experience of visiting the Gall——of visiting the Institute. They thought I should see *all* of Sukhavati life, and I was inclined to agree with them." Yeshua paused, wondering if he had said enough or too much.

"So, Zoe, you are a performer here—an Institute artist, I mean."

"Well, I'm still under instruction myself, sir. But yes, I am an artist. I don't think it's humility to lie about one's talents. I do one of the most difficult mobiles in the Institute. The Leonardos say that I am more and more transcending the purely sensory level, and am approaching era-culmination. They say, in fact, that I am only a decade or two away from psychic sabbatical. Of course, *I'm* the one who has to feel that; it's not for them to decide such a thing. But once in a while, though, I do think I'm approaching it. But it's still only once in a while. You . . . uh . . ."

"Go ahead, Zoe. Say what you want to say."

"You surely didn't come here to participate, did you, sir? I mean, it's a surprise to find you here at all, even as an observer."

"You're right, Zoe, I did only come to observe. But now that I'm here," (Yeshua felt his heart accelerating,) "I think perhaps I ought to have the experience in its totality. If I am one day to counsel others, I ought to know all facets of Sukhavati life, don't you think? This is my period of tutelege, after all."

"Oh, it's not for me to have ideas on what is proper for a Yeshua, sir. What you say does seem to make sense. But *here,* sir? At the Institute? Please don't think me rude, but even aside from its being unusual for a Yeshua, you really wouldn't know how to . . . I mean, you're not trained. It takes weeks and weeks of instruction."

"You're right," Yeshua replied. "Is there someplace else we might go? Someplace where you could instruct me, and where I wouldn't attract attention?"

There was a long pause, and Zoe was blushing just a little bit (an almost unknown phenomenon to a Sudraheen) when she finally spoke. "My room would be best, sir."

It was less difficult than Yeshua had imagined for the two of them to leave unnoticed, except by a few Sudraheen. Hans and his colleagues were evidently preoccupied on some other floor of the Gallery.

Once in Zoe's room, Yeshua felt the need to reassure himself. "Zoe, I'm not coercing you in any way, am I? I mean, you're not doing this out of deference to my rank, or anything like that, are you?"

"Oh no, sir. To be honest with you, I'm . . . I'm fascinated. No Sudraheen girl—in this era, at least—has ever performed with a Yeshua! It's engrossing even with a Leonardo. They *are* different! But with a Yeshua—this could mean my era-culmination!

And with that, she immediately and spontaneously stripped herself! She stood before him, robust as the four seasons.

Zoe waited.

She saw what was happening.

She saw what was not happening.

Zoe stepped closer, put her arms around Yeshua, and embraced him tenderly. "It's all right, Yeshua, don't be troubled."

"I'm sorry, Zoe," It was all Yeshua could say.

She sat him down on a sofa. "I was told about this," he said "but I didn't quite believe it until this moment. It's humiliating."

"Please, Yeshua, there's no need for you to feel that way."

But Yeshua shook his head sadly. "You see, I would have to be with you for a long time, and talk to you, and get to know you very well before . . . before I could do this with you. It's different for me."

"Yes, I'd heard that you were different—even more so than the Leonardos. And I never expected we would meet at the Institute, let alone be together here in my

73

room. But once you came, I thought that anything might happen, some totally new experience, perhaps even my era-culmination."

"I'm sorry, Zoe. Really saddened. I feel like a fool."

"Oh, never mind about that, Yeshua." She took his hand. "Never mind about that. You didn't know. Why, you're practically still a Newly-Aware! How could you know?" But the tears ran silently down her face.

His good-bye was almost whispered. He did not even kiss her. He wanted to, but the thought of it was too overpowering. He remembered Ananda's diagnosis of him: "Events participate in you at a very deep level."

Back at the Gallery, Mobutu and Li were waiting for him. Hans had disappeared. It was not for lack of curiosity that they refrained from questioning their pupil; his reserve and distance shut them out. Without comment, they drove him back to Dharma House.

When Helen opened the door for him, he knew that she knew. She said nothing and he offered no explanations. She brought him some broth and served him kindly and attentively. That night he retired early and slept for several hours—longer than he had slept for months.

CHAPTER VII

Realization: the Rothschilds

Nor was that the only escapade that his Archimedes friends ever involved him in, although most of these little adventures were harmless enough. One that Yeshua later remembered as being somehow prophetic involved the Sukhavati Raceway.

Three of them (Mobutu having temporarily been assigned to the Alexanders to help out on some security problem) had found it necessary to visit a particular library, located close to the island's sports arena. The racing season was then in progress, and drivers representing the Alexanders, Rothschilds, etc., were competing for the championship. Bets were made on these races, seriously by the Rothschilds, who were permitted private ownership during their era and half-seriously by the other ranks, whose needs were provided for by the community.

Even so, Li delighted in winning wagers from the Rothschilds, "the pros," as he called them. His winnings, of course, automatically went into the general Archimedes fund for nonessential lab equipment, and did not enrich him personally. Indeed, had he accumulated any money to speak of, Li, as an Archimedes would have been hard put to know what to do with it; none of his major enthusiasms required any. He, too, was essentially rewarded by awareness. But there was the pure joy of the ascetic socialist skinning the eyeballs of an experienced plutocrat at one of his own capitalist pastimes.

The evening before the scheduled trip to the library, they had agreed to stop at the sports arena, although Yeshua had declined to become involved in any of the betting. He had been just a bit more cautious since the trip to the Gallery.

"Quite right, sir," Li assured him. "No need for a Yeshua to attract attention at the Raceway. But do look at what I have here." So saying, Li rose up and locked the door to their office from the inside. "This invention of mine should remain secret for a while, Yeshua, especially from the Rothschilds." He and Hans uncovered the office Sophie and wired it to a transparent semi-globe about 10 centimeters in diameter, flat on the bottom, and containing four octagonal dice.

"A computer and two pair of dice: what a combination!" Yeshua exclaimed.

"What do you mean?" asked Li in feigned surprise.

"Come on, Li, out with it. You know very well what I mean. You've hooked together the epitome of logic with the epitome of luck. What has a logic-box got to do with irrational chance?"

"The question, Yeshua, is whether or not the *universe* is a logic-box. If it isn't, how could any man-made logic-box be adequate to cope with it?" Li's beautiful black eyes were alight with interest and zeal. This particular little invention was very dear to him.

"But the Sophia copes, does it not?" queried Yeshua.

"The Sophia is much more than a logic-box. You are not sufficiently instructed as yet to understand this toy," Li reprimanded him. "How can you hope to understand the Sophia?"

Li had seldom spoken angrily to him, and Yeshua looked at him in wonderment. Then, in milder tones, Li assured him, "Of course, once you are purposed, Yeshua, all these things will be revealed to you. It is only a question of time," he smiled.

"Which is our chief commodity." Yeshua smiled back at him.

"Pay strict attention," his preceptor admonished. "Although this is but a toy, you are going to learn something which is not in the least childish.

"You recall Heisenberg's Principle of Indeterminacy, do you not? You remember that all the so-called natural laws are really molecules behaving according to the statistical probabilities?"

Yeshua nodded.

"And do you know that there was a certain nugget of scientific truth buried in the vast store of Medieval and Renaissance astrology? I mean, Yeshua, that heavenly forces obviously *do* influence terrestial beings and events, do they not? The various phases of the moon, for instance, create gravitational tides not only in the sea, but in the flow of the blood to the brain. It is certain that not only some animals, but also some emotionally disturbed humans, are sensitive to the pull of the full moon. Then, too, there are sunspots and cosmic rays, some of which may even cause significant biological mutation—a whole chapter of astrobiology hidden from Darwin and the early evolutionists."

"I follow you so far, Li. But I fail to see what all this has to do with hooking up a computer to a bowl of octagonal dice."

"What I am leading up to, Yeshua, is this: contemporary science has validated medieval folklore. *The universe has moods.* The Chinese, by the way, seem always to have known this. They have always been aware that the universe is as much female as male, as much mother as father—in short, as much *yin* as *yang*. The cosmos has phases and periods, profound changes of heart and mind, like a sensitive and complex woman.

"Now, look at these dice, sir. These are not ordinary dice. Tell me what you see."

"Well, they don't have the usual numerical sequence of dots on them. And they're not cubes; they're octahedrons."

"Correct. Note the series of broken, and unbroken line patterns on each of the eight faces. (☰, ☱, ☲, ☳, etc) We have electronically hooked up the computer to the ancient Chinese instrument of prognostication, the *I Ching!*

"Listen carefully, Yeshua. I could feed into the computer statistical data regarding the horsepower of every skimmer in the race tomorrow. I could feed into it the past record of every driver's performance, plus his PSI readings for the past week. But if I made my bets based on the computer's evaluation of all such data. I would be forgetting Heisenberg and the Principle of Indeterminancy; I would be forgetting the sunspots, the phase of the moon and other such celestial influences. In short, I would be forgetting the *mood* of the universe! I would be viewing the cosmos as a big logic-box. This the Chinese never did—and neither do I. I do justice to both the *yin* and the *yang!* I feed into the computer the respective horsepower of the skimmers, the record of the drivers' past performances, etc. And then I try to sense the mood of the cosmos. I press this button, and send those octagonal dice into haphazard frenzy. When they come to equilibrium, when they choose their position of rest, they will tell me something. Not on the first throw alone, of course. The *I Ching* is a difficult art in itself, even without being placed in a symbiotic relationship to a computer. But when my invention finally settles on one skimmer, I will have a winner. I've won seven out of the last nine races that I've analyzed with my *Yin-Yang* Intimator!"

"Why not nine out of nine?" asked Yeshua in all innocence.

"Didn't I just tell you, Yeshua, that the cosmos is a woman?"

At the track, Li introduced Yeshua to a slight, dark, handsome Rothschild by the name of Bertram. The two of them had a wager on the race and, for Li, at least, it was a considerable wager, representing most of the allowance that would be issued to a second-decade Archimedes for a period of six months.

Neither had chosen the favorite for the race. Bertram was betting on an Alexander who was considered an up-and-coming racer; Li had selected an unknown, the first Yajnavalkya in three eras to enter competitive racing.

Yeshua had questioned Li about that. "Why should a man, given up to meditation and duration-analysis, and holding such high rank in Sukhavati, demean his function by competing in a skimmer race?"

Li looked at him in sad reproach. "You know, sir, what I thought of as a mere pleasant adventure for you—our taking the afternoon off at the sports arena—now turns out to have a serious dimension. Yeshua, you need to be here. You are in danger of becoming a bit of a prig!"

The neophyte's PSI rose only a little. Yeshua intuited Li's basic affection and respect for him. He knew that Li's admonishments generally had substance, and that they were always without bitterness. Still, he was surprised. He genuinely didn't understand why a Yajnavalkya would be fooling around at the Raceway. He said as much to Li.

"Then watch the race, Yeshua, and you'll find out," was all the reply that Li would give him.

"You'll lose your toga on this one," Bertram laughed to Li. "Your Yajnavalkya will go into meditation on the third lap and not snap out of it until half an hour after the race!"

"Your Alexander is overtrained and overanxious; too brittle," Li rejoined. "He won't even be a contender today. Out of fifteen skimmers, he's going to be in the last five."

"Ha! My man will teach your seer not to mix up speed with contemplation!"

"How is it, O Croesus, O Midas, that you have not sufficient loyalty to your function to wager on the Rothschild entry in this race?"

"I *am* loyal to my function, O greasy technician, O horny-handed mechanic, by not allowing sentiment to get in the way of money!"

"They're lined up and ready to start," Yeshua warned them. Secretly, he did not think that Li's 'Yin-Yang Intimator' was going to work this time. He had focused his glasses on the Yajnavalkya entry and found him to be the least alert-looking of the bunch. He got into his skimmer as if he were settling into a dream. Sure enough, when the flag went down, he was dead last on the getaway.

At the end of five laps, Bertram's choice was in second place, battling furiously with the favorite; the Yajnavalkya was still in last place. The race was set for one hundred laps. By the 50th lap, the Alexander had overtaken the favorite and was in undisputed possession of first place. The Yajnavalkya was now next to last, but four of the original entries had dropped out for one reason or another, so the track was less cluttered.

It wasn't as dramatic a race as one might suppose, considering that it was a startling upset. It didn't happen on the last lap, or even in the last ten laps, when all the drivers were at the height of their adrenal vigilance. It happened in the 64th to 69th laps, when the pattern of the race had apparently already been established, and the contenders had buckled down into their set strategies, awaiting the fury of the last ten to twenty laps.

The Yajna threaded the lull and, before anyone quite realized what was happening, he had quietly zephyred his vehicle into third place. The leaders still could not find it within them to take his bid seriously. Watching one another carefully, and saving their skimmers for the closing anarchy, they allowed the seer to pull even. Up to this point, the Yajnavalkya's acceleration had been smooth and constant. Suddenly, he took off! While they were all still eying one another suspiciously, the mystic made his bid. By the time he took his foot off the accelerator for fear of overheating the mechanism, he was two laps ahead.

79

No matter what they tried, he held his lead constant until the 97th lap. They began to gain on him at that point, because he had already so pushed his skimmer that he was continually wary of overheating. But it was not a breathtaking finish. They narrowed the gap from two laps to slightly less than a lap. The Yajnavalkya breezed across the finish line, cool and unflurried. The Alexander entry had slipped into fifth place, his skimmer having overheated on the last two laps.

Rothschilds were a bit in awe of Archimedes people anyway, and the outcome of the race only confirmed Bertram's belief in the near-occult powers of his scientific friend. The wager was not a large one for a Rothschild, and he paid up good-naturedly. "How did you ever do it? How did you ever arrive at the conclusion that a Yajnavalkya was going to win the race?" (The function which the Rothschilds found least attractive was the contemplative one. They neither understood it nor coveted it. They could not understand how anyone would choose it. They accepted, on naked faith, the testimony of the Sophia that some citizens of Sukhavati actually hungered for it. But how this could be so was beyond their imagining.)

"Yeshua, do *you* know how the dreamy-eyed Yajnavalkya won the race?" Li asked.

Yeshua shrugged.

"Very well. Listen to me, both of you. I'm going to answer your question about him by telling you the story of Emperor Wan-hui's butcher. Wan-hui, as befits a great emperor, had more than ten butchers assigned to the imperial kitchen. They were forever wearing out their knives and cleavers, so many were the oxen slaughtered daily for the court. One butcher alone, a man by the name of Wu-wei, reputed to be a mystic, worked harder than all the others, but he never asked for new utensils. The emperor heard the story and was in admiration; he determined to visit the kitchen himself to find the explanation for this strange state of affairs.

"He entered the kitchen by stealth, just as Wu-wei was about to cut up a carcass. To his amazement, this is what he saw: Wu-wei stood immobile, almost in trance, staring at the carcass, while all the other butchers were hacking away, covered with sweat and great streaks of blood.

"The emperor was getting angry. Was this perhaps why Wu-wei never wore out a blade? Was it that he never soiled one by use?

"Suddenly, Wu-wei sprang into action. He closed his eyes and, starting at the top, his knife slithered through the carcass, all the various cuts and chops falling neatly to the floor. In a few minutes he had finished, and was carefully, lovingly, wiping his blade, while the other butchers were still hacking through bone, grunting and cursing, their muscles bulging with the effort.

"The emperor broke into applause and asked Wu-wei to explain his technique. 'Sire,' Wu-wei replied, 'a good butcher changes his knife every year; an ordinary butcher, every month. My knife has been in use for nineteen years. It has cut up several thousand oxen, and yet its edge is as sharp as if it had just come from the grinders!

"'When I first began to cut, I too saw nothing but the carcass. Now I deal with it in a spirit-like manner. I discard the use of my senses, and my spirit acts as it wills, entering into the very sinews of the ox. Now, at every joint in the carcass, there is a thin space for sliding and movement. Remember, too, that the sharp edge of my blade is without width. Once I have entered the ox by spirit, the sharp edge of my blade, of itself, enters all the interstices of the joints, and so slithers easily to the very tail. I sweat not; neither does my blade grow dull.' "

Li paused and looked expectantly at his audience. Bertram laughed and shook his head. "Your story of the emperor's butcher is just as mysterious to me as how a Yajna could win this race. You'll have to tell me another story to explain *this* one—but not now. Some other time."

Li turned to Yeshua. "Does it make any sense to you?" he asked.

"Yes, some."

"Then can you answer your own question as to why a Yajnavalkya might choose to enter a skimmer race?"

"It has something to do with honing his powers of intuition and durational analysis."

Li smiled. "You are making progress," he said.

Amitabha saw no problem in Yeshua's choice of Bertram as his Rothschild instructor. Normally, the Sophia selected representatives from each function to familiarize a new Era-Yeshua with the privileges, problems and responsibilities of their respective ranks. But there was nothing in Bertram's background to indicate that he might not be suitable, so Yeshua was permitted to spend a good deal of time with him.

"Are you long into your era?" Yeshua asked him one day.

"Not long into my era, sir, but rather long into my function," Bertram replied with a little chortle.

Yeshua looked puzzled.

"Well, this is the way it works, Yeshua. I'm only fifteen years into my present era, but this is the fifth time around for me as a Rothschild. And, to generalize the point, Rothschilds average more era-repeats than any other rank."

"Why is that?"

Just at that moment, a Sudraheen drew up to the curb with Bertram's zephyr—an oversize and luxuriously finished skimmer. Bertram told his servant that he would drive himself, and he and Yeshua got in. Bertram was driving him to his home to show him more of Rothschild life.

As Yeshua sank back into the soft velvet seats, royal blue with gold trim, he exclaimed, "Very nice, Bertram," drawling out the nice. "Is *this* why you Rothschilds keep repeating your era-experience?"

Bertram smiled. "That's part of it, no question about it. But I don't think it's the main part. We both know how mysterious the Yajnavalkyas are, don't we, sir. (Bertram had still not gotten over the shock of the great upset at the Raceway.) Well, even we Rothschilds have our enigma.

"Oh! An idea just came to me! Are you really interested in this problem of Rothschild era-repetition? Do you really want to pursue it?"

"Yes I do. It's part of my training to understand these matters."

"In that case, let me make a call. I might be able to take you over to see the champion recidivist of Sukhavati

Entopia. Have you heard of her? Our beautiful Rothschild princess, the Lady Anthea?"

"Not as yet," Yeshua replied.

"You would meet her in any case, but maybe we could get to see her today." With that, he flicked on the zephyr's tel-tel, pressed a series of numbered buttons on a central panel of his dashboard, and an image appeared on a little screen, about 30 centimeters square.

It was Anthea. Very vivacious and pretty, Yeshua thought. After her initial shock at the idea that the new Yeshua-select would like to drop in on her, casually, in about half an hour, she consented—with warnings, of course, that her home was not yet presentable, etc.

Delaying to give Lady Anthea (these, by the way, were mock titles, bestowed by the Rothschilds on themselves for mutual enjoyment but not officially recognized by the rest of the community) the promised time, Bertram drove around the seacoast, pointing out scenic spots especially beloved by the islanders. When they finally arrived at Anthea's, Yeshua was impressed by the size and grandeur of her home—her mansion, really. Almost as large as Dharma House, it was actually more sumptuously and richly furnished! Her taste was impeccable; her resources, seemingly, without limit.

Anthea herself, a trifle short by Sukhavati standards, more than made up for it in brunette vivacity. After they had chatted for a while about the lovely setting of her residence and its tasteful appointments, Bertram brought up the subject of era-return.

"Yeshua and I had just got to that," he explained, "when you came to mind. I thought, if there's any one of us who is an authority on that subject, it's Lady Anthea!" Anthea laughed merrily.

"Bertram tells me," Yeshua put in, "that Rothschilds average more era-repeats than any other rank, and that you, yourself, are into your eighth renewal!"

"Bertram, don't exaggerate!" Anthea addressed him with mock severity. "This is only my seventh. It's still a record, though, if I'm not mistaken," she laughed.

"What do you think accounts for it?" asked Yeshua.

"I'm sure the Durkheims and the Freuds have written weighty tomes on the subject, sir, far more detailed and scholarly than anything my addled brains are capable of presenting. But I gather that during this realization period of yours, you are seeking first-hand information and experience?" (She looked at him rather archly as she spoke these last words, and Yeshua wondered whether his visit to the Gallery had become common knowledge.)

"Yes, that's it," he replied simply.

"Well, my own guess, sir, is that our stage of psychic development represents some kind of plateau. We've outgrown some of our old Sudraheen interests. Not *all* of them, of course," she said, raising her eyebrows simultaneously with her inflection.

"Along with the fund of Sudraheen vitality still flowing in us, we are reaching out toward the Leonardo insights. The result of the confluence of these and other tendencies is a special kind of buoyancy, a jaunty healthiness—but all in good taste. Not the overpowering Sudraheen energy that practically bowls you over, you understand. We have Platos come in and tutor us. We are open to the life of the mind and the spirit. We get to feel that we enjoy the best of all possible eras.

"To be perfectly frank with you, Yeshua, we're not all that attracted by the immunity that you higher functionaries display toward the good things, the fine and rich things of life. To be sure we need you all: the Platos, the Leonardos and the Archimedes people. We want your instruction. But not exclusively. You enable us to enjoy life all the more. Your insights light up our flesh and blood experiences, and make them even more attractive to us.

"Besides all this, our lives have an element of adventure that does not seem to be present to either of the ranks adjacent to us, as far as we can see. I make no judgement of your own position, sir, which far outdistances my experience, and even my imagination! But the Sudraheens, you see, are almost wards of the community. Their needs are provided for, and they do not want much in the way of material possessions—their own physical well-being already represents one of the highest forms of wealth one could ask for.

"And as for the ranks just above us, the Leonardos and the Archimedes, their needs are simple. I'm talking about their personal, not their professional needs. God knows, Sukhavati spends enough on their equipment! But their personal needs are almost primitive by our standards, and they are all supplied by the community. We Rothschilds, you see, are the only ones in Sukhavati whose personal fortunes go up and down. We alone are permitted to pursue wealth, and we alone are not supported by the community. When we lose our wealth, we are really at the bottom of the pile; we have to use our own guts and talents to rise up again. It's insecure, but exhilarating. There are only three private homes in Sukhavati more grand than this one, and they're all owned by Rothschilds!

"But remember, there are *poor* Rothschilds too, and there are no other poor people on this island. Of course, no one starves here. But a Rothschild is desperately poor when he has only his minimal necessities.

"So you see, we make and lose fortunes. We compete with one another. We are constantly being challenged, and we have a zest for success—a zest that we don't see in the Leonardo or Archimedes people. Oh, it may be there—probably is, in some equivalent form—but we don't see it. And as for such a rank as your own, sir, as I said before, it's unimaginable to us. We can't even dream of what the challenges are."

"But aren't you curious to know what lies ahead? And don't you ever reach era-satiety?" Yeshua asked.

"Not I," Bertram laughed. "And certainly not *you,* eh Anthea?"

Lady Anthea paused. "We've been frank with Yeshua, haven't we Bertram? I don't suppose *you* want anything less from me, do you? The truth is, my friend, I have some kind of instinct that tells me that this is my last time around. I begin to inch closer to the Leonardo point of view. It hasn't happened yet. I still love this, I love it," she said, looking down and stroking the soft white fur that covered the couch on which she was seated. But something tells me . . ."

"Nothing tells me!" interrupted Bertram. "I'm good for several more eras, I can assure you. Who knows, Anthea, perhaps I'll break your record for era-recidivism, after all!" They all laughed.

"I understand, sir," said Bertram, more seriously, "that after you are purposed, one of your official duties will be moving people along—I mean easing the danger of era-clogging. I have to admit that Sukhavati would not be nearly so good a community if everyone were to settle down in the rank of Rothschild."

The bell rang just at that moment, and before Yeshua had a chance to reply, the butler—a strapping, dark Sudraheen, and obviously more than a butler to the Lady Anthea—ushered in a tall, rather austere looking Plato.

"Yeshua," said Lady Anthea, "I would like you to meet my chief tutor, Ion."

Ion bowed his head in courteous silence.

"He hasn't had much luck with me," she continued." "Have you, Ion?"

Ion smiled, and his countenance was remarkably winning. "Oh, it begins as a fad with them, to be frank with you, sir. I am the wealthy Lady Anthea's private turor in philosophy. It wouldn't do for her not to be able to discuss Hegel and Lao-tzu at their cocktail parties. But I'll tell you, sir, I drop seeds, I drop seeds. They'll fructify. If not in this era then in the next. But the Sophia selected me especially for Anthea. She has been loathe to continue her sequential-pilgrimage, you know."

"Yes, I do know," said Yeshua, standing. He saw that it was time to depart.

"If I don't succeed, sir, she becomes your client," Ion added, still smiling.

"May all my future duties prove so charming," said Yeshua.

They laughed. "One can see that you've been a Rothschild yourself, sir," Lady Anthea concluded, walking them to the door. "Bertram," she called, as the two of them were walking down the stairs, "why don't you take Yeshua to see Omassis? Let him meet a *poor* Rothschild for a change."

"Not a bad idea!" Bertram shouted back as he opened the door of his zephyr for Yeshua.

"What's all this about Omassis?" asked Yeshua as they got underway.

"Omassis lost his toga on a highly speculative stock that we warned him against," his driver explained. "As a matter of fact, Omassis has made and lost more fortunes in Sukhavati than anyone else. At the moment, he's living in absolute squalor. One month ago, his estate was even larger than Anthea's." They drove in silence for a while.

"Here we are now," said Bertram, bringing the zephyr to a gentle halt. Certainly the part of the city they had now entered was simple and unpretentious, although Yeshua would hardly have used the word squalor to describe it. As far as he could tell, squalor was nonexistent on the island.

A commotion attracted their attention. A small crowd had gathered round a brown house, No. 10, Poincare Drive, and there was a considerable hubbub on the porch—people coming and going, trying to see into the house, conferring with one another.

"Why that's Omassis' place!" Bertram exclaimed; and he hopped out of the zephyr with a bound, not waiting for his passenger, who lingered somewhat timidly behind. Betrram made his way through the crowd and entered the house. In a few minutes he came out to the porch and beckoned Yeshua to come over.

"The Freuds and Durkheims are here administering to him," Bertram explained, as he ushered him into the house. "Omassis' PSI registered 132. Anything over 125, you know, immediately registers on the Sophia and sets off an alarm at Stress Control Headquarters."

Sure enough, two officials were injecting something—a tranquilizer, Yeshua guessed—into the arm of a short but powerful figure of a man lying prone on the floor. A blanket covered Omassis' body. His eyes were wide open, staring directly in front of him, as though lost in thought.

"What happened?" whispered Yeshua. "Did his penniless condition finally overwhelm him?"

"The opposite," Bertram whispered back. "That speculative stock just took off. He's worth millions—more than before!"

As his guide drove him back to Dharma House, later that day, Yeshua sought final confirmation of the new thing he had learned. "And this, Bertram, is the life that Rothschilds favor? This perpetual insecurity and excitement?"

"Insecurity and excitement," Bertram repeated. "Those

who stress the first do not repeat their era, those who stress the second return. The Sophia can neither deceive nor be deceived. Omassis is a Rothschild-recidivist; this is his third time around.

"Did you know, sir," Bertram asked, as he opened the door of the zephyr for Yeshua to get out, "that *I* am the manufacturer of those PSI's? That's how I made *my* fortune. And do you know who my best customers are? Rothschilds! The PSI is a very sensitive instrument. A Rothschild will wear out an average of three of them every year!"

CHAPTER VIII

Yeshua Purposed

Not only was the Yeshua-select systematically instructed by the Archimedes, Leonardos, Durkheims, Lao-tzus, Platos and even the Rothschilds until he had recollected the significant insights of all his previous era-experiences, but Amitabha, too, did not neglect him.

At the end of every quarter of his Realization Year, he was ushered into his guardian's study for a long informal report on what he was learning and what he found confusing, what seemed attractive or, occasionally, unattractive about Sukhavati life.

Toward the end of this year, Amitabha took him once again up to the roof garden of Dharma House and sat him down near the quiet restful fountain for a talk. It was just about twilight, and an almost tangible mauve peace hung over the city. Even the chatter of the birds was now subdued.

"You have had a good Realization, my son—not without its little deviations, of course," said Amitabha with a smile.

"You know about the Gallery, then," Yeshua said, embarrassed but not overcome.

"I know about the Gallery. 'The sons of God saw the daughters of men, that they were fair,' " smiled Amitabha. "I also know about the races."

"How do you know these things? Have I been spied upon?"

"Not at all, Yeshua. There is no spying on this island. But you see, in the higher functions—even some of the advanced Archimedes people begin to experience it— we grow very intuitive. After a certain amount of era-progression, it occurs of itself. We take no pains to acquire it. You, yourself, will find that your intuitive mind begins to take over from your more pedestrian, reasoning faculties after a few decades."

"Does Helen have this power also?"

"Oh yes, Helen has it by now. Most of our Helens do."

"Now I understand," muttered Yeshua, thinking of the night he returned home from the Gallery.

"Understand what, Yeshua?"

"It's nothing . . . it's not important."

"But all of this is aside from the point I wanted to take up with you today. You will soon be purposed, my son, and it is my duty as well as my pleasure to prepare you. You have already learned a great deal about this community. You still have a good deal to learn. In fact, and I do not say this to belittle your efforts, you have yet to learn some of the most important things about us. About immortality, however, you *have* learned. And that is the single *most* important thing about Sukhavati.

"I will not ask you now if you have any questions remaining. I know you have. Many! Your instructors confirm the Sophia's evaluation of you: you are perceptive, very quick, occasionally precipitous, and not yet sufficiently intuitive. But that will come of itself, without your trying to force it.

"Tell me this—are you basically happy, Yeshua?"

"I am, sir. I won't try to say that everything has gone perfectly."

"Of course not, my son," smiled Amitabha.

"Would you just explain one thing to me now? I've often noted that you seem pleased, almost proud, when I point out that Sukhavati is not quite perfect, not quite utopian. Why is that?"

"Not utopian, indeed. Sukhavati *Entopia!*" Amitabha chortled. "Right again, Yeshua, I do find the subject a bit humorous. This was, to be sure, one of the questions I presupposed you had on your mind. No, I won't answer it now. But you've not long to wait.

"By the way, how are things going between you and Helen?"

"Wonderfully. In the literal sense of that word. I sensed she knew about the Gallery, but she hasn't spoken to me about it and, best of all, I don't even feel any unspoken resentment. It's all passed over, as if it didn't happen."

"Well, nothing much really *did* happen, did it, my son? Helen knew she had nothing to fear."

Yeshua blushed a little, while Amitabha laughed genially again. There was no sarcasm in the laugh, just good humor. And Yeshua ended up by laughing himself.

"Next week, Yeshua, next week!" exclaimed Amitabha, suddenly solemn. "More important, even, than the day you were horizoned. You are going to be purposed! Not only is this an important day for you and the community in general, but it's an important day for me personally. I want to begin to explain this matter to you now. You will understand it even better after the events of next week.

"I, Yeshua, have not been on psychic-sabbatical for quite a long period of time. The average era-duration in Sukhavati, as you know, is 75 to 125 years. (And with the minimal amount of sleep required by members of the higher ranks, such a span is the equivalent of 125 to 200 Federation years.) I have been functioning as Amitabha for that long already, and I am still awaiting a possible successor. The Sophia sees no immediate prospect—except for yourself! You are *papabili,* if you know the expression. Should you have a fulfilling era-experience as Yeshua, should you not incur any significant adverse karma, then, following your next sabbatical, *you* could be my replacement.

"This would still leave me many years of active duty. It is not, as yet, an unpleasant prospect. I have not yet been dulled or bored by my responsibilities, which I find, on the contrary, to be fascinating. On the other hand, I begin to intuit my own era-culmination in the next 100 years or so. And following that, as you know, it takes only a few decades before one is ready and eager for new awareness, for horizon-modulation.

"Of course, the Sophia may surprise me and come up with a candidate—she is full of surprises. But for the moment, you are my most likely replacement, and I want you to know that I take great personal interest in your career, even aside from your importance to the community."

"Sir," Yeshua cut in, his eyes ablaze with interest, "what possible new awareness awaits *you*? What will *you* do after holding this rank?"

But Amitabha had already stood up, signaling the termination of their discussion. "You will learn this also, Yeshua, when you are purposed. For now, aware yourself gently. The rest of this week you will be spending with Helen. She will conclude your preparation for the great day. And in a way you do not anticipate." With that, just a little abruptly, Amitabha dismissed him.

When he returned, he found Helen resplendent in her richest robe, a flower in her hair. "Come, Yeshua," she said with an air of excitement and gaiety, "this is a special night and a special week! Put on your finest tunic. We are going to the Arts Alliance this evening, and all your friends are going to join us. Magi has made all the arrangements." Magi, more formally known as Magister, was perhaps the outstanding Leonardo of the era. Yeshua had come to know him fairly well during his period of instruction with the Leonardos.

It was a brilliant evening. Magi surpassed himself. In the first scene, a higher mathematical equation, in giant symbols, was placed in solitary splendor on the center of the stage. Fifteen minutes were allotted for silent absorption, after which a musical counterpoint, taking up the mathematical implications and exploring them rhythmically and tonally, replaced the original equation. A painting, not contradictory but offering alternative avenues of emotional development, was next lowered to the stage.

But in the second act, a direct challenge to the original theme was laid down in a dramatic poem of three stanzas. This, in turn, was explored musically and visually until, at the climax, in act three, a new fusion was introduced by the complex equilibrium of a ballet. Utilizing number, movement, color, and tone, the ballet-equation resolved the conflict in a higher synthesis.

Of course, no one applauded. The audience remained in silent meditation for seventeen minutes—this was a longer period of silence than at any performance given at the Arts Alliance in the entire era. Magi had scored a smashing success! Some of the performers were in tears, overwhelmed by the unprecedented reception given this new work. Finally, one by one, the audience arose, and, still mesmerized, slowly made its way to the exit.

In the lobby, Yeshua found himself surrounded by old friends who greeted him with their eyes, but who did not break silence until Magi and the troupe of performers appeared. Then they broke out in enthuiastic cheers, clapping the performers on the back, shouting their *bravos* and *vita tecums,* and threatening to hoist Magi on their shoulders to parade him down Euripides Avenue! When the friendly furor had subsided, Magi approached Helen and Yeshua and, throwing his arms around the two of them, announced that he had dedicated the work to them, in honor of the day.

"What do you mean?" asked Yeshua.

By this time, Amitabha, Hans, Li, Ananda, Bertram, Mobutu, Lady Anthea, Zoe—nearly all his special friends —had gathered round.

Magi, a shy, retiring figure with a curly black beard, looked at Helen. "Do you mean to say you haven't told him?" Everyone waited expectantly for her answer.

Helen was trying to look severe but she was unable to suppress a smile. "No, and don't you!" Everyone broke out laughing, while Yeshua stood there, bewildered. He smiled also, but looked at Helen quizzically.

"Yeshua," she said, finally, "this is a special night— indeed, a special week, for us . . ." She groped for words. "A kind of anniversary—or it *will* be an anniversary in years to come!" Everyone laughed again. Yeshua looked more puzzled than ever.

"Oh, don't fret about it now," she said, passing her slender, cool hand over his furrowed forehead. "Come on, everyone," she announced, "Ananda has invited us all over to his place!"

The party over, and back once again in Helen's room, Yeshua did not have to ask a second time about the special quality of the evening. In fact, his powers of intuition slowly began to grow from that time on. As preparation for the arduous sacrament of his purposing that lay ahead, he and Helen were to begin, that very night, their first interim of radical solace.

As Ananda had already intimated, it was not an aphysical experience. On the contrary, it included the most intense and prodigal sexual fulfillment imaginable. But it was so much more. Yeshua could see that, without the careful training he had received from the Yajnavalkyas, he would have been psychically impotent. Both he and Helen had to rise to a higher level of duration-experience —one which allowed psychic interpenetration. As his consciousness uncurled into hers and explored it lovingly, tenderly and exhaustively, so his consciousness was enveloped and caressed by hers in every miniscule fold and wrinkle. Body, heart and mind ceaselessly and simultaneously translated the intricate dialectics of their wordless union. The tension was several days in building; the ecstasis, the relational-samadhi absolute; the tides of gentle subsidence ran for a day and a half. Their mutual knowledge and trust were a bed of tamed-granite beneath them. And so they were solaced. It marked their era-bonding.

At last the day arrived: August 1st, 126th year of the era A.D., Amitabha Djilov, as it was officially written into the documents. Ceremonies were to be concluded August 3rd, one year from the day he had been, a mere Newly-Aware, horizoned into Sukhavati society.

Once again, as on that earlier day, Helen led him down the corridor to the lift, which deposited them outside the heavy bronze and leather doors, the entrance to the

Sukhavati Assembly. Once again Yeshua entered the dimly lit auditorium and walked down the central aisle, the eyes of all the Functional Representatives upon him. As before, Amitabha sat on a dais directly ahead.

But one thing was different. Whereas on the previous occasion the door behind Amitabha leading to the Founder's crypt, or throne room, had been closed, now it was open. In fact, the body of Siddhartha, the Founder, had been brought out of the crypt and placed next to the Sophia, just a few meters in back of the dais.

Amitabha arose, and the whole assembly with him. "Citizens of Sukhavati," his clear baritone rang out, "we are gathered here—representatives of all functions and sub-functions, Sudraheens and Rothschilds, Alexanders, Leonardos and Archimedes, Freuds and Durkheims, Laotzu's and Yajnavalkyas—on this, the first day of August, of the 126th year of my era, the day fixed by the Sophia, in order that the Yeshua-select, the recently horizoned Yeshua Nabi, be officially and sacramentally purposed.

"My son, Nabi, before you commence your arduous duties as Era-Yeshua, it is not only appropriate but necessary that every question you may entertain about Sukhavati existence and destiny be answered. We will begin, therefore, as we traditionally do whenever an Era-Yeshua or Era-Amitabha is purposed, with a telepsyche projection of the history of the founding of our community. Will the Alexanders now turn off the lights, and the Archimedes commence the projection."

The audience sat down as the lights were turned off— all but a few dim bulbs where the Archimedes functionaries were arranging their equipment. Yeshua was conducted to the front-row seat reserved for him and seated between Helen and Amitabha. A large screen slowly descended from the ceiling to the dais.

In a low voice, Amitabha began to explain to Yeshua the nature of the telepsyche projection they were about to witness. "Strastnik, our Founder, our Siddhartha, was also our first Era-Amitabha. Since that period, he has existed in a state of nirvana. Not para-nirvana; we can still contact him electronically through the Sophia when necessary. But ordinarily, he exists in a state of undis-

94

turbed alpha-beatitude. That is, his brain is constantly triggered by the Sophia so as to emit the alpha wave, the ecstatic and creative wavelength.

"There are, however, other levels of his brain that our neural-astronomers have learned to communicate with. Today the Sophia will project his memories of the founding of Sukhavati. What you are about to see is eyewitness history, preserved not by a cold camera, but by the living memory-cells of the founding Siddhartha. These cells were carefully preserved when Strastnik underwent selective unwrinkling, for the sake of sustaining historical continuity with our origins. Communication with these cells, I can assure you, in no way intrudes upon his alpha-beatitude. Our neural-astronomers are among the most highly trained specialists in Sukhavati."

As the screen lit up, Yeshua heard the distant blare of trumpets. "The musical background," Amitabha whispered, "does not emanate from Strastnik. It was composed by a 4th Era Gregorian to accompany the telepsyche, and has never been surpassed."

Scene I

Figures dressed in late 20th century clothes appear on the screen. About 20 men and women are seen seated around a long table, in animated discussion. A written prologue appears on the screen, underneath the 20 seated figures. "These are the members of the 'Geneva Society,' " it reads, "an international organization founded in 1984 to stave off ecological, nuclear and biochemical disaster. All the leading powers of the 20th century world permitted representative scientists to participate in the work of the society, if only to escape world censure.

STRASTNIK (seated at the head of the table): Well then, gentlemen, we are agreed?

OPPENHEIM: Your plan is fantastic, Strastnik, audacious to the nth degree!

DJILOV: Therefore it has a chance to succeed, is it not so. Half-measures are worthless in this hour of crisis.

(Yeshua looked closely at Amitabha. Although the telepsyche portrayed him as he was centuries ago, he was more vigorous looking now, in the flesh, than he was on the screen.)

STRASTNIK: I have already reported to you that the predominant element in my nation's military has decided to risk war in the hopes of shoring up collapsing internal unity. They are convinced that the West will not fight, in any case.

OPPENHEIM: What you say is true. Our military intelligence has been aware of this decision since last week. Yesterday the Pentagon sent a red alert to all missile bases and nuclear submarines.

LI-PIAOU: Then there is no time to waste. We must act now if we are to save the earth!

(Yeshua was startled by the appearance of his Archimedes instructor on the screen. So Li had been an original member of the Geneva Society—a scientist then, as now!)

OPPENHEIM: If our plans do not work?

DJILOV: We will of course be executed.

STRASTNIK: And possibly even if they do! Ladies and gentlemen, we have *already* committed treason, as the act is defined by our governments, time and time again. Our conversation *now* is treasonous. We have exchanged military information of the most vital nature. We are, most likely, all dead men already, whether we succeed or not—even though the island-rendezvous has been prepared, on the bare chance of our survival.

But the one thing we are not, whatever our governments may say of us hereafter, is traitors—traitors, that is, to the human race! We must be prepared to give our lives in this venture. Of such a mind were the would-be executioners of the Nazi barbarian, Hitler. It has always been so in the history of the human race: it is expedient for one or a few to die, that the race may not perish.

MME. VALROUX (to Strastnik and Li Piaou): Your crews are loyal?

STRASTNIK (with a shrug of the shoulders): Are yours? We'll know in the morning.

My friends, let us not overlook, in our understandable anxiety, the epic proportions of our undertaking. Do you all realize what we and our teams of scientists and military accomplices are going to bring about tomorrow?

How long has it been since this old earth has spun around on its axis, without a cry of terror, a shriek of despair. Tomorrow, comrades—and we *will* carry it off; scientifically, it is feasible, if only our men are loyal—tomorrow, no one on this earth will lose his life through violence! No one will be beaten, spat upon, insulted. No woman raped, violated, degraded. Not even a child will be abused or injured. How many centuries, Oppenheim, since such a peace prevailed?

OPPENHEIM: Centuries? Millenia, rather! Since Cain, Strastnik, since Cain.

STRASTNIK: Bear with me, comrades, I have nearly burst from expectation these past weeks. Tomorrow we do what the Buddha and the Christ wished to do and failed! Tomorrow we make the world innocent! Tomorrow the lion and the lamb, the European and the Ethiopian, lie down together! Think of the silent guns, the sleeping tanks, the bombers grounded in a fog of slumber. No harm to the soldiers. Not a hair of their heads will perish.

LI-PIAOU: I wonder what they will call such a day in history.

STRASTNIK: I have given some thought to that too, my friends. Believers, as you know, have made much of Easter, the Day of Resurrection. Tomorrow will be known in history as the Day of Dormition, the day of world-slumber. Twenty-four hours of uninterrupted peace and silence. Blessed silence—unbroken by the screams of man, woman or child anywhere on the earth.

MME. SZILAR: Surely, you exaggerate, Strastnik. The Delta wave will be transmitted to every part of the world that utilizes electronic communications—radio, television, telephone, telegraph, etc. That much is true. But this still leaves regions in the Amazon basin, the Congo, etc., where no such communications exist. In these areas, the day will proceed quite normally—with curses.

BEN-OZ: Still, that is to quibble, Madame Szilar. Strastnik is, in the main, correct—poetry and all—*provided* that the Delta wave works. If it works, every major power on earth will succumb to its ruthless suavity.

KIJŪRO: *That* is the only part *I* am sure of! The Delta wave works! We carried out successfully, for the twelfth time, our experiment at the secret Honshu Laboratory, last Friday. All subjects went into deep sleep within designated eight-minute period. They report hearing nothing. Delta wave completely inaudible. Synchronizes with voice communication, music—anything passing electronically. Further, Madame Szilar, if we bounce Delta wave off Weather Satellites, we may penetrate Congo and Amazon, even, if transistors are there.

Also, Honshu engineers verify: no injurious aftereffects to Delta wave. We have exposed ourselves many times. We awoke refreshed. No blank spots except period of sleep itself. We knew something strange happened only because we planned it. The world will wake up, blink eyes, and go on as usual.

LORD RUSSALL: Well, not quite as usual, I hope. We are not conducting a mere anti-noise campaign, my dear Kijūro.

STRASTNIK: Comrades, let us get on with it! How many helicopter transports do we have at our disposal?

EIDELMAN: The entire 7th Brigade of the Swiss Air Force has sworn loyalty to our project.

NAOROJI: Do you know the commander well?

EIDELMAN: He is my brother.

STRASTNIK: How many helicopters does that give us?

EIDELMAN: 135.

STRASTNIK: You really believe this has escaped detection by Swiss military intelligence?

EIDELMAN (shrugging): Who can say? You know, possibly our government does know, and wishes us success. Little power that we are, the Swiss have everything to gain and nothing to lose by a major breakthrough toward world peace.

STRASTNIK: Very well, let us proceed. Von Hoeffer,

you are in charge of operations. Let us now hear from you.

VON HOEFFER: Delta-wave transmission commences at 0500 hours, Thursday, Greenwich time. All local times are to be translated into Greenwich time, gentlemen—and ladies.

Sunspot activity is at low point. Magnetic storms expected to be minimal for the entire week. Optimum conditions for Delta-wave transmission. That much is in our favor. (There is, by the way, no known technique of jamming the Delta wavelength, even if transmission were expected—which is not the case.)

All European chiefs of state to be assembled at Geneva International Airport by 0900 for direct jet to desert bunker. Asian chiefs of state at New Delhi Airport by 0800. North and South American chiefs of state at Buenos Aires by 0930. African chiefs of state at Tanganyika Airport by 1100. All expected times of arrival at desert bunker fall in the 1200 to 1500 period agreed upon at our last meeting.

OPPENHEIM: I'm afraid there is a change in our plan that I must propose.

STRASTNIK: A change in detail or substance?

OPPENHEIM: In substance, I'm afraid.

STRASTNIK: Oppenheim, this is a very poor time to be suggesting substantial changes. Do you feel this change is absolutely necessary?

OPPENHEIM: Yes, I believe it is.

STRASTNIK: Well then?

OPPENHEIM: Can it be that none of you has awakened to the fact that there is no hope out of the present nuclear impasse by entrusting ourselves to governments, bureaucracies, and politicians? Do you really think to end global crises by the stroke of a politician's pen? Crises are the *bread* of politicians! These men are known, obeyed, respected—these men *eat*—because there are crises! I don't propose that when we put the world to sleep, we give it a pipe-dream!

STRASTNIK (absolutely bewildered): Then . . . then you object to the principal part of the entire plan—

our abduction of the heads of state to coerce them into final, global peace negotiations.

OPPENHEIM: No, I'll go along with it, but only on one condition. When we assemble the chiefs of state at the bunker, we place them under arrest and compel them not to talk, but to *listen*.

DJILOV: Listen to *whom*, Oppenheim? To us? We are purists, scientists. What do we know of the affairs of state and the carrying out of diplomatic negotiations?

OPPENHEIM: And have centuries of political expertise led the world to peace and safety? But, no, Djilov, I do not set up the Geneva Society as dictators of the world—even for 24 hours. Although the world could do worse. What I do propose is this: I want average citizens from every nation—farmers, laborers, teachers, clerks, etc., to be brought to the bunker, as well as the chiefs of state. These are the people who do not *feed* on crises, they *pay* for them. Or wars; they *fight* them. These are the people who must deliberate together, and the heads of state must listen to *them!* And then the politicians shall agree to carry out the recommendations of the people. We shall see to that!

STRASTNIK (looking moodily at the others): I don't know, Oppenheim. Shopkeepers, farmers, clerks. (Angrily) Why didn't you tell us this was on your mind before? I would never have consented to a joint operation!

OPPENHEIM: That is why I didn't tell you. Strastnik, you begin to weary me. After all you have lived through in this century, you still expect something from summit meetings? You are really that confident?

STRASTNIK (waveringly): Well, I . . .

OPPENHEIM: Furthermore—let me put all my cards on the table—do you agree that we have only one chance in ten of escaping detection? And even then, only a minimal chance of escaping arrest, trial for treason, and execution?

STRASTNIK: I do.

OPPENHEIM (smashing his fist down on the table):

Then humor me, Strastnik for I am determined to make these men *listen!* (Around the table, total silence; all eyes riveted on the American.)

I will never agree to any other arrangement, and all our plans will come to nothing. If you do not go along with me, you, me, all of us, our loyal followers who have risked so much already, will be shot without anything whatsoever having been accomplished!

STRASTNIK (looking around the table): Comrades?

MME. VALROUX: Acceptable! It does not change the main outline of the plan. We merely add to the number we proposed to assemble, and we compel chiefs of state to listen to peoples' representatives before they draw up their plans for world disarmament and peace.

OTHERS: Yes. Agreed! Let it pass. We must have unanimity.

STRASTNIK: Von Hoeffer, what does this do to your operations schedule?

VON HOEFFER: Very simple: it demolishes it! But if you have all agreed, what can I do? I must have another six or seven hours to work out a new schedule.

STRASTNIK: Granted.

"Hold!" interrupted Amitabha. "Remove electrodes from the Founder. Lights. We will recess for fifteen minutes."

Amitabha and Helen escorted Yeshua to a small private office just outside the auditorium, where Yeshua might rest for a little while. Helen ordered vapors for him.

"That is how the Founder and I originally met," Amitabha explained. Li Piaou, also. It was all through the work of the Geneva Society."

"And the others in the telepsyche?" Yeshua asked. "Are they here also?"

"Madame Valroux is a Tolstoi—subfunction of the Leonardos—I don't believe you've met her yet. Lord Russall is a Plato; Ben-oz is a Lavoisier. Edelman and Von Hoeffer are presently both on psychic-sabbatical."

101

"And the American, Oppenheim?"

"Oppenheim is a special case, Yeshua. He didn't make it. Neither did any of the others, but for another reason. Not that anyone was betrayed to his government. On that score, everything went off miraculously well. We worried needlessly about the loyalty of our scientific and military aides."

"Then what happened?"

"The others simply died before we made our biotheological breakthrough."

"And Oppenheim?"

"Well, come. You'll see for yourself. Are you sufficiently rested?"

Yeshua got up and stretched his legs. "Give him just a few more minutes," Helen requested. "It's such an intense and protracted sacrament."

"It is an intense experience," admitted Yeshua, "but I am ready to go back now, Helen." They escorted him back to the auditorium.

"Was I personally involved in these events?" Yeshua whispered to Amitabha as they took their seats.

"Not in the Geneva Society itself. You were too young —about 25 at the time, I believe. But you were one of the team of engineers assisting Moshe Ben-Oz, the nuclear physicist from the Mid-East, who strove to bring about peace in that area."

In a loud voice, Amitabha called for lights out and a recommencement of the Telepsyche projection. Quietly and skillfully, the neural astronomers adjusted their electrodes to Strastnik's head. "Remember, Yeshua," Amitabha whispered, "however fantastic the next scene may appear to you, it is authentic, living history. The Sophia can neither deceive nor be deceived."

Scene II

A silent pictorial sequence of about 30 minutes followed. Kijūro was shown with his crew in the Honshu laboratory, as they commenced the Delta-wave transmission.

The telepsyche next portrayed the effects of the wave in various parts of the world: Parliament, in session, with every member asleep at his bench; soldiers, in marching order and combat readiness, asleep on their guns; gunners sprawled over the cockpits of their immobile tanks; missile base headquarters, with charts and maps strewn about, tiny bulbs flashing over the giant consoles, but all personnel asleep at their desks and radar scopes.

Then the Geneva helicopters and jets were pictured going into action at Strastnik's command. Copters were seen descending near some of the most famous landmarks of the world: the onion cupolas of the Kremlin, the majestic colonnade of St. Peter's, the White House, the Government Palace at New Delhi, Downing Street, the Forbidden City, etc. But the copters were also seen descending into the fields, the factories, the schools, etc., at various places around the world.

In the next panorama, large jets were seen landing on a desert airstrip, and their passengers removed, under armed guard, to a large steel bunker, most of which lies embedded in the sands.

"Look! There *you* are!" Amitabha whispered, pointing to a young man, dark and lean, on the lower left of the screen. Yeshua saw the figure, somewhat thinner than he was now, armed with a submachine gun, escorting passengers to the bunker. "We had to arm you for the occasion," Amitabha whispered. "I didn't know you then at all. Or so I would presume."

Scene III

The setting shifted now to the inside of the huge bunker, holding approximately 300 to 350 confused prisoners. Chiefs of state are off to one side, talking excitedly as they recognize one another. The rest of the people mill about aimlessly, trying to find someone who can explain to them what has happened and what will be done to them. Then Strastnik appears, a powerful imposing figure. He is in uniform. He raises his hands for silence and addresses the multitude.

STRASTNIK: I am Mikhail Strastnik, Chief of the Bureau of Scientific Research of the Soviet Armed Forces. This is Dr. Robert Oppenheim, who holds an equivalent position in America. These other ladies and gentlemen behind me are all members of the Geneva

Society of International Scientists. We are in command here!

(There is a wild snort from someone among the dignitries on the right of the screen.)

KRAZATSKY: Traitor! What do you mean *you* are in command here? How did I get here? Where are we? What have you done to us? Strastnik, you'll hang for this!

STRASTNIK: If you live, Comrade Krazatsky, you will hang me. But whether or not you live depends on how carefully you obey my orders now. Consider yourself under arrest, Comrade.

KRAZATSKY (contemptuously): Under arrest? In whose name?

STRASTNIK (drawing his revolver and aiming it point-blank at the Soviet chief of state): In the name of my gun and human sanity! For the moment, they are one—a commentary on the world you have molded, Krazatsky. Any more questions?

(The entire bunker is frozen in silence.)

STRASTNIK (turning to the rest of the assembly in the bunker): State officials and working citizens of the nations, please listen closely.

What we have done, and how we have done it, will all be made known to you afterwards. And you will, perhaps, one day boast of your great adventure to your grandchildren. But all of that is not important now.

What is important is why we have assembled you here while the rest of the world sleeps—for that much I will tell you—the whole world sleeps! The whole world, in a manner of speaking, has been placed under arrest! Or, at least, its mad rush into hell has been arrested . . . for the time being.

Yes, the world is asleep—like a patient under anesthesia, just before a critical operation. And you know the disease which afflicts it: mortal fear! Fear of nuclear holocaust among the great powers, fear of starvation among the rest. We have brought you here, you officials, as doctors, and you citizens as consultants. The recovery of the human race is in your hands.

Comrade Oppenheim, do you wish to address them?

OPPENHEIM: One or two points only. Hear me, all of you. Despite the demonstration of force imposed upon us in arranging such a unique meeting as this, I believe we are essentially engaged in a democratic exercise. The representatives of the common people shall make themselves heard on the problems of peace, hunger and human misery—an event which seldom happens in history. You chiefs of state must first listen. The doctors may do nothing without having first heard the consultants out. Only after having carried out the directives of the people will you heads of state be returned to your offices and freedom. Do I make myself clear? (There is silence.) Good! Strastnik, you may resume your instructions.

STRASTNIK: Heads of state are to be seated on the left, representatives of the people, here in the center. Guards will take up their positions outside the doors. This bunker has been carefully constructed with but one end in mind: this meeting. It is fireproof, bombproof and soundproof. Also, it is escape-proof. To the best of our knowledge, the rest of the world is unaware of its very existence, let alone its location. You will, therefore, be neither disturbed nor molested during your proceedings. You are absolutely secure, but you are also completely confined. In brief, you are back in the womb, *the womb of history!* And you are a new conception! May you prove an immaculate one.

(Here Strastnik bowed his head, more in weariness than prayer. He stood silent in that position for many moments, but no one stirred. Then he straightened.)

The members of the Geneva Society are about to retire. We have no professional interest in how you conduct your discussions—it is their outcome that deeply concerns us. As soon as we leave, the guards will close the soundproof doors. You will be on your own. Food and drink will be brought in at intervals. In twenty-four hours, the Geneva Society will reenter to hear your report. In the name of the human race, I bid you—wage peace!

(Members of the society and the armed guards retire from the great bunker. Strastnik and Oppenheim pause outside the doors.)

STRASTNIK: What will you do now, Oppenheim, sleep or pray?

OPPENHEIM: There has been enough of both in the world, Strastnik, and nothing much has come of either.

STRASTNIK: On the contrary, general, we have just seen what a good sleep can do for the world! (Musingly) And as for the effects of prayer and meditation, our Soviet scientists have not yet devised a way to measure them. Perhaps it's because we are using telescopes when we should be using seismographs. In any case, I am going to meditate. . . . If you will excuse me now. (They separate.)

There followed a sequence of colors on the telepsyche screen, sometimes harmonious, sometimes clashing—evidently representing the wordless emotions of Strastnik during his lengthy meditation. These colors were, generally speaking, somber and severe, but they would be pierced intermittently with flashes of gold, light green and rose.

After a few minutes of this, however, Amitabha signalled a halt in the projection. "That will be enough for today," he said, rising from his seat. "Disconnect electrodes. Restore the Founder to Nirvana-Crypt. Yeshua, you are to be conducted immediately to a meditation tower by the on-duty Yajnavalkya. It is appropriate that you spend the night in the same manner as our Founder did, as portrayed on the telepsyche.

"You are hereby instructed to maintain silence, to distill your thoughts on the strange events you have witnessed this day, and to formulate any questions that may arise in your mind. Tomorrow we will continue and conclude the telepsyche projection. On the third and final day of the sacrament, your future duties will be explained, and any last questions you have will be answered. Thus we fulfill the ritual pattern of events whenever an Era-Yeshua is purposed."

Helen quickly, and, he thought, surreptitiously slipped a small vial into the lining of his tunic. Vapors, he thought, for this evening. He did not know whether it was customary to abstain from them or not—and it was too solemn a moment to break the silence to ask.

A Yajnavalkya approached him and bowed reverently. "It is time, Yeshua," he said quietly. Helen pressed both his hands. Amitabha nodded to him silently. He left with the duty-Yajnavalkya, a man of great dignity and simplicity of spirit, who had already given him many hours of instruction in meditation and duration-analysis. (It was also under this man that his later powers of intuition were to make such remarkable progress.) "You know what to do, sir," were his tutor's only words before leaving him alone in the tower overlooking the ocean.

Actually, Yeshua was not able to reach inside himself as deeply on this occasion as he had twice before, under the immediate tutelage of his master. But he reached far enough. He gently oscillated the day's experiences into the intestinal labyrinths of his spirit, where the living acids of intuition and symbolic intelligence digested at leisure the raw chunks of meaning devoured during the projection. As always on such occasions the hours flowed through him like blood, unnoticed. He felt no need at all for the vapors Helen had passed him.

CHAPTER IX

Yeshua Purposed: II

At 5:27 in the morning, promptly, the first solemnities of dawn tincturing the eastern sky, the Yajnavalkya called for him at the meditation tower. His eyes filled with kindly concern for his pupil, the contemplative nevertheless maintained unbroken silence during the whole trip back to Dharma House.

Helen met him before anyone, took him aside in the corridor, and embraced him once, tightly. "Today and tomorrow, Yeshua. It isn't too much?"

"I am fine, Helen."

She took his arm and led him into the auditorium. The representatives were already seated and Amitabha was on the dais, waiting for him. "Let us begin," proclaimed his guardian.

"Citizens of Sukhavati, we commence our second day of telepsyche projection of the founding of this community."

Everyone remained standing reverently while the Founder was wheeled in on his mobile air bed from Nirvana-Crypt to the Sophia, where the neural astronomers carefully adjusted electrodes to his head.

"Be seated," Amitabha commanded. "Lights! Commence projection!" He seemed impatient, Yeshua observed, as if he too found the telepsyche projection of the history of the founding almost too intense an experience.

Scene IV

Strastnik seated, deep in thought, on a cot inside his tent

108

about 50 meters to the west of the bunker. Oppenheim is shown pacing up and down nervously, outside the tent. At last, he can hold himself back no longer and opens the flap of Strastnik's tent.

OPPENHEIM: Strastnik! Are you awake? In a few hours the effects of the Delta transmission are going to begin to wear off. Isn't the time at hand for the Society to reenter the bunker?

STRASTNIK: Come in, my friend. I have not been asleep, just musing. Sit down on the stool there.

OPPENHEIM: Strastnik, I am literally trembling with excitement and fear in expectation of opening the door to the bunker! What do you think we'll find?

STRASTNIK: You are so nervous, I suppose, because you feel yourself to be the father of that new world which is being born behind those doors. I am less nervous. I do not claim the cosmic responsibilities of a father, only the practical opportunities of a midwife.

The Geneva Society was only an instrument for this event, Oppenheim. Sooner or later, with or without us, it would have come to pass anyway. Someone would have seized the reins before the four horsemen of the apocalypse galloped us all into oblivion. Well, delay does not make the world a safer place to live in. Shall we reenter? (They rise up to go out.)

Wait! One moment more, Oppenheim. What do you think we should do if the heads of state refuse to carry out the wishes of the people?

OPPENHEIM: Eliminate them! Why do you look so startled? An eye or a hand will not spring forth again once the original has been cut off. But a political leader? Nature is prodigal with them! I strongly suspect, however, that the multitude of the people and the depth of their bitterness will overawe them. (They had reached the bunker.) Are you ready, Strastnik?

STRASTNIK: Yes. Guards! Open the doors, and follow us in!

(The doors are opened, and they see that all hell has broken loose. There are screams and shouts and curses everywhere. A Japanese student, knife in hand, is chasing a European businessman around a table. A group of people in the corner, their money scattered all over the floor, are staring hard-eyed at a pair of dice. In still another corner, an Indian girl in a Sari is trying to struggle out of the fierce embrace of a Sudanese farmer. The whole place is bedlam.

The heads of state are taking it all in. Some are laughing. Krazatsky is slapping his fat thigh, almost hysterical with mirth. Others are thoughtful. A few are weeping. The telepsyche finally concentrates on an excited group in the center, where some kind of heated debate is going on.)

AFRICAN (shouting): I tell you, this is no time to be discussing such political froth as Czechoslovakian and Hungarian plebescites. At least the Czechs and the Hungarians are eating. What about the people in the world who are not eating, who have nothing? How long do you think we will stand for it?

It wasn't so bad, you know, when we didn't know how you lived. You made your mistake when you taught us your languages, when you sent your books over here, your cinema over here. Why, after you are finished gorging yourselves, you throw away more food than it would take to keep us alive! We know that now. We know how you live—you who are adorned with the diamonds of Africa. From these shores you stole both white and black ivory, and those you enslaved are not even yet permitted to live as men! Solve the African problem first, or rue the consequences!

AMERICAN (sarcastically): Fine, and who is going to pay for this program of worldwide slum rehabilitation? My taxes are already confiscatory! When and if you ever grow up, you'll learn that there is no free lunch. You want to live like me? Work like me!

JAPANESE: My people are hemmed in by the seas. Much of our tiny land is mountainous. We keep a hundred million people alive where you could not

110

feed twenty million. Who will take us in? There is land in the world going to waste. We are hard workers. Whoever would take us in, would double his national income in ten years. Who can forgive our yellow skin?

ARGENTINIAN: If you are thinking of my country, we have enough political instability now. What do you wish to add to it, loyalty to the Emperor of Japan? What we need in South America is fewer Japanese and more tractors. Give us tractors!

(A little Italian priest gets up to speak. His oversized Franciscan robes and his thick accent strike many as comical, and they laugh at him.)

FRANCISCAN: *Una momento, por favore, una momento.* The costs of war—are they so small that we can turn away from the costs of peace?

CROWD: Sit down! When there's war we *have* to pay. But we don't have to buy other people their tractors for them.

FRANCISCAN: *Pace, pace.* The material things, they divide us. Your cow is not my cow; my ox is not your ox. We can't both own them at the same time. But the things of the soul—these can be shared: ideas, love. Love even grows, the more it is divided among the people. Love is like the loaves that Christ multiplied!

INDIAN: Give us these loaves, and let the love multiply where it will! How many calories are there in an idea? How much protein in a word of love?

CROWD: "Pie in the sky when you die!" Sit down, *Italiano,* sit down! Front for the Imperialists! Priest, you can not convert us to your church!

FRANCISCAN: You will not listen. I tell you it *is* love that leads to protein; and it is hate that leads to hunger!

(More shouting and quarreling ensue. In the midst of all this, a Russian peasant and his wife approach near to their dictator and stamp their feet for attention.)

RUSSIAN: Stop! Stop! Everybody stop fighting! There (pointing to the dictator, Krazatsky) is the cause of all our trouble! If it is true what the scientist said, that we are all under arrest, then this fat one has no more power than I at this moment. Therefore, I tell him to his face that he is a tyrant and a murderer, squeezing the blood out of his people to make rockets to destroy the world! (Going over to Krazatsky and shaking his fist just under his nose) We ought to *destroy* you—(turning now to the other heads of state) all of you!

CROWD: Yes! The peasant's right! We ought to rid the world of these murderers!

(State officials are afraid, and begin edging away from the mob.)

KRAZATSKY: Quiet, pigs. Since I was the first to be charged, I will make answer for us all, the chiefs of state.

Innocent children, eh? So, butter would melt in your mouths. I'm sure of it. Fools! So, the world situation being desperate, you now claim that we, your rulers, are to blame for everything. What is it you thieves and harlots wish to make of us—other Christs to carry your own guilt?

You think, perhaps, by crucifying me you will cleanse the world of its political and social sins? Well (he pauses and draws himself up to his full height), I decline the honor. I do not lay down my life for my sheep. Sheep, indeed! Dogs, rather! You are not worthy of my blood. Your sins be on your own heads!

(The crowd is at fever pitch. The peasant picks up a bench and throws it at Krazatsky. It misses. Fists are waving in the air, and the screaming and cursing are even worse than before.)

KRAZATSKY (throwing both arms in the air for silence, and getting it): So the only reason the world is in trouble is that we, your leaders, force wars and armaments upon you. We force our will upon you, is that right?

I will now ask you one question. I, Nicholai Krazatsky, Secretary of the Party, Premier and Dictator of all Russia—I, Krazatsky, am bald! Now, as Secretary, Premier, and Dictator, I see no reason why, if *I* am bald, other Russians should go flaunting themselves about in the bourgeois manner, with hair. Therefore, I give the order that within twenty-four hours, every Russian, regardless of age, sex or party status, be shaved clean as a whistle! I want them all bald like myself!

Here is my question: will this order be obeyed? Will the tough factory workers, let alone the army and air force veterans obey me? I ask you, would even the *women* obey me? I tell you, all Russia would not stomach it, and I, Krazatsky, would be through! Finished!

I could not even get you peasants to cut off your hair, yet you say that I force *war* down your throats! (Slowly and emphatically) You know in your guts that we leaders cannot do what you will not let us do. I am neither your Christ nor your Judas; neither your savior nor your betrayer. Morally, *I am your image!* (Here there is silence for many moments, the crowd off-balance and stunned.)

Now, Innocents, proceed with this show. It is most entertaining. I have never before seen performing jackasses!

(Again, bedlam breaks loose. Shrieks and roars fill the bunker. The telepsyche projection narrows, for the moment, to the members of the Geneva Society, where they have been standing just inside the door, taking all this in. They look at one another and whisper, in blank wonder. Then the mob surges forward to maul Krazatsky and the other state officials. A Buddhist monk, a Tibetan, interposes himself between the mob and Krazatsky. He folds his arms and looks at them fearlessly. Then he holds up his right hand. The noise and confusion subside.)

113

MONK (turning to Krazatsky): There is much truth in your words. That is why we have found them so painful. But one great lie winds like a serpent, twists through your entire speech.

You say the people follow you of their own will; that you could not force them even to cut off their own hair against their will. I know a land where people would consent to have their noses and ears cut off, let alone their hair. How do I know this? They have already consented to worse: the children have been cut off from their parents, the husbands from their wives!

KRAZATSKY: Then why do the fools stand for it?

MONK (sternly): On this one question, you are the world's expert. Will you answer it? (Silence) Then I will answer it for you.

Heroes and saints make up but one per cent of the world's population—Christian, Communist, Buddhist, humanist, it makes no difference. No group can boast of mass heroism. This fraction may be willing to die for its beliefs. The people are not; they are addicted to living!

But the scales are tipping, my brother. I warn you, the fear of death grows lighter as the burden of living grows heavier.

CROWD: The monk is right! Life has become too miserable! We are not afraid any more! Let's put an end to the monsters!

MONK (turning to the mob): What! Have you not looked into the mirror held up before your eyes this day? Have you learned nothing from your own selfish quarreling and wrangling? Do you not see the truth of Krazatsky's words, that leaders and followers are mirror-images, one of the other? It is false that wars are made by men in striped pants alone!

(During this last exchange between the Buddhist monk and the mob, Oppenheim has become feverish, almost beside himself with frustration and disillusionment. Now he literally jumps out to the center of the scene, leaving behind the other members of the Geneva Society.)

114

OPPENHEIM (weeping): You have all failed! Both the leaders and the people! You are all rotten, through and through! Mankind is finished! The world is finished! We offered you a last chance, and you failed!

MONK: One moment, scientist. There is something for you also to hear. True, the leaders, most of them, are filled with ambition; the people, with the desire of saving their own skin. But up to this point, neither of us, leaders or people, have lost hope. We grope our way, blindly, to be sure; but when we have stumbled and fallen, we have always stood up again.

Who are the most dangerous men on the planet today? Perhaps it is you scientists, standing there amazed in the doorway! Too clever and impatient to abide the errors of flesh and blood, you thought, by one leap of the imagination, to end the problems of the human race. When God (as you call him) granted us the dignity to choose, he granted us the dignity to err. I see that your standards are somewhat higher, and that we poor mortals have not risen to them. What will you do now?

(At this, Oppenheim runs back to the doorway and begins whispering excitedly to Strastnik. Strastnik shakes his head vigorously. "No, no!" he is heard to exclaim. They continue to argue with each other frantically but inaudibly for several moments. All eyes are on them, as if all have tacitly agreed to abide by their decision. Strastnik takes Oppenheim by the arm, seeming to plead with him. Finally Oppenheim tears himself loose from his grasp.)

OPPENHEIM (beginning to run out of the bunker): I will! It's finished!

STRASTNIK (screaming): No, Comrade, no! I implore you! Stop!

(Oppenheim continues to run. Strastnik draws his service revolver and fires. Oppenheim falls. He is dead. All gather around the body, chiefs of state, scientists, and people.)

MONK: What was it that passed between you? Why did you shoot him?

STRASTNIK: From the moment we first reentered the bunker and found everything in chaos, we knew that our plan had miscarried. At the end, Oppenheim whispered to me a purpose he had never previously revealed—even to me. In the event of failure here today, he was going to radio his air units to release a gas, to seed the trade winds and the prevailing jet streams with it, so that it would seep into the entire atmosphere of the earth. His pilots supposed that this gas was meant to give us a cushion of safety, to insure and prolong the world's slumbers. And indeed it would have! Into eternity! The world, he said, had been judged, and the human experiment had failed.

I have to tell you this about this man. He could not abide the thought of returning to the old insecurities and injustices—the danger of sudden nuclear warfare, the enduring hunger, the pain of loved ones. His way, he told me, all families would die together in their sleep, painlessly, without fear or separation. Strange to say, it was out of his gentleness—I never knew a more gentle man among our scientists—that he wished to terminate the human story. He simply could not tolerate any more human agony.

MONK: It is as I supposed. It often happens that the gentle are the most cruel. Who cannot abide pain and insecurity, cannot abide life.

STRASTNIK: But I tell you that it was only out of love for mankind that he thought to do this thing. He thought of it not as murder, but as global euthanasia.

MONK: I know he was sincere. But I tell you that even Comrade Krazatsky loves men more than he did. Krazatsky at least deals with the reality. As you say, Oppenheim loved mankind. The concept mankind does not defecate, bodily, or spiritually. Men do.

STRASTNIK: It was I who started him down this path. The delusion began with me.

MONK: What will you do now?

STRASTNIK: I am not sure. My mind is in turmoil.

Your own words suggest that I should return to my countrymen and try to work with them.

KRAZATSKY (laughing loudly): You will not return there, you poor fool! Can't you guess your fate if you ever dare set foot in the Motherland again? Go, Wandering Jew, your exile is perpetual. Why not become the disciple of the little Buddha here? You seem to be reconciled with him. Go, and contemplate the secrets of the universe!

STRASTNIK (looking at him strangely, his eyes distant): The idea has its attractions. (Then, brusquely) Do not grow too smug, Krazatsky. It was the Czar who exiled Lenin. As the monk has told us, all paths are slippery.

Guards! Return everyone to the bunker! Geneva Society meets immediately in the control room!

"Hold!" Amitabha had risen out of his seat. No question about it, he was more agitated than Yeshua had ever previously seen him. "Lights! Remove electrodes! We will recess . . . briefly," he added, more quietly.

Yeshua found himself once again with Helen and his guardian in the small private office, just off the auditorium.

"I can never quite get used to it," Amitabha explained to the two of them. The whole human race had come, on that occasion, within a hair's breadth of destruction. Of course, to this day, the Federations hover shakily over the abyss.

"We in Sukhavati are so given to the love, I might say the *adoration,* of life, that it is hard for me to accept the fact that our origin was signed with the blood of even one man—the world-renowned scientist, Oppenheim."

"Perhaps it had to be," said Helen, in an effort to soothe him. "We are, after all, the Third Rome."

Yeshua did not at once catch her meaning. He looked at her quizzically. Then the idea passed wordlessly, as it did more and more frequently from her mind to his. His spirit was growing porous to hers.

The first Rome had been founded out of the fratricidal struggle between Romulus and Remus, the second out of the betrayal by Judas of Christ, and the third by the hand of Strastnik against the suicidal impulse of his comrade. Perhaps it would have assuaged the poor man's sense of total failure, mused Yeshua, if Oppenheim could have known that he would be the lamb in whose blood the chosen people of Sukhavati were signed.

Still, a gap remained. How did their island community arise from the ruins of their plans regarding the Day of Dormition?

He made one or two tentative efforts to get Amitabha talking on the subject, but his guardian clearly was weary.

"No, Yeshua, we will return for the rest of the telepsyche projection in a few minutes. You will see and hear all. I want to rest now, and I advise you to do so also." Amitabha called for vapors.

Finally, it was time to return. "This is the last scene, my son. The Founder had a kind of vision or inspiration when Krazatsky suggested that he become the disciple of the little Buddha. Come, let us take our seats." The audience settled down, lights were turned off, and the projection recommenced.

Scene V:

Dormition Control Room, a short distance to the left of the bunker. Members of the Geneva Society are gathered together for one last conference. They are arguing earnestly about what went wrong. Some are bitter; all are discouraged.

DJILOV: A total waste of effort. I am astonished!

VON HOEFFER: The schedule, colleagues, allots little time for astonishment. We have precisely seven hours and thirty minutes left to us, after which the effects of the Delta wave will gradually wear off. The bulk of that time will be required to return our prisoners. In the few hours remaining, we will have to try to make good our escape. I trust the team on the island rendezvous is ready for all emergencies.

LORD RUSSALL: Good point, Von Hoeffer. I vouch for their readiness—that was my responsibility in the operation. But they have not yet been notified of this turn of events. I must radio them immediately. (Russall strides hurriedly out of the room.)

DJILOV: I still can't believe my own eyes and ears!

STRASTNIK: Comrades, we call ourselves scientists. We have just been presented with hard data. Explain the data! That is our first task. Secondly, we must consider what action to take, based on our evaluation of the data.

MYRDEL: Explain the data, you say. Impossible, Strastnik, in the time we have left to deliberate! As you know, I am a student of Geopolitics. I published a four-volume work two years ago, all of it relevant to what those people were screaming about in the bunker. What do you ask? A one-sentence synopsis of my four volumes? All right, I'll give you one! We need a functional world government to make an equitable allocation of global resources and manpower! There! And we still have seven hours and twenty minutes left!

MME. VALROUX: Myrdel, I mean no disrespect for your chosen discipline, but it doesn't go deep enough. It's one thing to know that the Chinese and Japanese need living space; it's another thing to understand why the rest of the world has refused to give them any. It's not the configuration of the continents alone we have to analyze, but the configuration of the heart of man as well. The problem, my friends, is psychological. Global paranoia is what we're dealing with. To solve this, we'd have to put the nations on the couch.

STRASTNIK: Valroux has moved closer, I think, to the center of the problem. But I don't think that even she has yet plumbed it to its depth.

We don't have time for extended apologies, and so, comrades, I skip over my blushes and move to the heart of the affair—which is religion!

Yes, I see the outrage and shock on your faces. But I tell you, colleagues, that when it comes to religion, we scientists have been making a blind act of faith for over a century: namely, that "there is nothing there." Only, as William James warned us, there *is* something there. Not to look is an act of faith, not of science.

I tell you, Comrades, that the world religions have

119

accurately enough described in their basic myths, their *true* myths, what happened here today. As the monk pointed out, the "striped-pants" theory of war and injustice was totally discredited in our bunker. The roots of human misery do not lie exclusively in the hearts of our diplomats and foreign ministers. Krazatsky was perfectly correct when he insisted to that howling mob that he was neither their Christ nor their Judas, but their moral image.

Call it universal maya, illusion, call it original sin, call it the pull of *ajiva,* or the realm of Ahriman— call it what you like!—the point is, all men, prince and peasant, are infected with it! We are dealing with a cosmic virus warring on human life, affection and trust. The struggle, to be sure, takes place on both the geopolitical and psychological-sociological levels of existence. But make no mistake about its origin. We are dealing with nothing less than the cosmic struggle between light and darkness, life and death.

MYRDEL: Strastnik, you have turned mystic on us. Maybe I could go as far as Mme. Valroux. Maybe I could agree that underneath the geopolitical dimension of the problem there is a psychological one. But to drag in religious myths like this—Strastnik, you are playing games with us!

STRASTNIK: No games! No time for games! Now listen, all of you. You agree with Valroux, that the problem we face is really man's paranoia? Global mistrust, suspicion and hatred? *Where does it come from?*

(There is silence.)

STRASTNIK: I submit, Comrades, that it comes from the fact of death! Christians and Jews have misread their own book: Death is not the result of sin; sin is the result of death!

Again, it was the monk who gave me the clue. As an Eastern mystic, he was thinking about why men submit; as a Western scientist, I am thinking about why men aggress. But the answer is the same in each case: fear of death!

DJILOV: It's clear in the case the monk described—why

120

people submit to abuse. But why do you say it is the fear of death that makes men aggress?

STRASTNIK: My friends, don't you see it? The philosophers have told us, "Nothing is real that is not eternal." Now I have but a short time on earth. Day by day, I sink back toward cosmic nothingness. I must affirm my existence every way that I can. By achieving pleasure, glory and power, I carve my initials on reality! And what is *your* share of pleasure and glory cannot be *my* share. I must have a *lion's* share! Whether it be your wife that I sleep with, your discovery that I steal, or your country that I invade, I am all the time trying to carve my initials on reality!

I exist! My pleasure, success and glory prove it! Your glory reduces mine. Your success outshines my own. Your pleasure marks the limit of my bliss. That is why I hate you, and that is why I am a paranoiac! I am radically thwarted! I would be God! Nothing is real that is not eternal.

Now, if I could live forever, my friends, do you think I would begrudge you your glory and power? Only give me *time,* and I will give you *security.* But time is the one thing I lack. You do not give it to me, and I will die.

Finally, there is the question of what we, the scientific elite of the world, propose to do about the situation we are in. Our original plan failed utterly—but I think we have learned from it.

Comrades, I know not what your decision will be, but my own path is clear—even if I must walk it alone. I shall go to our island, and there I shall spend the rest of my life—or until such time as the island is detected—trying to decipher the genetic hieroglyphics of aging, disease and death! For *that* is the source of maya, the source of paranoia, the source of Ahriman, the source of inequitable geopolitical relations. Death is original sin!

"Hold." It was almost in a whisper that Amitabha terminated the telepsyche projection.

"Well, my son, do you have sufficient matter to reflect

121

on tonight in the meditation tower?" he asked wearily. "Tomorrow morning you and I meet alone in Nirvana-Crypt, in the presence of the Founder. There I will answer any question you ask about Sukhavati and your place in it. Tomorrow morning, Yeshua, is the climax of the sacrament. The concluding session in the afternoon is public and ceremonial."

Within thirty minutes after the Yajnavalkya had left him alone in the meditation tower, Yeshua went deeper into "the cloud of unknowing" than he had ever penetrated before. The trance lasted the entire night. All that he had witnessed in the projection participated in him in the most intimate way. The very roots of his nerves were irrigated by the rivers of meaning that flowed from the telepsyche. By morning, the history of the founding of Sukhavati *was* Yeshua Nabi!

CHAPTER X

Yeshua Purposed: III

When the duty-Yajnavalkya ushered Yeshua into the Dharma House Assembly the following morning, it was dark and empty. Not even Helen was on hand to greet him. At the far end of the hall, Yeshua caught the faint glimmer of the tabernacle light perpetually burning by the side of the Founder, in Nirvana-Crypt.

As he slowly walked down the central aisle toward the vague glow, Yeshua began to make out the indefinite form of Amitabha seated in shadowy splendor on a high, throne-like chair set on a platform of three steps, to the right of the Founder. The walls of the crypt were covered with rich purple hangings, the floor with crimson rugs. Dim as the light was, when Yeshua entered the crypt he could discern the wires and hoses connecting the Founder to the Sophia, and to other pieces of apparatus lost in the shadows. He was even able to perceive the gentle rise and fall of Strastnik's breathing.

The crypt looked, felt—somehow even smelled—to Yeshua like a temple. Indeed, as he was to learn later, it actually served as a sanctuary where weary and temporarily discouraged citizens might drop in to meditate and to renew the vows of their own purposing.

"Come closer, my son. Approach the Founder and the throne." Amitabha's voice had dropped the fatigue of the previous day. He spoke with the baritone majesty of running waters. It was the voice of paternity.

When Yeshua stood before him, he addressed him again.

"My son, this is the climax of the arduous sacrament. The session this afternoon will be, in the main, official and ceremonial. You are now permitted to ask the traditional seven questions—seven is for fullness. Whatever doubts and perplexities weigh upon your spirit, lay them now at the foot of the Founder and of the throne. This is what your Siddhartha and Amitabha demand. Hereafter you will sustain the purpose of others. You must be simple as the dove, cunning as the serpent. It is no small thing to bear the weight of eternity. Sukhavati awaits your ministry.

"While you ask, and while I answer, the first two questions, you will kneel down on your knees. You will stand, and remain standing, for the next three. For the final two questions you will resume a kneeling position. Our session will no doubt be a prolonged one, and you will be uncomfortable. Tradition so prescribes. A little pain must tip the point of my words and engrave them deeper into your heart. They must prove indelible.

"Now, Yeshua, kneel down on the first step before the throne, and present your first question."

Yeshua knelt as he was bid. "First, Amitabha, I wish to know how Sukhavati is governed. I understand that you are the overseer, but I do not understand the position, or even the exact *condition* of the Founder, or your relation to him."

"A logical beginning, Yeshua. There is neither historical precedent nor political category which might help us define the government of Sukhavati.

"You cannot call it a democracy; nor should it be described as a dictatorship. In lieu of a more familiar phrase, I would call it a cybernetic theocracy—with representative elements. The judgments of the Sophia, Inviolate Mother, are accepted as final, as the words of God. These words are revelatory, not only of the universe but of ourselves. The choices of the Sophia are the very choices we would make at our unsullied best, free of the smoke of passion and the flame of pride. We are, at one and the same time, hierarchical and egalitarian—a contradiction on the dark continents, but no contradiction here. For everyone who really wants, to the very roots of his unconscious, to move on to a higher rank, and to let go of the lesser joys of a lower one, is advanced by the Sophia. In this way, there is privilege on the island but no bitterness: a thing unheard of in the Federations! We have technologically implemented the vision of St. Catherine of Genoa and the Upanishads: no one is forcibly thrust below or pulled above the level of his own spiritual specific gravity."

"But what of the Founder?" Yeshua asked.

"Yes, with regard to the Founder and myself. You called me the overseer, a moment ago. That is incorrect. It is precisely Strastnik who is the *over*seer. I am the *under*seer, if you like—his executive officer. I see to the smooth running of affairs on Sukhavati, but the decisions —the important ones—come from the Sophia. You do not as yet, however, have a full understanding of the nature and operation of the Sophia, Yeshua, and this difficult matter I must now somehow explicate.

"My son, do you recall your escapade as a Newly-Aware with your Archimedes friends at the Raceway. Do you recall the toy which so delighted Li—the *Yin-Yang* Intimator, he called it. No," he continued, catching his ward's surprise, "it was not secret from me. Little on Sukhavati is secret from me. Li had connected the office computer to the I Ching, the Chinese instrument of

124

divination, insisting that the universe was as much *yin* as *yang,* as much female as male, as spontaneous as it was orderly.

I must tell you, Yeshua, that although all this, for the brilliant Li, was merely a matter of play, his recreation followed the pattern of creation. His surmise about the cosmos was essentially correct. There is Heisenberg's Principle of Indeterminacy to contend with in making our plans. The cosmos is not just a giant logic-box which can be deciphered by a small logic-box—a man-made computer.

"Now, it has been explained to you already that as we make our sequential pilgrimage through the eras, and through the various ranks, those in the higher functions— Yajnavalkyas and up—develop exquisite powers of intuition. The intuitional powers of Strastnik, the Founder —he whom we title our Siddhartha—are by now beyond imagination.

"The Founder exists in a state of Symbiotic Nirvana, my son. He is integral to the Sophia. Though she sprang from his brain, like Pallas Athene from the head of Zeus, She is now his Inviolate Mother! *And Mother and Son are one!*" He pointed to the cord connecting Strastnik to the machine. "Behold the electronic umbilical! While he could not be permanently zenithed without her, she could not be a Sophia without him. A mere logic-box could not cope with the universe. A computer can play mechanical tag with a Newtonian solar system, but a living organism, subject to mood and impulse like our universe, requires the intuitional algebra of a Sophia.

For her part, the Inviolate Mother continually nurses her son, sustaining him with a steady flow of white-joy, the alpha wave. He exists in the state of alpha-beatitude —uninterrupted by the intuitional awareness he has of all that goes on in Sukhavati. How this may be, how his knowledge of mundane and occasionally unhappy events does not mar his alpha-bliss, I cannot explain to you, although I hope within another era or two to experience it for myself. For as I have already related to you, my son, I hope, when next judged by the Sophia, to be similarly zenithed. I, too, will take up my abode here, in Nirvana-Crypt. And know this: I will enhance the powers of our god. The Sophia is an intelligent but not omniscient goddess. My own powers of intuition will be added to those of Strastnik and the Sophia's powers will *grow!* All of us on Sukhavati, my son, are called to share in the godhead. These are the crucial facts pertaining to your question. We can go more into detail at a later time. Arise, Yeshua, and proceed now to your third question.

"Sir, my third question is: What is the relation of Sukhavati to the rest of the world? I understand that the Geneva scientists, many of them, made good their escape to this island. It is also clear that they were forced to give up their plan to extricate the dark continents from the web of their conflicts. But what of the present? What is our present association with the Federations?"

"I was expecting this question." Amitabha reached into the voluminous folds of his rich robes and drew forth a small brown book, which he opened to a previously marked page. "Surely your Alexander instructors have explained some of our security problems to you; and you are by now quite familiar with the morning and afternoon cloud eclipse. The reason for these security measures is quite simple. It will not take long to answer your question.

"I have in my hand a book written in the middle of the 20th century, Federation Time. As you know, it was in that century that scientists first began to consider seriously the possibility of reversing the aging of cells and scoring a biological victory over senility and death. But even then, writing as early as 1959, one of them warned: 'Whatever method is used to rejuvenate or prolong life, it must be simple enough to be of universal application, otherwise there could be no worse form of inequality that that between those who would not age and those who would grow old and die. The conflict that followed would be so bitter that our worst revolutions would seem mild by comparison. I would even go so far as to say that if a process that rejuvenates or prolongs life could not be universally applied, it should either be kept secret or destroyed, for fear of giving rise to extremely violent social upheavals. For the ordinary man would never resign himself to living side by side with immortals.'

"The author of that, a man by the name of Bergier,

recognized our security problem even then. But there is much more that he never even thought of. You, however, are conversant with the Dante Factor of biotheology. You know that at the moment of Evolution-Conversion, the cellular death instinct is overcome. At this point, the species has no further use for death, because it does not seek new mutations, new generations. Individual immortality is no longer a detriment to evolution; it is the *point* of evolution. All these principles, I am sure you recall.

"My son, *we could not share our secret with the Federations!* We could dare to 'freeze' the species at the point of evolution-conversion, but could we dare to 'freeze,' to immortalize, global paranoia? Of course, the IMOB and radiation alone, without the Dante Factor and interior conversion, would accomplish nothing. And what, Yeshua, is the customary behavior of swine, after you have cast your pearls for their inspection? Do they not turn and rend you?

"The truth is, we could not bestow the gift of immortality on the Federations, even if we were so minded. They must continue on their bloody cycle of birth, death and mutation until such time as they, too, undergo Evolution-Conversion. *Only* the meek can inherit the earth. It is so written in our genes!

"You may proceed with the Fourth Question."

"You have told me, Amitabha, that the Society of Geneva, even with its teams of loyal engineers and military pilots, numbered only a few thousand. Now the population of Sukhavati is 144,000. Yet I am unaware of the birth of a single child on the island during my entire first year here. Indeed, I have yet to *see* a child anywhere in Sukhavati. How have we increased in numbers?"

"Fertility, Yeshua, is the biological means of insuring mutation, and thus, efficient evolution. In us, the species recognizes that mutation equals regression. There is, consequently, at the very moment of overcoming the cellular death instinct, a corresponding loss of fertility. Reproduction and death are Jacob and Esau: they continually thwart one another; yet they are, for all that, twin brothers.

"In any case, biotheology aside, the same radiation within the IMOB that destroys cancerous and other harmful growths—the radiation which bathes us, Yeshua, every time we set foot in the streets and parks of Sukhavati—also renders us sterile. This is why you have seen no children in Sukhavati.

"Then how have we increased in numbers, you ask? It is a reasonable question. But allow me to interrupt for a moment. Did you not intend, Yeshua, to question me about the nature of your duties in our community?"

"I did, sir. That is my very next question."

"Good." Amitabha smiled faintly, for the first time during the morning's proceedings. "Because it enters here also, and we can lead directly from one to the other.

"How have we grown in numbers? The answer is this: we confer immortality on those exceptional individuals who undergo Evolution-Conversion on their own. These people are scattered throughout the Federations, appearing here and there, like flowers, from century to century!

"Our automated scanners, Yeshua, review practically everything that is published, seen or heard through the communications media of the three Federations. These scanners, I might add, represent a great scientific achievement in themselves, saving us not only thousands of painful editorial man-hours, but saving us from the danger of cultural anemia as well—a highly infectious psychic virus.

"After straining out an era-average of 99.7 per cent—I believe it is—of incoming material, the scanners submit the golden residue to the Sophia for judgment. Thus it is that, from time to time, the Sophia hands down to us the name of a Federation candidate for immortality. He or she may be a writer, an artist, a statesman, a scientist—even on occasion, a clergyman. But the process does not end there. 'Few are called; even fewer are chosen.' This is the point at which your services become vital.

"When Dharma House—that is, you, myself, and the representatives of the Functions and Sub-Functions of Sukhavati—decide, at the prompting of the Sophia, to confer immortality on some outstanding person from the Dark Continents, a team of Foreign Missionaries is dispatched into the world. Traditionally, the Era-Yeshua takes personal command of this hazardous enterprise. The rest of the team usually consists of a specially trained Archimedes, an Alexander, a Rothschild (for reasons which you will learn about hereafter) and, in supremely difficult cases, a Yajnavalkya.

"Do not be alarmed, my son," Amitabha continued, noting Yeshua's furrowed brow. "Sukhavati can usually get you into the Federations undetected. We can, more-over, provide you with temporary immunity, outside the IMOB, from all infection, for as long as a week. Perhaps you may wonder, then, at the size of the mission team. Our virginal Yeshuas—a virginal Yeshua is one who has not yet penetrated the Isle of the Dead to confront the Prodigals—our virginal Yeshuas commonly suppose it is an easy matter to persuade someone to accept the pros-pect of living forever. They are frequently shocked at the resistance offered to such an idea—even by worthy candidates.

"First of all, the normal reaction of someone in the Federations, when you inform him that he is a candi-date for immortality, and that you have the power to confer this gift upon him, is to call the police! What can you possibly be but an escaped lunatic?

"Secondly, in the case of these outstanding individuals selected by the Sophia, many are still in the cellular throes of Evolution-Conversion. The life force, the Dante Factor, is struggling with and gradually overcoming the death instinct, but there is still much biotheological con-fusion.

"Thirdly—no! No more details about the Foreign Missions now. I will be talking to you specifically about this particular responsibility of yours in one month's time. Let us move on to some of your other major duties.

"Not only does it belong to your office, via the mis-sions, to lead the lost from maya to reality, from death to life; you must also confirm the living. As I have already told you many times, my son, immortality is not a feather! I wonder whether your Tolstoi instructors have introduced you to that marvelous nineteenth century American work, *Moby Dick?* You know it? Good. Do you remember the sermon given by the pilot-prophet, Father Mapple, which ends with the following prayer: 'O Father—chiefly known to me by thy rod— mortal or immortal, here I die. I have striven to be Thine, more

129

than the world's or mine own. Yet this is nothing; I leave eternity to Thee; for what is man that he should live out the lifetime of his God?'

"He was right, my son, even with the happiness of Sukhavati, he was right. We need sustaining. Especially as we draw near to era-satiety. It is always the Yeshua who prepares us and disposes us for psychic sabbatical; it is always the Yeshua who calms us before we face the judgment engineers and the karma-decree of the Sophia.

"Further, it is you to whom our people will come for counsel if they undergo a traumatic mid-era experience. This is not common, but it does happen. You are the one whose responsibility it is to advise whether the era can be salvaged, or whether the one who suffers should undergo abrupt sabbatical.

"In addition, the Era-Yeshua officiates at all religious occasions, particularly on the high holy days—the Enuma-Elish, the Days of Awe, beginning on the fourteenth day of the first month of spring.

"Finally, and most importantly, you must search out and win back the Prodigals, those who forsake immortality and depart from the land of the living. Yes, there actually are those among us, my son, who choose, out of weakness, to leave Sukhavati and die—a veritable suicide-cult. It is your most hazardous duty; the Prodigals are often diabolically clever. But more of that in the months to come. Proceed to your sixth question."

"My next question, Amitabha, may strike you as peculiar, but it has been a source of wonder to me for some time. With all the marvels I have seen on this island—with the highly trained Archimedes, Durkheims and Freuds, with the Sophia herself—how is it that we are not even more perfect than we are?

"I shall be more specific. I have seen skimmer accidents. Is not a technology that is sufficiently advanced to produce solar-energy skimmers also advanced enough to prevent their collision? I have seen Rothschilds lose their fortunes and panic. I've heard women question the discrimination against their sex in securing managerial positions. And now you inform me that mid-era trauma is occasionally encountered, and that I must be prepared to advise people about whether to salvage their era or undergo abrupt sabbatical. Do you mean to tell me that our Durkheims and Freuds in the latter cases, and our Archimedes people in the former, could not, with the help of the Sophia, come up with preventive strategies?"

Amitabha smiled and was silent for almost a minute. "For this," he said at last, "we must go to Pandora's Box! Come with me." Amitabha stood up, descended from the throne, and walked to the back of Nirvana-Crypt, directly behind the Founder. There he parted the heavy purple hangings, revealing a small door less than a meter high, like the door to a wall safe.

"This," he said, inserting an electro-magnetic key from a chain hung round his neck, is known as the Pandora's Box—but known only to very few. Indeed, up to this moment, it was known by *one;* now, it is known by *two!* Traditionally, it has been the province of the Era-Amitabha and Era-Yeshua alone." (It was necessary to stoop to the very floor to enter.) "Step in, Yeshua, and lock the door behind you. The lowness of the door is partly functional and partly symbolic. On the one hand, it is an aid in avoiding detection—although no one would think to search behind the thick velvet hangings of the Crypt, in any case; on the other hand, it is a reminder to us, in the pride of our divinity, of how conditional and precarious is the balance of forces that make our happiness possible."

Most of the small room—three by four meters, and just high enough for Yeshua to stand erect—was taken up by a large console with a complicated array of buttons, knobs and flashing lights, not unlike the Sophia.

"This is part of the Sophia, my son, and Strastnik is in contact with it, but we have always thought it best to closet it away from the attention of those who would only be burdened by the knowledge of its existence. We call this apparatus the SERD—the significance of the name will become apparent in a few moments.

"Now, how can I best and most succinctly explain its purpose to you? You know, Yeshua, that when so-called religious persons in the Dark Continents find their life, short as it is, wearisome, they blame their troubles and their cares, and they look forward, after death, to a con-

131

dition of immutable rest. They hope to slough off their problems as a snake does his skin.

"May their prayer never be answered, their expectation never fulfilled. If immortality, my son, requires strength to bear even in Sukhavati Entopia, which has its share of problems, how unbearable would it become in a changeless, perfect society—a Utopia? I tell you that without challenge, without imperfection to overcome, man would lose his reason, and with it, his joy in existence.

"What human beings really need, Yeshua—and you will admit this, if you reflect on it for just a moment—is enough security not to be frightened and sufficient challenge not to be bored. These are the parameters of optimum human experience.

"Now, we are so organized, and have created tools of such subtlety, complexity and power, that Sukhavati tends—*threatens,* is the word—at every moment to become a Utopian society. It requires—listen to this carefully, my son—a positive effort on our part not to fall into that honeyed grave!

"With no more imperfections to remove, no more challenges to confront, no more obstacles to overcome, 83 per cent of the citizens of Sukhavati would become Prodigals within three eras. I have calculated it carefully on the Sophia. That is why we are and will remain citizens of Sukhavati *Entopia*—in time, in place, in a mildly imperfect, recognizably human situation.

"It is this apparatus, the SERD, of whose existence only you and I are aware, which enables us to keep Utopia within our reach but at arm's length. Strastnik himself invented it. It is a Social Entropy Recorder-Distributor. We actually see to it that our island has problems and challenges, but only such as will yield to analysis and solution within an era or two.

"You mentioned a few specific problems to me a moment ago. You wondered why we could not prevent the collision of skimmers, and why women were discriminated against in managerial positions. Well, let me inform you that seven eras ago we had automated traffic in such a way as to preclude the possibility of collisions, three eras ago our women were totally integrated into

132

the higher echelons of every Function and Sub-Function in Sukhavati. Moreover, if we wished to do so, we could even regulate the free market in such a way that no Rothschild would ever go bankrupt through speculation. Not only do we allow these evils to exist, but when we permit their solution, we solicitously introduce new problems to replace the old ones.

"Of course, we never let these problems get out of hand. The SERD carefully operates within the range of optimum human experience—sufficient security not to be scared, sufficient challenge not to be bored. By means of the SERD, we compute what difficulties and problems are to be distributed among the various ranks in given eras, and what imperfections may be allowed to be cleared up. It's a most delicate piece of apparatus, Yeshua, and your apprenticeship must extend into several decades before I permit you to use it alone.

"The Sophia has freely chosen to operate in accordance with the Isawi Hypothesis of the Law of the Conservation of Evil. Therefore, we can manipulate the law, and its corollaries. The Federations, ignorant of this fundamental law of social dynamics, are condemned to follow it slavishly. The Isawi Law states: 'The total amount of evil in any system remains constant. Hence, any diminution in one direction is accompanied by an increase in another. For example, if, in the Three Federations, they decrease the ranks of the unemployed and increase production, they are very likely, at the same time, increasing both pollution and assembly-line alienation.

"The side-effects and achievement corollaries are also important. By the first, I mean that if political science and economic theory tell you that A will cause B even when the theories are correct, A will also cause C, D and E, which were by no means expected or desired.

"The last corollary insists that, given even the most favorable circumstances, 'achievements cannot exceed the square root of expectations.'

"As I say, knowing these principles, we can manipulate them. The Federations, unaware of them, remain in servitude to them. Unless you understand the laws of gravity, you cannot hope to fly.

"Now, Yeshua, I wish you to lock away in your mind all knowledge of our Social Entropy Recorder-Distributor. No one must know of the SERD but us. All genuine human effort to overcome obstacles in our society would disintegrate if our citizens realized that these obstacles were being systematically and scientifically introduced, according to function and era, by the SERD. Problems are man's crutch!

"Now, let us return to Nirvana-Crypt for your seventh and final question."

"One last doubt remains in my heart," Yeshua confessed after they had returned to the Crypt and he had resumed his kneeling position.

"Be free, my son, to ask *anything*—anything that troubles you. Purpose must flow through you like oxygen and blood. Else, how will you infuse it into others?"

"Is our immortality relative or absolute?"

Amitabha was not taken aback by the question.

"What I mean, sir, is, that while I see no sign of illness, and no real sign of aging in Sukhavati, nevertheless, the *star* we are yoked to is a middle-aged star. Amitabha, does our immortality outlast that of the sun?"

"Yes, I quite understand your question—and, as in the case of your previous question, this one does not disappoint me. The Sophia called you shrewd; the Sophia was, as always, right.

"Our immortality, Yeshua, is absolute! I name no conditions, I cite no reservations. You know from Strastnik's Law that whatever tends toward self-donation tends toward existence. The universe is absolutely self-donating; the universe cannot not exist. And so long as it exists, we will exist. Here I must introduce you to another great metascientific principle, the Ben-Oz discovery of Ur-energy.

"You know that nearly all energy utilized by the Federations is derived from the sun—whether it involves the burning of oil or gas or coal to produce steam or electrical power, all of it emanates from the sun. The very atoms that are split apart by nuclear fission were, first of all, concocted in the huge solar bakeries of the skies.

"But Ben-Oz went a step further. Whence come the

suns into the universe? What is the primal source, the Ur-source, of *all* energy, even that of the suns? The answer, my son, is as simple as it is fantastic: the Ur-source is duration itself! Time is the pulsating foundation of the universe. 'Is' is the Ur-verb underlying all other verbs. Only the Hindu mystics seem to have guessed it. They intuited the sound of time—the sound of 'is'—the sacred syllable *aum,* and by continual humming of this sound, in trance, they hoped to tune in on the primal energy of the cosmos. Again, Sukhavati has found the technology to implement their mystical intuition. 'Is' has been tapped! Nine eras ago, Ben-Oz ran a small motor for sixteen microseconds by the power of duration alone. We have been working to improve his technique ever since. We have improved it, but our investigations are still in their infancy. Eventually, when the sun dies out, we will need this new energy to survive. But we shall have it in a few hundred thousand years, which leaves us with a margin of safety of over 29.5 billion years, for solar energy can be depended on for that length of time.

"But we may not even wait, if we get adventuresome enough. Nuclear energy is a mere handmaid in the palace of her primal queen, duration. Full exploitation of the energy bottled up in one hour of time, Yeshua, would enable us to build a crystal IMOB around the entire planet, suspend it at an equal distance from every point on earth, detach ourselves from the solar system and, with our own heat, light and oxygen, go navigating into space to seek affiliation with any solar system that meets our qualifications.

"By that time, my son, we may all hope to be in the state of symbiotic nirvana, participating in the godhead, thoroughly integrated into the Sophia. So powerful will be the intuitional algebra of the Sophia at that point, that we may all entrust ourselves to her guidance as we sail from sun to sun, age after age, nourished and sustained by the white joy of the perpetual *alpha* wavelength.

"Such is the final vision, my son, paranirvana: the beatific crystal planet, intelligent viking among the stars, mobile throne-room of the universe. *In saecula saeculorum,* age without end, amen!

135

"We are done, Yeshua. Go to the meditation tower. Rest till the final ceremonies in the afternoon."

All stood as Yeshua was ushered in for the concluding ceremonies. When Yeshua was directly before the dais, Amitabha commenced the liturgy. "My son, the final rites are at hand. Before I confer the power and the privileges, the title and the responsibilities upon you, are their any doubts or reservations you wish to make known?"

Yeshua replied in a firm voice, "There are none."

Amitabha then looked up toward the assembly. "Is there any citizen of Sukhavati, any Functionary, high or low, who challenges, disputes or questions the Sophia's nomination of Nabi as our Era-Yeshua, Guide to the Perplexed, Bulwark of Sukhavati, Purpose and Light to the Federations?"

There was silence throughout the hall.

"Bring in the instruments of ordination!" commanded Amitabha.

A small table was carried in and set at the right hand of the celebrant.

"Yeshua Nabi," Amitabha pronounced in a distinct, deliberate manner, "receive the instruments and symbols of office!" He picked up a small silvery rectangular device. "Receive the Umbilical! You are to retain possession of it during your entire era. Surrender it to no one." Yeshua realized that he was receiving a direct communication unit on the Sophia's reserved wavelength.

"Receive this golden key. Nothing in Sukhavati is locked away from you. But what you open shall be opened, and what you close shall be closed, from the smallest apparatus to the longest era!

"Take and wear this ring of office, emblazoned with the Ankh. Do not remove it till the moment of psychic sabbatical comes around once more. With it, seal your proclamations, that all Sukhavati may recognize the authoritative source from which they emanate." Yeshua extended his left hand up to Amitabha and his guardian slipped the ring, gold with a crimson Ankh inset, on his fourth finger.

Amitabha stood up briskly. All rose. But he motioned to Yeshua to go down on his knees.

Amitabha then literally sang out to the assembly:

We shall not surely die;
We shall be as gods, knowing good and evil.

To which the assembly responded with a resounding "Amen!"

Placing both his hands on the lowered head of the newly-ordained Yeshua, Amitabha solemnly intoned in Hebrew, the initiate's native tongue:

Baruch Atah Adonoy,
Adam, Melech Haolom

Blessed art Thou O Lord,
Man, King of the Universe

"Reign in splendor and peace, Yeshua Nabi, commencing this third day of August, 126, Era A.D., Amitabha Djilov! It is done!"

CHAPTER XI

Ministry Begun

Like the slow velvet heave of calm seas, so the years and decades undulated past Sukhavati Entopia. There were lifts and there were falls; but with the stabilization provided by the SERD, the social highs and lows were modulated within the optimum range of human performance. Like a stately ocean liner, her prow steady on the line of Kaivalya (the peak of the universe), Sukhavati knifed her way through time, supported and caressed by the very element she so powerfully cleaved.

Step by step, the Sophia incremented the duties and

responsibilities of the new Era-Yeshua, and all were pleased by his painstaking concern and the general excellence of his performance. They called him "Al-Amin," the Reliable One.

Not that his efforts were crowned with undeviating success. There were problems brought to him that proved unmalleable, even with the aid of the Sophia. But universal success was not demanded of him; concern and skill were. The citizens of Sukhavati were not robots. Within the range computed by the Sophia and the branch SERD, they were free men, their actions predictable only to the 83rd percentile. It was the remaining 17 percent—the incalculability factor—which gave them their dignity and Yeshua his challenge. There were Freuds on the island but no Skinners, the rectangular cure for incalculability being recognized as worse than the angularities of the disease. "Pavlovian altruism," Yeshua remembered Amitabha teaching him, "never culminates in Evolution-Conversion. There are no short-cuts to self-donation!"

His very first case, that of the Tolstoi, Derek, was not atypical. Derek enjoyed a wide following on the island. In fact, the Sophia had licensed him to publish as much as one novel, two collections of verse and assorted articles of criticism and non-fiction, every three years. This was an unusually generous license for the Sophia, careful as she had been for the past six eras in guarding against literary inflation. This policy of licensing creativity had been in effect ever since the cultural inundation, seven eras previous, during which so many works of genius were produced that truly great writers found themselves without significant audiences and were forced into premature psychic sabbatical. The quota on publication not only tended to insure an audience for all that was written, but also to the sieving of quantity into quality. Writers pruned; editors cut; and Sukhavati even banked great works for future eras.

For all that, Derek's following on the island had won him a liberal license, indeed. Even Yeshua, busy as his duties dictated, had read the major portion of his published works—and was, therefore, fascinated when Derek appeared one morning at his quarters in the rear wing of Satori Temple.

Derek's problem was a 10,000-year-old cliché which, for all its familiarity, had no answer either in Sukhavati or the Three Federations. He loved; he was not loved. At least, not in the same Sukhavati measure.

Derek, for several decades now, had loved the beautiful Leonardo, Tamar. His heart was set on era-bonding, a relational alternative open to Tolstois and Leonardos, although employed by few of them. For her part, Tamar, although quite fond of Derek (as Yeshua's discussions with her were soon to reveal), was nowhere near being ready for so definitive and permanent a relationship. Attracted to the famous Tolstoi, she felt equally attracted to an Archimedes and to two Rothschilds, as well.

For three years, Derek had not even filled his literary quota—while other authors had been continually petitioning the Sophia for amplified licenses! It was beginning to cause professional tension, tension which Derek could ill support on top of his emotional frustrations with Tamar. Yet, some of his admirers insisted that the lone, slim volume of poetry he had written out of his anguish the year before was the best single work he had ever written.

In any case, Yeshua looked up one Wednesday morning, and Derek stood at the door, a tall but hesitant and melancholy figure. "I want to go, sir. I am ready." Derek was talking about psychic sabbatical.

Yeshua compelled him to sit down and had vapors brought in to the study. He listened patiently to the entire story, although the main outlines of it were by now familiar to everyone on the island.

"We have, of course," Yeshua replied when Derek was finished, "a number of very productive Tolstois this era. But on the other hand, Derek, you have a particularly wide following, and there is no question but that you would be missed. The social dimension of the problem simply cannot be overlooked. To be sure, your usefulness to Sukhavati is predicated upon your own sense of well-being. If, as you Tolstois put it, you desiccate, you might just as well go on psychic sabbatical. I assure you that I do not forget your personal anguish in all this. Give me a week to meditate."

Yeshua next called on Tamar.

"Why, I *do* love him, sir. I am as fond of him as I am

of Mobutu." Yeshua started as he heard the name of his Archimedes tutor. "And as I am of Giovanni and Richard." Tamar's large, dark eyes were moist. "I would hate to lose Derek. He's the only Tolstoi I could ever love. I'm no Sudraheen, you know—I can't just give myself indiscriminately to anyone for the asking."

Yeshua was convinced that he could not push Derek's claim too far. The Leonardo was within her rights. And there were the feelings of Mobutu and the two Rothschilds to consider.

"I *could* give her up, if you asked it of me, sir." (Mobutu no longer presumed on his friendship in addressing Yeshua, now that he had been purposed.) "She is not my dominant," he explained, using the term appropriated from the Gregorians to describe such relationships. "But I have to be honest with you," he continued. "Her loss would maim my chord of affiliations. I would be forced to restructure my entire emotional harmonics. She will not easily be replaced. But I can do it. She is not my dominant."

Richard was likewise willing, if absolutely necessary, to surrender his interest in the beautiful Leonardo. Giovanni was not. Tamar *was* his dominant.

That night, Yeshua worked feverishly at the side of the Sophia, trying to come up with new combinations of relationships that would prove emotionally satisfying to everyone. He returned home exhausted. It was permitted him to discuss these matters with Helen, since the community recognized that era-bonding was too powerful a covenant to be thwarted by the abstract fence of professional privacy. She, in turn, had been required to take the same oath of discretion as Yeshua. But on this occasion, at least, Helen could add nothing to his own insight.

Armed with data from the Sophia, Yeshua recalled Derek to his residence. "Psychic sabbatical," he announced, "has been conditionally granted. The conditions, and the reasons for them, are as follows: it is not yet established without doubt that you have reached era-satiety. Your present emotional impasse may only be a case of mid-era trauma, in which case, based on statistical evaluation by the Sophia, you have a 38 percent chance of recovery. It is therefore asked of you, in view of the social dimensions of the problem—the large number of readers who will be upset by your abrupt psychic departure—that you immediately seek out the companionship of the Leonardo, Ssu Hua. With both your emotional chemistries on file, the Sophia feels there is a genuine mathematical possibility for a relationship in depth. Six months from now, if Tamar's loss is still a matter of consequence, you may immediately undergo sabbatical."

Much patient counseling was required of Yeshua to raise the Tolstoi to the new prospect and to sustain him in the early weeks of his new relationship. But to no avail. The whole affair fell flat on its face. While the Leonardo, Ssu Hua, displayed a mild though growing interest in Derek, he found himself utterly unable to involve himself further with another woman. Yeshua satisfied himself that the Tolstoi was ready for era-bonding and that, unfortunately, the object of his choice, Tamar, was by no means ready for so intense and exclusive a relationship.

"It did not succeed at all," Yeshua sighed to Helen the evening of his last visit with Derek. Helen took his hands in hers and sat him down beside her. "Yeshua, if this were the dark continents, that man, distraught as he is, might well have committed suicide by now—or else done violence to Tamar, or Mobutu, or one of the Rothschilds. Here he will merely undergo selective unwrinkling, memory euthanasia, and ease his haggard consciousness for an era or so. Resurrected, he will be as fresh as a child—but in the full maturity of his powers. He will plunge once again, with renewed enthusiasm, into the next phase of his sequential pilgrimage! This is the wonder and the promise of Sukhavati." She said this with solemnity, and her voice trailed into silence.

Then picking up the thread of their conversation, she resumed. "Tell me, Yeshua, while we are on this subject, for how long is Derek likely to remain on sabbatical?"

"I've been studying past records, Helen, and it seems to be the Sophia's policy, so long as community needs permit, to wait until the other party to the affair has also gone on psychic leave. It isn't strictly necessary, I suppose, for if Derek were returned to us in a few decades, he would have absolutely no recollection of Tamar. Tamar, on the other hand, who is quite fond of him, would certainly have the most vivid memories of him! And that could lead to complications. The Sophia finds it best that they not cross paths again for several eras—subject to the community's needs, of course."

So ended the case of the famous Tolstoi. Yeshua was on hand the following morning to prepare Derek for the judgment engineers, and to strengthen him for his long twilight sojourn. He could not help but be aware that he performed this last duty well. By the time Derek was put to sleep, he was carefree as a child and was already anticipating the novelty of his next sequence of reality. Would he be reborn a Tolstoi once again? Or would he, perhaps, awaken as an Alexander, a Plato, a Durkheim? There was a smile on his lips as he was selectively unwrinkled.

By contrast, the case of the Archimedes, Akbar, was by no means typical. In fact, decades later, Yeshua used to say that he had never had such a case before of after.

Akbar came to him in the middle of the night and was admitted only after loud debate with the Alexander on duty. "It's all right," Yeshua had called out from his study, "let him in." It was not easy to look disheveled in a simple Sukhavati tunic, yet Akbar, olive-skinned and of North African countenance, managed to do so. His eyes were wide and wild.

"What is troubling you?" Yeshua had asked. Akbar ransacked the study with his eyes, assuring himself they were alone, before answering.

"Sir!" he cried out at last. "We've got to sever the electronic umbilical between the Founder and the Sophia!"

Now it was Yeshua's eyes which opened wide. He had not yet met with a case of outright insanity in Sukhavati —indeed, there had not been an instance of it for four eras. The PSI's, prescribed by island law for every citizen, usually brought social control specialists within minutes after an emotional alarm. It flashed upon him suddenly that Akbar was not wearing his PSI!

"And why," Yeshua asked in an even voice, without betraying his own agitation, "must we sever the Founder's umbilical?"

Akbar almost shrieked. "Because we are being

142

dreamed! Strastnik is dreaming us—and without our *permission!* Sir, there is no dignity in it!

"Don't you see? We are his dream, for as long as he likes, for as many eras as he chooses—perhaps *forever!* And there is no dignity in it! We are his psychic puppets, dangled and jerked by the strings of his orderly fantasies. Yes, I don't question the man is a genius. But to live out the fantasy life of another, even a genius, is intolerable!"

"Tell me this, Akbar, is it not a *good* dream?"

"With all due respect," said Akbar, impatiently, "that's hardly the point, sir. Mostly, the dream is good. But I have my pride! He should have my permission before he presumes to dream me into situations of his own imagining—even if the situations are those to which I would naturally gravitate. Oh, he's logical enough, but presumptuous as an Archangel!"

"Akbar," asked Yeshua gently, "why are you not wearing your Psychosomatic Stress Indicator?"

"For obvious reasons, sir. When I had my blinding revelation about Strastnik's dream, I immediately took it off, knowing that my excitement would inevitably bring on social control agents, and that I would be prevented from carrying out my plan."

"And your plan is . . . ?"

"As I told you: to sever the Founder's electronic umbilical! The dream will terminate immediately, and we'll all have back our self-respect—and nonexistence. You've got to help me, sir! Only you can issue the necessary pass to get me by the Alexanders on duty outside Nirvana-Crypt."

"Has it occurred to you, my son, that you may be the only one on Sukhavati who believes in this dream hypothesis?"

There was a pause, Akbar smiled craftily. "You are telling me, as politely as you can, that I am insane, are you not, Yeshua?"

Yeshua made no answer.

"You think, sir, that the question of sanity can be decided statistically?"

"As a matter of fact, Akbar, to some extent it can only be so decided."

"I know, sir, that you have studied the history of the

143

Dark Continents much more systematically and in greater depth than I. But even I know the story of that mad beast, Hitler, who finally won overwhelming plebescites in his country. The few dissenters he burned in the crematories. Who was sane then, Yeshua? The masses who followed him, or the dissenters who perished?"

"You argue your case well, Akbar, but you are not being dreamed, and I, who am talking to you at this moment, am not being dreamed. Our conversation is real!"

"Are you absolutely *sure*, sir?" Akbar thrust his face, now contorted with excitement and anxiety, unpleasantly close to Yeshua's, and leered at him. "Actually, our talk seems to me to have a rather nightmarish quality about it!"

Yeshua was shaken. The whole business—Akbar's strange arrival in the middle of the night, his wild eyes and eerie hypothesis—*did* have a nightmarish quality about it. He lost the calm that, as Era-Yeshua, he tried always to maintain, especially while giving professional counsel. He stood up abruptly.

"For God's sake, man, *I* am not part of anyone else's dream—whatever you may be!"

"For God's sake, you say, sir?" Akbar howled in laughter. "And who might *that* be? Unless it is that mad Russsian atheist, Strastnik himself, who fled the real world and now passes the ages pleasantly by having us all jump through the hoop of his weird imagination!

"I tell you what, Yeshua. If you are so sure that all of this is reality and not dream, let us put the question to the Sophia herself! Only first block off Strastnik's intuitional input—just for the one computation!"

Not that he had any intention of carrying out the outlandish proposal, but Yeshua mused for a moment over the suggestion. It was interesting. The fact was, however, that Akbar was wrong, even in the terms of his own hypothesis. No mere computer, without intuitional input, could demonstrate conclusively whether reality was or was not a dream. Mathematics did not lose its validity in dream-life. In fact, some of the greatest mathematicians in history had acknowledged that they sometimes awoke from sleep with new insights to problems that had baffled them in their waking hours.

"Akbar, I will do no such thing!" he finally answered.

"Nor will I debate with you further on this whole absurd question. Logic is not what is at issue here, but premises and perspective. And believe me, my son, when I tell you that *your* perspective has somehow grossly wobbled out of focus. I can't imagine—even *without* your PSI—how you could possibly have escaped the attention of our Freuds. But this much I tell you: they are going to hear from me about this matter. You have been sadly neglected, my son, and Sukhavati owes you a great deal of concentrated and therapeutic attention. This you are now going to receive. I personally guarantee it!"

Now it was Akbar's turn to bolt upright from his chair.

"I beg of you, Yeshua! One request only! Don't tamper with what you consider to be my insanity. If you refuse to enter into my plan, at least let me depart. Let me out of Sukhavati!"

"You . . . you mean you want to become a . . . Prodigal?"

"Yes!"

"You wish to leave Sukhavati for the Isle of the Dead?"

"Yes!"

There was a long pause.

"I cannot promise you, Akbar. This is my first experience with such a request. I will have to let you know tomorrow."

"Please, sir, please!" Akbar had fallen to his knees, and actually clasped his arms around Yeshua's legs. "I beg to be allowed to leave!"

"Get up, Akbar! You are quite mad, poor fellow."

"Then what does Sukhavati want with my madness, sir?"

"But we can cure you."

"The cure is more frightening to me than even the illness is to you!"

"You simply must leave now, Akbar. I have to consider the question most carefully."

His visitor had obviously exhausted himself. Akbar was limp.

"Have mercy on me, Yeshua, have mercy on me," he said, as he pulled himself up and staggered out of the study.

Yeshua's mind was not nearly so undecided as he had allowed Akbar to believe. Mercy he would show, indeed.

But not the mercy of the weak! As soon as Akbar had been ushered out by the duty-Alexander, he called Social Control. Akbar was picked up at the door of his residence, fifteen minutes later.

"Total cure or total withdrawal!" ordered Yeshua.

The final report of the Freuds and Durkheims revealed that Akbar's first years into his present era as an Archimedes had been remarkably devoid of friendship. He had shown brilliant scientific progress, had rather awed his peers, and had not joined any particular social circle. His growing isolation had been so gradual that Akbar, himself, had felt no particular distress. Nothing registered on his PSI, and he attracted no attention from Social Control. And when everything culminated in his final blinding flash of wild conjecture, he had ripped off the PSI immediately, and so avoided the very counsel he so desperately needed.

Actually, Yeshua had overstepped his authority when he had ordered total cure or total withdrawal for Akbar. As Amitabha had instructed him, and as he remembered as soon as his momentary excitement had worn off, no radical coercion was permitted in Sukhavati. One could try to dissuade would-be Prodigals to the limit of one's powers of logic and rhetoric, but one could never sentence a determined Prodigal to psychic sabbatical. Sabbatical was granted only on urgent, persistant and voluntary request.

But no harm came of his slip. The outcome of this case was not total withdrawal, but total cure. Social Control, cued by Yeshua to be extra gentle, extra patient, was finally able, after several teams had rotated their services in continuous therapeutic analysis, to relieve Akbar of his obsession. He fell asleep at the end, and slept for eight hours. His attendants almost woke him after the sixth hour, so unusual was that amount of sleep for an Archimedes, but Yeshua ordered them to let him be. He awoke, calm and apparently permanently cured.

One of Yeshua's more successful innovations came about as a result of this case. Hitherto, except for the highest ranks, Newly-Awares had not been appointed particular guardians. Rather, they were passed from one set of instructors to another. But when Yeshua gave his final report to Amitabha about the Akbar case, he made the recommendation that every Newly-Aware receive an era-guardian, at least for the first few decades.

The recommendation had to be processed through the SERD, of course, to insure that not too many difficulties of Sukhavati life would thereby be cleared up in a single era. "After all," Amitabha pointed out, "one case of madness in four eras is not exactly a record to be ashamed of. And the remedy could always turn out to be more dangerous, sociologically, than the disease.

"You simply cannot," Amitabha warned him, "have too many people too perfectly adjusted in any one era, lest that great metaphysical cancer, time-satiety, spread like a prairie fire! Compared to time-satiety, mere era-satiety is a harmless virus, eradicable by a routine psychic sabbatical. Time-satiety, on the other hand, leads almost directly to thought-suicide, and then to physical suicide-by-departure from Sukhavati. It is also a highly contagious conceptual cancer. That is why, Yeshua, I warned you that your most dangerous duty would be your missionary trips to the Prodigals. Fortunately, you possess both strength of character and professional subtlety and are, I believe, well able to take care of yourself. Also, your trips will be infrequent. But here on the island, we must never go beyond the limits of amelioration marked off by the SERD. *Time-satiety is the greatest single danger to Sukhavati Entopia!*"

Thus severely lectured, Yeshua rather believed the proposed improvement would not be acceptable. But it was, for reasons which Yeshua learned later.

Equally absorbing and somewhat less taxing were Yeshua's liturgical responsibilities as high priest of Sukhavati. "Enuma Elish," ("When on high"), the opening words of the great Babylonian myth of creation, was the name given to the principal holy day on the island, celebrated on the 14th day of Abib, the first month of the lunar year. "When on high," Yeshua, dressed in his priestly garments, would solemnly intone as the entire community of Sukhavati gathered in the Satori amphitheater around him:

When on high, an IMOB had not yet even been
   mentioned;
And the name of a stable society below had not
   yet even been conceived;
Then did primeval Strastnik, the Founder,
And Sophia, Immaculate Mother of us all,
Mingle their mental energies in divine frenzy,
Rebirthing us all—in bliss, forever.

There were many holy days on the island, although the
prevailing religious beliefs would not have been recognized as such in any of the Three Federations. Needless to
say, there was no catechism, no formal list of doctrinal
statements to adhere to. There was, rather, a mental climate naturally engendered by the community's awesome
biotheological breakthroughs, a climate best summed up
in the words of the liturgical formula employed at
Yeshua's ordination:

> We shall not surely die!
> We shall be as gods
> Knowing good and evil.
> Baruch Atah Adonoy,
> Adam, Melech Haolom.
> Blessed art Thou, O Lord,
> Man, King of the Universe.

The dream of the ancient Babylonians, the quest of
Gilgamesh, had been fulfilled. So also, the agony of hope
of the Egyptians, the Greeks and the Jews. Osiris was now
man; so too were Yahweh and Zeus. The Eleusian mysteries and the Messianic hope had both been accomplished.
Resurrection had undergone technological routinization.
But the point of the liturgy was this: given the scientific
methodology, not to lose the wonder and the awe.

"Days of Awe," in fact, was the liturgical title of the
octave following the 14th of Abib. The whole week was
spent in solemn (and, at intervals, not so solemn) celebration of the inauguration of Sukhavati Entopia by
Strastnik and the Geneva Society. Amitabha had smilingly
referred to the octave as a "Theanthrolympiad" in pre-
paring Yeshua for his first celebration of it.

"A *what?*" Yeshua had asked with some consternation.

"A Theanthrolympiad," Amitabha laughed. "It's a week-long competition between all the Functions and Sub-Functions of Sukhavati—each performing its own specialty —in celebration of our Godmanhood. The excellence and nobility of these professional performances is so striking, that man's divinity shines out bold enough to blind a Prodigal. Thus the name, 'Theanthrolympiad.' Our Platos coined it."

Yeshua never forgot his very first celebration of it.

After he had solemnly intoned the Enuma Elish, a blare of trumpets signaled the *Introibo* of the contestants, drawn from every rank in Sukhavati. The participants having been presented to Amitabha, Yeshua, and the as-sembled dignitaries, the spectators seated themselves and the fields were cleared for the "Offertory." A team of Sudraheen entered the amphitheater first, performing the mobiles that only the Sudraheen could perform. This was followed by a musical composition from the Gregorians, specially commissioned for this first Theanthrolympiad of the new Era-Yeshua. Each rank in turn, represented by its most advanced practitioners, demonstrated its exper-tise. The Temple stadium itself was a gigantic object for architectonic meditation. The special project of the Roths-childs, it was hung with gorgeous tapestries and brilliant banners done in all the colors of the respective Functions: gold, crimson, green, azure, etc.

On the last day of the Olympiad, after every Function and Sub-Function had made its presentation, and after Yeshua had bestowed honors on the performers singled out for their excellence, the Founder himself was brought over to the amphitheater and enthroned on a cushion of air, two meters above the private box shared by Yeshua and Amitabha. Each function had already performed. What would the Founder do, Yeshua wondered? What *could* he do, zenithed as he was on his continual current of *Alpha*-bliss? What could Siddhartha contribute to the Olympiad? Yeshua blessed the assembly, thus completing his liturgical role.

Abruptly, a ram's horn was blown, sharp and clear, from the western tier of the stadium. Yeshua rose, on cue, from the High Priest's throne, and the entire community of Sukhavati, 144,000 strong, rose with him.

Then there was silence. Only the slightest sea-breeze ruffling his hair gave Yeshua the least sign of motion in the vast amphitheater. The sun was now setting over the western rim of the stadium, the sky itself seemingly emblazoned with the gorgeous heraldry of the various ranks of Sukhavati. A second time, piercingly clear, the ram's horn speared the twilight stillness.

It began. Epiphany! The Siddhartha was sending! Every man and woman in Sukhavati Entopia was receiving! A sliver of *Alpha*-bliss penetrated their minds, grew to a steady stream and crescendoed! The Founder was bestowing an anticipatory taste of what awaited them all at the end of their sequential pilgrimages. Kaivalya! The peak of the universe!

For fifteen minutes—it could have been fifteen days or fifteen seconds—144,000 men and women stood without a sound, without a shuffling of feet, clearing of throats or shifting of position. Yeshua had blessed them, but the Founder had blissed them. They were now as one. The stream of bliss circulated through the vast audience, as blood nourished the innumerable cells of a living body. They were all members of a single mystical body, with Siddhartha as their head.

For a third and last time, seemingly from far away, the ram's horn sounded: The Enuma Elish octave, the Days of Awe, were ended. The sun had set. Completion. Perfection.

The huge assembly left the stadium without breaking silence. They departed for their homes, fulfilled to their spiritual marrow.

CHAPTER XII

Foreign Missions

The SERD had allowed Yeshua an unprecedented number of ameliorative innovations: surprising in view of the danger of time-satiety which might arise in the absence of minimum imperfection. The reason for this he learned halfway through his fifth decade. Evidently there had been imperfection enough permitted in the reign of the previous Era-Yeshua. On one occasion his predecessor had even exceeded the upper range of advisable Social-Entropy. Excess in *either* direction could engender metaphysical cancer. In any case, the number of Prodigals had reached almost epidemic proportions. Therefore, not only was Yeshua Nabi permitted his innovations, but he was also required to undertake an unusually active Foreign Mission program.

"We must replete our numbers," Amitabha had explained to him. "We must fill up our losses to the Prodigals. More than that, the Founder has been beaming *Alpha*-waves into the Federations—casting his net, you might say. There are never many takers. ('Many are called, but few are chosen,' if you recall the saying.) Yet, there are relatively more individuals worthy of immortality who are trapped in the Dark Continents now than in the last three eras. It's a kind of cosmic rhythm that the Sophia is tuned to: when the number of Prodigals rises, so too does the number of those who have undergone Evolution-Conversion in the Dark Continents. Prepare yourself, my son, for a strenuous decade."

And with that, Amitabha had turned him over to Marcus. Marcus was Era-Centurion of the entire Alexander function. Lean and muscular, with short-cropped black hair, he truly looked the part. In fact, Yeshua, upon meeting him, had wondered whether in all of Marcus' sequential pilgrimages, he had ever been anything other than an Alexander. It was certainly difficult to picture him as a Leonardo, a Plato, a Rothschild, etc. Marcus gave him an orderly but hurried tour of the Security Wing of Social Control headquarters. The centurion had been overworked, the last few decades, by the large number of PSI alarms and the increasing number of Prodigals.

Two weeks later, Yeshua having become more knowledgeable in this area of Sukhavati professional life, he was recalled by Amitabha for his first Foreign Mission assignment. As Yeshua came into his study, Amitabha silently handed him a list of five names. When they were seated, he explained. "This is the high-priority list submitted by the Sophia. The men and women on this list have been designated 'WELL'—Worthy of Eternal Life and Love. You are being sent, O Divine Physician, not to the sick but to the well!" A smile flickered over Amitabha's face. Then he grew solemn again. "Kindly note the first name on the list."

It was a Russian name. Aleksandr Myshkin. Yeshua recognized it at once. Myshkin was one of the greatest writers presently alive in the Three Federations. Branch scanners were employed by the Sophia to peruse virtually everything published in the Federations. They were in continual operation, and any work meriting the attention of either specialized scholars or the general reading public of Sukhavati was instantly translated and made available. Aleksandr Myshkin was surely one of the most avidly followed Federation authors on the island.

"You know his story, do you not, Yeshua?" Amitabha asked. "Let me go over the main outlines of it, anyway, just to refresh your memory.

"Aleksandr Myshkin, writer, eleven years in a concentration camp, slave labor, for publishing works denouncing the quality of life in the Eastern Federation. Released after eleven years, he promptly wrote another article, condemning anew the tyranny over mind exercised in that federation. I quote: 'It is no longer tolerable that our literature has been enduring censorship for centuries. . . . No one can bar the road to the truth, and to advance its cause I am prepared to accept even death.' For this article, smuggled out and published in the Western Federation, the authorities once again placed Myshkin in detention—this time in a mental institution!

"Released again, he spoke out again. And he's on his way, right now, to a camp from which no prisoner has ever returned. His novels—you have read them, haven't you?—have been a beacon, lighting up the dark night of the soul throughout the Eastern Federation. Even in the East, where it is extremely dangerous to read him, his admirers have painstakingly copied his condemned works and secretly circulated them, sometimes page by page.

"Yeshua, I rejoice that the object of your very first Foreign Mission should be the conferring of immortality on Aleksandr Myshkin!" Here, Amitabha paused for several moments. "And yet," he continued, "I regret—I have to admit it—that your very first mission takes you to the Eastern Federation, the most difficult region of the world to penetrate. Hazards are maximum, my son," he said solemnly, "but so is the prize! I am giving you Marcus, the best man we have for this mission. Follow his counsel religiously."

Back at the Security Wing of Social Control headquarters, Marcus briefed him in more detail on the imminent mission.

"It won't be easy, sir. As I'm sure you are aware, that federation is notoriously more strict than the other two regarding border patrols, examination of papers and internal security in general. On the other hand, our scanners keep scrupulously up to date regarding documentation forms, currency, dress—even contemporary slang. Security has a Yajnavalkya-adjunct, permanently assigned, to aid us in our more difficult cases. You are scheduled to receive five or six intensive hypnotic sessions with him and a branch linguistic-computer. Sir, by the end of that time, you will not only have mastered grammatical Russian and Mandarin Chinese, but even contemporary obscenity in both languages! You'll need fortifying, though! Take my word for it. They'll stretch your brain for you, they will. Be forewarned, sir."

"I understand," Yeshua said in a tone of voice that indicated he was still seeking assurance on the point, "that we can be immunized for as long as a week outside the IMOB."

"Yes, one week." Marcus looked solemn. Then he brightened, leaned over, and clamped his strong sinewy hand on Yeshua's shoulder. "Never fear, sir. I've done it before—dozens of times to the other two federations, and twice into the Eastern Federation—with your predecessor, you know. We made it.

"Now, suppose you fill me in on the man we are going in for." Yeshua related the background of Aleksandr Myshkin. When he was finished, Marcus shook his head solemnly from side to side.

"That *is* a risky mission, sir. There is no use belittling either the difficulties or the risks. It would be a tricky business to penetrate the borders and arrange for the escape of even a respected scientist or musician. But the Sophia is directing us to free a condemned criminal imprisoned in a concentration camp—and probably in solitary confinement, at that. A tomb, within a prison, within a dictatorship! We have to pass, both ways, through three concentric circles of hell. And on the way back, accompanied by the prisoner himself! It will take some doing.

"We will need a Rothschild on the mission team to handle the diplomatic formalities and amenities. We'll need a first-rate Archimedes, with all the miniaturized electronic gear he can carry. And, for this particular assignment, I believe we had better take along a Yajnavalkya, also."

"Why a Yajnavalkya?" Yeshua asked. "I can see the necessity for someone of your own professional background, and also the utility of an Archimedes—even a Rothschild. But why on earth a Yajnavalkya?"

"I am afraid you will probably find that out, sir. And, if you pardon me, you'll be damned glad we took him along!" Marcus' tone was sharp. "If the Sophia hadn't assigned us this mission, I would have sworn it could not be accomplished! But I know the Sophia trades on possibilities, not impossibilities. She can neither deceive nor be deceived. So be it."

Yeshua was next shown the marine skimmer which

could sift in under all radar and infra-red detection systems. The skimmer was designed to cover the distance of several thousand miles in a matter of hours. "We could do it even faster, sir," Marcus boasted, "but we don't know the effects of ULTRA—top ionization power—on our immunities outside the IMOB."

By custom as well as by privilege of rank, it was Yeshua's prerogative to choose the members of his Foreign Mission team. Inasmuch as it was his first mission assignment, however, he relied heavily of the centurion's advice. Marcus strongly recommended a Rothschild by the name of Hilary: "Extremely cool man in a crisis. Thoroughly practical. I've served with him before." The Yajnavalkya adjunct to Sukhavati Security was, similarly, a logical choice, and Marcus had full faith in him. For the mission-Archimedes, however, Marcus presented Yeshua with a list of three candidates, all of whom, in his judgment, were equally suitable. Yeshua spotted Hans' name on the list, and chose him immediately.

The Mission Team was called to Yeshua's study the very next day and briefed on the difficult assignment. A schedule was drawn up providing each man with a series of intensive hypnotic sessions under the direction of the Security-Yajnavalkya, utilizing a branch linguistic-computer. Not in his entire five-decade experience had Yeshua needed as much sleep (up to three hours), or as much protein-broth (two bowls every eighteen hours), as he needed during this training period. Truly, it felt like his brain was being stretched. By the end of the month, he confided to Helen, "I feel as weak as a Newly-Aware." But he knew Russian, he knew Mandarin Chinese, and he could be both polite and obscene in the two languages.

The Yajnavalkya had laughed at his groanings and assured him, "In the Federations, the average person utilizes less than a third of his total brain capacity. Here we go up to about 38 or 40 per cent of capacity in an average era of 120 solar years. The brightest Archimedes or Plato among us is still operating at less than 50 per cent of capacity. It has been estimated that there are about as many neural connections in the brain as there are stars in the known universe! You will all survive."

Helen and Yeshua felt especially close to each other

during the last week preceding the mission. To be sure, the Sophia had predicated a mere 13 per cent chance of premature discovery by the Eastern Federation. On the other hand, chances for total mission success were estimated at only 42 per cent, so it was obviously going to be arduous. Helen knew all this. No effort was made by any member of the mission to withhold information from her.

On the final evening before his scheduled departure, Helen complained seriously of Sukhavati policy for the first time since he had known her.

"They ask a lot," she said in a low but bitter voice, "of an Era-Yeshua—and they ask a lot of me, too. If you were a soldier in one of the Federation armies, going to war somewhere on the Dark Continents, what would you really be risking? The remainder of your short life—anywhere from 30 to 50 years—and painful, troubled years, at that! But look what *you* are being asked to risk: a lifetime of successive lives; unending life! You risk your whole eternity! What if they do discover you and detain you for more than a week, so that you lose your immunization? I will lose you for my entire eternity! Even their Ghandi and their Socrates and their Jesus only surrendered a few decades of trouble-filled years. And they say of those men, 'Greater love than this, no man hath, than to lay down his life for his friends.' Do you realize what *you* will be laying down? Time! Time, itself! And for whom? For a man you've never even met! It doesn't seem fair."

"Aware yourself gently, Helen," Yeshua smiled. Your PSI is beginning to gyrate. Remember, the Sophia estimates a 13 per cent chance of *detection*, not apprehension. There's a difference. You know Hans, and you know his reputation. You have met both Marcus and Hilary. The Security-Yajnavalkya is an old friend of yours. None of these are men to be trifled with. We will cope.

"As for Myshkin, the man we are sent to rescue—you must know, even better than I, with your phenomenal intuitive powers, just how remarkable a personality he is. If I'm not mistaken, Helen, you've read everything the man has ever written—twice! The Sophia has designated him WELL, Helen, and the Sophia does not confer

156

immortality casually. This man has spent the larger part of his life in slave-labor camps, prisons and mental institutions, and the Eastern Federation has still not been able to break his spirit. His spirit cries out from behind bars, and the Sophia has heard him!

It seemed to the Mission Team that most of Sukhavati had turned out to bid them farewell at the dock.

"It's not always this dramatic," Marcus informed Yeshua in an undertone as they approached the marine skimmer which would have them at the main Pacific Port of the Eastern Federation in about five hours. "When we leave for the Western or Southern Federation, it's usually only our own friends and associates who come down to see us off. But they all know about Myshkin, and they all know the Sophia's estimate of risk and failure. They are down here to honor us. There's always a chance we won't be back. We give up a great deal more than a mere lifetime if we are not back in a week."

Amitabha himself was on hand for the solemn moment of departure. He admonished them against taking any extraordinary risks in the effort to liberate Myshkin. "We want him, yes. But our first priority"—he said this, looking straight at Marcus—"is the safe return of our Era-Yeshua. Is that clear, Centurion?"

Then, taking in the whole team with his glance and pronouncing each word distinctly and emphatically, he added: "Every one of you is precious. A trade-off would not constitute an even trade. We do not trade gods for men."

Yeshua's first and dearest guide on the island, Ananda, took him by the hand but had little to say. "Take care, sir." The words were almost whispered. It was a poignant moment for them both. Li, Mobutu, Zoe, Bertram, Anthea, Magi—all were there, embracing him, shaking his hand, wishing him well. Helen was not there. Their farewell had been private. It had been long and mostly silent. But very dear.

"Cast off the bow line!" Marcus commanded, when the mission team was finally aboard. The glistening white bow of the sea skimmer swung 15 degrees to open water.

"Cast off, amidships! Cast off stern line!" The orders

157

came in rapid succession. "All engines ahead one-third." Hans operated the throttle. The sea skimmer—her superstructure modeled precisely after that of an Eastern Federation patrol boat, slowly and gracefully glided her way toward IMOB Sluice No. 7. Yeshua waved once to his friends, slowly fading out of sight on the Sukhavati dock.

In a few minutes, they were within hailing distance of the sluice. The Alexander on watch saluted them and then hunched over his controls. Slowly, almost lethargically, the heavy transparent plastic gate slid up. Yeshua himself was feeling a bit lethargic—the effect of the radiological immunization treatment they had all received the evening before. Marcus had forewarned him of the symptoms.

But all that lethargy blew off like summer haze as soon as the skimmer launched out into the open sea. Yeshua had completely forgotten about the extreme southern latitude of Sukhavati! The island under the IMOB was warmed by solar energy and atomic fusion to the point that palm trees and orange groves flourished there in abundance. The frigid air outside the IMOB now greeted Yeshua with all the subtlety of a punch to the jaw. He was freezing! But Hilary was already distributing winter gear, modeled after the style used in the Eastern Federation Navy. It was authentic, right down to the crimson epaulettes and the insignia on the brass buttons.

Once the course had been established and the ionic thrust set on automatic, the mission team assembled in Yeshua's quarters to go over their plan of operations.

"All of you have been on at least one previous mission," Yeshua began, "and Marcus has been on over a dozen. I have not. I consider my command nominal, therefore, until such time as we face a situation lacking precedent. Marcus will lead the discussion."

"Let me remind you, gentlemen," said Marcus, rising, as he nearly always did when he had anything of consequence to say, "that one man alone among us is authorized to conduct discussions with Eastern Federation officials—not Yeshua; not myself; but Hilary! He is the most fluent of us in the two major languages of the East. He is the most knowledgeable with regard to diplomatic procedures and social amenities. He has not been a Rothschild these 89 years," Marcus smiled, "for nothing. The rest of us will speak when spoken to.

"You all have your official papers—in fact, two sets of them, depending on which identity it becomes necessary to assume. Once we have reached port, we will switch our naval attire for army uniforms—all except Yeshua. Yeshua will be dressed as a civilian. He is assuming the identity of a comparatively high-ranking member of the ruling party—someone not so important that the mention of his name would conjure up a face, but someone too important to forbid access to Federation facilities. He will pose as Third Assistant Minister of State Security, Department of Internal Affairs.

"Once inside the prison where Myshkin is currently being held, Hilary is to remain with the prison commandant, if at all possible, preoccupying the staff with his lively conversation and military gossip. I will remain with him. Concealed in an inside pocket, I carry a memory-laser of 250 volts. Should we arouse suspicion, I can confuse them sufficiently to prevent coherent reporting of what goes on. Hans, whose uniform, you will note, is large and bulky—not an unusual fit in the Eastern Federation—is carrying several miniaturized items of emergency electronic gear. He will accompany Yeshua and Yajnavalkya as backup, while they deal directly with the prisoner and his guards.

"Yeshua, you will of course demand a private cell for interrogation. Naturally, we are aware of just how private such a cell will be. Your very first action, once inside the cell, Hans, will be to jam every electronic sensor they have planted. Count on a minimum of four." Hans nodded.

"I will now call on our Security-Yajnavalkya," said Marcus, rather formally, according to his custom, "to add any advice he might find appropriate."

"Yes, there is something I want to explain—to Yeshua, particularly." The Security-Yajnavalkya was a mild-mannered, tranquil-looking man—they weren't all that way. Some of the most contemplative of them were actually quite fierce-looking. But, four decades of service with the Alexanders notwithstanding, and leading the

159

most active life imaginable, the Security Yajnavalkya remained an extremely gentle and soft-spoken individual—until the moment for decisive action! His behavior on those occasions had won him the sobriquet, in security circles, of "Instant Acceleration." "He defies the laws of Newtonian physics," said an Archimedes who had seen him in action.

"Yeshua," Yajnavalkya continued, I am sure that Amitabha cautioned you about the probable unbelief and initial hostility of the very people you are sent to rescue. I myself have been on three previous foreign missions. The first reaction of our intended beneficiaries was, in each case, to call for the police. (Fortunately, Myshkin is not likely to do *that*). But in all three missions, they supposed that I was insane.

"Even after you establish your credibility by giving evidence"—here he turned toward Hans—"of your advanced scientific achievements, so that they begin to take you seriously, their reaction is still an uncertain business. To be sure, I have seen overwhelming joy at the thought that we really could confer immortality. But, believe it or not, there is frequently some reluctance. It's not always easy to persuade someone to live forever. If I were an Archimedes, I'd say that eternity had a psychological mass roughly equal to the the weight of time divided by the square of the psychic energy of the individual confronting it. The less dynamic the personality, the more terrifying the burden of immortality. There's no question, but that it demands a certain kind of heroism to embrace eternity."

"In the case of Myshkin," Yeshua broke in, "I don't think we have to worry about either his psychic energy or his heroism."

"You are most likely correct, sir. But I do want you to know that there are cases on record of the flat refusal of immortality. And in the case of Myshkin, we have to add onto his initial confusion at hearing our proposal, his general disgust with life as he has known it in the Dark Continents—harrassed by his government, mocked by the authorized critics, etc. At this moment, he may be longing more for the cessation than the prolongation of life!"

"Hmmm. What *do* we do, then," Yeshua asked, "if Myshkin refuses to come with us?"

"It goes without saying, sir, that we cannot kill. We may never directly add to the kingdom of death. We are, even genetically, committed to life. Yet we may not, on the other hand, allow him—or anyone else—to broadcast the news of our existence to the Three Federations. The reasons for this, I am sure, Amitabha has rehearsed with you many times.

"That leaves us with just two possibilities: the memory-laser, in extreme emergency—although that comes too close to violence to constitute our first choice. Except under laboratory conditions, I think you are all aware that the laser is too imprecise an instrument. It stupefies rather large areas of the brain, and the victims also attract the attention and wonder of the authorities.

"No, our first choice would be to leave Myshkin, finally, so confused regarding the reality of the whole confrontation with us, that he would be too embarrassed to discuss it with anyone. I must say, Marcus, that my admonition regarding the laser extends as well to its use on prison officials. It ought to be only our instrument of last resort."

"Acknowledged." Marcus rose again. "I am now going to put our skimmer into high thrust. Expected time of arrival" (he glanced down at his watch)—"four hours and twenty minutes. From this point on, gentlemen, it will not be a comfortable ride. I might have been able to diminish the vibration, but not with this additional weight, this superstructure we have built on for disguise. So get set, gentlemen. Any last communications? We won't even be able to talk, you know, above the level of vibration. No further word? Then, Hans, full speed, all engines!"

It was totally unlike any previous skimmer trip Yeshua had ever taken. They were now hovering over a rough and shifting ocean instead of a smooth concrete surface, and ploughing through pockets of raw frigid air instead of the light, balmy breezes of Sukhavati. As the hard rhythm of the waves and cold air-pockets massaged his vertebrae, Yeshua felt all the tension go out of him. Physically and spiritually, he stretched out his body and

161

extended his senses to the wind, spray and sun. His nerves hung in the sea air like clean wash on a line, refreshed and invigorated. He was with experienced men, completely equipped, with only a 13 per cent probability of detection, according to the Sophia. He pushed all the way back in his heavily cushioned seat, eased up on his seat belt, and enjoyed the vast expanse of space.

"Space! That's the one thing we lack," he mused. "Until such time as the dark continents yield to life and compassion, until the great mutation-conversion. Should that occur, we would have all of this." He pondered the problem of IMOB engineering that such a global conversion would entail. "First," he thought, "the huge metropolitan centers would be enclosed, and then protected IMOB channels could be constructed to connect them—enclosed highways and even sea lanes. But eventually, Amitabha's vision of the crystal planet would have to be implemented."

He tried to picture in his mind how the earth looked as it hung in space. Billions of years ago, it had once been a ball of red molten rock, a lithosphere. It had, after a billion years or two, taken on the fluid aquamarine and blue tints of a hydrosphere and atmosphere. After life evolved, the earth had turned green with growth: a biosphere. Then, as a Western Federation scientist and philosopher had pictured it, the earth had turned phosphorescent, covered with a layer of thought: a Noosphere. And lastly, mused Yeshua, the entire planet, after mutation-conversion, would be enclosed in a crystal IMOB—a diamond sparkling in space forever: an ecstosphere! Serenity has no color but transparency, he mused.

The hours passed rapidly as he sat thus lost in thought. The ionic thrust had now definitely been cut to half power; he could feel it. The ride had grown much smoother, the wind, less outrageous against his face. Then he heard, abruptly, the ringing of the ship's bell. Three bells! The prearranged signal to alert the mission team that Eastern Federation patrol boats had been sighted.

As had been expected, there had been no trouble at all with early radar or infrared detection systems. They were already quite close to one of the few great Federation ports on the Pacific Ocean. The test would come after they landed. Their speed had now dropped off to a mere

162

15 knots—normal cruising speed for a patrol boat on routine duty. Marcus shouted. Turning his head, Yeshua saw him pointing off the starboard bow. Land! Just a few minutes later, and Yeshua could begin to make out the shapes of the taller buildings of the port. It was about 5 p.m., Pacific Federation time. The weather was still brisk, but no longer freezing: autumnal.

As they slid into the harbor, their hull, like that of any Federation patrol boat, now firmly planted in the water, none of the other vessels paid them the slightest attention. It was a vast port with scores of ships and boats of all sizes—some of them at anchor, some just coming into harbor, others making way to open sea. The Sophia had evidently chosen a code number for their ship and ship's radio that fitted in perfectly with the present disposition of the Eastern Federation Navy. It would have taken a team of clerks, pouring over admiralty lists for days, to discover there was no such launch as theirs in commission.

The dock loomed dead ahead. Hilary threw over a line, and three obliging Federation seamen helped tie them up. Hilary thanked them and chatted briefly but briskly with them in Russian. Marcus ordered everyone but Yajnavalkya ashore for an hour or so, to accustom neighboring ships and personnel to their presence. So far, so good.

Upon their return to the skimmer, they all descended below, where they exchanged their navy uniforms for army garb—except for Yeshua, who was assuming the identity of a high-ranking party official, and who changed into civilian clothes. They waited, then, until dark: about 6:30. They waited further, till about 7 p.m., for an especially quiet moment on the docks. All naval personnel seemed to have returned to their respective ships for their meal. When no one was visible on the dock nearest them, they emerged in their army attire. There were a sufficient number of Federation soldiers attached to the harbor defense forces so that the five of them continued to enjoy universal disinterest. But now their first test was at hand.

At the gate leading out of the dock area, Hilary saluted the officer in charge, presented his papers, and introduced

Yeshua as Victor Semyonovich Adumov, Third Assistant Minister of State Security, Department of Internal Affairs. All went smoothly. Army transport was arranged, and Hilary, declining the loan of an enlisted man as chauffeur, took the wheel himself.

These successes, however, were trivial; air transport was another matter entirely. The prison of Mavrino, their ultimate destination, lay a good 2,500 miles to the west and Eastern Federation air transport was never easily arranged. At the army airport, Hilary went into a lengthy huddle with one of the resident senior officers. Even after the introduction of Minister Adumov, whose position, although not overwhelming, was still consequential, it was necessary to pass rubles, as well as official papers, from hand to hand.

Hilary and Yeshua at last walked back to their little group, huddled in the waiting room of the commandant's office. They were taut, but triumphant! "It's been arranged," Yeshua announced softly. A flight in three hours. "Go and eat now." They had been forewarned that, distasteful as it might be to them, they would have to eat and drink the food of the Federations when it seemed appropriate, in order to avoid arousing curiosity.

Aboard the plane, seated among the other passengers, they held their communications to a minimum. Once, the door to the pilot's cabin opened and the pilot looked over his passengers, pausing and staring hard—so it seemed to them—when his eyes fastened on Hilary and Yeshua. But then he climbed back into his cabin and shut the door, and they did not see him again for the remainder of the trip.

It was a night flight. Marcus stealthily passed word that they should all sleep, or pretend sleep as best they could. Only Yajnavalkya, it turned out, truly slept, or else— Yeshua resolved to find out which, later on—he put himself in a state of trance at least as deep as sleep. Because they were flying westward, it was not yet quite light when they arrived at the Eastern Federation Army Airport, outside the city of Omsk.

Again, they had to show papers and secure army transport to Mavrino, a high-security, hard-labor camp, under the administration of GULAG (Chief Admmistration for

Corrective Labor Camps). On this occasion, however, the officer in charge seemed only half awake. It was, in fact, only 3 a.m., Federation Central time. If anything, the Major on duty was a bit in awe of the Third Assistant Minister of State Security. He could not recognize Adumov by face, but the name certainly was not unfamiliar. The Sophia had been sociologically on target.

They would not, however, entrust Hilary with a vehicle. Their complaint: too many air force vehicles were never returned by infantry personnel. Inter-service jealousy. An air force corporal, therefore, drove them the entire distance, 42 kilometers, to the Mavrino prison camp. And they were unable, all that time, to rehearse their plans for the next phase of the daring operation.

It was five a.m., and still dark, upon their arrival at Mavrino. The officer on duty did not choose to interpret their unexpected presence as a pleasant surprise. He was too sleepy. Also, too grumpy. He fussed over their papers. Hilary, using the name Major Bokynin, was as charming as the early hour would allow. But it was all wasted.

"This is a dangerous man that you have come to see. What you can possibly want with him I have no idea," the duty-officer mumbled over and through his glass of steaming tea. "You will have to see Colonel Klimensky. I, myself, cannot authorize this visit."

"What time does the Colonel arrive?" Hilary asked.

"Eight-thirty."

"Impossible! You are asking the Third Assistant Minister of State Security, Victor Semyonovich Adumov, to cool his heels for over three hours!"

At a lift of Hilary's eyebrow, Yeshua moved in for the kill.

"What is your name, my man?" Yeshua asked brusquely.

"Lieutenant Shutov."

"Write that name down, Major. Well, Lieutenant Shutov, I am due back in Moscow in time for a conference with the First Minister tomorrow evening, about this prisoner. It looks now as if I shall miss my flight. You are willing to take full responsibility for this delay, are you not? Write down his answer, Major Bokynin."

"Well, I . . ."

"Come, come, Lieutenant, yes or no—let's have it!"

"Sir, I have had strict orders regarding the prisoner, Myshkin. He's to be allowed no visitors. He is a dangerous enemy of the state."

"And I, Lieutenant? I remind you of whom? His wife? His accomplice in crime? In which category do you place me? Relative or friend of this enemy of the Eastern Federation? It has to be one or the other!" Yeshua let go an authentic barrage of Slavic profanity.

"Up!" he screamed at the junior officer. "Be quick about it! Arrange a private cell where I can interrogate this prisoner alone, with my aides!"

The Lieutenant, now thoroughly cowed, jumped out of his chair and summoned a guard. "Wake the prisoner Myshkin," he ordered him, "and escort him to the interrogation room."

Marcus nudged Yeshua. "Not the interrogation room!" Yeshua swore loudly, remembering the electronic sensors. "Give me an empty cell. I prefer it. Prisoners freeze up in the interrogation room. Makes it twice as difficult to get anything out of them."

"Take the prisoner to cell 14, second tier, "the lieutenant told the guard.

The mission team sat down in the office and waited in silence.

In five minutes the guard was back. "Myshkin threw a fit," he grumbled to the lieutenant. "You know how cheeky he is. Demanded to know why he was being awakened half an hour before regulations prescribe! Swears he won't answer questions for *anyone*."

The duty officer looked pointedly at Yeshua.

"Never mind about that," Yeshua said calmly. "We have our ways. Just conduct me and my aides to the prisoner. Major Bokynin and Captain Shikin will wait for us here with you."

The guard led them down a dank corridor permeated with the odor of stale urine, then up a flight of stairs to the second tier of cells. Outside cell 14, he came to a halt, jangled his keys, and opened the steel door.

Inside the cell, a small, wiry figure with jet-black hair

and eyes stood against the far wall, glaring at them angrily.

"Leave us," Yeshua ordered the guard. The guard slammed the cell door shut behind them. Hans immediately pulled out a miniature electronic detection device and went over the entire cell with it. The prisoner, meanwhile, eyed him with hostility, but with wonder, also.

Hans found, without much trouble, two listening devices implanted in the ceiling near the single light bulb that lit the cell. He ripped them out. "It's all right now," he said to Yeshua. "That's all there are." "Certain?" Yeshua asked. "Certain."

Yeshua addressed him for the first time. "We are not Eastern Federation officials," he said quietly, but in a clear, firm voice. "We are not here to interrogate you or to torment you. We have come to rescue you."

Slowly, a look of understanding mixed with caution and suspicion passed over the prisoner's countenance.

"You are from the West, then? How am I to know this for certain?"

Yeshua decided to go along with Myshkin's surmise for a little while. To blurt out at once the full import of their mission would have placed too great a strain on Myshkin's credulity.

"How am I to know," the prisoner went on, "that this is not another plot to discredit me entirely, to depict me as an agent of the Western Federation—a man who has sold out his own people? Then you could not only destroy me physically but, what is much more important, destroy my life's work, as well!"

"Myshkin, what would constitute a proof in your eyes?" Yeshua asked.

"Intelligent, intelligent," the prisoner reflected. He was shivering in the cold cell, clothed as he was in thin, coarse cotton prison grab. "I frankly don't know how you could convince me you were not party agents sent to entrap me in some phony escape plot. But there's more to it than that. . . .

"You know what?" he continued, "I tend to believe you—just by your faces, your presence, the non-verbal signs! You just don't come across to me as party men or double agents. But even if I were fully to trust you, there is another problem. I don't think I want to go with you. If I were to escape to the Western Federation, I would lose some part—perhaps the major part—of the power I now wield over men's souls here in the East. Have I endured so much over these last two decades to end my life in bourgeois comfort and safety, while my friends and followers live on in danger and oppression?"

"We have hardly come here," Yeshua answered sharply, "to offer you bourgeois comfort and security. We too, you see, are risking our lives."

"Yes, that is true," mused Myshkin. "If what you say is so, you are risking your lives for me. Tell me why."

"With us, Myshkin, you could go on unhampered with your life's work. You could speak from the shores of a free federation. You would, in your own person, be a second Statue of Liberty, a torch for the world!"

"Horrible!" the prisoner practically spat out of his mouth. "I don't want to be a Statue of Liberty! I don't want to be a statue of anything! Was it by being a frozen, divine statue that Jesus Christ changed the world? It was the moment they began to make statues of him that he ceased to be a world force. I tell you that, without the blood and the nails, the sweat and the urine, Christ would have been just another wordy moralist. It is absolutely necessary to pay the price of your own book first. If it's a steep book, it's a steep price! You offer me physical safety and moral oblivion."

The prisoner paused. "Besides," he added in a sad, low tone, "your federation is hardly the archetype of the civilization I hope for. You have your own slaveries and your own degradations. I will not go."

Yajnavalkya spoke. "Tell him, Yeshua. You have to, now."

The three missioners looked at one another. Yeshua nodded his head. "All right," he said.

"Myshkin, our tale is a strange one. But paradoxically, it may be easier to convince you of its truth than to convince you that we are Western Federation agents.

"Friend, we are from none of the world's federations."

The prisoner looked at them in fright. Then he shook his head in disgust. "I see," he said, when he had regained his composure. "You are from outer space, come to take me to some suburban galaxy. I might have known!"

"Nothing like that, Myshkin—and there's precious little time for sarcasm, that I'll tell you. Does the name Strastnik mean anything to you?"

"Strastnik? Strastnik? Do you speak of the Soviet scientist—a great one, they say—who, legend has it, simply disappeared some centuries ago, after trying to engineer a new world order?"

"That is the one."

"Are you trying to tell me that the legend is to be taken seriously? That there is something to that whole business?"

"There *is* something to that business. Strastnik and the Geneva Society were thwarted in their attempt to establish global peace, but they did bring into being a new kind of community—small, but in several important respects, unique. This community, Myshkin, does not have its location in outer space. We have come from it. To you."

"You know," mused the captive, "among the Eastern Federation intellectuals, this has been a half-hope, half-dream for hundreds of years, passed on from one generation to another." He sighed. "To think that Strastnik made it, that he actually started something!" His eyes were glistening now.

Then, abruptly, he drew himself erect. "This changes nothing! Even were I to credit your new tale, the same objection applies as to your story about coming from outer space. How do I know you are not trying to entrap me in some absurd escape plan in order to discredit me forever?" It was clear that he had again retreated behind a wall of hostility.

"We didn't make up the space story. *You* did. Anyway, Myshkin, I think we can prove to you that we come from a community that the world knows nothing about. But look, my friend, we have very little time. We must all be out of here well before the commandant, Colonel Klimensky returns. Our papers appear to be in order, but they won't bear checking out at Eastern Federation Headquarters. Now, probably the quickest—albeit the crudest—way of demonstrating that our highly improbable tale is indeed within the realm of possibility, is to

169

show you a few scientific feats well beyond the achievements of any of the three Federations' scientists. Then the decision will be up to you. I myself admit that possibility is not certainty. Once we have demonstrated the possibility, you will have to decide whether you trust us or not. Like most of the crucial decisions in a man's life, this one will also come down to your human intuition."

Yeshua checked his watch. "We have less than an hour left. Hans—!"

Hans, who had remained in the background all this while, now stepped forward and removed several pieces of miniaturized equipment from his voluminous outer coat.

In a corner of the damp and dirty cell stood a single rickety wooden table and chair. "I propose," said Hans quietly, to aim this little instrument at the table in the corner and to send it floating upward till it rests against the ceiling." With a slight buzz and a beam of bluish light, he proceeded to do so.

The prisoner looked at him wide-eyed. "You destroyed gravity!"

"No. I *used* gravity—but I reversed its field."

For a moment, the prisoner looked convinced—convinced of everything! Then he snapped out of it.

"It might have been hypnotism! You could make me believe I had seen anything!"

"Myshkin," said Yeshua with some exasperation, "I cannot demonstrate to you that you are not hypnotized, because such a demonstration could very well be part of the hypnosis, correct?"

"Correct."

"Do you think you are hypnotized? Pinch yourself! Do you feel normal pain? Count to ten. Think of your son's middle name. Do you feel that your state of consciousness is in any way altered?"

"No, I can't say that I do—for what *that's* worth.

"Did I not tell you," said Yeshua, "that ultimately this would be a test not of your powers of logic, but of your intuition?"

Hans had, in the meanwhile, set up a miniature Audio. "Will you consent," he asked the prisoner respectfully, to listen to a few minutes of our music?"

"Your *music!*," Myshkin repeated in amazement.

"Yes. It is different from any music you have ever heard. This music will actually nourish you, warm you, strengthen you in mind and body."

The prisoner still looked suspicious, but consented to put on the earphones.

"I want you to turn it off as soon as I give you a signal—as soon as I raise my right arm. Agreed?"

"Agreed." Hans smiled at him. "Please sit down."

Hans set the controls and turned on the switch. First, a look of childlike wonder, then one of total rapture, passed over the captive's countenance. Hans looked at a dial on the Audio. "He is an exquisitely sensitive reactor," he whispered to the others. "Much above average."

Myshkin did not raise his arm and, when after a lapse of several minutes, Hans made a move to turn the Audio off, the listener thrust him away. In spite of the tension they were under, the three missioners had to laugh. Finally, after six and a half minutes, Yeshua signaled Hans, who abruptly switched the Audio off. There was simply not a minute to spare. Myshkin slowly, almost languorously, removed the earphones from his head.

"It was . . . it was . . . outstanding." That was all he could say. The prisoner felt marvelously well—as if he had slept for eight hours instead of the regulation five, as if he had eaten three meals instead of one and a half, as if he were warmly clothed instead of bone-chilled in his coarse cotton garb.

Yeshua, feeling desperate for time, now seized him by the shoulders and shook him!

"Tell me now, do we still seem to be liars, hypnotizers, double agents?"

"No."

"Do you believe us, then?"

"I tend to believe you . . . I believe you."

"Good! Then you will come with us?"

There was no reply.

"Myshkin, will you come with us?"

"No."

It was the turn of his would-be rescuers to be astounded. They thought they had won him over.

"Why not?" Yeshua exploded. Yajnavalkya put a cau-

171

tioning hand on his shoulder. The guards might be nearby in the passageway.

"My reasons are the same as before. Whether it be escape to the Western Federation or to Strastnik's community, it's still an escape. It would destroy the meaning of my life."

The three men looked at one another. "Now tell him *all*," said Yajnavalkya.

"Myshkin," Yeshua began quietly, "prepare yourself for a shock. You have seen a few of our instruments—toys, really. Now it is time to tell you the great thing we have to offer you. My friend, we have vanquished illness and pain. We have vanquished the aging process. *Myshkin, we have vanquished death! We live forever!*"

"Live forever? I . . . I don't believe you!"

"What would motivate us to tell you so stupendous a lie?"

"Perhaps . . . perhaps you are men of good will who truly wish to remove me from this hell-hole, and you tell me such a thing to entice me because, up to this point, I have refused to leave with you. You can't understand why I wish to stay, so you quickly conjure up the greatest possible inducement to get me to accompany you."

Hans produced a small vial of liquid and a hypodermic needle. "This," he explained to the prisoner, "is a standard, old-fashioned truth serum, still much in vogue among your Federation security people. Let me first administer a dose to you, so that you can test its efficacy. Even when you deliberately try to lie, it will be impossible. Then I will administer the same drug to our spokesman here, and you can put any question to him you like—including whether or not we have overcome disease, aging and death."

Myshkin appeared shaken by the suggestion.

"No! I don't agree to that! You might administer a tranquilizer that would render me helpless, and thus steal me away from Mavrino."

"My God, man!" Yeshua exclaimed. "You speak of this place as if it were your castle, your home—and of us, as if we were kidnappers!"

"Yes."

Again the three men looked at one another, in doubt how to proceed.

"Aleksandr, time does not permit me to explain in detail. It is not merely the biological fact of everlasting life we offer—the *quality* of life in our society is almost unimaginable to you in your present misery. The beauty, the peace, the intellectual—yes, and the physical—satisfactions are beyond Federation words to articulate."

"It is not necessary that you should explain all that in detail," replied the convict. "I presumed as much after the first half-hour of conversing with you gentlemen. It's not *entirely* unimaginable to me. Imagination is my first faculty." He smiled at them. "Ask the Union of Eastern Federation Writers."

Yeshua grabbed him by the arms. "Think, man, think! We are not fooling with you! There is no dying, no death where we come from! We want you to be part of us! Do you think we make this offer casually? Why, our community has followed your career for years! Every word that you have written has been scanned and analyzed scores of times. You are WELL—worthy of eternal life and love! We have so judged you. You must come with us!"

"No."

Yeshua groaned. "Time has run out. Why, Aleksandr, do you refuse life and choose death?"

The prisoner paused a few moments before answering. Then he said quietly, "Do you know that you gentlemen are torturing me worse than my captors? You ask me the cosmic question, and you demand an answer in fifteen minutes' time. I gave you my gut reaction: No! Perhaps after months of unhurried reflection I would have given you a less wise and a more cowardly one. In a way, I'm glad you gave me so short a time to make up my mind. I will not cop out."

"For the last time," Yeshua spoke wearily, "this would not be a betrayal of your friends. You would not be washing your hands of the Eastern Federation. We in Suk . . . in our small community, have plans that involve the entire planet. We don't simply consign it to oblivion. One day——"

"One day. That's the key phrase. One day. You gentle-

173

men, if your fantastic story is true—as it may be—you gentlemen have *forever* to work out our salvation. We have only these few years—years like a string of pearls—to finger. And mostly, our rulers keep our hands in 'govno' so we cannot even savour the pearls. You want me to play God in a way that not even Jesus Christ played God. I can't desert my comrades in the here-and-now. In Mavrino."

"You are sure this is love, and not pride?"

"How *can* I be sure? I hope it is love."

"So you choose death over life," said Yeshua sadly.

"So it would seem to you."

"So be it."

Yajnavalkya leaned forward and whispered something in Yeshua's ear. Yeshua slowly, sadly nodded affirmation.

"You are a tough nut, Myshkin," Yeshua said stiffly. "You fall for nothing. We nearly had you toward the end, though. Listen. Our Federation cannot take the chance that you might break under future interrogation—yes, that's right. Our *Federation! Y*our first guess was the best."

While Yeshua was talking, Hans had slipped behind the prisoner. Suddenly, he thrust a needle into his arm. Myshkin leaped into the air, but Yajnavalkya was like a cat upon him.

"That was the sedation you were so worried about," said Yeshua. "But don't worry. We're not taking you back with us to the West. We want no reluctant escapees with us. Too chancy. We've got to make good our own escape now.

"You won't repeat any of this—you won't even be sure the crazy thing happened! A table and chair rising to the ceiling, indeed! To whom would you tell such a tale? You're probably dreaming, Myshkin. You *are* dreaming. Either that, or you're going *insane*. Dreaming is preferable. Why make a fantasy permanent? You know where they'll put you if you tell such a story. Sleep on, Myshkin. You're worn out from exhaustion, cold and lack of nourishment. Anyone could have illusions and fantasies in your physical condition. Demand more calories! You

174

know how to do it. You're not afraid of them—you've proved that many times.

"Myshkin! Myshkin! Are you sleeping?" Yeshua passed his hands before the man's eyes. His eyes were still open, but they did not flicker. "Good. We won't have to use anything stronger on him. I would hate to leave such a man with a psychic scar."

They lay the prisoner on the cot and summoned the guard. "Myshkin will be indisposed for several hours," Yeshua said curtly. "We had to use drugs to get the information we wanted. When he wakes up, he'll be a little confused in his head. Leave him alone for a day or two and give him a few decent meals, or he's liable to drop dead on you. I want him to live—do you understand? I may need more information from him in the future."

Returning quickly to Lieutenant Shutov's office, they rejoined Marcus and Hilary, tended their official thanks, and secured transportation back to the Eastern Federation Air Terminal near Omsk. It was 6:30 a.m. There were still two hours before Colonel Klimensky was due to arrive at Mavrino Prison. With a bit of luck, he would not check them out for a day or two. They needed only an eight- to ten-hour start to be out of the Federation and out of danger.

They were not to receive it.

The Mavrino Commandant was a stickler for protocol. Highly incensed that he had received no advance notice of a visit by someone of the comparatively high rank of Third Assistant Minister of State Security, he phoned Federation Security Headquarters. There, after several minutes of confused checking, they told him that Victor Semyonovich Adumov was presumably in Peking, and had expressed no intention of stopping off at Mavrino Prison to interview the prisoner Myshkin. They could not swear that the Third Assistant Minister would not do such a thing, but it would be a highly irregular procedure, and was much unlike his customary behavior. No, they had not been able to reach him at Peking.

When their plane landed at the Pacific Air Terminal, the five uninvited visitors to the Eastern Federation were met by an armed guard and escorted into the office of the commanding officer, Major General Dobroumov. Just before they were ushered into his presence, Yajnavalkya leaned forward and whispered, unaccountably, into Yeshua's ear, "Peking." Yeshua, already highly nervous, wondered if his aide was becoming erratic under the strain.

The general, a tall, imposing man with a barrel chest and baritone voice, was very calm as he looked them up and down. "Your papers, please," he ordered. As he examined the documents quickly but professionally, he remarked to them, "Colonel Klimensky over at Mavrino is highly incensed at you all—especially you, Comrade Adumov—for not forewarning him of your impending visit. More than that. Checking headquarters, he finds that you are supposed to be elsewhere—not enjoying long conversations with the enemy of the state, Myshkin."

"Ah yes," said Yeshua, recalling at that moment Yajnavalkya's extraordinary powers of intuition. "I have been in Peking, discussing cultural matters with the Minister of Internal Security there. They have relaxed their stiff controls, you know, over writers and artists, in that province of the Federation. My talks there led to my decision to confer with Myshkin. I wanted to see if he, too—like so many of our Federation writers—would listen to reason. He enjoys tremendous prestige in the West, you know. It would be something to reclaim him."

"Yes I do know. I read him myself."

This last remark was most unexpected. Myshkin was forbidden reading and, indeed, only one or two of his works had ever been openly published in the East.

"To know what the Underground is thinking," the general explained cooly.

"And how did you get here from Peking, gentlemen?" he asked them.

"Why, we flew, of course."

"I see. Today is Thursday. You took a flight on Tuesday or Wednesday, I suppose?"

"Yes, Wed . . . Tuesday," Yeshua replied, feeling Yajnavalkya's foot on his toes.

"Excuse my thoughtlessness, Comrade Adumov. Please sit down," said the general, pointing to a single chair at the side of his desk. Yeshua did not know whether the general had noticed Yajnavalkya's signals, but in any case, he was now effectively separated from his aide and forced onto the powers of his own intuition. These were not inconsiderable, but he wished now that he had done more meditation during his early decades in Sukhavati.

"Now, let me see," the general continued. "Was that the morning or evening flight out of Peking?"

"The . . . uh . . . morning, I believe."

"And Major Yang Chiou arranged air transport for you, I suppose? He usually handles our personnel."

"Why yes, Major Yang Chiou, to be sure."

The general sent his guards out of the office. When they were all alone with him for the first time, he said quietly, "You are frauds."

They looked at one another in consternation.

"You are Western Federation agents," he continued, eying them thoughtfully. There is no morning flight out of Peking to our air base. There is no Major Yang Chiou. He is a purely fictitious character. Your papers appear to be in order, but they are forgeries, I am sure. If you like, I can put you on televised intercom, to be checked out by the First Minister." He paused. "I don't hear any urgent demand for that kind of corroboration."

Yeshua did not give the prearranged signal for emergency action. His aides were waiting anxiously for it. But now it was his own intuition, not Yajnavalkya's, that came into play. There was something subtle and strange about this Eastern Federation general who continued to sit there cooly and talk to them, believing they were foreign agents, and even taking the risk of dismissing his armed guards.

"General Dobroumov, you have indeed found us out," Yeshua replied, gambling on the accuracy of his premonitions. "Now what do you propose to do with us?"

"You have noted that I have dismissed the guards. We are quite alone here."

"Yes, I have noted precisely that. Why did you order them out?"

"Because," the general half rose from his desk, his hands gripping the sides until his knuckles were white, "because I would die for him!"

Once again the three men looked at one another in bewilderment.

"For Myshkin?" asked Yeshua incredulously.

"For Myshkin, you fools! Why have you not brought him out of Mavrino? I could almost have guaranteed his escape to the West, had you brought him this far. The Underground has no contact at Mavrino, but here we are fairly effective. And now I must get *you* out of the Federation—at no small risk to my personal safety, I assure you of that—lest your capture compromise Myshkin even further!"

The general picked up his phone. "Get me Colonel Klimensky at the Mavrino Prison Labor Camp, District of Omsk."

There was a minute or two of complete silence. Then the general spoke again. "Colonel Klimensky, this is General Dobroumov at the Pacific Air Terminal. The Third Minister, Adumov, and his aides are with me. Yes, I checked their story out. Yes, they flew in from Peking. Unexpected trip. Surely, unauthorized, but they needed some crucial information which only your prisoner could provide. Certainly I have had them checked by Security Headquarters over the television intercom! Do you take me for a baby? That's all right, Colonel, no need to apologize. Your zeal and thoroughness in this affair have been commendable, and will be reported by me to headquarters. No, do not trouble yourself any further. It's in my hands now, and I'll see to everything."

Without giving Yeshua and his men so much as a glance, the general picked up a second phone and ordered ground transportation to the harbor area for the Third Minister and his aides.

"How did you know we wanted to get to the harbor?" Yeshua asked.

"It's the only feasible way of getting into the Eastern Federation undetected. We use it all the time."

"What will happen to you when the real Victor Semyonovich Adumov returns from Peking and is questioned about his unauthorized trip to Mavrino?"

"Gentlemen, my work is over. I would have died to get him out. I will die for considerably less. But I will

178

never implicate him, never fear. I won't wait for them to torture me, I promise you that."

Yajnavalkya and Marcus remembered it at almost the same moment. Marcus mumbled something to Yeshua, who immediately turned to the General and said, "In the Underground you are Father Zossima, are you not?"

Amitabha was not too surprised. "The universe is not a logic-box," he said meditatively. "A surprise-free incursion into the Eastern Federation would have been a bigger surprise than the one you returned with." They had brought home not the writer, Myshkin, but his protector in the underground, the legendary Father Zossima! An Era-Yeshua had the authority in critical situations, on Federation territory, to declare a man WELL. Yeshua had so declared. Dobroumov had accepted.

Chapter XIII

Foreign Missions: II

It must not be supposed that every foreign mission involved the same degree of personal danger for Yeshua and the members of his mission team as the last described. Incursions into the Western and Central Federations, whose internal security systems were more relaxed, allowed them all much more peace of mind—and no one more than Helen. As a matter of fact, she was permitted to accompany him on one of the more memorable missions of his sixth decade—memorable, not because of any inherent peril, but because of the variety of interesting tasks assigned the missioners.

"We are doubling up on our mission objectives,"

Amitabha explained to him one late afternoon, in the quiet of his familiar study, "because we want to clear the decks, so to speak, for your seventh decade. The seventh, my son, is the decade traditionally set aside for work with the Prodigals. Remember," he smiled almost sadly, "despite your many mission ventures, you are still a metaphysical virgin until you confront the Prodigals on their own territory." Amitabha stood up and walked to the window. Looking out to the west, one could just make out the brown scrubby island, ten kilometers beyond the IMOB, which was known in Sukhavati as the "Isle of the Dead."

"That trip," said Amitabha, pointing to the island takes a quarter of an hour. It's the longest journey you'll ever make as Era-Yeshua.

"But to get back to your present mission. I'm sure you have been following our scanners closely regarding the recent election in the Western Federation. You know there were several attempts on the life of the Social Evolution Party candidate for Prime Minister, George McDonald—attempts by elements within the State Stability Party. But have you heard the latest reports? Did you know that since his overwhelming defeat in the election, his own Evolution Party has disavowed him, and there has been another attempt at assassination—this time, it is believed, by members of his own campaign committee! They look upon him as a political leper, a one-man contagion who might mortally infect the entire party. They may even be correct about that: the Evolution Party at this moment is in a state of disintegration.

"McDonald, himself, is in utter despair. One of our Yajnavalkyas informs us that he is sure the man is fighting down the temptation to suicide. The Sophia, moreover, has looked into his case and, just last night, declared him WELL—in the Sukhavati sense of the term. His rescue will be your first objective on this mission."

For some unknown reason, Amitabha broke into a smile. "Yeshua, you have a treat in store for you. Unless I am mistaken, you have not yet seen the new device employed by the Sophia to evaluate the special class of people known as politicians. Our Archimedes people, working closely with our Freuds and Lippmans, devised it. They call it a Veriscope.

"Your good friend, Mobutu, happens to be one of our leading experts with the new device, and I'm going to give him the pleasure of demonstrating to you just how the Sophia arrived at her decision respecting McDonald." With that he walked over to his desk and issued a brief command over the intercom.

In a very few minutes, Mobutu stood at the entrance of the study, grinning like a genial African god (which of course he was). He and Yeshua had not seen one another for several months, owing to his intensive research on the new device. The two men embraced warmly. After they had chatted awhile, Amitabha bid the Archimedes conduct Yeshua to the laboratory where the Veriscope was in operation.

"You know," said Mobutu, when the two of them were alone in his private lab, "that our scanners review all that is written in the books and more significant journals of each of the Federations. And they also evaluate all that comes over their radio and television networks. This enables the Sophia to make judgments regarding the probable course of events in the Federations, as well as to sieve out those who might possibly have undergone Evolution-Conversion—those whom she might decree WELL. But of all the different types of men and women evaluated by the Sophia, the politicians cause the most trouble. That is because, scan their words as we may, we are never quite sure what they mean. Master of ambiguity, doctor of deception—all of them! This is where the Veriscope comes in. Here, let me show you how it works."

Mobutu flicked two switches. "I'm going to use the last pre-election tapes, rather than live input. The evaluation has already been made, and it will be easier for you to understand just what this new instrument accomplishes."

The Veriscope was rather disappointing in appearance to Yeshua. It looked like nothing more than a Federation television set, plugged into a transparent plastic box containing a complicated maze of wiring and electronic gear. This plastic box itself was plugged into the Sophia's circuits.

An image flickered across the Veriscope screen. It was the face of the newly-elected Prime Minister of the Western Federation, Ricardo Saxon, whose victory at the polls had been devastating. He was talking vehemently, and Mobutu had to turn the volume down. The Veriscope, he explained, worked on the same basic principle as the Federation lie-detector, but with much greater sophistication and subtlety.

"Whereas the lie-detector contents itself with an examination of pulse and heartbeat to decide when the speaker is telling the truth, the Veriscope," said Mobutu, patting the instrument affectionately, "uses much more sensitive measurements, involving dilation of pupils, contraction of the eyelids, tension of crucial facial muscles—especially those about the mouth—and an analysis of the voice. All this data is collected and analyzed against the sociopolitical background of the speech, and the speaker's personality structure. That's where the Lippmans and the Freuds come in.

"The Sophia integrates the totality of data and translates the politicians' words into what the man is *really* saying. Thus, while the prime minister is speaking, you can see and hear him on a regular Federation channel, and then, about fifteen minutes later, you can see and hear him over again, on the Veriscope, saying what he really *believes*—and in his very own voice, too. The elements of his voice have been computerized, so as to enable the Veriscope to state its conclusions in the speaker's own tones and accents."

Mobutu turned the volume up again. The prime minister was loudly orating: "The citizens of the Western Federation know that the Stability Party stands for full employment, for the dignity of labor—as opposed to the indignities of GAP, the opposition's Government Alms Program. The people of the Western Federation, a great and alert citizenry, know that we are the party of balanced budget and stable prices. We are the party of peace and disarmament—but," here the voice rose to a crescendo, "peace with honor, and disarmament without dishonor!"

"Now," said Mobutu, switching off the regular television tape, "let us play back that speech on the Veriscope."

The candidate's voice came back as loud and clear as

182

before, but now he was saying: "The people of the Western Federation would know, if they were not adolescents, preoccupied with sex and ball games, that in my previous term, unemployment rose by several million, our budget deficit exceeded the combined deficits of the last three administrations taken together, and that inflation has gone up another 18 per cent. Moreover, the vast majority of our citizens would know, if they were not as slow-witted as they are silent, that I requested another four billion pounds from Parliament to implement our military outlay two months after signing the arms agreement with the Eastern Federation. Finally, Mr. McDonald would, by his reformed tax program, have the first families of the Federation face the indignity of daily labor. He does not understand that welfare is for the rich, who will not be enervated by it!"

"It's unbelievable!" Yeshua laughed aloud. "Why, it's his very own voice!"

"Yes, and it's a highly accurate rendering of what he was really thinking, too. The eyelids, the pupils, voice analysis, facial muscles, together with the political situation of the Stability Party and Saxon's own personality drives—all these are constituents of the Veriscope's translation. The translation is automatically fed into the Sophia, which, you see, can neither deceive nor be deceived—not even by federation politicians!" Mobutu switched off the device.

Yeshua stood up reluctantly. He would willingly have heard more. "I wonder what would happen," he mused, "if our Rothschilds were to flood the Western Federation market with these sets."

"I'll tell you what would happen," Mobutu replied. "No one would get elected!"

"Well, I suppose I'm exaggerating a little. George McDonald, by the way, according to our Veriscope analysis, compiled the amazing ATC index of 48 per cent!"

"ATC?" asked Yeshua perplexedly.

"Average Truth Content," answered Mobutu. "In fact, on selected issues he went as high as 52 per cent. That hasn't been equaled in 65 years of Western Federation politics. And listen to this—I really did some research on it—that score was last surpassed 286 years ago, by a candidate from Venezuela running for Federation Parliament. On one key issue, the Venezuelan had a 98 per cent ATC index. He was shot the day after his speech, of course. But it didn't matter much. He was spared the knowledge that his opponent won in a landslide."

"But if McDonald only achieved a 48 per cent ATC index, I'm surprised the Sophia has declared him WELL," Yeshua protested.

"Given the socio-political situation in the Western Federation," Mobutu explained; "and given the spiritual climate of his place and century, it's a *heroic* ATC, sir! His opponent registered a mere 8 per cent ATC—going down to minus three per cent on selected issues!"

"How can you possibly get less than zero ATC? Even if you tell only lies, you should get zero."

"The Sophia lays down an extra penalty for lying in situations when it is not even useful or necessary to lie!" Mobutu paused to let this sink in. "McDonald on the other hand did risk his life to say some things he felt had to be said.

"I think it is now time I returned you to Amitabha, sir. He has more to say to you before you leave on this mission."

Back again in the study, Amitabha called for vapors. The atmosphere was so much more relaxed than it had been when Yeshua was being briefed for his journey to the Eastern Federation.

"You'll have little or no trouble penetrating the West," Amitabha said to him, but there is one detail of this case that could be troublesome. McDonald is married, happily married. If you recall your expedition to rescue Myshkin, he hadn't lived with his wife for so many years—what with being placed in labor camps, insane asylums, etc.— that he was, for all practical purposes, a bachelor. As for Dobroumov, his wife had died. He was free to come with you. McDonald is not free. His wife—Sarah, if I'm not mistaken—is very much part of his scene. Actually, the Sophia is looking into her case as well; if she were also declared WELL, your problem would be greatly simplified. This, however, is not yet and may never be the case. It's more difficult to come to a decision in her case, since she has not spoken publicly or published as much as her husband. The question is, will his wife be willing to let him depart with you? And even if she should be willing, will he consent to leave her behind? Marriage, as you know, is the closest the Federations come to era-bonding. Of course their *adhesive* marriages are now down to seven per cent. But the McDonald marriage may be in this category."

This emboldened Yeshua to make the plea he had almost resolved to make in any case.

"Sir, in view of the difficulty you have pointed out, I would like very much to have one or more women members on my mission team. It would, I feel, be a distinct disadvantage in dealing with a relationship such as exists between McDonald and his wife to have only male missioners with me."

"Actually, Yeshua, you've been pushing harder and harder for the advancement of women into highly responsible positions for the last two decades, haven't you?"

"That is so, sir. But now I feel the opportune moment has arrived. I cannot let it pass without an urgent appeal."

"Well, we must put it to the SERD, Yeshua. I will not stand in the way of your policy if the SERD approves. But I am highly doubtful that it will."

It was labor trouble that advanced the position of women on Sukhavati. Six months previously, the whole Leonardo Function had risen as one man and refused to aware the Yajnavalkyas further until what they considered a basic injustice had been corrected. The strike, for that is exactly what it was (although the Leonardos called it "a focus of moral awareness") was surprising on several counts. First, such a thing had never occurred before in Sukhavati, at least during the past several eras. And second, the Leonardos enjoyed their relationship with the Yajnavalkyas more, it seemed, than with any other function. But that, as it turned out, was part of the problem. Traditionally, the lion's share of Yajnavalkya-tutoring went to the Platos, who were considered next in line, logically and chronologically, in the scale of rebirth. Having probed intellectually about as deep as man's mind could probe, a Plato's next step on his sequential pilgrimage, it was felt, would be the contemplative experience, in which he would begin to taste, to savor, the truths he had hitherto talked about.

Sometimes it turned out this way, but often it did not. The Platos, as a matter of fact, proved to have a number of notorious recidivists among themselves. The Yajnavalkyas would gladly have given more of their time to the Leonardos who, although supposedly further down on the scale of awareness, were keen to share that raw experience of being, which was the major preoccupation of the seers. Also, the seers sorely missed, during the entire strike, that esthetic awareness which the Leonardos brought to a razor's edge in them. Besides all this, the Yajnavalkyas secrectly agreed with the Leonardos that the Platos were getting too much tutoring in meditation. "They learn to articulate about meditation, to verbalize about the various interior states, and to conceptualize about the value of spiritual search. "In short," complained the Yajnavalkyas, "the Platos do everything but meditate!" Thus the recidivism.

Yeshua was able to arbitrate the three-way conflict with professional skill and economy. "Were the Leonardos willing to make up with their own awareness the loss in awareness that was suffered by the Platos in yielding Yajnavalkya time to them? They were. Were the Platos willing to make this exchange of awareness? They were. Was the whole transaction agreeable to the Yajnavalkyas? It most certainly was. The strike was over.

But it had achieved an unintended goal. The increment of unrest in Sukhavati eased the SERD's approval of still another of Yeshua's ameliorations—the upward mobility of women. He was given formal permission to take with him, on his next foreign mission, two women out of a team of four. As his Alexander, he chose Zenobia, who had worked effectively for three decades in her function and had never been given a post comparable to her abilities. And he chose Helen.

He declined the services of the Security Yajnavalkya, deeming the danger of a trip to the Western Federation too slight to require his assistance. Hilary was a repeat—his diplomatic and social maneuverability were awesome. And Yeshua asked Mobutu to come along as Mission Archimedes. For several reasons. One being his closeness to the McDonald case through his work on the Veriscope, and the other being his familiarity with the OR, about which more must be said later. There were actually three separate objectives to this foreign mission, the most complicated ever attempted by Yeshua in six decades.

To Yeshua's amazement, Helen was ambivalent about participating in the mission. "I thought," said Yeshua, "you would be overjoyed—not only because we would be working together, but because you would also be advancing the cause of women throughout the island. If our mission objectives are achieved, I am certain that more and more responsible positions, in every function, will be opened up for women."

"Yes," Helen replied with a rip in her voice, "I feel that dimension of the assignment keenly, believe me, Yeshua. It's just my role in this particular mission that upsets me. I am being brought along to deal with a distraught wife who must somehow be persuaded to release her husband, to give him up forever. Our own relationship—what I feel for you—inhibits my enthusiasm."

"But think what's at stake, Helen. Are we to lose this man who, according to the Sophia, has already undergone a conversion-mutation? Are we to lose him to the Great Absurd, to the everlasting Imperium of Ice and Silence?" He knew that Helen reacted almost as violently to the imagery of death and dissolution as he did himself.

"I am coming, Yeshua. There was never any real doubt in my heart about that. It's just that I would have registered more enthusiasm for another sort of mission. In any case, I have no scruples about our other two objectives, and I'll enjoy *that* part of the missions. The first part, for me at least, is naked duty."

Yeshua called his newly appointed mission team together almost immediately. After he had congratulated Zenobia on her selection as Mission Archimedes, and after explaining their threefold objective, he asked for comments and questions.

He turned to Hilary, in particular. "Of all of us, Hilary, you probably have the most knowledge of how human nature operates in the three Federations. What do you think is going to happen in the McDonald case? Have you had any experience with a case like this in the past, where the Sophia decrees either the husband or the wife to be WELL, but not both?"

Hilary smiled sadly. "You mean, when two are in the field, and one is taken and one is left; when two are grinding at the mill, and one is taken and one is left; what happens? Does the elected one pick up and leave? Or does his very election instigate feelings of guilt and betrayal, so that he or she refuses to leave the less fortunate spouse?

"Well, sir, it all depends on what era you're talking about. The dark continents do change, Yeshua, although they remain dark. Up to five or six hundreds years ago, I think the old Federation adage still held true:

> Higamous, hogamous, woman's monogamous;
> Hogamous, higamous, man is polygamous.

"That is to say, sir, that if the Sophia elected the wife, she would refuse to leave her husband behind. She could not tolerate the thought of another woman getting him in her clutches, I suppose, or perhaps her love was just too urgent, too single-minded."

"More likely the latter," cooly contributed Zenobia.

"But the last three or four hundred years, you know, have seen the predominance of non-adhesive, sequential monogamy in the West, and I believe that we face much less of a problem now in implementing these split decrees of the Sophia. Of course, if the McDonald marriage is one of the remaining adhesive types, we are in trouble."

"I think we are in trouble," said Yeshua.

Their marine skimmer departed the very next evening. They wished to enter the Western Federation early the following afternoon. Zenobia had advised against assuming the guise of naval personnel. She had suggested that, with a mixed crew of women and men on board, they assume the identities of wealthy socialites out on a pleasure cruise. This seemed plausible to Yeshua, and the Sophia had provided them with the necessary documentation.

The trip was uneventful, except for the added pleasure Yeshua derived from the presence of Helen. As nearly always, they escaped detection in their incursion into Western Federation waters. At 2 p.m., on a Wednesday afternoon in early May, they tied up at a dock owned by an exclusive yacht club, twenty kilometers from the largest port on the Atlantic coast. They immediately made their appearance, in the most expensive federation sport clothes they had, in the bar of the club. Federation liquor seemed harsh and ineffective to them, but Zenobia insisted, just as Marcus had done, that they eat and drink when it seemed appropriate.

"I am going to place a call now to McDonald campaign headquarters," said Yeshua in a low voice. "I hope that somebody is still around. I'll join you in the dining room shortly."

Entering the teleview booth, Yeshua smoothed back his thick black hair, checking his appearance in the mirror provided in every booth. Satisfied that his appearance conformed in every detail to upper-class western standards, Yeshua took out the number retrieved for him by the Sophia: "Party Headquarters, 914-631-3200." But would he find anyone there or not? The disastrous campaign had been over for more than a week. The teleview rang for almost a minute.

Already halfway out of the booth, Yeshua was finally rewarded by a click and the appearance in the viewer of a young man with a luxurious handlebar mustache. "McDonald Headquarters," he announced listlessly. "Who is calling, please?"

"My name is Geoffrey Cannon," Yeshua answered with casual authority. "I'm a Canadian industrialist. In aluminium. Listen, I know you McDonald people did your best, and that your party is in the hole for 55 million pounds. I may be able to help you a little on the debt. I can't pay it all off by myself, you understand; I'm not in that league. But I can get help. That is, if you are interested."

"Are we ever interested!" the mustache quivered on the other end. "Wait just a minute, till I get you Walt Jenson! I'm just minding the store."

Yeshua recognized the name as that of the Secretary-Treasurer of the Social Evolution Party.

A gray-haired, portly gentleman with a large, fleshy nose appeared on the viewer. "Mr. Cannon, how do you do? I'm Walt Jenson, treasurer of the Evolution Party. Understand you may be able to help us."

"Yes. A few of my colleagues and I got together the other day and decided we ought to make a stab at reviving your party. Most of the money men are on the other side——"

"How well I know——"

"And we figured that if the Evolution party ever got back on its feet, you people would not forget the loyal backers who stood by you when you were down and out. Am I correct?"

"You are so right! What kind of help do you think you can give us? We're down 60 million pounds, you know."

"Fifty-five, isn't it? Well we think we can scrape together nine or ten million of it, anyway, if you think it's worthwhile. We lost a big backer just this morning—might have been good for four or five million, all by himself. But we know others like him."

"Oh, we think ten million pounds is eminently worthwhile, don't worry about that." Jenson laughed.

"There's one thing, Mr. Jenson. This is my first fling at politics."

"Yes, I know. Your name is completely unfamiliar to me, and I credit myself with knowing just about every millionaire whose hobby it is to med . . . to take part in election campaigns."

"Right. I'm new at it, and, well . . . I want to have a little something to talk about when I go home to British Columbia. Look, I want to meet McDonald. Can you arrange it?"

"That will take some arranging. He's exhausted, as you can imagine. And to tell you the truth, he's feeling very down. Almost no one outside the immediate family gets in to see him these days. However, what you are doing for the party is important; you may be the spearhead of our comeback. I'll do my level best to persuade him to see you. Now you can't stay with him for more than a few minutes, you understand—supposing I can arrange for you to get in at all."

"That would be fine. Just get me an appointment. I'm at the Silver Surf Yacht Club. The number is 201-436-3233."

"Fine. You'll be there for the next hour or two?"

"Most likely. We haven't even ordered dinner yet."

"Very good. Check back with you, soon as I can."

Yeshua rejoined his party in the dining room. "They're going to try to get me an appointment. McDonald is seeing virtually no one these days."

Their dinner, the finest that money could buy in the Western Federation, gave them little pleasure. For Helen and Yeshua, it was actually a problem to get it down, but Zenobia insisted that they at least go through the motions. Mr. Geoffrey Cannon was called to the teleview in the middle of dessert.

"It's all been arranged," smiled Yeshua as he rejoined his group. "We have an appointment for 3:30 tomorrow afternoon. But he lives out West, you know, and that's where he's been hiding out this past week, trying to regain his equilibrium."

"And," Zenobia added professionally, "avoid assassination."

"Yes, you are right," said Yeshua, nodding his head in slow affirmation. For the moment, he had forgotten that although he, himself, felt comparatively relaxed on this mission, McDonald's life was in real danger.

"Yet," thought Yeshua, as he settled back into his soft recliner on the plane, "it surely is much easier to travel here than in the East. No demand for official papers every time you buy a ticket. No guards looking you over." He felt a tap on his shoulder. It was an air-terminal policeman.

"Come with me, please," the officer announced firmly.

Yeshua was shocked. He looked at the others, bewildered. They looked back at him in equal confusion.

"Yes, surely, officer," he finally replied. "May I ask what the trouble is?"

"Just follow me to the terminal police office. We have a few questions we'd like you to answer."

"But the plane leaves in fifteen minutes, and my companions are all aboard. Will I miss my flight?"

"That depends on how quickly and satisfactorily you answer our questions."

Fortunately, the office itself was close by the boarding area. A slight gray-haired man of about 60, in civilian clothes, was waiting for them as they came in. He flashed his badge at Yeshua, and immediately began questioning him.

"You are Mr. Geoffrey Cannon, of British Columbia?"

"Why yes, I am. Would you mind telling me what this is all about?"

Through the glass partition of the door, Yeshua spotted Zenobia. She had left the plane and followed them to the terminal office. Prearranged emergency-action plans had been rehearsed many times, but Yeshua still hoped it would not become necessary to resort to them. Their emergency plans were both highly effective and physically non-violent, but they could leave psychic scars, and they could complicate the achievement of their mission objectives.

"You have been in contact with Mr. McDonald, the Evolution Party candidate?" the agent continued.

"Well, yes, I have, but I don't see how that is anyone else's business but my own. How did you know I made the call?"

The agent saw fit to ignore the last question; he replied to the first. "It's the Prime Minister's business, as well. He's been wanting to know the whereabouts of Mr. McDonald ever since the election—for McDonald's safety, of course. We have reason to believe that you are going to see him personally. You would be doing him a favor if you would tell us where he could be found. No? We will obtain the information anyway, one way or another. But in the intervening time, he will not be safeguarded against assassination. Suit yourself.

"By the way," he continued in a dry, even tone of voice, "you're throwing away quite a few pounds on a leaky boat. Why don't you get aboard the ship of state? Just a friendly tip. You can go now."

They got back to their plane just seconds before the gangway was closed off. As the plane took off, Yeshua, seated between Helen and Zenobia, said to them in a whisper, "That was unexpectedly spooky. I didn't think we would be making any calls at air-terminal police stations on *this* trip! I wonder if they are still planning anything against the life of McDonald."

"No," Zenobia whispered back. "He must be worth more to them now alive and pathetic than dead and martyred. Actually, you could even have given them his location, except for your promise to Jenson. The Stability Party is probably quite sincere about wanting to keep him alive—now that the election is over."

Yeshua nodded his head in agreement. He hadn't looked at it in quite that light. Zenobia was proving every bit as perspicacious as Marcus.

They were met at the airport by Walter Jenson. They, of course, recognized him at once, having studied the pictures of everyone of prominence in both parties. He was inspecting the incoming passengers, but without much idea what his guests would look like, other than that they would include Mr. and Mrs. Cannon and three associates, two men and a woman.

Yeshua walked over to him and introduced himself and his party. Jenson immediately whisked them all into his own car. "No limousine or chauffeur," thought Yeshua, "the Evolution Party must really have hit bottom." It was a drive of an hour and a half, the last 45 minutes of which took them off the highway and onto a country road leading to the MacDonald ranch.

A very hefty and humorless guard looked them over cautiously. He searched the men in the group and looked like he wanted to search the women as well, before admitting them. The arrival of Sarah McDonald spared the ladies this embarrassment.

"It's all right, John, we were expecting these people," she said to the guard.

"How do you do, Mr. Cannon. I'm Sarah McDonald," she said, extending her hand to Yeshua in a friendly manner. The strain of the last few weeks, however, was deeply etched into her face. Still, she stood erect and proud.

"We are grateful for your support," she continued, "at a time when everyone we know is turning away from my husband as if he carried the plague.

"I'm sorry to say your visit will have to be a very brief one. George really shouldn't be seeing anyone at all right now."

Yeshua thought her a rather impressive woman, her strength of will in inverse proportion to her physical slightness.

"Of course, Mrs. McDonald," Yeshua replied. "We're grateful to have the opportunity at all."

The defeated candidate received them in his study. He was slumped into his arm chair, a blanket over his knees, his face haggard and empty.

"There are just a few questions," said Hilary, as politely as he could, "which we must discuss privately with Mr. McDonald."

Sarah looked at Jenson. He nodded affirmatively. "I'll just be in the next room, dear," she said to her husband, "if you need me." He followed her out of the room with his eyes.

As soon as Jenson and Mrs. McDonald had gone, Yeshua began.

"Mr. McDonald, there's no use wasting time beating around the bush. Your wife said to make this brief. We can solve your problems for you, if you will allow us!"

"Do you mean the whole 55 million pounds?" the exhausted man gasped, his thin gray hair falling astray over his forehead. A bit of light seemed to come back into his face.

"The whole 55 million! And more than that—the chance of a comeback!" The political situation was, of course, uppermost in McDonald's mind, and Yeshua went along with it while he gradually prepared him for the real purpose of his visit. Nothing he said was an outright lie. He *was* offering a comeback—more of one than McDonald realized the universe contained.

"You are that wealthy and powerful?" McDonald asked incredulously.

"We are that wealthy and powerful."

"But I must have you checked out. Jenson hadn't ever heard of you, and he knows all the millionaires in the Federation."

"He knows all the millionaires who have dabbled in politics," said Hilary. "But we are newcomers. This seemed to us an opportune moment to get involved."

"If you mean you are getting in on the ground floor," McDonald smiled, sickly, "you are certainly right. The Social-Evolution party is a veritable bargain-basement for anyone still interested."

The sour grin gradually faded away. "You gentlemen

will have to excuse my suspicions. A man can look mighty foolish if he takes his supporters' words for everything."

They all remembered a damaging incident in his recent political campaign. "Of course," said Hilary. "But you can check us out at your leisure. Let's get to the point, first."

"The point? Ah, yes. The point. I understand . . . this is a hoax! You came for a favor. How could anyone be as wealthy and powerful as you claim to be, and still be so naive? What favor could I possibly bestow on anyone! I couldn't get you appointed dog-catcher in British Columbia! Gentlemen, get out of my home!"

"*That's* not the point, Mr. McDonald," said Yeshua. "There is no position you can possibly offer us, but there is one we can offer you. And we hope you will accept it."

McDonald sat straight up for the first time since they had entered. "What are you, anyway? Eastern Federation agents? You could not get me *any* post in the West! There is no position open to me today in Western Federation public life. But that doesn't mean I'll defect!"

"Believe me, Mr. McDonald," said Yeshua, as soothingly as possible, we are not Eastern Federation agents. But we are not from the West, either. Our story is a strange one, and you barely have the physical or psychic strength to absorb it just now. We could give you something to revive your energies, but you wouldn't trust us enough, at this point, to receive it, so we'll just have to take our chances.

"First, I want you to witness a brief scientific experiment." He nodded to Mobutu.

Mobutu quickly assembled his miniature gravitation director and focused it on the heavy steel desk to the left of the study. The desk rose smoothly to the height of two meters and floated gently in space.

McDonald's face flushed. His eyes opened wide.

"Put it down, Mobutu," Yeshua ordered. The steel desk slowly descended to the floor.

"Eastern Federation scientists might have invented that, without our agents knowing about it," said McDonald lamely.

"They never invented *this*," said Yeshua, removing a

195

small vial from his inside pocket. "I'm going to breathe these vapors deeply, to demonstrate that you have nothing to fear. If you would breathe some in after me, most of your depleted energies would be restored to you almost instantly." Yeshua breathed deeply, snorting loudly, his nose right above the vial. There could be no mistake about the genuineness of his action. Yeshua almost glowed with vitality. He handed the vial to McDonald.

The veteran statesman hesitated, half wanting to try it, so painful was his exhaustion. Yet he was half afraid of falling into some kind of a crazy trap.

"Please, Mr. McDonald, it really is all right." Helen spoke for the first time. Her concern was so manifest, her whole presence so lovely and reassuring, that McDonald was won over.

Seizing the vial, he threw caution to the winds and breathed in deeply. Desperately! It went through him like sunlight. Three layers of fatigue unrolled from his face, one after the other. He looked almost normal again. Only the lines on his forehead remained. "Ahh," he sighed, leaning back in his chair.

He was silent a long time.

Then he said simply, "O.K. gentlemen. Where do you come from?"

Yeshua told him their story, as gently as he could.

Despite all the evidence of his senses, despite his own restored vitality, even despite his having heard the legend of the Geneva Society and rumors of the existence of Strastnik's community, McDonald simply could not bring himself to credit their story. "It's just not possible," he said flatly. He racked his brains to find some other explanation, some other rational motivation, for the presence of the five people in his study.

"Maybe you do come from somewhere outside of the three Federations," he finally admitted. "But I still can't buy the immortality business. You're just raising the ante, hoping I'll go with you. Of course, I am finished in Federation politics," he added in a low voice, more to himself than to anyone else. "The Stability Party is in for the next 20 years, I imagine."

"I don't want to weaken our case," Zenobia broke in, "but the truth is that the Sophia—that is, our calculations

—indicate that the Prime Minister is likely to be in for a bit of trouble himself in a few years. Yet, what you said is true: your own work in the Western Federation is about finished."

Then he asked the question.

"What about my wife? Does she get to go too?"

The missioners looked at one another in consternation. This was the moment they had been dreading from the beginning.

Yeshua shook his head sadly. "It appears that only you are eligible."

"Then it's impossible!" he roared at them. "I don't believe your claims to eternal life anyway, but even if I did, I couldn't ditch Sarah. Don't you see," he asked with tears welling up in his eyes, "how she sticks to me in my hour of total defeat and humiliation? Why, I'm the laughing stock of the Federation. I know that. The only reason I've been able to bear it so far is that she shares it with me. What kind of a lousy cop-out are you proposing, anyway!"

And for the second time he ordered them out of the house!

"Sarah!" he called, and moved for the door.

But before he could get there, it burst open from the other side.

"I heard the whole thing, George. I was worried that they were taking so much time with you, and I listened. You can't imagine how well and strong you look! They did it to you! George, they're telling the truth. I feel it. I know it. You must go with them, darling." Her own eyes were now full.

"Without you?"

"Without me!" She burst into sobs.

They clung to one another for a few moments. Then, getting control of herself, she began to reason with him.

"Listen, George, we're grandparents already. We've had a full and blessed life together. Only our old age is left to us now. You can . . ." (She noted for the first time how beautiful Helen looked.) ". . . start over, on that island of theirs." She hesitated for a moment, as if she were reconsidering that prospect.

Then she threw herself once again in her husband's

197

arms, sobbing. "You must go, George. I love you! I love you! But you must go with them!"

It was too much for Helen. She seized Yeshua by the arm. She herself was weeping silently. "You must do something, Yeshua. This relationship is adhesive. We are tearing raw flesh!"

Yeshua looked directly into her eyes for a long moment. Then he turned away, closed his eyes, and went into trance. Everyone, even the McDonalds, gathered around him in wonder.

For several minutes there was complete silence. Then Yeshua, returning from a far place, slowly opened his eyes, still full of dream and distance.

"The answer came back affirmative. The Sophia has declared her WELL!"

Helen and Zenobia threw their arms around the McDonalds, who were still utterly confused by Yeshua's strange words and behavior. "That means you are *both* to come! You will be together!" They shouted and laughed and wept, all of them. Only Yeshua stood apart somewhat, in great happiness, but quite still. He was talking in a low voice, but they did not even hear him in their outburst of joy.

"It happened," Yeshua muttered, almost to himself, "at the moment she gave internal consent to his leaving her. She was still behind the door, listening and struggling with herself. She offered him up, and thus experienced her own conversion-mutation. I felt it." Yeshua's quiet beatitude was greater even than the joyful release of everyone else. This was, for him, one of the most awesome acts of his sixth decade. He had intuited Sarah McDonald's conversion-mutation, and had thereby saved one, perhaps two human beings from the Void, the Great Absurd. Truly, it was no small thing to be Era-Yeshua, shepherd of the flock. And it was Helen who had precipitated his action. She was indeed his helpmate.

Later, when enough of the excitement had worn off for everyone to begin making practical departure plans—a more complicated matter, now that the Prime Minister was watching McDonald's every move—the retired politician made one last effort for his party.

"Tell me, Mr. Cannon, were you just trying to humor

me when you told me that you could pay off the entire party debt?"

"No, we are prepared to do that, provided it does not attract too much attention."

"Sir," said Zenobia, "it had better be done by installments. Such a huge lump sum would arouse the curiosity of the Prime Minister's agents."

"How does this community of yours, Sukha . . . Sukha . . .?"

"Sukhavati."

"Yes. How does it come to have so much wealth, so much of our currency?"

Hilary laughed. "We have a professional group whose task it is to protect the financial interests of the island. From time to time, one of the group will accompany Yeshua—Mr. Cannon—on these trips to the Federations and place some strategic investments. Lately, we've had the additional help of an instrument known as the *Yin-Yang* Intimater. If you should become one of our group, Mr. McDonald, I'll be glad to explain these things to you in detail. Suffice it to say, our community has several numbered accounts in a network of Western Federation banks, and we have only to direct them to start payment into the account of the Social Evolution Party—payments to be completed in, say, four years time, just to allay surprise and suspicion."

The McDonalds were sent to an address in British Columbia to await the missioners, while Yeshua and his group set about achieving their other two objectives. The move fit in with the stories of Mr. Cannon, the Canadian millionaire, that were now being spread about in Stability Party circles. It was, moreover, Zenobia's opinion that removing the McDonalds that far from the Federation's capital in Mexico City might relax the Prime Minister's agents a bit. As it turned out, no one ever heard from the McDonalds again. It was rumored in the opposition party that he had changed his name and given up all interest in politics, to find a new home in the Canadian woods.

"Stocking salmon streams, I hear," laughed the Home Secretary to the Prime Minister, a few weeks later. "He always was a bit of an ecology nut, you know."

"Yes, I know," said the leader of the Western Federation, cheerful and dapper since his overwhelming victory. "The reporters always used to say he was in love with life. That gets in the way of politics, though." He smiled thoughtfully. "Especially foreign policy."

Mobutu was the crucial man in achieving both the remaining objectives. Their second task was basically similar to the first, in that it involved the rescue of another public figure in danger of assassination. John Baldwin was a Black leader in the Federation Civil Rights Movement. The race problem had remained the single longest, most persistent social problem in the Western world. It had, of course, undergone changes since the time of the Geneva Society, but what had not changed was the distrust and dislike of one man for another based on a difference in skin pigmentation. What had changed in the last thousand years or so, was the pigmentation itself.

Early in the millenium, it looked as if the chromosomal structure of the black race was being modified through reproductive affiliation with caucasians. In the West, by that time, few people were accurately described by the word "black." Those who were not white were, at most, tan, umber, manganese brown, etc.

But around mid-millenium, the axis of the earth, in another of its innumerable angular shifts, slipped a sufficient number of degrees to alter the climatic conditions in the southern tier of provinces in the Western Federation. After many more centuries had gone by, the Blacks were indeed black once again, and the whites were now umber, proceeding toward manganese brown.

Following two centuries of desperate scientific experimentation, there had been a breakthrough—not in race relations, but in pigmentation-control. Governor Benson, hard-driving, popular leader of one of the larger southern provinces, convoked an emergency session of the provincial legislature to announce the news.

"Pigmental retrogression has been successfully halted by Professor Franklin, at the Province University laboratory!" announced the Governor. There was a standing ovation. Benson finally gavelled them down.

"There are, however, certain modifications which have

200

to be accepted, Franklin informs me. I have convoked the assembly today for a vote that will be crucial to the people of our great province for thousands of generations to come.

"By the injection of graduated doses of chemical chlorophyll, the ingredient essential to the production of carbohydrates in plants through the process of photosynthesis, pigmental retrogression can unquestionably be terminated. However, after the absorption of 680 cc. of chlorophyll, it does result, in a slight, but, believe me, not unattractive greenish tint.

"Gentlemen, are we to acquiesce in a total confusion and amalgamation of the two races?" (Loud "no's" from the audience.) "Or are we to sustain the separation that God ordained from the beginning?" (Loud affirmations.) "Gentlemen, I propose to you the veritable creation of a new race: the Chlorcasian!"

The governor was overwhelmed by the members of the provincial legislature, who rolled across the floor in a tidal wave of reelection inevitability. It was decided to dispense with a formal roll-call vote. The motion was carried by unanimous acclamation. The citizens of the province began their series of injections within the month.

And so, the centuries-old conflict between the races went on. There was a difference btween the southern and northern tier of provinces, to be sure. In the North, the Blacks were now concentrated in urban reservations, over which they had finally gained control. Indeed, for a brief period three centuries before the birth of John Baldwin, they had successfully asserted an independent status for their alliance of free Black city-states; and they had even secured recognition from the World Federation. Tariffs and import duties had been levied on all goods coming into the urban reservations from the Federation, and ambassadors had been sent to represent them at the Federation capital. But these sovereign ghettoes had finally been suppressed in bloody street-to-street fighting, although the Blacks held onto the official positions of leadership. It was too dangerous for anyone else to take up residence there.

In the southern tier of provinces, the Blacks were still quoting the ancient adage: "Up North, they don't care how high you get, so long as you don't get too close; down South, they don't care how close you get, so long as you don't get too high." But even down South, there tended to be more and more bloodshed, as explosives and firearms became progressively more available and more skillfully miniaturized.

Into such a scene was John Baldwin born, lifelong advocate of non-violence and brotherhood disciple of Jesus, Gandhi, Tolstoi and John XXIII. He was, of course, loathed by racists, of all colors.

Now, having last been seen boarding a plane to Canada, he disappeared from public view. Some years later he received the posthumous accolade of "Pontifex," "bridge-builder," the first layman—and a Baptist at that—to receive the title from Rome (so far had the Ecumenical Movement progressed in 1000 years). It seemed certain that he and his entire family (who had accompanied him) had met with foul play somewhere between the federation capital and his ultimate (but unknown) destination in Canada. There had been three attempts on his life in the preceding two years, and there was no question but that powerful and organized forces were out to eliminate him. Even among his own brothers, he was under attack, dismissed as a Tom by many who were determined to re-establish the "Sovereign Ghettoes of the West."

Baldwin and his wife had been marked by the Sophia for a long time. She had shared both his dedication and his danger. But it was not the policy of the Sophia to liberate even those decreed WELL during the time-period of their usefulness to the Dark Continents. The three Federations desperately needed those men and women who had undergone conversion mutation, and it was Sukhavati strategy to allow them to work until almost the last minute of their personal safety. It was nearly always the case that such persons ended their careers in the same painful situation as Jesus, Socrates, Gandhi, etc. The non-violent are invariably lightning rods for the violent.

It was Mobutu who quietly explained all this, and much else besides, to John Baldwin in his neat, middle-class apartment in the Federation capital. Baldwin and his wife, Clare, did not ask a great number of questions. The tempo of assassination attempts had markedly increased at the very time they felt their moral influence waning. It was a period of increased hatred and militancy. This tension, they knew, would be released only in blood. They asked Mobutu and Yeshua two principal questions: What were the social conditions and race relations like on their island, and what would be the status of their children?

The first was more easily answered than the second. Yeshua had once remarked to Amitabha upon the absence of children in Sukhavati, and had been told that there were, in fact, a very few children being raised and educated in a single building on the Southwest promontory of the island. They were the children of returned Prodigals and Federation converts. Inhabitants of Sukhavati, of course, had no children, since one of the biological effects of conversion-mutation was sterility—immortality rendered procreation irrelevant, even undesirable. In the course of his training, Yeshua had looked into the status of these children, and he knew the answer to the Baldwins' question.

The two of them, he explained, had been declared WELL by the Sophia, in the light of a lifetime of evidence regarding their benevolence and self-sacrifice. There was, of course, no such accumulation of evidence in the case of their children. They had not been declared WELL, and such a decree was never gained by inheritance. They would have to earn it in their own right.

But in view of the wholesome—one might say, the optimum—surroundings and influences their children would enjoy in Sukhavati, there was every reason to believe that when they reached adulthood, they too would win the Sophia's approving judgment.

And even in case they did not, and were exiled to the island of the Prodigals, they would be no worse off than they were in the Dark Continents. There they would live a normal lifespan and die in peace. Here, in the Western Federation, they were subject to insult, abuse and premature termination.

The missioners did not go out of their way to correct the universal impression that the Baldwin family had met with foul play. Perhaps the report of their deaths would eventually help bring about the reconciliation of the races —if only for a few years. Peace in the Dark Continents seemed to require more sacrifices than an Aztec divinity.

Only the third objective remained. They had three days of radiological immunity outside the IMOB left to them in which to achieve it. It was Mobutu who again directed this phase of their operations.

The OR had been assembled by the combined efforts of the Freuds, Durkheims, Toynbees and Archimedes functionaries. As that list might suggest, it was a delicate and highly complicated piece of miniaturized apparatus.

"The Option-Rotor," Mobutu had laughingly explained to him, "can best be understood in terms of an anecdote the Toynbees like to tell against themselves. You know, Yeshua, that historians are always looking for the broad, sweeping principles that give some kind of discernible shape and coherence to the mass and jumble of recorded facts. Grand plans and patterns of historical causality have been imposed on the humble, shapeless data from St. Augustine right to through to Karl Marx. But grand patterns and principles of historical causality aside, historians know that even world-changing events are often the result of unforeseen and quite fortuitous details. Let me tell you the anecdote by way of citing an example.

"You know that the foundation, the great molding influence on the Western Federation—even the Eastern, to some extent—was the ancient Roman Empire. The direction the Empire took is the direction transmitted to the Federation. Now, at a critical point in Roman history, following the assassination of Julius Caesar, three men jockeyed for power: Octavian, later known as Augustus, the nephew of Caesar; Lepidus, Caesar's old cavalry commander; and Marc Antony, Caesar's trusted friend and Acting Consul at the time of his death. Lepidus was easily out-maneuvered; the struggle for supremacy lay between Augustus and Antony. They were men of markedly different policies and proclivities, and it mattered a great deal to the Empire—and indirectly to the future Western Federation—which man won. (This is not my specialty, as you know, Yeshua. I'm telling you only what I have learned from the Toynbees.)

"Antony, more at home in the East than Augustus, might have amalgamated an Empire so diverse and cosmopolitan that the tensions which persist to this day between East and West might then have been nipped in the bud. Augustus stood for the sole supremacy of Rome, with lenience to the conquered, but no nonsense.

"As you know, Augustus won. He totally defeated the forces of Marc Antony. Why? Some Grand Plan of history favoring the West? Some Hegelian or Marxist pattern of thesis, antithesis, synthesis? No. Antony fell in love with the beautiful Egyptian princess, Cleopatra, and subsequently removed himself for too long a period from his Italian base. Augustus was able to propagate rumors about him to the effect that he intended to bequeath Roman provinces in the East to Cleopatra and her sons.

"Now comes the question: *Suppose Cleopatra's nose had been just a few centimeters longer?* Would Antony have fallen in love with her? Would he have removed himself from his Italian base? Would Augustus have been able to defeat him? Would East and West now form one single Federation?

"The Toynbees call this 'the Principle of Cleopatra's Nose,' and laugh as we all do when we hear the story, it is not entirely romantic drivel. As a matter of fact, it fits in rather nicely with Heisenberg's Principle of Indeterminacy. It isn't that history is entirely without intelligent order or pattern, but the facts are mere pellets of clay until a great historian squeezes them together and molds them into recognizable form. And yet, it remains true that a few apparently haphazard details can alter great destinies.

"This is where the OR, the Option-Rotor, comes in. Hooked into the Sophia and supplied with all the information processed by the scanners, the Veriscope and the calculated probabilities of Federation developments, the OR narrows in on the 'details of destiny'—those chance events or non-events which can swing world history into one channel or another. And it suggests options: if chance 'A' does not take place and chance 'B' does, will it be a fortuitous turn in Federation history or not? You see, we try to keep the Federations going, partly out of love for humanity, partly in self-defense. A cobalt war between the

205

Federations might render the entire planet uninhabitable. We have twice short-circuited chains of causation that could have resulted in such a war. And our third objective on this mission is to do it again!"

Such was the background of their last objective. George Marshall Hendricks, the son of General Thomas J. Hendricks, commander of the entire Federation's missile strike force, was slated to catch flight 503 from the capital to Buenos Aires, where he was to attend a coming-out party for the sister of his college roommate, Estelle Valencia y Santiago. The Santiago family owned and controlled the largest munitions cartel in the Southern Hemisphere. The OR evaluated the meeting of these two young people as "Extremely Unfortuitous" for world peace. After much spinning of electronic gears, it came up with another option.

Mobuto assured Yeshua, as his superior prepared to board a pane back to the Atlantic Coast, that he would join the entire group at their rendezvous, the Silver Surf Yacht Club, in 24 hours. "This is not a difficult assignment, sir. I cannot only handle it by myself, but I can do it better that way. A partner might actually get in the way."

In the men's room of the air terminal of the Federation capital, Mobuto took off his expensive sport clothes and changed into a porter's uniform. Flight 503 to Buenos Aires was due to leave at 4:28. At precisely 4:16, Mobutu spotted young Hendricks coming through the main gate of the terminal, where he had taken up his post.

"Bags, sir?"

"Yes, please. Would you kindly take me to Pan-Federation Airlines, and quickly! I'm taking a 4:28 plane."

"Yes, sir! Follow me. Have you there right away."

Seven minutes later, at the extreme western end of the terminal, Mobutu deposited Hendricks at the ticket counter, received a rather generous tip, and disappeared into the crowd.

It was very late, but there was still time, thought Hendricks.

"Ticket for the 503 flight to Buenos Aires, please."

"The 503 to Buenos Aires? We have no such flight, sir."

"What do you mean, you have no such flight! Look, here it is, right in this printed schedule!"

"I'm sorry sir. You're holding a schedule for Pan-Federation Airlines."

"Yes, of course I am!"

"This is the counter for the *Trans*-Federation Airline."

"Oh my God, that stupid porter! I can't catch the flight now! It's already 4:26!"

"We have a flight to Buenos Aires, sir, that leaves in 45 minutes, if that's any help."

Hendricks calculated the time schedule for the party, the dance and the banquet. "Yes, I'll take a ticket. Round-trip, please. I can still make it for most of the evening."

By the time Mobutu returned to the Silver-Surf Yacht Club, Yeshua had assembled all the McDonalds and Baldwins, Indeed, he had them safely anchored out in the marine skimmer, in open water.

"How did the third objective go, Mobutu?" Yeshua asked.

Mobutu explained how he had handled it.

"So he will never meet Miss Santiago?"

"No, he'll meet her, all right."

"I don't understand. I thought the Option-Rotor had given you another alternative!"

"It did! One of the passengers on board Trans-Federation flight 356 is Jennifer Moore, classmate of both Hendricks and his roommate, Juan Santiago. She is supposed to be Santiago's date. But the OR calculates a high compatibility between Hendricks and Moore. An unexpected marriage is in the making, and an unexpected rift is developing right now between the Hendricks and Santiago clans—two families that are better off not united by ties of blood, lest the world be the bloodier for it."

So ended the memorable, totally successful, most complicated foreign mission of Yeshua Nabi's sixth decade.

Chapter XIV

The Ezekiel Hypothesis

The uninterrupted week of communal festivity and celebration that heralded their return from this magnificent
mission was not so welcome to Yeshua, much as he enjoyed it, as the first sentence uttered by Amitabha in their
next official conference.

"I have withheld from you, my son, news of a project
which, if successful, would henceforth eliminate the need
for you or your successors to confront the Prodigals on
the Isle of the Dead!"

Yeshua almost rose from his chair in Amitabha's study!
It was the very eve of his seventh decade—the decade
traditionally reserved for work with the Prodigals. His
metaphysical virginity was virtually at an end.

"But why have you withheld such news?" he asked.

"Because the whole project was so tenuous and unlike-
ly, I did not want to raise false hopes unnecessarily.
Project Resurrection, as we call it, has now, however, taken
a stride toward reality, and while there is by no means a
guarantee—or even a high probability—of success, it does
seem time to alert you about the new possibilities.

"You know, Yeshua, that we hazard your journey to
the Isle of the Dead for two reasons: first, in the hope of
reclaiming lost souls from the Null Imperium; second, to
replete our numbers. The Sophia has found that population of between 140,000 and 150,000 citizens—roughly
12,000 in each of our 12 major Functions and Sub-Functions—suits our needs best. We will, of course, always
feel the pressure of the first motive: reclamation of the

lost. But possibly this new project will remove some of the pressure of the second: repletion of numbers. By the same token, it might also reduce the number of foreign missions required of you, and happily restore to Sukhavati more of your needed presence.

"But even aside from the practical utility of Project Resurrection, its intrinsic interest is overwhelming. Spiritually and intellectually, this is going to be a great treat and a welcome respite for you—one which you have thoroughly earned, I assure you.

"The whole project hinges on the validity of what will one day go down in the Archimedes' text books as the Ezekiel Hypothesis. You are familiar with this curious name?"

"Yes. The name of a Biblical prophet, was it not? Some kind of poetic visionary, as I recall him."

"You recall him accurately. Yahweh brought him into a plain, the Bible says, covered with heaps of bones —'and they were exceedingly dry.' And Yahweh said to him, 'Son of man, dost thou think these bones shall live? Prophecy concerning these bones, and say to them: "Behold, I will send spirit into you, and you shall live!" And the bones were fleshed.'

"We have an Archimedes, Yeshua—probably the greatest of the last three eras—who thinks he can fulfill the prophesy of Ezekiel! Come, I am going to introduce you to him. His name is Ikhnaton. Some of his colleagues think he is slightly mad, but I suspect he is simply out in front of his era."

En route to Tathagata Central Laboratories in Amitabha's private skimmer, Yeshua's superior picked up the thread of their conversation.

"And would you care to guess who might be his chief assistant in this project? Your tutor, Hans! That is one of the reasons, aside from Mobutu's special utility in the McDonald and Baldwin cases, that Hans did not accompany you on the last great mission. Brilliant as both Li and Mobutu are, Hans is heir-apparent to Ikhnaton, who, by the way, is well along into his era. This is probably the last great breakthrough we can expect from him. In fact, he hinted to me that after Project Resurrection is concluded—one way or the other—he would be checking in with you about psychic sabbatical. So I thought it prudent that someone of Hans' caliber be present at every stage of the experimentation. Indeed, Hans has a corollary of his own that he has appended to the Ezekiel Hypothesis. But here we are, and they can explain these abstruse matters to you more easily than I."

They had arrived at Tathagata Central, the largest scientific complex on Sukhavati. Everything on the island was small by Federation standards, yet, for quality of equipment, for rapid dissemination of knowledge and techniques, for bold and imaginative scientific conjecture and ingenious, practical devices for testing such conjecture, there was nothing on the Dark Continents to touch Tathagata Lab.

Yeshua was formally introduced to the senior Archimedes. Ikhnaton looked to be about as advanced in age as it was possible to look in Sukhavati—say, 40 years old, by Federation measure. A touch of gray showed in his straight red hair. Yet, withal, he had a striking coutenance and a frame overflowing with movement and animation—a wild bird of a man! Hard to believe that he was contemplating psychic sabbatical. But Yeshua had met such types before. Active, almost obsessed with work until the last moment, yet perfectly clear in their minds about having reached and passed their peak moment, their professional consummation. They were not interested in "harvest years." Evidently, Ikhnaton was convinced that Project Resurrection, win, lose or draw, represented his own era-culmination. Yeshua had, of course, heard much about him; he was a near-legendary figure in Sukhavati. But curiously, he had never before been personally introduced to the senior Archimedes.

Ikhnaton was friendly, but not at all overwhelmed by the presence of the Era-Yeshua. "Glad you have come," he smiled, and immediately plunged into an explanation of Project Resurrection.

"No use in long preambles, sir. I can tell you in ten seconds just how I got interested in this whole affair. I was daydreaming one day—that's the most important thing I do, you know—on the names of our different functions and sub-functions: Platos, Alexanders, Freuds etc. And the thought came to me, wouldn't it be interesting to be joined by the very prototypes after whom we have named our professionals! Wouldn't our Platos love to hold a symposium with *Plato!* Wouldn't our Leonardos love to show their creations to *Leonardo!*

"After all, we confer immortality on deserving but far less eminent personages from the dark continents. Is it absolutely certain that the burnt out stars of the human firmament cannot be rekindled out of the dark of oblivion? I thought to myself, if the Sophia licenses my mission, I shall invade the Dark Imperium and bestow the gift of Sukhavati life on the heroes of the past! Reclaim them from the slime of primeval nullity!"

"It sounds like a dream!"

"It *is* a dream, Yeshua. I told you, it came to me as a daydream. But that does not exclude the possibility of its realization. Let me explain some of the basic principles of the Ezekiel Hypothesis to you.

"The entire hypothesis is simply another extension of the basic natural law of conservation of energy. We know that light from the early period of the universe—perhaps from the original explosion itself—still radiates at the edges of space. Now, if light, heat, chemical and electrical energy cannot be destroyed, but only altered or transformed, think of the immense expenditures of thought, will, emotion, passion, idealism, ambition, etc., that are released into the cosmos by every human being in the course of a lifetime. Even brute physical and chemical energy enjoys immortality. Does this living, cunning meta-energy, alone, suffer annihilation? Does the law of conservation of energy apply only up to the point of what is most precious in the unverse? Siddhartha forbid!

"I tell you it's all out there—all that psychic energy of Plato, Leonardo da Vinci, Sigmund Freud! I know that all the 'respectable' scientists have avoided like the plague the kind of research we are doing. I know that only the superstitious crackpots of the Dark Continents have ever put any stock in this. But let me tell you something: in science as in ethics, it sometimes happens that the harlots and the publicans enter the kingdom before the respectable folk!

"But to be more precise, both the scientists and the

211

crackpots have been wrong about these things. Let me give you an example.

"On the Dark Continents, to this day, the curious and the grief-stricken will occasionally employ a medium to contact, as they believe, the soul of a departed loved one. The more respected scientists refuse to touch such investigations with a ten-foot pole. I say the scientists are wrong, because from time to time, something *does* transpire at these seances! But the mediums and their employers are wrong too, I believe, in supposing that they achieve contact with actual living personages in some other and better world.

"What these mediums—those of them who possess genuine powers of extrasensory perception—get in contact with is not a living person, but vibrant energy-clusters of thought, will and emotion that were released into the cosmos by the deceased during the course of his long and varied lifetime! All this expended psychic energy is still hovering at the edge of time-space, available to anyone who knows how to tune in on the right wavelength. This the genuine medium—most of them are phonies, to be sure—is able to do. Energy—and I maintain, *especially* psychic energy, meta-energy—defies destruction. Brute chemical and physical energy resist the void by mere existential inertia. But the energy of intelligence and will does far more. It claws a niche for itself in the cosmos, as into the lining of its natural placenta! The Dark Imperium knows no solvent that can unglue a psychic cluster from its niche in the cosmos! This may or may not be heresy around here, but even if it is, I maintain it is based on scientific fact, and Sukhavati may have to modify the whole dogmatic structure of its biotheology!"

"If you are correct," Yeshua put in, "there really is no urgency in our missions to the Dark Continents. We were mistaken when we supposed we were rescuing the WELL from everlasting death."

"You were rescuing them from everlasting oblivion and inutility. That's a *kind* of death—perhaps worse, even, than nullity. And your own risk, outside the IMOB, is also quite real. Although I must say, if Project Resurrection works, we could reach out into the cosmos and fetch you back to Sukhavati, even if you should die out there in the dark continents."

"But would it be *me* you bring back? You were saying a moment ago that the mediums and their employers were mistaken in supposing that they had contacted actual living persons in some other world."

"Very keen, Yeshua. Yes, we had better go into that question in more detail. Sir, a psychic energy cluster is no more a living person than oxygen is water, even though, in each case, the former is the active component of the latter. Human beings are psychosomatic wholes, and mere psychic energy is not in any way a living soul unless and until it is viably incarnated. Federation scientists wrongly suppose death to be the annihilation of the person, whereas it is merely his disorganization. What if Sukhavati scientists could engineer a reorganization? Could we not recall and recycle those psychic clusters decreed WELL by the Sophia, and find them suitable cellular habitations?

"This is where the Ezekiel Hypothesis comes in. In many cases, we possess, or are in a position to acquire actual physical fragments from the bodies of the deceased. While we do not have a single physical atom from the remains of Plato, we can easily locate the remains of Freud, and probably even some bone fragments of Leonardo. (One of the less attractive assignments we will have to impose on every member of our project team is to take turns at grave-location and tissue-borrowing. Not body-snatching or grave-robbing, mind you! We are not thieves! We propose to return to the cosmos much more than we borrow.)

"Now, with even the tiniest bit of authentic body tissue, no matter how small, we believe we can, by our breakthroughs in atomic genetics, reconstitute a complete, viable, 'tailor-made' cellular habitation for the psychic energy cluster.

"Note that our task is twofold: first, to tune in on the appropriate wavelength and induce to earth, by psychomagnetic processes, the energy-cluster decreed WELL by the Sophia; and second, to reconstitute an authentic celluar habitation tailored to the personality we are reorganizing."

"My God!"

"You called me, sir?"

They both laughed at the quip. And it was just as well for Yeshua, whose PSI had begun to hover at the mark that, sustained for more than five minutes, would bring the Social Control people running.

"You see, then, Yeshua, the critical importance of Project Resurrection," Ikhnaton continued, the hot light once again flaring up in his eyes. "If the Dark Continents do not prove amenable to salvation, we can still repopulate the earth by selective resurrection of outstanding personalities from the past history of the human race. By our technical and biotheological breakthroughs, we have already made the Buddhist vision of karmic rebirth a reality. It is time to do the same for the Judeo-Christian dream of resurrection.

"I ask you, would it not be a grandeur to recall a St. Francis of Assisi, a Gandhi or an Einstein to Sukhavati society—not to mention the historical Buddha or Jesus? We ought *certainly* to confer immortality on Jesus, it seems to me. He's as worthy of Godhood as any of us!"

Yeshua's PSI again swung up to the danger mark! But it was Amitabha, just rejoining them, who took up the questioning. He appeared very agitated by Ikhnaton's last oracular remark.

"Do you mean to say that you have hopes of restoring life even to persons whose bodily remains are not available to us—men like the Buddha and Jesus?"

"Yes. Hopes. I do not use a stronger word."

"But," continued Amitabha, "how can you even have hopes? As I understand the Ezekiel Hypothesis, you need to find a viable cellular habitation for the recalled energy cluster. In fact, unless I am mistaken, the habitation serves as the principal means of induction—a kind of material vacuum demanding psychic occupation by the appropriate cluster."

"That is correct."

"But if you do not possess so much as a single cell of the historical Buddha or Jesus, not even atomic genetics can multiply authentic tissue for you."

"That is also correct."

"Then how do you get a viable habitation?"

"The Yajnavalkyas, the Freuds and the Leonardos must come to our rescue! We depend on the Yajnavalkyas

214

to intuit the basic personality—indeed, to tune in on the actual wavelength of the psychic energy cluster in question. We depend on the Freuds to deduce, in more scientific terms, the basic character structure. Finally, we depend on the Leonardos, putting everything together, to give us an esthetically precise model of the appropriate bodily habitation—what it would look like, sound like, even feel like to the touch. Our atomic geneticists will work under their continual supervision. Of course, there is always the chance that we may come across a stray cell. Believe me, I'd love to get my hands on some of the treasured relics on the Dark Continents:—a hair of Mohammed, a thorn from the crown of thorns or a thread from that shroud of Turin, the imprint of the Buddha's foot, etc. I'd need only thirty seconds to detect authentic cells in any of them, given the equipment we now have at our command. Lacking these, however, I still have hopes that the Leonardos could do the job for us, as regards appropriate cellular habitation."

"*Ikhnaton, do it!*" shouted Amitabha. His face was flushed and perspiring! Yeshua was certain he had never seen him so agitated.

"Sir, I am delighted to be given the assignment. I was certain, myself, that Jesus was WELL. But may I have your permission to attempt the easier task first? We do have some fragments of—believe it or not—that great 17th century Archimedes, Sir Isaac Newton. We lifted them, Yeshua, on one of your missions, and you never even knew it. That eccentric gentleman is one of my favorite people, and if it checks out with the Sophia, I should love to aim my first incarnation-duct in the direction of his energy cluster. Should it prove successful, we would immediately call in the Yajnavalkyas, Freuds and Leonardos, to get to work on an immaculate body for Jesus."

"I will have the judgment engineers check with the Sophia immediately!" Amitabha whispered some directions to an Alexander in attendance at the lab. "In the meantime," he said, having dismissed his aide, "I must speak to Yeshua at once."

"Sir, we have not yet gone into Hans' Literary Corollary. Don't you think———"

"Later, later!" exclaimed Amitabha. "I simply must talk to Yeshua now.

Taking Yeshua by the arm, the Overseer of Sukhavati led him to the private office always reserved for him at Tathagata Central Laboratories. When they had both entered, Amitabha quickly closed and locked the door: a most unusual procedure anywhere on Sukhavati!

"Yeshua," he said in a low, hurried voice, "not even the gifted Ikhnaton realizes the full implications of Project Resurrection! It's not just a matter of replenishing our numbers or enlivening Sukhavati society by introducing outstanding personalities from the past. The full significance of the project occurred to me when he was talking to you about recalling the Buddha or Jesus. *It's a chance to intervene decisively in the affairs of the Dark Continents—to trigger a gigantic wave of conversion-mutations all over the three Federations!*"

"I'm sorry, sir. I sense the extreme importance of what you are saying. But there are pieces missing in the puzzle."

"Don't you see, my son? Except for isolated rescue missions and a few alterations in Federation affairs as suggested by the OR, we have never before dared to intervene crucially in the concerns of the Federations. We embrace—you might say, we are gentically committed to—nonviolence. They espouse violence. Once aware of our existence and location, they would make short work of us. You understand all this—we have talked about it many times."

"I'm beginning to catch your meaning. You feel that Project Resurrection puts us in a position where we might hazard a major intervention."

"Yes! Yes!" Amitabha was now almost beside himself with excitement! He had taken the precaution, Yeshua observed, of removing his PSI as soon as he had closed the door to the private office. "If Ikhnaton should be successful in this fantastic project, Sukhavati would have at its disposal the talents and services of the great charismatic leaders of all time: Moses, Jesus, Buddha, Socrates, Mohammed, Confucius, Lao Tzu! Once we had properly horizoned and purposed these men, their simultaneous appearance on the Dark Continents and their unamimous witness to Sukhavati values would prove irresistible! There would be global conversion-mutation!

Amitabha stopped, his mouth still open, trying to realize the full import of his own words. Then he began again, almost in a whisper. "Thus would we accomplish our ultimate vision: the earth at peace, the state of mutual love prevailing, we would construct our planetary IMOB. And eventually, zenithed, every one of us would sail through space forever, from sun to sun—the Crystal Planet, intelligent Viking among the stars, mobile throne-room of the universe!"

Yeshua had to take Amitabha by the arm and lead him to a chair. His eyes were glazed with the vision.

The two men sat in silence for several minutes, reflecting. Finally, his customary balance and calm returning, Amitabha spoke in almost normal tones, "Of course, we would not chance such intervention unless affairs in the Dark Continents took a disastrous turn, such that the planet itself might be endangered by a cobalt war. Should there be a recognizable pattern of evolution and progress in Federation history, we could simply wait for the appropriate moment to announce our existence. A Jesus or a Buddha would still be helpful in such a case, but we would not risk either them or ourselves unless it became absolutely necessary.

"You know, my son,"—his voice was altogether conversational now—"the problem is that we have never been able to discern a pattern, at least an *ethical* pattern in Federation affairs. Is the world getting better? We don't know. Is it getting worse? We don't know. Does it merely remain the same? We don't know. And very great decisions—including whether or not Sukhavati intervenes decisively in Federation affairs—hang on the answers to these questions. Less than the Sudraheens and the Rothschilds, less even than the Platos, do our Toynbees offer us certainties in their conjectures."

"Isn't the Isawi Hypothesis of the 'Conservation of Evil' relevant here?" asked Yeshua.

"It's relevant, but still hypothetical. It works in our system, but we have not, as yet, incontrovertible evidence that it is operable in the Federation."

217

"Then why not put the question to the Sophia?" Yeshua asked innocently.

"Put the question? Do you realize the prolonged agony of labor that is compressed in those three words? It would be an enormous undertaking, Yeshua, to program such a project for the Sophia. You would have to devise a code whereby you could signify in mathematical logic every significant episode of Federation history. How else could the Sophia determine the drift?"

"But we wouldn't have to work with each separate event, sir. Do you remember the German concept—Hegel's, I believe—of *Zeitgeist?* The spirit of the times? You know, every historical period hangs together in such a way that even the art and architecture, let us say, are not really different in spirit from the economy or the technology? There is a certain spirit of the times, a certain *Zeitgeist*, which not only the common man but even the genius absorbs with his mother's milk.

"Now I believe that with a team of skilled Archimedes —give me Li and Mobutu to start with—and . . . and a proficient group of Yajnavalkyas—sir, a plan is occurring to me as I talk. I believe it is possible to analyze and mathematize for the Sophia the essential *Zeitgeist* of each successive period of Federation history—from the early Babylonian, Inca and Chinese civilizations, right through the Middle Ages, Ming Dynasty, Renaissance, Marxist and Industrial Revolutions, the formation of the three Federations, etc. Give me six months, and I can put the question to the Sophia! You will know the drift of Federation history!"

"Impossible, Yeshua. More like six years than six months."

"Even so, sir. It's vital information, is it not? When we resurrect the great leaders of the past, when we incarnate the Buddha and the Christ, won't we need to know how to use their services? Whether to send them out on foreign mission to the Federations? Your vision of the Crystal Planet, sir—is it not worth the interruption? Besides, who knows how long it will take Ikhnaton to verify the Ezekiel Hypothesis? He's starting with Sir Isaac Newton, is he not? It will be some time before he can, without any cell tissue whatsoever, create a viable habitation for Jesus. Give me permission, sir."

Amitabha smiled. "As always, my son, you are very persuasive. Very well. Permission granted. But Yeshua, warn Li and Mobutu that this is no Gallery escapade, no *Yin-Yang* prank of prognostication! You said six months, and I will hold you to it. Yeshua, I can keep no secrets from you: The Sophia has lately been indicating that a moment of IT is approaching! We must be ready.

Yeshua shuddered with excitement and anticipation not unmixed with fear. IT—Interior Transformation— had last occurred in the third era, with the invention of the SERD. Sukhavati had then been verging on a utopian condition, and losses to the Prodigals had skyrocketed. The SERD had changed the whole nature of Sukhavati life and had guaranteed its uninterrupted entopian status. A whole millenium had gone tranquilly by, and now, in *his* era, IT was at hand once again! Most likely, Yeshua thought, it involved the second coming of the Buddha, Christ and the other great charismatic leaders of the world.

"Well, then," Yeshua finally replied, "we have even more impetus to accomplish our task. Sir, I give you my personal word that we will finish in six months."

The very next morning, Yeshua assembled his crew and commandeered his resources. They took over the whole history wing of Satori University, plus a suite of offices in the basement to program their information. The Yajnavalkyas, however, required absolute quiet, and could not work with the rest of them. It was they who had to do the crucial Hegel-work: to summarize, spiritually, the essence of complicated periods of history, some of them centuries long. For them, Yeshua arranged the temporary takeover of the university meditation towers, from which he ran direct lines of audio-visual communication down to their basement offices. As soon as a Yajnavalkya, having pored over the history, literature and art forms of a given epoch for weeks, would experience a culminating seizure, a moment of synthetic historical satori, he would switch on audio-visual and communicate—as much by poetry, countenance and song as by logic and prose— the essential *Zeitgeist* of the period under study. This, in turn, down in the basement offices, would be translated by picked crews of Archimedes, together with Whitehead

219

and Russell sub-functionaires, into appropriate mathematical symbols.

The interminable details of their prolonged and Herculean mental labor aside, suffice it to say that six months later—having gone the entire time with no sleep, not even the few hours to which they were accustomed, and looking like imminent prospects for psychic sabbatical, they assembled at Dharma House with a completed program to be submitted to the Sophia. In all this time, they had neither spoken to Amitabha about their progress nor been spoken to by him about developments in Project Resurrection. They had been completely barricaded against interruption in the basement offices and meditation towers of Satori University.

Having been ushered immediately into Amitabha's study, Yeshua was just about to explode with the happy news that he had completed the necessary programing, when Amitabha placed a finger over his lips for silence and beckoned him over to the rear window of his study.

Yeshua joined him at the alcove. Holding aside the drapes for better vision, Amitabha pointed to a group of people—two groups of people, to be exact—assembled in the gardens to the rear of Dharma House. In the first group, thirty or forty Archimedes—Yeshua recognized many of them—were gathered around a slight figure in white knee breeches and a blue velvet waistcoat, who had one arm around a small mounted telescope and was pointing to the sun with the other.

Yeshua's mouth fell open. "Sir Isaac?" he asked. Amitabha nodded in slow affirmation.

The other group was larger—about one or two hundred citizens of all ranks and functions of Sukhavati. They were seated on the grass, listening in rapt attention to a tall man with long brown hair who wore a coarse brown woolen robe and open sandals. Yeshua couldn't even frame the question. He merely looked at Amitabha in astonished wonder, and Amitabha said, "Yes."

It was three days before Yeshua and his crew gathered in the still solemnity of Nirvana-Crypt to run the *Zeitgeist*-Evaluation Program through the Sophia. Amitabha, of course, joined them for the occasion, the culminating moment of six months of mind-bending labor. They had a full three-day respite to digest the fact which all Sukhavati had known two weeks earlier: the Ezekiel Hypothesis had tested out. Project Resurrection was a stupefying success!

"Gratifying, the good time you have made, gentlemen," said Amitabha when he arrived. "You are sure the program checks out? No crucial historical periods omitted?"

"All our data was double-checked by a standby crew, sir," Yeshua replied, "and to the best of our knowledge, all human error has now been eliminated. Of course, what the various historical periods offer by way of documentary and cultural illumination varies both quantitatively and qualitatively. But we are now convinced that, until such time as Federation archeologists and historians come up with revolutionary new findings, this represents the most complete and accurate programing attainable by Sukhavati analysts."

"Very good." Amitabha rewarded them all with a smile of approval. "Let us submit your work to the Sophia immediately. We will purpose Jesus in a year's time, and we must decide whether or not we will send him on a mission to the Dark Continents. Proceed, gentlemen.

Li adjusted the electronic controls and smoothly, almost silently, ran the program through the Sophia. It was a lengthy program, and nearly two hours were consumed by the process. Amitabha had stepped out to answer a message when they summoned him back for the Sophia's verdict.

"You are ready?" Amitabha asked. "Then let us have the Sophia's answer."

Li fed in the first question which, translated from the mathematical logic into which it had been coded, read simply: "Are the affairs of the three Federations in decline? Does the world move toward inevitable disaster?"

There was a smooth electronic whirr, and the Sophia printed out a short statement in symbolic logic. Li, the expert here, quickly pulled out his well-worn code book and deciphered it.

"Negative," he read. "The affairs of the Federations are not in decline, nor does the world move toward inevitable disaster!"

The whole crew was alive with pleasure and excitement. Not only had their program been validated—the Sophia would not have operated with it had it been significantly inadequate—but the Sophia's verdict was a joyful one. No cobalt war was to be feared in the Dark Continents. At least, such a war was not inevitable. It might not be necessary, after all, to risk their Newly-Aware, Jesus, on a mission to the Federations. (He was now in demand everywhere in Sukhavati. Every Function and Sub-Function on the island wished to speak to him.)

Amitabha quieted them. "There are still two alternatives," he reminded the technicians. "Proceed with the second question."

Li fed it in and they waited—now in happy anticipation—for the answer. The question was: "Are the affairs of the Federations progressing? Is the world moving toward peace and justice for all? After the electronic-intuitive transaction had occurred, Li ripped off the printed reply and decoded it.

"Negative!" he read. Everyone stiffened. "The affairs of the Federations are not progressing toward peace and justice for all men."

"Well," said Amitabha, his brow furrowed with care, "that leaves only the third alternative. The world grows neither better nor worse, but essentially remains the same as it has always been. To tell you the truth, that was my own suspicion. It merely confirms the Isawi Law of the Conservation of Evil." He turned to his aide and asked him to summon his skimmer.

"Wait, Amitabha," Yeshua asked. "Please stay with us for the final question. It will only take a minute, sir."

"Very well, Yeshua, since you request it. But I hardly see the point in remaining."

Li quickly fed in the last question. Translated, it read: "Do the affairs of the Federations remain essentially the same, so that no movement relevant to conversion-mutation is discernible?"

A few seconds later, Li tore off the printed reply. "Negative. The affairs of the Federations do not remain essentially the same. Movements relevant to conversion-mutation are discernible!"

Amitabha slumped to a chair, his intention to leave the

Crypt forgotten. Crew members looked at one another in consternation. Had their program gone awry? Had it so completely thrown off the delicate mechanism of the Sophia that it could commit gross errors in logic? Li pulled out his code book and began to go over the message. Mobutu and a Yajnavalkya began studying the mathematical logic of the last question on the program. Something had gone terribly wrong.

"There seems to be a direct contradiction here," said Amitabha, his countenance pale and troubled. In all his years as Overseer he had never known the Sophia to be caught in a contradiction. Indeed, the records of Sukhavati, so far as he knew them—and his knowledge here was encyclopedic—revealed no such instance. "But the Sophia, as we all know," he said emphatically, "can neither deceive nor be deceived!"

"The world, according to the Sophia, is growing neither better nor worse, yet the world does not remain the same. Gentlemen, six months of uninterrupted labor placed too great a strain on your resources, superb as these are, both mental and electronic. I am to blame, not to have foreseen it," he said kindly. "You will relax for the next two weeks, and we will come back to your program—bringing in, perhaps, a crew of fresh technicians to restudy the problem."

"Wait! Please wait just a few minutes more, sir," Yeshua pleaded. He was convinced that their programing had been painstakingly accurate. He, Mobutu and Li had each checked it out independently of one another. One of them might make a mistake; but for the three of them—and two of them such superb technicians as Li and Mobutu—to make the identical errors, seemed virtually impossible.

"I believe the Sophia is telling us something. Now if we can all just concentrate on it for a moment. Have we truly exhausted all the possibilities? Is there no other question that can be submitted to the Sophia, based on our program?"

There was absolute silence for several minutes. The strain was growing intolerable. Then Yeshua's face slowly began to relax. A smile played around the corners of his mouth. Like the morning tide, his confidence and equilibrium rolled back in, filling up the depression lines on his countenance. Everyone finally turned toward him.

"Gentlemen, we have been ignoring a fourth alternative, implicit in the three negations of the Sophia. There has been no contradiction. Li, may I have your code book for a moment?"

Li handed it over. Yeshua thumbed through, rapidly composing still another question to put to the Sophia. "Here," he said at last, "feed this in."

Li dutifully fed the question in, and a few moments later ripped off the printed reply, handing it over immediately to Yeshua. Yeshua, in great haste, decoded the two lines of symbolic logic, and exclaimed in triumph, "That's it! We all missed the fourth alternative!"

"Do get on with it, Yeshua!" Amitabha reminded him. "We haven't the vaguest idea of what you are talking about."

"Excuse me, sir. Let me read the reply to my question: "Affirmative! The affairs of the Federations grow better *and* worse. They are approaching culmination point!"

"I don't quite understand," came back the troubled reply. "It still sounds like garbled programing. How can the world be getting better *and*—Oh!" He groaned. "Oh. I see." He smiled wearily. "How did I ever miss it! The possibility was implicit in everything the Sophia said."

"Now Li and Mobutu brightened. It was a chain reaction. Li began to laugh. Some of the other technicians, however, still had not resolved the apparent contradiction. Yeshua explained.

"What the Sophia is telling us is that, from the bow-and-arrow to depth psychology and the cobalt bomb, every breakthrough made by man has been used *both* for good and evil. With their new knowledge of personality structure, Federation scientists can now cure a high percentage of cases of insanity; they can also brainwash entire populations. In the Dark Continents, both have been done. Inevitably. With the power obtainable from nuclear fusion and the cobalt-exchange, they can desalinate the oceans and turn the Sahara desert back into the garden it once was; they can also erase entire populations. Both will occur in the Federations. Every breakthrough will be used for all it is worth, in *both* ways. Therefore, the world grows better and worse at the same time. It does not remain the same. We have come up with a refinement of the Isawi Law of the Conservation of Evil. Each successive breakthrough actually raises the stakes, increases the tension between the creative and destructive forces on earth. Soon, with unlimited energy at their disposal, the Federations will be in a position to make every man a king—or every man a robot. The Sophia swears that both will occur."

"The way these things happen," Li interjected, "I look for every man a robot-king!"

"Perhaps," said Yeshua. "That's not yet perfectly clear. But one thing is clear: we are approaching global culmination!"

"Better *and* worse, better *and* worse . . ." Amitabha was still ruminating over the new vista opened up by the Sophia. "The only certitude we have," he smiled at last, "is the certitude of radical ambiguity. The wheat and the tares most assuredly do grow together. Our Newly-Aware spoke the truth."

"Will you be sending him into the Federations under these conditions?" asked Yeshua. There was no doubt whom he was talking about.

"The question, as our biotheologians would say, is not ripe. We must be patient a while longer." The Overseer was himself once more: strong, persevering, benevolent.

"Short of total intervention in Federation affairs, there are still a few types of minor involvement we have never yet tried," Yeshua added as an afterthought.

"What do you have in mind, Yeshua?"

"It is really an idea that the senior centurion, Marcus, has in mind. He wants permission to send out flying Mo-Tzu squads around the Federations, wherever they are needed."

"Flying Mo-Tzu squads! Whatever in the world is that?"

"If you don't mind, I'll ask Li to explain it. He has done a little preliminary research, in case we get interested."

"Mo-Tzu," Li explained with a smile, "was an ancient Chinese sage, almost a contemporary of Confucius, which puts him back to about 500 B.C., Federation time. He abhorred warfare and expressed his abhorrence in a rather

225

practical Chinese fashion: he became a genius at military defense. Not offense, mind you; strictly defense. Thereafter, whenever he would hear of some contemplated aggression, even hundreds of miles away, he and his disciples would set out and, by forced marches, would manage to arrive on the scene, however bloody their feet, before the onset of battle. Then they would teach the intended victims of the aggression how to build earthworks, moats, battlements, etc., to withstand the attack. So you see, paradoxically, his very pacifism led to his becoming a military genius—but only in defense!"

Amitabha smiled. "It's a good story—as Federation stories go. But what does all this have to do with Marcus?"

"Marcus," said Yeshua," wants to drop ideas for weapons systems around the Federations in such a way that the smaller powers, who might be facing aggression on the part of the superpowers, would believe that they had stumbled onto the military secrets of their enemies. Thus, they could build advanced defense systems, never suspecting who their unknown benefactor really was."

Amitabha wasn't sure how seriously he should take the suggestion. "Sounds problematical," he smiled once more. "We'll talk more about it, but remember, we are genetically committed to nonviolence. The burden of proof is on the Mo-Tzu squad: can they guarantee that the promulgation of advanced weapons systems will deter rather than incite war? Enough for now. Let us see how Ikhnaton's Newly-Awares are faring."

For several weeks, the citizens of Sukhavati were enthralled by the resurrected beneficiaries of Ikhnaton's project. So intense was the interest and intellectual excitement that the SERD imposed a curfew, two days a week, on the Arts Alliance, the Institute of Amatory Mobiles, the Olympiad Raceway and other popular places of entertainment. "Overcoming boredom is part of our Entopian challenge," Amitabha explained. "Keep the citizens at too high a pitch of interest for too long a time, and *everything* would eventually lose its intellectual salt—the cosmos itself would become a bore!"

As it turned out, Amitabha's fears were groundless. Sukhavati interest in the Newly-Awares wore thin. The trouble started with Newton. The junior Archimedes began to shake their heads over the 17th century genius. Yeshua heard them muttering to themselves after their sessions with the exotic arrival. He decided to speak to Hans about the matter.

"Sir Isaac," Hans coolly announced, "is stupid!"

Yeshua, even knowing his friend's proclivity for shocking statements, was shocked! "Hans, don't be so patronizing. Naturally, the man is far behind the times. Even Federation scientists, let alone our Archimedes functionaries, must be way ahead of him. But Hans, science is cumulative! We stand on his shoulders! He was the first to sling a mathematical lasso around the solar system and tie it down to our charts. Remember it was as gigantic an intellectual achievement for primitive man to invent the first wheel, as for Cowper to modify Einstein's laws and give us a Unified Field Theory! We stand on the shoulders of the past."

"Sir Isaac," Hans repeated with dignity, "is stupid."

Yeshua was now truly annoyed. "Hans, you will please explain your remark."

"We did not expect for a minute, sir, that this Newly-Aware would prove *au courant* with Cowper's Unified Field Theory, or with Einstein's Laws of Relativity, for that matter. But we did expect he would be interested in hearing something about such matters!"

"He ... he is not interested?"

"Sir Isaac, sir, is stupid. He refuses to enter into discussions of any matters other than his own 17th century mechanical laws of physics. We cannot interest him even in the basic laws of biotheology, the laws which govern Sukhavati immortality. Yeshua, I tell you that you learned more in one day as a Newly-Aware than this fellow has learned since his arrival. Something is terribly wrong, and I'm beginning to have a feeling about what it is. I'm still accumulating evidence. If my theory firms up, I will report to you immediately."

"No, best report directly to Amitabha. According to the Sophia, Sukhavati is awaiting IT, and Amitabha believes the transformation has something to do with Project Resurrection. It is of the utmost importance that any new findings be communicated to him at once."

It was Yeshua himself who picked up the first clue that there was something amiss with his fellow Israeli, Ikhnaton's other Newly-Aware.

Yeshua had begun to follow him everywhere, feeling attracted to him even beyond what mere intellectual curiosity could account for. He listened as this first-century rabbi entered into discussions with the Sudraheen, the Rothschilds, the Alexanders, etc. To his astonishment, he realized that the new incarnate was saying different things to different men—pleasing them all, but contradicting himself in the process! At first, it wasn't noticeable to the citizens of Sukhavati, since they tended to meet with him separately, function by function. But to Yeshua, who accompanied him everywhere, the contradictions were both painful and obvious.

To the Sudraheen, the new incarnate preached, "Blessed are the lowly, the meek of heart." But to the Rothschilds, he said, "I have come that you may have life, and have it more abundantly." And he pointed out that the movement he had started so many years ago had come to number billions of adherents, and had built up an organization to rival any corporate structure in Sukhavati or the Federations.

"The kingdom of heaven is taken by storm," he preached to the Alexanders. And, as the rank of Alexander was not a particularly high one in Sukhavati, Yeshua listened nervously as this restless rabbi went on to urge, "Liberation now—the moment of *kairos* is at hand!"

As the glamor of his arrival wore off, moreover, his audiences began to challenge his statements. Not infrequently, he was left downcast, at a loss for words. "Blessed are the poor," he made the mistake of saying to the Leonardos, whose esthetic tastes were very expensive. "But, sir, we *have no poor*," one of them had finally replied.

"You . . . you have no poor?"

"We have no poor."

"But the poor ye shall have *always* with you!"

"Sir, there are no poor on Sukhavati!"

The reclaimed one was silent. Finally, he said in a disheartened tone, "A prophet is nowhere without honor, save in his own city."

More and more frequently, this pattern came to be repeated. The rabbi would say, "Blessed are those who mourn." And his audience would explain that no one on Sukhavati mourned, owing to the general availability of psychic sabbatical. He would say, "Blessed are those who suffer persecution for justice' sake," and his audience would explain that there was no such persecution on the island; since, possessing immortality, they had no need to aggress against the person or the rights of another.

His following dwindled. He ceased to attract attention. Finally, people began to go out of their way to avoid him altogether. It wasn't that he had no charm. No, the charisma was still there; but somehow, he could not sensibly apply his teachings to the Sukhavati situation. It was all rote delivery. Even worse, for someone like Yeshua who followed him everwhere, there were these terrible contradictions in his message.

The day came when Yeshua could stand it no longer. For lack of a better audience, the Newly-Aware had begun to address the trees and the stones of Sukhavati! It was time to report to Amitabha.

He blurted it out as soon as they were alone in the study. "Sir, have you talked to Hans? Things are not right with the New Incarnates."

There was a long pause.

"This morning, at 5:25, according to the Alexander on duty," Amitabha solemnly replied, "your friend Hans passed through sluice No. 7. He has gone over to the Prodigals!"

Yeshua fell back into his chair. He said nothing at all for some time. Helen and Amitabha aside, he probably felt closer to Hans than to any other person on the island.

"You are quite sure of this?" he finally asked.

"Quite sure, my son," Amitabha replied sadly.

"Do you know why?"

"Yes, I know why."

Yeshua waited for the explanation. It seemed to be more than Amitabha could bear to offer one. He called for vapors.

"It was his Literary Corollary to Ikhnaton's Hypothesis," said Amitabha, when he had regained his composure.

229

"It didn't work? I don't understand. One scientific disappointment out of dozens of brilliant successes would not bring Hans to the point of despair. Besides, he could have spoken to me about psychic sabbatical!"

"You have it reversed, Yeshua. The only part of the Ezekiel Hypothesis that *does* work is the Literary Corollary!"

"But why should the success of his own hypothesis prove so terrible?"

"I guess, Yeshua, that you never actually had the corollary explained to you. No, you didn't. I recall drawing you aside to speak to you privately, when Ikhnaton wanted to go into it. Did Hans ever discuss it with you?"

"No. He did say that he found Sir Isaac's behavior peculiar, and that he thought he knew what might be wrong with Ikhnaton's project, but he never went into his own theory. And then I became very involved with the other New Incarnate."

"Well, my son, as with so many other brilliant scientific discoveries of your tutor, Hans first thought up the corollary as a joke, a prank. But the more he thought about it, the more convinced he became that there might be something to it. If you wait for just a moment, I'll get the tape we have of his explanation of the corollary to the crew of Project Resurrection."

Amitabha buzzed his aide, and in a few minutes the designated tape was brought to the study. The Overseer inserted it into place and switched on the speaker. It cut through them both to hear the familiar mock-pompous voice of their departed friend.

"Well gentlemen," Hans began. "It is my contention that the Senior Archimedes, our own esteemed Ikhanaton, genius though he is, has only scratched the surface with his Ezekiel Hypothesis! His scientific ambition walks—limps, actually. Mine soars! He hopes to reclaim only the real, historical psychic energy clusters from the placenta of time-space. What kind of a victory over the Null Imperium is that? A skirmish, a battle perhaps, but certainly not a war!

"Is he creating anything new? He will be the first to admit that he is only involved in a job of reclamation and recycling. He hopes to rekindle the burnt-out stars of the past.

"Now what is it, by contrast, that *I* propose to do? Gentlemen, listen closely. It is one thing to bring back great men; it is another to bring back the *dreams* of great men! Will you, esteemed Senior Archimedes, bring back Shakespeare? Then I will bring back Hamlet! Will you bring back Dostoievsky? Then I will bring back Alyosha Karamazov! I will bring back Achilles and Oedipus and Don Quixote—any fictional hero or heroine you like, provided only that the Sophia pronounce him WELL! *This,* gentlemen, is my Literary Corollary. Would it not be a delight to go to the Arts Alliance and see Hamlet portray himself on the stage?

"Some of you look skeptical. How does it work, you ask? Well, with scientists as brilliant as yourselves, I can play the role of Confucius—who will be glad to relate to you personally, once Ikhnaton incarnates him for you, that he would lift but one corner of the cloth for his students and would expect them to lift the other three corners by themselves. You get my drift?

"Good! Well, realize then, my friends and colleagues, that according to the same law of conservation of energy appealed to by Ikhanaton, the vast amount of thought, passion and interpretation poured into such purely fictional characters as Hamlet, Oedipus, Don Quixote, etc., must *also* exist on the fringes of the space-time continuum! In fact, if I may be a bit obvious, whom do men know more about: Homer or Achilles! We are not even sure that Homer really existed, but does anyone have any doubts about Achilles? Yes, you reply, but it's a mere literary existence, bound by the narrow dimensions of a book. Wrong! Gentlemen, in the past millenium, in the year 1984 to be exact, there was a minor bureaucrat in Brooklyn—that was in the old United States—who helped amalgamate the new Western Federation. His name was James Edwin MacIntyre. I know, because I've just been reading about him. He was 5 feet 9 inches tall, weighed 175 pounds and lived at 14 Somerset Street. A thoroughly real person. Have you ever heard of him? You shake your heads. Neither has anyone else, these past thousands of years. He's a footnote I dug out of an old history book just for the occasion.

"Gentlemen, may I remind you that we are discussing the conservation of energy—and meta-energy, at that! In whom, do you suppose, has there been the greater energy-accumulation of speculation, interpretation and passion—James Edwin MacIntyre, real flesh and blood, or Hamlet, whose nerves were woven out of air and imagination?

"What an energy-cluster is Hamlet's, gentlemen! This I will swear to you: James Edwin MacIntyre's entire cluster compares to that which has accumulated about the character of Hamlet as a mote compares to the sun. If Ikhnaton likes, he can bring back MacIntyre; I, gentlemen—the Sophia permitting—will bring back Hamlet!"

The tape came to an end. Amitabha stood up and removed it from the machine.

"I still fail to see what there is about the Literary Corollary "that would drive Hans to commit metaphysical suicide, said Yeshua, "particularly if his imaginative theorizing turned out to be valid—as you say it did."

"Yeshua, what I said was that the Literary Corollary was the *only* part of the entire project that turned out to be valid!"

"Do you mean . . . ?"

"Yes. That was not the real Sir Isaac Newton our Archimedes were talking to. The only psychic energy clusters Ikhnaton could find turned out to be clusters of thought and interpretation *about* the actual historical personages!"

"Then that is why Sir Isaac was so stupid!"

"Precisely. He could only enter into discussions of the real Newton's theories. His entire cluster was composed of such thought, passion and speculation."

"And the restless Israeli?"

"The same—a bundle of interpretations of what the human race has felt and believed to be true about Jesus of Nazareth."

"That explains . . ."

"Yes, it does."

"What happens now to the . . . to the . . . ?"

"That's precisely the problem, Yeshua. You don't know

what to call them, because we don't really know what they are. I suppose we'll put them in the children's wing of our residence for liberated Federation WELLs. They *are* children, really. Quite helpless, totally unable to initiate a free action. Even the children will get bored with them, I'm sure. You know, my son, they are not really 'Incarnates' in the full sense of the word. I mean, we have not incarnated actual psychic clusters. There is no real personality present in either case. It would not offend our genetic commitment against violence, I think, if we should have to destroy them—for their own good, of course. Well, we can wait a bit on that. Wait and see whether they make any progress in the children's wing. They are not human, really—just literary figures. The 'Literary Jesus' and the 'Literary Newton.' "

"And what about poor Hans? It is still unbelievable to me that he could take this step, merely because his corollary came true. Why, Amitabha. *Why?*"

"We have his last words in Sukhavati, Yeshua. When he had formed a firm conclusion about the failure of Project Resurrection and the success of the Literary Corollary, he was overheard by Mobutu to utter the words: *'Nothing in Sukhavati is serious.'* "

"But of all people to say that! He was such an unserious person himself!"

"Was he, Yeshua? By the way, my son—someone left with him."

"Who was that, sir?"

"The Sudraheen, Zoe.

"And next month, Yeshua, you set out for the Isle of the Dead yourself. The confrontation with the Prodigals is now a necessity."

CHAPTER XV

The Prodigals

"Ion, I must tell you frankly that I was quite surprised when you were recommended to me by the Security Yajnavalkya." Yeshua was operating out of his own study, recruiting, as carefully as possible, the mission team which would accompany him to the nearby Isle of the Dead. "That you worked well with Rothschilds, I know," he continued, "but the Prodigals are a far cry from Rothschilds! Do you have any idea why you were recommended over the heads of Platos who had even represented their function in the last Olympiad?"

"I am certainly not the fastest mind on the island, sir," said Ion, with one of his sudden infectious smiles that completely transformed his long, austere face. "I rather imagine," he continued, "that I was recommended as much for my weaknesses as my strengths. Indeed, in this case I suppose that my weakness *is* my strength."

"As you must gather, Ion, I do not follow you at all."

"My story, sir, is not sweet, but it is short. I once nearly succumbed to time-satiety myself. It was a few decades before your rebirth, Yeshua. It was your predecessor who saved me—salvaged my immortality. Now, in a way, I'm innoculated, at least in *this* era, against the arguments of the Prodigals. Once tempted and saved, it's almost unheard of, you know, to fall again in any one era. I know their ideas and feelings pretty well, I imagine."

"I see," said Yeshua. "Tell me, Ion, you say my predecessor saved you from going over to the Prodigals. Did he reclaim many of *them?*"

"Not many, sir. When you have had time to read these," Ion said, tapping the three-volume study on his desk, which Amitabha had left for him to read, "you'll learn that no Era-Yeshua has ever reclaimed as many as 25 per cent of the Prodigal population. Ten per cent has been considered a good average—and that is about the achievement of your predecessor. Perhaps a point or two above."

"Do you, yourself, have any recommendations to make as to who should be our mission Freud or Durkheim?"

"Not for a Freud, I'm afraid. I don't really know any of them that intimately. But I do have a Durkheim friend, Jeremy, whose era-experience has, to some degree, paralleled my own. I should think he might be especially suited for work among the Prodigals."

A check of central files indicated exactly where Jeremy would be working at 10:23 on a Wednesday morning, and a summons from Yeshua was more than adequate authority for him to drop his assigned task. In a very short time, he appeared before them at their conference table. Short, energetic, mustache bristling, he was fascinated by the opportunity to work alongside his old friend Ion as well as the reigning Yeshua. He had, moreover, a Freud in mind—one, Warren, by name, who had specialized in healing mid-era trauma. Yeshua had heard of him and, indeed, had referred several cases to him in the past.

Here, however, they hit a snag. Warren, though interested professionally, had recently lost a good friend to the Prodigals and, emotionally, did not quite feel up to making the journey to the Isle of the Dead. Nevertheless, he was able to suggest to them another Freud who eventually proved suitable. Not only was she suitable but, Yeshua thought, extremely beautiful, as well. Her name was Lila. Originally from the Indian sub-continent, she was now into her ninth decade as a very successful Sukhavati Freud.

And so the recruiting progressed—entirely through personal contact. Yeshua found it remarkable, in contrast to his foreign missions, how little public attention was

235

paid to this journey to the Isle of the Dead. As a matter of fact, the community tended to avoid any public mention of the Prodigals. The literature, the press, the theater, never focused attention on the problem. This omission was all the more striking, in view of the positive encouragement given the media by the Sophia to point out all defects and imperfections in Sukhavati society. There seemed to be a kind of voluntary censorship. By tacit consent, the whole subject of the Prodigals was left alone—or rather, left in the capable hands of Amitabha, Yeshua and the designated professionals of the mission teams.

There was, of course, the three-volume study, privately commissioned by Amitabha and brought forth with painstaking labor by a team of Freuds and Durkheims. The next few weeks were given over by the team to the study of this work.

Squeezed down to the barest essentials, this study's conclusions were that Prodigals typically came from the middle ranks of the Sukhavati social spectrum. Both the Sudraheen and the Yajnavalkya functions were relatively immune. Leonardos, Archimedes Platos, etc., were not. There were virtually no other correlations that could be made. Prodigals had neither markedly higher nor markedly lower intelligence than other members of the community. Some Prodigals had been outstanding; a few of them were men and women of genius. But most of them could boast only average professional achievement, while a few had indicated even less than median ability.

Mid-era trauma *could* lead to metaphysical-suicide, but more often, when it was not successfully resolved in the first place, it led merely to psychic sabbatical. It hardly ranked as the chief reason for turning Prodigal.

There *was* no chief reason! Almost anything, it appeared, could eventually lead to a decision to flee Sukhavati. Things that one person could handle easily were things that someone else could not handle at all. Sometimes there were not even "things" in the Prodigal's casehistory. At times, successful Gregorians, Alexanders, Leonardos, apparently problem-free, not even approaching mid-era trauma, would take themselves off and not be

236

heard from again. And, as Ion had said, only a small percentage were ever reclaimed.

"Ion," groaned Yeshua, after two weeks of intense study and discussion had yielded virtually no significant insights, "why does a man do it—throw away not just a life, but an unending life of lives, an eternal sequence of predominantly blissful experiences? How can a man do it —choose the Null Imperium, congealed infinitely, over the continuity and warmth of life in Sukhavati?"

"The only thing I think we've learned, sir, is that there are as many answers as there are Prodigals. Each one seems to have his own reasons."

"Ion," said Lila softly, why did *you* almost join them? Are you able to talk about that?"

"The subject is still a little tender for me, to tell you the truth, but the problem is so important, I suppose it warrants the pain. I have, in fact, a theory that is not touched on in these three volumes," he added, indicating the bound studies. "It is based on my own experiences. I suspect that some part of what I felt then may be felt by every Prodigal, according to his or her own personality and capacity. And now, you see, I've just contradicted what I said a moment ago about each Prodigal having his own reasons. But it's not really a complete contradiction. The truth, here, just happens to be complicated."

"The truth is complicated everywhere," Lila put in, her gentle smile reassuring him.

"To come directly to the point, what I felt in Sukhavati was the lack of absolutes. The climate on our island—the total climate, mental, physical, and emotional—is temperate, moderate, equitable. We avoid extremes and absolutes. As a Plato, I particularly felt the absence of intellectual absolutes. We cannot get to the *bottom* of things—the bottom of reality, the bottom of the universe. Others, less speculative than I, probably feel the absence of absolutes in some other way."

"But Ion, is that a fair critique of our society?" asked Jeremy. "Surely we are light-years ahead of the Federations in our scientific and biotheological investigations. And our own era is, of course, much further ahead than all previous eras, even on Sukhavati. We are zeroing in on what you call 'absolute reality' more and more, with each successive era. And with us, of course, a man can come back to reap the scientific fruits of the investigatory seeds that he may have planted in a previous era."

"Jeremy, that's like counting with high numbers. We count with higher numbers than the Federation scientists. But the gap between high numbers and infinity is just as great as the gap between low numbers and infinity."

"But you can't *reach* infinity. It's impossible. And it's insane to try."

"I know," said Ion simply. He smiled his winning smile once again. "That's why I'm not a Prodigal."

There was a pause in the conversation.

"You are suggesting . . . ?" said Yeshua.

"I am suggesting that the hunger for infinity—at once a little insane and very human—is the one constant we will find in the Prodigal phenomenon. I experienced it after my own fashion as a Plato; a Leonardo, a Tolstoi, a Toynbee, would feel it another way. I call it Ultimacy Deficiency, UD. You won't find it in the three-volume report, but I lived through it. UD with us is like VD in the Federations—a universal inconvenience and, sporadically, a fatal one. There or here, if you invite ten people to your home, one of them has it."

"I think he's onto something," Lila mused.

"I do, too," said Yeshua, "and therefore, I propose adding another member to our team—the Security-Yajnavalkya." It had not been the tradition to utilize either Rothschilds or Yajnavalkyas on missions to the Prodigals, but rather to use representatives of the middle functions, which suffered the greatest losses. It had been believed that, having much in common, a fellow functionary could make the stronger appeal.

"How will that help us, Yeshua?" Lila asked.

"Because meditation opens the sluice gate of the only ultimacy, the only infinity, available to man. These Prodigals have fled real life to await 'pie in the sky when they die.' Yajnavalkya can give them *sky!*"

The material and security aspects of the trip were as easy to negotiate as the mental and emotional aspects were strenuous. In contrast to a foray into the Dark Continents, this was a journey of about 12 kilometers, a matter of a few minutes in the marine skimmer. No uniforms or disguises would be necessary, and practically no supplies or equipment. They would all, of course, have to receive the standard radiological immunization treatment —12 kilometers or 1200 kilometers made no difference; outside the IMOB was outside the IMOB. The temporal limit of their journey remained the same—one week. But there was no fear of forcible detention on the Isle of the Dead. Traditionally, the Prodigals were as anxious to be rid of them as they were to get back to Sukhavati.

There were still two conversations worthy of report, however, before Yeshua's departure. One of them was unexpected; both of them were stressful. On his last evening at home before the mission, Amitabha made an unannounced and rather sudden appearance.

"I must talk to you for just a few minutes, my son— but without any interruption. You know that we are awaiting a moment of IT. The Sophia has now indicated that Interior Transformation is *imminent—an event rivaling in importance the founding of Sukhavati itself!*"

Yeshua stopped in the very middle of a breath and exhaled only several seconds later. He needed every bit of the control which his Yajnavalkya master had inculcated. This news, on top of his forthcoming journey to the Isle of the Dead, taxed his emotional equilibrium to the limit.

He was able, nevertheless, to ask objectively, "Do you have as yet any indication as to the nature of the event?" But he could feel his heart pounding.

"None! Except that the failure of Project Resurrection seems to have something to do with it. Just what, however, the Sophia does not specify."

"I wonder," Yeshua said, almost in annoyance, "how the Sophia can determine that *something* is going to happen without knowing a little about *what* is going to happen. It's not logical."

Amitabha smiled wearily. "Must I really repeat one of your first lessons in Sukhavati? The Sophia, Yeshua, as you well understand, is not a logic-box. You know how Weather-Control detects and reports the beginnings of an electrical storm hours before it reaches the IMOB. So has the Sophia intuited a new cosmic mood drifting into our part of the universe. Great events are imminent. IT is imminent! That is all I know. All I can say to you, my son, is be very watchful—there is no end to the argumentative guile of the Prodigals—and return to us as soon as possible." With that, Amitabha stood up, embraced him warmly, and left.

As for Helen, she had been on edge even before Amitabha's unexpected visit; after it, there was no containing her. She implored Yeshua to call off the mission. "Why should you go? Let us leave the Prodigals to themselves. I know that some great change is going to take place shortly. I want you near me, Yeshua!"

Yeshua offered the obvious pacifiers: there was virtually no physical danger, their immunization was good for a week, and they hoped to be back in much less time than that. "We don't even worry about detection," he added. "We *announce* ourselves. And we certainly don't worry about forcible detention; they can't wait till we get off their island. Should an emergency arise, Amitabha can contact us immediately, and I can be home within a few hours. So what is it, Helen, that makes you so fearful?"

"I don't know, Yeshua," she replied helplessly, "I don't know."

The mission team left early the next morning. Dawn was only just reconnoitering the eastern horizon with her delicate orange probes. As their marine skimmer slid through sluice No. 4, the traditional IMOB gate for home missions, they passed into a frigid wet morning of sleet and icy rain. It was always a shock to realize just how near the frigid zone Sukhavati lay.

A vise of foreboding and silence constrained them as they skimmed the surface of the rough and choppy sea. They made for the little cove on the southeast coast, the closest thing to a harbor that the Isle of the Dead afforded. Soon they could make out a few scrubby fir trees and a small village of thatched huts. Dark smoke drifted somberly over the chimneys. Now they were very near. There was no one down at the cove to greet them. Indeed, there was no one in sight.

Yeshua broke silence. "Is the village deserted?"

"There never is anyone about, sir, when a Sukhavati delegation arrives," Ion replied. "Expect no act of hospitality whatsoever. Remember, they look upon us as man-hunters—slavers, in a way."

"Stop all engines," Yeshua commanded. The skimmer slid gently into the sea and glided to shore. Jeremy had to leap from the bow of the ship to a rock, where he received the starboard line and made it fast to the gnarled trunk of a stunted pine.

When they were all ashore, Yeshua pointed silently to the nearest hut, and they all made their way up a short, rocky incline to the village. The earth was hard and barren. The gusts were freezing. Yeshua tied the strings of his parka more tightly about his neck. They had now reached the first hut.

Yeshua knocked loudly three times on the makeshift door of rotten timbers which seemed to have been plucked out of the sea. There was no answer. And yet, there was a thin column of black smoke continuing to trickle out of the chimney.

Yeshua knocked again. "Anyone here?" he shouted.

After another pause, there was a muffled noise behind the door, and it creaked open a few centimeters.

Yeshua stepped back in alarm. There, sticking his head through the door was an extremely old man! Even on his trips to the Federations, Yeshua had never really beheld advanced old age at such close range. There were, to be sure, entire reservations set aside for the aged of the Dark Continents, but he had never had occasion to visit them. Now he recoiled in horror. The withered, toothless face disgusted him, terrified him! Death had written his signature all over the man's face. He was already no more than a shadow, fading swiftly into the Null!

Before Yeshua could recover sufficiently even to ask a question, the old man, contorted and grim, leaned out the door, bent around to his left and pointed. He pointed clearly to the third hut on the left, the topmost hut on the little incline. Then the villager pulled himself back, like a wizened old turtle withdrawing its head, and slammed the door. They could hear him barring it against any further interruption.

Yeshua turned and walked up the incline to the hut which had been pointed out. The others followed without comment. Again, Yeshua knocked. This time the door opened promptly. A woman, middle-aged by Federation standards, a babushka tied round her still dark hair, faced them calmly. Her countenance was open but distant.

"I am Yeshua," he announced quietly.

"We know," she replied.

"These are my friends. We were directed to your cabin —I'm not sure why—by one of your neighbors. May we come in?"

She did not reply, but left the door ajar and stood to one side so that they might let themselves in if they chose. They entered one by one, Yeshua first.

The room—there were only two in the dwelling—was sparsely furnished. A crude table, a few unmatched wooden chairs, an open fireplace on which a kettle was heating. The floor was of rough planking except near the hearth, where there was some stonework.

Standing near the fire—in fact, warming his hands over it—was a man, sturdy, erect and, Yeshua guessed, also middle-aged. His countenance was remarkably like that of the woman's: calm, open and alert, but also reserved and almost aloof. He turned around to view them squarely as they crowded into the room.

"I am Yeshua."

"I am Jeremiah."

Yeshua noticed that he wore a small black skullcap which contrasted sharply with his long blond hair. His beard, too, was long and blond, with just a touch of gray.

Yeshua had been briefed regarding the identity of the leading inhabitants of the Isle—in which category the people before him obviously belonged—but Jeremiah was not a name that he recognized. His looks must have reflected his puzzlement, for the man presently explained:

"Many of us take up new names when we leave Sukhavati. Passing through the IMOB is a kind of baptism, a Hegira to us, as you can imagine. I was previously a Leonardo, Eric." Yeshua's face lit up in recognition. "Svenson was my Federation name." The entire mission team now understood that they were in the presence of

242

the headman, or Abba, as they called him, of the Prodigal community.

"This is my wife Judith," he continued, "formally a Durkheim, Regina, Federation name, McBride."

It all fell into place in Yeshua's mind. Eric had taken over leadership of the Prodigals since the death, six months previously, of the Rothschild, Maximillian. He had lately married the Durkheim, Regina, although era-bonding was hardly ever elected by either of their functions on Sukhavati. "A dangerous and formidable antagonist," Yeshua's intelligence reports had described him.

"May we sit down?" Yeshua asked.

Jeremiah extended his hand, palm up, to the chairs. It was plain that he wished them to understand they were not his invited guests, although he intended no deliberate discourtesy. He remained standing by the fire.

"You know, I suppose, why we are here," Yeshua said.

"We know that you have come here, to the Isle of the Living, to try to persuade us to return to hell." He said this in a normal conversational tone. "You will not succeed."

Yeshua looked at his associates in amazement. Only Ion seemed not have lost his poise.

"Why," asked Ion quietly, "do you refer to Sukhavati, the 'Good Place,' as hell? Were you so very unhappy there?"

"What *is* hell?" Jeremiah asked. "Are you sure you would know when you were in it?"

None of the missioners made answer.

"Then I will define it for you," replied their interrogator, raising his voice. "Medieval imagery aside, hell is the state of permanent separation from God, who is infinite goodness and truth. Here, on the Isle of the Living, we are not permanently separated from Him. We hope one day to be joined to Him in an everlasting union. It will be more even than era-bonding; it will be eternal bonding. In such a union, neither partner will ever experience era-satiety or require horizon-modulation." Here, he smiled at them.

Almost at once, however, he grew serious again. "But as long as you misguided ones continue in your present situation in Sukhavati, era after era, rebirth after rebirth, you are, though no one of you realizes it, in a state of hell! You permanently separate yourselves from Him, who is absolute goodness and truth!"

"But was it so *unpleasant* on Sukhavati?" Lila interrupted with a smile of her own. "How can you call it hell, *really?*"

Jeremiah exploded. "Hell," he roared, "is *triviality!* The delectation, absorption and, finally, the suffocation of the soul in endless pleasant triviality!"

Ion took over. "You consider the founding of Sukhavati trivial?"

"Yes."

"The great scientific breakthroughs we have made?"

"Toys!"

"The conquest over death itself?"

"A trap!"

"Why a trap?" Jeremy asked, sincerely puzzled by the man.

"For the reason I've already explained," he answered impatiently. "You cannot creep and crawl to God through the eras. It requires a *leap!* The leap of dying! You people are cowering in a technological womb, refusing birth! You have covered your womb with fine tapestries, and you have air-conditioned it, but it is still only a womb! For love of it, you refuse life—everlasting life!"

Yeshua did not find this turn of their dialogue very profitable. "Jeremiah," he said, in an effort to change the subject, "would you mind telling us how all this began in your case? What started your disaffection with Sukhavati?"

"It will do no harm, I suppose. Yes, I will tell you. It's a strange tale, actually. My guess is, I'm the only Freedman who ever escaped Sukhavati by this particular route.

"In the fourth decade of my last era as a Leonardo, I became much interested in the history of painting. By my fifth decade, I had settled down as a specialist in 20th century art. The period fascinated me—kaleidoscopic, no central thrust, religious works, nihilistic works, everything. But it was the religious paintings that began to preoccupy me, particularly the fantastic work of an artist by the name of Chagall. To understand this artist I had to acquire a background in one of the Federation religions—Judaism, particularly the Hasidic movement. My fascination grew and grew. I put off psychic sabbatical twice, so engrossed did I become in my studies.

"Now comes the part which is difficult to explain. Through my readings in Hasidic literature, I began to sense the presence of . . . Him whom we call *Ribbono Shel Olom,* the Master of the Universe. Do you know whom I mean? Sukhavati, with all its achievements—the Arts-Alliance, the Gallery, the Theanthrolympiad—now seemed to me dust and ashes. Ignorant of the fullness of the law and tradition though I am, I have become, so far as is possible for me, a Hasid, a follower of the *Baal Shem Tov,* Master of the Name. Judith, my wife, is also a convert."

He had come to the end of his story. For a moment he rested his head against his chest. Then he looked up and, in a strong voice, concluded. "She and I believe that all that you people represent comes from another kingdom —*sitra achra,* 'the other side'! It is not the work of God. Sukhavati is a work of darkness. Indeed, it is the crown of darkness!"

Now Ion was aroused. "This is all fantasy," he said in a controlled but commanding voice. "How do you *know* what will happen to you after you leap, after you die? We, at least, know what will happen to us when we go on psychic sabbatical. We will be equitably—even mathematically—judged, and we will rise again. We will rise to the station and life-experience appropriate for us. We can demonstrate *our* immortality! What can *you* demonstrate? *Nothing!"*

Judith's voice was low and musical. "The Rabbi of Besht," she said, "once related the following parable: We read in the Talmud that only 49 of the 50 doors of understanding were opened to Moses. For the 50th, the Master of the Universe substituted faith. When it comes to the Infinite, even Moses cannot demonstrate; he must believe. Beyond a certain point of inquiry, both the learned and the simple are in a like condition. Only he who can pass through the 50th door is blessed."

"But it is so bleak; so cold on the Isle of the D—

on your island," Jeremy protested. He had pulled his chair closer to the fire and had not removed his outer garments at all. "Isn't this, truly, a joyless existence, compared to what you once possessed in Sukhavati? And this union with God that you seek—that's all in the unknown future, is it not? It seems to me," he concluded with a sad smile, "that you have given up much and gained little."

"In the Book of Chronicles," Judith replied, still without a trace of irritation, "it is written, 'Let the heart of them rejoice that seek the Lord.' Of this, the Apelier Reb had to say, 'When one seeks certain objects, he feels no gladness until his quest is successful. But when one seeks the Lord, *Ribbono Shel Olom,* the very act of seeking rejoices the heart of the seeker.' Do you think," she asked with a smile, "that we need to stage an Olympiad or construct a Gallery in order to rejoice?"

Ion groaned. "I have not yet read the Talmud, I admit. Somehow, I thought that was the one work which would never be relevant in Sukhavati. But I have read—and this may surprise you—a little of the Hasidic fathers. And it seems to me that the two of you are leaving something out of the picture—even from your own point of view."

Jeremiah and Judith looked at one another in surprise. "What is that?" Jeremiah asked with real curiosity.

"Did not the Rabbi of Bunham," Ion continued, as Jeremiah's eyebrows arched in amazement, "once compare the universe to an unfinished vessel? An unfinished vessel!" he repeated accusingly. "We, on Sukhavati, are completing the work. You Prodigals are abandoning it. How is it you do not prize the gift of immortality, which would enable you to complete the task set before you by your God—his work of creation?"

For once, Jeremiah had no answer. He stood, reflecting on the question, his mouth slightly open.

It was Judith who answered. "Do you think, then, it is only by achievements in mathematics, physics and philosophy that we complete the work of creation? No. I tell you, it is by suffering and dying, also. Otherwise," she added in a low voice, almost a whisper, "the Messiah cannot come!"

"Oh, I see," said Ion, with a frown, "Now you are

saying that Sukhavati, in addition to its other errors, tends to postpone the coming of the Messiah?"

Judith and Jeremiah answered simultaneously: "Yes!"

The missioners again looked at one another in perplexity, not knowing how to pursue the dialogue.

"When I became a student of history," Jeremiah added quietly, "I used to think that the clearest indication of the Adversary's hand was the success of a Hitler, a Stalin. I know better. Violence bears within it the seeds of its own destruction. I now believe the Adversary's master card is not terror, but endless . . . pleasant . . . triviality." His voice trailed into silence. He was clearly exhausted.

Jeremy made an effort to continue the discussion. "Who is this Ad——?"

"Never mind, Jeremy," Yeshua interrupted. He had understood these Prodigals very well, and had concluded that it was absolutely useless to prolong the discussion further. Their time was short. They had been instructed to return to Sukhavati as soon as possible. There were many other Prodigals they must talk to.

Still, there was one point of information that would be useful to them. "Are the others here all of the same mind as you?" he asked.

Jeremiah recovered a bit and laughed softly. "Sometimes it doesn't seem so. In fact, we think that one or two in our community are not fully sane—assuming anyone is."

"*We* are," said Ion.

"That is probably," said Judith, "the prevailing form of insanity on Sukhavati. It is unreal for human beings not to participate in the partial absurdity of the universe. Your total coherence is inhuman."

"Please," Yeshua brought them back. "My question was whether you were all of the same mind. Your answer was, 'Sometimes it doesn't *seem* so.' Does that mean that, essentially and for the most part, you *are* of the same mind?"

"Yes," answered Jeremiah, "essentially and for the most part. We are certainly not all Hasids, or even Jews, but we are all followers of 'the Way'—all members of the Catholic Israel of God. We may be Zen, or Roman or

247

Lutheran, but we all acknowledge something greater in the Cosmos than human beings. We walk on different paths, but they are all paths of righteousness—part of the holy network of roads we call 'the Way.' "

"The great thing," Judith added, smiling again, "is that faith is non-Euclidean. Our parallel paths meet in infinity. Do you know the words of the 20th century writer: 'All that goes up must converge'?"

Yeshua rose to leave and the others followed. His heart was unexpectedly heavy. There was so much that was good in these two, but it was hopeless to continue the dialogue. "We respect your feelings," he said to Judith and Jeremiah in parting. "Needless to say, we believe you are making a mistake that is as horrible as it is unnecessary. You know that we will always welcome your return to Sukhavati with open arms. There you can be reclaimed and recycled. But if you die here, outside the IMOB, you will most assuredly be swallowed up by the Null."

Jeremiah shrugged. "By your lights," he said.

They filed out silently, leaving Jeremiah and Judith staring after them, their backs to the fire.

There was, unfortunately, no time at all for them, once outside the hut, to confer together about what had just transpired. Raucous laughter and shouting enveloped them the moment they stepped out into the piercing air.

"Akbar! Akbar!" exclaimed Yeshua. I thought you had been cured!"

"And so I have been! But not by your Freuds, I'll tell you that!" The North African's dark eyes were flashing, his arms gesticulating in every direction. His appearance was altogether a wild one.

"Yes, I'm cured," Akbar continued, at the top of his lungs. "I'm cured of my base servitude, my psychic slavery to the whims and fantasies of your founder, God and slave-master—Strastnik! I no longer jump through the hoop of his dreams. You poor puppets! I exist now in my own right, stand on my own two feet! And do you know what you high and mighty missioners are? I'll tell you what you are—frail and drifting cobwebs of thought, spun out by a bored Sophia!

248

"I challenge you: show yourselves men! Stay here with us on the Isle of the Free! You can become real, too—if you've got the guts!"

"Akbar, Akbar," said Lila softly—she had known him in her professional capacity on Sukhavati. "Such bold words. Such angry words. Here you will die. You most assuredly will die if you do not return home with us to Sukhavati. Are you not afraid to die?"

"More of your Freudish trickery," he sneered. He pulled himself erect, folded his arms across his chest and looked her squarely in the eye. "While I am, death is not. When death is, I am not. Therefore, death is no concern of mine. I am a man!"

"Again, brave words, Akbar—but not your own. And only words! They are the words of Epicurus, and do you know where Epicurus is now? He is primeval silence. He has been swallowed up by the Null.

"No, Akbar, my friend. No matter what fine words you use to describe your new existential manhood and freedom, I want you to remember this: death is simply the black bag, the old black bag. They will surely stuff you in it if you do not return with us!"

There was quiet, for the first time since their exit from the hut. They could all see that Lila had touched a nerve. She knew her patient.

Then Akbar began to whimper. Tears streamed down his face. Finally, he was rent by mighty sobs. He fell to his knees and clutched Lila's legs. "Take me home," he wept. "Take me back with you. They'll put me in the black bag!"

Lila put her arms around his head, trying to comfort him, but still he wept. He was in great anxiety now. "No matter what these religious fanatics say about the Garden, the Vision and the World to Come," he sobbed, "death is still the old black bag! Lila, Yeshua, don't let them get me! Please don't let them!"

Lila and Yeshua looked at each other. They had saved their first Prodigal, albeit a partially deranged one. No matter. He could be selectively unwrinkled, placed on psychic sabbatical and reclaimed for future eras. He was *alive!* That was the important thing.

They approached the next hut, a little lower down the hill, to the right of Jeremiah's. There was no particular system of covering the Isle that Yeshua had in mind; they would simply make their rounds and speak to anyone who was willing to converse with them.

Jeremy knocked on the door. No answer. He knocked a second time. A feeble voice was heard from within, bidding them enter. Jeremy slowly opened the ill-fitting door, which scraped along the earthen floor. It was quite dark inside, and there was a disgusting, sour odor. No mistake; someone had vomited in the room, and not too long ago. An old coat had been nailed over the one window, further reducing the light. In the far corner, on the left, Jeremy made out a shapeless bulge of a couch, and on it, covered with a ragged quilt, lay an old man—quite ill, to judge from his pale, haggard face and weak voice.

Illness! Yeshua shuddered. He had certainly seen sick people in the Federations, but never the desperately ill, never those close to death in the hospital wards of the Dark Continents.

The man on the couch attempted to turn, so as to see them better, but the movement sent a flash of pain through his body. He fell back with a weak groan.

"Is that you, Judith?" he finally gasped. "Come in, come in."

"No, I'm sorry, sir. It is not Judith," said Jeremy. "We are visitors from Sukhavati. Yeshua is with us."

The countenance of the old man became, if possible, paler than before. "Ah yes, I was told that your vessel had been sighted."

"May we come in and speak with you for awhile?" Yeshua asked.

"If you like." His tone was fearful but not unfriendly.

"May we ask your name?"

"I am Abraham. You see," he smiled feebly, "I have left my father's house and have traveled to a strange land."

"And before, in Sukhavati?"

"I was a Plato. I was called Philo. My Federation name was Weiss." Ion's face lit up; this man had been one of the most revered philosophers on the island four or five decades ago.

"And have you also embraced religion, old man?" Yajnavalkya asked. He had maintained his customary silence up to this point, but something about this wretchedly ill old man touched him, some kind of nobility on the old man's suffering countenance.

"I have become a Christian," he answered. And, turning his head so as to look directly at Yeshua, he added, "I follow Him whose name you bear, O 'Shepherd of the Flock.' " He smiled gently and turned his head away.

"Do you agree, then, with Jeremiah," Ion asked, "that we are, as he puts it, *sitra achra,* the work of the other side?"

The old man looked a little embarassed. "Jeremiah is a very strong and forthright personality. For myself, I reject your way of life, but I think . . ." he paused, as much for breath as for reflection. "I think that you know not what you do. I think that perhaps you are not from hell, but *limbo!"*

"You mean," said Ion, "that we are innocent and childish?"

"Infants!" Old Abraham smiled again. His own half-toothless smile was childlike.

Yeshua had gradually adjusted himself to the room and its occupant. He no longer found the old man repulsive. On the contrary. Despite the rags and offensive odors, he found in Abraham an elusive and intangible charm.

"Abraham," he said kindly, "do you realize that you are close to death?"

"I *am* close to death."

"We could still reclaim you, Abraham. As a Christian, you must value life."

"I do."

"Then you will come with us?" There was a new note of hope and excitement in Yeshua's voice.

But Abraham only sighed. "You must have gone through this already with Jeremiah. Our views on these matters, you know, are basically the same. Why weary yourselves and me any further?"

Seeing their disappointment, he attempted a further explanation. "You must understand, my friends, here, on this isle, I am in Israel. Holy Land. The jumping-off

251

point for eternity. This whole earth—with the solitary exception of tiny Sukhavati—is Israel!" His voice was gathering strength as he went on. Now he half-rose from the couch: "You, alone, on all the earth are deprived of eternity! You are deprived of it because you believe you already possess it. You count yourself rich—and you are; healthy—and you are; powerful and intelligent—and you are. You count yourselves WELL—and you are *not!* Because, my friends, Christ comes not to heal the well, but the sick. If, after all, Jeremiah should be right, and Sukhavati does derive from hell, I want you to understand one thing: Hell is always locked from the inside!"

There was silence. The old man's sudden resurgence had put them in awe.

"And you, if you were really a Christian," Yeshua finally broke in rather sternly, "would return with us to Sukhavati. Christ is the very prototype of our community! God-man is what he claimed to be, and God-men is what we have become! He came that you might have life, and have it more abundantly. It is *we* who offer that abundance. Abundance without end!"

"You . . . you put yourselves on His level?" gasped Abraham.

"Higher!" Yeshua replied without the slightest hesitation. "Christ saw our day and was glad! When the disciples were in awe of his miracles, he prophesied to them: 'Greater things than these shall you do.' On Sukhavati we have done them. He saved Lazarus; we have saved the 144,000! And we stand ready to save all who are worthy. *You* are worthy." In a voice of solemn command, Yeshua now addressed him. "Arise, Abraham, take up thy bed and walk—come back with us to Sukhavati!"

The old man screamed! "Go away, go away! You are frightening me!" Then he fell back to the couch and lay totally inert. For a moment, they were afraid that he had died at their hands, so faint was his breathing. Finally, his eyes opened once again and his lips began to move. They had to strain to catch his whisper.

"Do you know why I was so terrified?" he muttered, looking at Yeshua. "It's because you are so like Him! You speak not as one who has been taught in the schools, but as one with authority. You promise happiness; you promise unending life. It is all so *nearly* true that it is horrifying. Perhaps you are, after all, *sitra achra!*"

Abraham turned his face to the wall, unwilling to speak with them further.

Yeshua gazed sadly at the others and shook his head. They had failed once more. They rose silently and began to file out.

It was Lila who heard him. Abraham had turned toward them again, and had called after them feebly. "Wait," he said. "I am sorry for my outburst. I still believe you know not what you do." He was fighting for breath. "Remember, this is Israel, holy soil. The land of the living. You are welcome here. I implore you. Leave your father's home, for your father, Strastnik is the father of lies!" He was gasping now; they were alarmed. "Leave your father's home. Abide in the land that the Lord will show you—is showing you now!" He fell back on the couch.

They watched him for several minutes before they realized that he had been swallowed by the Null! Neither Yeshua nor the others had ever seen it before.

It totally overpowered Ion. The old man had simply ceased to be, before his very eyes. His legs buckled, and Yajnavalkya and Lila had to help him out. They, too, had found the scene horrible. Once out in the open air, Lila went behind a clump of battered pines and threw up.

But strangely enough, it did not so affect Jeremy and Yeshua. They remained in the hut for a few moments after the others had rushed Ion out. Old Abraham lay peacefully on his bed. And that is what they felt: peace, not horror. The two men looked at each other and realized they were experiencing the same thing. Finally, Yeshua said, "Shalom, old man," and walked out. Jeremy followed. The two did not discuss the matter further.

When they rejoined the others, Lila was saying, "I wonder if we should try to make some arrangements for Abraham."

"No," said Ion, still shaky over what he had witnessed. "Let us leave the dead to bury the dead." He could take no more of it.

So it continued. For the most part, they found themselves unsuccessful. It is true that here and there they were able to win back a Prodigal, but this usually turned out to be what the inhabitants called a postulant—someone who had only come to the Isle of the Dead in the last two or three years, and who was not yet considered stable in his vocation.

All hopes of quickly filling their skimmer with reclaimed Prodigals and making an early return to Sukhavati were abandoned. Besides, it was very important to Yeshua, personally, to find Hans and Zoe and talk with them. The Prodigals were being very protective of them, since they had only been on the Isle for a month and were not judged ready to confront a delegation from Sukhavati. It was impossible to elicit any information regarding their whereabouts. The missioners thus found it necessary to appropriate one of the larger abandoned shacks and make it into a temporary headquarters for themselves and their reclaimed Prodigals. It was clear that they were here for the entire week.

It was Yajnavalkya who partially salvaged the mission. Of all the members of the team that Yeshua had assembled, he turned out to be the most effective. Finally, he asked permission to detach himself from the group to work alone. It was granted. Yeshua had thought all along that events might turn out so. Adding Yajnavalkya to the team had been an inspiration. Exactly how he operated they did not know. Nor did they ask, convinced as they were that none of them would be able to duplicate his expertise, in any case. Yeshua had it in mind, however, to question him in detail upon their return to Sukhavati. He was sure that Yajnavalkya, by drawing the Prodigals into deep meditation, was able to satisfy the emptiness which Ion had identified as UD, Ultimacy Deficiency.

But another question that Yeshua would have to confront was his own ineffectiveness—and *growing* ineffectiveness—on this mission. Never, in six full decades of service, had he proved so inept. Here also, he had an intimation of the truth, but he did not want to face it. Face it shortly, he must. He knew his time of respite was brief. But for the moment, he could not.

On the sixth and final morning of their stay on the

Isle of the Dead, they were all sitting around a sputtering fire in the deserted shack. Yajnavalkya had sent them three more reclaimed Prodigals during the night. No one had rested very well. Despite the noisy fire (the brushwood had been wet with sleet and ice), the hut was still extremely cold. You could see your breath in the damp air. Except for the crackling fire, the room was perfectly still. The reclaimees sent them by Yajnavalkya were completely worn out by their strenuous experience with him, and in no mood for further conversation. Yeshua was just as pleased, for at that point he could not have given them any. Most of them sat, knees up, on the earthen floor near the fire, staring dreamily into the embers. One or two paced up and down, lost in their own reflections.

Suddenly, loud cries were heard outside the hut, emanating from a point near the cove.

"Out! Out, you fraud! I gave you a fair test. Any real seer would have known how to conduct himself. You failed! All your so-called duration-analysis is mere breath-and-spinal cord technology, kindergarten mysticism. Even your *Alpha*-bliss is a vulgar resonance of the nerve-chords, spiritual masturbation. That's what you're teaching people—spiritual masturbation!"

Yeshua and the other missioners rushed out of their hut to the scene of the commotion. A small crowd of Prodigals had gathered at the bottom of the hill, near the very last hut before the cove. There they saw a rather short man, an Oriental, dressed in a long, tattered woolen robe. His shaved head and flailing arms bobbed in the air as he stood shouting at poor Yajnavalkya. The latter, highly mortified, was vainly attempting to quiet his antagonist. They stood there, oblivious to the driving sleet and rain on this dark, chill morning.

Yeshua strode over to the two of them, made his identity known, and asked the angry Prodigal his name.

"My name is Takuan, after the Zen master whose teaching I have adopted. My neighbors here call me Basho, however." Now he lowered his voice for the first time and smiled a little. "They seem to think it suits my personality. In Samsara—that is, Sukhavati—I was a Freud, Chuang Tzu."

Lila gasped. "I remember you! You were my instructor

255

for many months when I was a Newly-Aware! It must have been all of 90 or 95 years ago."

"Indeed. I am surprised that you remember the time. Time means nothing to you people." His voice had regained its sternness, but it was less loud than before.

"What was the nature of the test," asked Yeshua, hoping to initiate some kind of civil dialogue, "that you administered to Yajnavalkya?"

"The same test that the master Nan-in once gave to his disciple, Tenno, who was passing himself off as a teacher of mysticism."

"Would you explain it to us?" asked Yeshua courteously.

"Surely," said Basho, somewhat mollified. "But I don't know if you will be able to understand it. Look around you. It's a rainy day. I welcomed this great Sukhavati mystic of yours into my home. And, as he was soaking wet and chilled, I had bade him remove his outer coat, hand it on a peg above my wooden clogs, and join me at the fire, to warm himself.

"That was when he told me he was a mystic. A Yajnavalkya, no less. And he offered to introduce me to the ecstasies of meditation. I am always willing to learn from a master, but first I like to be sure I am in the hands of a master.

"So I said to him, simply, 'Tell me, O Yajnavalkya, when you hung up your coat to dry a moment ago, did you hang it on the peg to the left or to the right of my clogs?'

"And do you know that this prince of concentration, this high potentate of focused reflection, could not even recapture the location of his soaking wet coat. He was completely unable to answer my question. Now, when the Zen monk Tenno found that he was unable to answer the identical question put to him by the Abbot Nan-in; he gave up teaching Zen and, like an honest man, went back to his apprenticeship for six more years of meditation. And that is my advice to this Sukhavati mystic!"

"But the recall of such details has nothing to do with mysticism," protested Yajnavalkya, his habitual calm reserve completely shot.

"It has nothing to do with *beginners!*" Basho exploded.

"All novices in meditation begin by withdrawing into themselves and dismissing the world as unreal, as maya. They think the Buddha-reality cannot possibly be found in a wet coat or a pair of wooden clogs. They are all for the peaks of Himalaya, these novices. It is only years later, after much courageous striving, humiliation and purifying, that a few of them are privileged to behold the transfiguration of mud, of straw, of a wooden bowl. I don't think you even know where the mystery *is,* O Transcendental One, let alone how to delineate it! But I'll tell you this, for your own future enlightenment: you won't find the mystery with your Sunday mind; you will only find it with your everyday mind."

Yeshua mediated. "The intricacies of the higher flights of the spirit, I leave to you both," he said. "But surely, Basho, you have been present at the solemn moment of the Theanthrolympiad, during the Days of Awe, when the Siddhartha blesses us and bestows upon each of us a taste of his own *Alpha*-bliss."

"I have been present many times, Yeshua," he replied, unruffled.

"And surely you do not find that experience either trivial or fraudulent."

"I do!" he snapped back. "I used the phrase 'spiritual masturbation' a moment back, and I stick to that description of the experience. All the Sophia really does is trigger a few brain centers. Brain-bliss is not the point of meditation! It's normally just a *sign* that the real work—the emptying-out of the pigsty, the renovation of the madhouse—has been carried out: a back-breaking, soul-hollowing effort that usually takes years. The Sophia bypasses the real work and gives us the sign—the sign without the substance. And wrong signs are lies. They lead to wrong turns, smash-ups, fatalities!"

Yeshua stared at him in disbelief. "Are you implying," his voice quivered," that the Founder himself does not experience Ultimacy, that he did not attain the Absolute when he was zenithed, and that we will not, either?"

"There is no doubt about it," answered Basho, cooly. *"Alpha*-bliss is a relatively low and vulgar phenomenon in the life of meditation. And in this case, it's more like a psychic short-circuit than a real event in the growth of the spirit. Wires are being crossed long before the poor little spirit is deserving of the experience. Listen, if you want to play with the switchboard of the brain, you can push buttons endlessly: sex buttons, fear buttons, aggression buttons—yes, and spiritual ecstasy buttons. Even drugs and slow breathing can do that much. But to mistake this playful technology for the true work of the spirit is, I must tell you, a mere beginner's error—unfortunately, one fraught with grave consequences. *Alpha*-bliss is a psychic lollypop. Those who suck on it forever remain infants into eternity."

"Even if what you say is true, which I doubt," Yeshua answered (Yajnavalkya apparently wanted no more part in the dialogue), "we have the *time* to reach the Absolute. We don't claim perfection. We are Entopians, after all. But we progress! Through all the ages, we progress. You do not! Time comes to a stop for each of you!"

"Time! Time, indeed! You think you are masters of it," Basho retorted. "Time: 'Queen Solvent for all that is rich and complex!'" He laughed sardonically. "I say to you, you are in a condition exactly the reverse of what you suppose! Your religious symbol is a clock—a timepiece with an *ankh*, the Egyptian symbol of eternity, adorning it. You loll in time, you bathe in it, you roll over and frolic in it like the salt ocean from which you evolved. You believe in time; you think that you love, honor and revere it.

"I say, you step on time, spit on it and desecrate it! You throw it away as if it were refuse—which, in effect, it is, in Sukhavati. What, after all, are your judgment engineers but psychic sanitation men. You can no longer value the present moment than a multimillionaire can value a penny. Same reason. You have too much. It's become unreal.

"Enough of my long discourse. I'm going to tell you a short Zen story. If you get it, you understand me; if you don't, I've been talking to the wind. Are you ready? Yajnavalkya, I ask you to excuse my crudeness.

"Once a nobleman came to Takuan, the Zen monk, to ask how he could more profitably pass the time. This nobleman, by reason of his rank and position, was forced to sit for many hours a day in stiff and formal ceremony,

258

receiving homage from officials. Takuan wrote his answer down in just eight Chinese characters and handed the slip of paper to the nobleman. Translated literally, his message read:

Not twice, this day.
Inch time, foot gem."

With that, Basho smiled, bowed courteously, walked back to his ramshackle little hut, and slammed the door behind him.

The Sukhavati emissaries huddled together, looking at one another blankly. It was Yeshua who understood it first.

"Not twice, this day. That means, I think, that *this* day—today, this moment—will never come again, for all eternity.

"Inch time, foot gem. I suppose he was saying that each minute is worth a dozen times its weight in diamonds."

"Why?" asked Lila.

"Because it's irrecoverable."

They all stood for a minute, lost in reverie. Then Yeshua snapped them out of it. "It is time to return to Sukhavati. Our immunization expires tomorrow. They obviously do not intend to allow us to talk to Hans and Zoe, so there is no point in further delay. Jeremy and I will go aboard the skimmer and make the necessary preparations. The rest of you will go back to our hut to escort our reclaimees. We will all meet aboard the marine skimmer in one hour."

They departed silently—all except Jeremy.

"May I speak with you a moment, sir?"

Yeshua turned about to face him.

"I'm not returning, Yeshua."

"I know." In the background, Yeshua could see the lively, pretty Leonardo, Maritta, that Jeremy had tried to reclaim. But Maritta, alone, was not the answer. Jeremy was a man who pushed questions to the end.

Jeremy stood there, waiting, not without apprehension, for Yeshua's impassioned reaction. It never came.

"Good-bye Jeremy."

"Good-bye, sir."

Yeshua turned and walked slowly to the cove.

When he got aboard the skimmer, Yeshua went below to inspect the engines. There he found Hans and Zoe.

The three embraced as if they had not seen one another for a quarter of an era. Yeshua and Zoe had tears in their eyes. Finally, Yeshua stepped back, grasping each of them by an arm.

"Does this mean, you have resolved to return to Sukhavati?" he asked in a low and tremulous voice.

"No, Yeshua," Zoe replied softly. "But we had to see you; we had to try to explain. The others didn't want us to. They were afraid you would overwhelm us with persuasive reasons why we should go back. So we hid in the last place anyone would think to look for us—your missioners *or* the Prodigals."

"I'm so happy you did. It saddened me to think I might not see you again. And I must tell you, frankly, that it still saddens me to think of the two of you dying here on this island."

Zoe placed two fingers on Yeshua's mouth. "Please don't say anything to break our resolution, Yeshua. We're weak enough, God knows. We just want to explain why, to an old friend."

Hans bowed his head.

At last, Yeshua said, "All right, Hans. Why?"

Hans threw up his hands and began to pace up and down the small engine room. "I hardly know where to begin," he said. "There was the example of men like Myshkin, who would not trade 'meaning' for longevity. There was the symbolic failure of Project Resurrection— you have to agree that a literary Jesus is an inadequate substitute for the original Galilean. You know that my whole era I have—how do they say it in the Federations? —horsed around with one brilliant but ineffectual stunt after another. Yeshua, I can't explain! I can explain Cowper's Unified Field theory, but I can't explain why I'm choosing this—" He waved his arm in the direction of the Isle of the Dead, "over Sukhavati. Hans groaned aloud. "Zoe, you've got to do the explaining for me!"

Yeshua turned to face her squarely. She was still beautiful, but not exactly in the way she had been. Her face certainly showed the emotional wear and tear she had been through in recent days.

"Well, I'm not so learned as Hans, Yeshua—yet he and I love each other. I think my answer will do for us both. Do you remember, Yeshua, when you first saw me?"

"I will never forget it, Zoe. It was my first day as a Newly-Aware. Ananda was giving me my first introduction to Sukhavati. I met you in a shop. I forget just what kind——"

"Fabrication Unit No. 6," she reminded him.

"And I was very attracted to you."

"Yes, I could tell. But nothing came of that, did it Yeshua? And the second time you met me, do you remember that, too?"

"Of course I do, Zoe," he replied with a tinge of embarrassment.

"It was at the Gallery, wasn't it?"

"Yes, Zoe, but——"

"As important a person as you were, you were so attracted to me that you came to my apartment."

"Zoe——"

"No, let me continue, Yeshua, it's important. You came in, and I had never been so excited! I thought that an experience with you would surely lead to era-culmination. But nothing happened, did it?

Yeshua groaned. "I'm sorry, Zoe. You know I didn't——"

"Yeshua, you still don't understand. Now listen to me carefully. The important thing was not that you hurt me, or trifled with me, or that there was no dignity in our meeting. All of that is so, but not important just now. What is important is that, in a short time, *none of it mattered*—my hurt, your hurt, our mutual ignorance, the mutual indignity. I got over it. You got over it. We get over *everything* in Sukhavati. Psychic sabbatical *guarantees* that we can get over everything." Zoe began to weep quietly.

"Do you see what she's saying, Yeshua?" Hans asked, taking Zoe in his arms. "It's the preposition, 'over'. It's an inhuman preposition in the context of human relationships. On Sukhavati, we don't 'go through,' we 'get over.'

261

It's a world of totalitarian playfulness. I sensed that, and behaved accordingly."

Yeshua was silent. Even if he had had an answer to make, he had promised Zoe that he would not contest their decision.

"Maybe Sukhavati was filled with love when Strastnik founded it," Hans continued. "But there is such a thing as devolution as well as evolution. And I think the original self-donation has now devolved to a kind of carefree tolerance: 'You can't really hurt me, you know, so why should I hurt you?' There is no relationship in Sukhavati which can not be permanently terminated at the first sign of a little boredom.

"For some reason," Hans concluded, "the knowledge that we are going to die has added a totally new dimension to life. How I treat Zoe, how she treats me, *counts!* We're not going to 'get over' one another, we are not going to be selectively unwrinkled and placed on psychic sabbatical. Now I'm *alive;* before, I was buoyant."

Yeshua managed a little sad smile. Hans hadn't lost all his buoyancy, either. He looked at his watch. "Zoe, Hans—you must go. The others will be returning shortly." Once more, the three embraced. A long, last embrace. Without further words, they parted. The return trip was uneventful.

CHAPTER XVI

'*It*'

On arrival in Sukhavati, Yeshua made straight for his own residence. Leaping the stairs three at a time, he rushed to his private quarters. Helen was actually looking at the door when he came in.

"You have betrayed Sukhavati, Yeshua." There were no histrionics, but it was a terrible moment for them both.

"I have not yet taken any action, Helen! I have returned home."

"But in your heart, you have already betrayed her."

"Helen, I don't know at this moment *where* my heart is. But what if I should be faced with the choice of betraying Sukhavati or betraying myself?"

"And what if I should be faced with the choice of staying with you or remaining in Sukhavati?"

Then they threw themselves into one another's arms and wept. Wept bitterly. When they had cried themselves out—even then, Yeshua had taken the precaution of removing their PSI's—Yeshua asked, "Helen, if it did come to that, what would you do?"

"Yeshua, I don't know. Tell me what happened with the Prodigals. I can feel the drift of your experiences, but this time it's necessary that I hear them in detail.

First he told her of Jeremiah and Judith, of their great faith in *Ribbono Shel Olom* and their fear of *sitra achra*. Then he narrated Lila's successful reclamation of the deranged Akbar. When he came to the part about the black bag, Helen shuddered. She shuddered again when he described his first-hand observations of extreme old age, mortal illness and the death of old Abraham. Basho's attack on Yajnavalkya she found to be a source of equal amusement and alarm. Finally, Yeshua repeated, almost word for word, Zoe's evaluation of life on Sukhavati.

"Do you think that's a fair charge, Yeshua—that here we get over everyone and everything?"

"What would you do if I left?" he asked in return. "Would you come with me? Continue on in your era? Or go on psychic sabbatical?"

"Certainly not continue on! How could you even think that? Yeshua, my soul is porous to yours. You and I are one. But the black bag, Yeshua, the black bag!" She burst into tears once again. "Hell, limbo, *sitra achra*, spiritual masturbation—these are all words. But the black bag is real! Real! Real! I'm frightened of it! I want to *be*, to

263

exist, to laugh, to love, to be warm, to be solaced! You ask me to walk with you into the Null."

He held her close. For a long time they sat silently, embracing, rocking gently back and forth. After a while, she began to sing from the Song of Solomon:

> Upon my bed by night
> I sought him whom my soul loves;
> I sought him, but found him not:
> I called him, but he gave no answer.
> I will rise now and go about the city,
> In the streets and in the squares:
> I will seek him whom my soul loves.

And he recited back:

> Set me as a seal upon your heart,
>   as a seal upon your arm;
> For love is strong as death,
>   and jealousy as cruel as the grave.

She smiled, looked up at him, and quoted from the Book of Ruth:

> Where you go, I will go,
> And where you lodge I will lodge;
> Your people shall be my people,
> And your God my God.
> Where you die I will die,
> And there will I be buried.
> May the Lord do so to me and more also,
> If aught but death parts me from thee.

"Is that your decision, Helen?"

"That is my decision, Yeshua."

"This moment means more to me"—the tears streamed openly down his face—"than the moment of my rebirth, the day I was horizoned, the week I was purposed. More even, than the night you and I were first solaced. But we must decide this together. Stay or go, our decision will be mutual."

"Yes, yes!" She felt her strength coming back to her. "It

is the greatest moment of my era also—and although I can't prove it," she laughed, "of any of my eras!" They laughed together. "No," she said, taking his head in her arms, "I don't ever want to get over you! No selective memory-euthanasia! No discretionary unwrinkling!"

They were solaced that night, and it went beyond all their past solacing.

At 3 p.m. on the third day following Yeshua's return, Amitabha placed a call to his residence. He had intuited that it would have been useless to call earlier.

"Yeshua," he said to him over the audio-visual, "you really ought to have come directly to Dharma House with your report on the Prodigals. When you did not, I refrained from calling you for as long as I possibly could. But I must tell you that at 12 noon, today, the Sophia named the day and almost the hour of Sukhavati's Interior Transformation. *It will occur this very evening!* Yeshua, I must have you with me in Nirvana-Crypt, by the side of the Sophia!"

Nothing Amitabha could have said, fitted in better with the plan that Yeshua was formulating. "Sir," he asked, "may I bring Helen with me?"

"That goes without saying, Yeshua."

"When Amitabha had switched off, Yeshua outlined his plan to Helen. She refused at first to help him. "You'd be within your rights," she said, "But Yeshua, that would be too much for me."

"How else could we ever find out?" he replied." How else could we ever know for sure? Helen, I loathe the black bag as much as anyone in Sukhavati. More, perhaps. I was not chosen Era-Yeshua by the Sophia without reason. But we've simply got to get to the bottom of the whole thing. Helen, what is the basic article of faith on Sukhavati?"

"That the Sophia can neither deceive nor be deceived."

"Very well. If we find that's true, we stay. If it's false, we go over to the Prodigals!"

Finally, Helen agreed to help in the plan. It involved measures so extreme that she trembled in anticipation, but she could come up with no alternative.

Helen took the wheel on their drive to Dharma House. Never had Sukhavati seemed so tranquil as at this moment, thought Yeshua. It was 6 p.m. The four-hour working day had ended an hour ago. The citizens had already reached home or the recreation center of their choice for the evening. The streets were very quiet, and that particular fragrance which Yeshua had found nowhere else in all his travels—that combination of brisk sea air with the lazy redolence of tropical flowers—was particularly marked in the early evening stillness.

> Baruch Atah Adonoy.
> Adam, Melech Haolom.

> Blessed art thou, O Lord,
> Man, King of the Universe.

He was recalling the words and the scene of his ordination. Amitabha had placed his hands on Yeshua's head. It was no lightweight benediction. "Reign in splendor and peace, Yeshua Nabi, commencing this 3rd day of August, 126, Era A.D., Amitabha Djilov. It is done!" Yeshua's memory of the day was positively photographic. So indelibly had he been purposed that it was alive in him yet, 70 years later.

"Perhaps," he said aloud to Helen, "we will not have to give all this up, after all." He knew without words that she was experiencing the exquisite beauty of the city exactly as he.

He had asked seven questions on the last day of his arduous sacrament. Seven represented fullness. Now he had an eighth.

They were ushered immediately into Nirvana-Crypt by the Alexander on duty. As soon as they entered, the door behind them was electronically sealed. Only Amitabha was in the Crypt, sitting by the side of the Sophia, in silent vigil. IT, the moment of Interior Transformation— "as great an event as the founding of Sukhavati"—was at hand. He had dressed himself in his rich official robes.

"Good evening, sir," said Yeshua.

"Amitabha nodded cooly and bid them occupy the two

266

chairs which they could now make out in the dark crypt, one on either side of him.

"I will not attempt to dissemble the fact, Yeshua, that I know that the purpose within you is paralytic. What was once a blazing fire, warming and enlightening all Sukhavati, is now a damp smouldering glimmer, near to extinction. In your seven decades of service, you could not have chosen a worse moment for metaphysical infection. How we need you now! Are you truly lost to us, or can you be healed? Helen, I know also that you are in a similar condition. But that does not surprise me."

"The hands placed on my head during my ordination as Era-Yeshua were not light ones, sir. I did return home from the Prodigals. Partly for Helen, it is true, but partly because my Sukhavati purpose is etched in diamonds and fire within me. It is not totally extinguished yet. Possibly you can revive the flame before the moment of Interior Transformation arrives. I don't know.

"One thing I do know, the oxygen which my flame of purpose needs is the oxygen of truth. For 70 years, the seven questions you answered on the day I was purposed have sufficed. Now I have another question."

"What is your question, Yeshua? I will do my best to answer it."

"I mean no disrespect, Amitabha, but this is a question which I must have answered for me by the Sophia."

"What is the question?"

"Is there a God?"

Amitabha sat stunned for several moments. Then, recovering, he laughed out loud. "You must be joking, Yeshua. This is childishness!"

Helen spoke up for the first time. "We're not joking, Amitabha, and we don't care how childish it may seem to others. That is the question we want the Sophia to answer —the Sophia who can neither deceive nor be deceived!"

"Sir," said Yeshua, "what we are really asking is not so childish. The question behind all other questions is: *Why is anything?* We know Strastnik's first law of biotheology: "What is freely and absolutely self-donating cannot not be." But we no longer believe there is anything about

267

atomic particles or cosmic electricity that is freely and absolutely self-donating. Thus our question about God. Perhaps *He* is self-donation."

"Metaphysical cancer!" pronounced the Overseer. "There is no doubt about it. You have caught it from the Prodigals! They lust insatiably, insanely, after meaning. Paradise is not sufficient; they must have absolute meaning too! The whole universe, in its opacity, is not enough for them. They will have ultimate meaning or nothing at all. So be it! They are their own judgment engineers! They will get what they secretly want—the Null Imperium! And so will you both, unless you come to your senses!"

"Perhaps Sukhavati does not hold a monopoly on immortality," suggested Yeshua.

"I don't follow," Amitabha replied.

"It's a corollary that Hans proposed to one of the laws of biotheology. It was never officially accepted, but I thought it made sense."

"Much good it did that renegade Archimedes! Well, what was his theory?"

"His theory was this: nature, the universe or God—whichever one, or all three in combination—never seems to create a craving for which there is not a possible satisfaction. Living things hunger; there is food. They thirst; there is water. Animals and men have sexual drives; there is the availability of an opposite sex. Now of all the animals, only man is aware beforehand of his inevitable death, and ever since the Stone Age, he has hungered, thirsted and yearned for continuity and survival! *Is this drive alone, of all the drives implanted by nature, doomed to be thwarted?*"

"There is food, Yeshua; but men starve. There is water; and men die of thirst. There is sexual hunger, but some men are forced into celibacy—prisoners and the like. Hans proves nothing."

"No, Amitabha. You overlook a crucial point. Hans did not suggest that no one ever dies of hunger or thirst. He says that nature did not implant the drive without their being the *possibility* of its satisfaction. I may die of thirst because I am in a desert where there is no water.

But thirst was not created in the world without the simultaneous and necessary creation of water to quench it. Water exists! You have to get to it."

"And therefore, you suggest, so does immortality?"

"Yes."

"You are correct, Yeshua! So it does. Right here on Sukhavati! But you have to get to it!"

"And prior to the existence of Sukhavati?" Yeshua pressed. "Could no one obtain it? Was there no possibility to satisfy this drive for continuity and survival, which is so strong in man?"

"The drive, Yeshua, was nature's way of telling man to get on with the job—to create his *own* immortality, since god or nature had been so parsimonious!"

"But——"

"Really, Yeshua, are we to carry on this dialogue forever? The questions you raise are unanswerable. They lead to endless semantic circles."

"Then let us put the question to the Sophia—who can neither deceive nor be deceived!"

"The question has never come up on Sukhavati! We have no need of a God. We have no old age, no illness, no death—none of the breaking points that societies on the dark continents must contend with. Any Durkheim will tell you that the Federations need gods to serve as bridges over the breaking points, or their societies might collapse. If a man works from nine to five all his life for his family, and then his family is wiped out in some absurd accident, why should he get up and work again? They need gods. They need 'larger meanings'—giant theological blotters—to soak up the absurdities. Sukhavati has no such need. We have no breaking points. We bend a little—the SERD makes sure that we do. It's healthy for us. But we don't break. We don't die. When we reach era-satiety, we go on psychic sabbatical. Where is there room for God in our system?"

"Even after primitive man learned that he needed air to live," replied Yeshua, "he did not know he needed oxygen. The oxygen was in the air, but he had no knowledge of it. It is possible that Sukhavati lives in ignorance of the munificence of Yahweh."

269

"Yahweh, is it? You can't program Yahweh into a computer."

"The Sophia, of course, is more than that, Amitabha." Yeshua could not refrain from smiling. "And you have had to tell me so many times. No special programing is necessary for this question. For well over a thousand years, the Sophia has been making measurements, comparisons, judgments, about men and the world they live in. By this time, the Sophia has reached an opinion on the probability of a planned or unplanned universe, on cosmic order or cosmic entropy."

"You insist on playing this charade at what is perhaps the most critical moment in Sukhavati's history? Is there no other way to reach you, to reason with you?"

"No other way."

"Then ask and be damned! Literally!"

Helen inserted the question, which the two of them had carefully coded beforehand, into the Sophia. There was the customary quiet electronic whirr. Then it jammed! The Sophia stopped and started erratically, in an unprecedented manner. Finally, she regurgitated the coded insert and switched off.

"I told you you couldn't program Yahweh into the Sophia," Amitabha snapped. His face was very red, and one of the vessels in his neck was swollen to the point of bursting.

"Re-insert the question!" Yeshua ordered. "The Sophia has the cumulative information to answer this question. She just went into temporary shock, that is all. It will pass."

Helen reinserted the coded question. Again the Sophia sputtered, coughed and rejected the message.

"Will you not at last desist, before you throw her delicate symbiotic balance off center!" Amitabha shouted.

"Once more!" ordered Yeshua.

The erratic stopping and starting finally gave way to the familiar smooth whirr. A coded tear sheet popped up. Yeshua seized it and frantically decoded it. Then he let it drop from his hands, his face bewildered and thoughtful.

"Yeshua, *please!*" said Helen. "What was the answer?"

"ABIDE, NOT KNOWING."

All three were lost in silence.

Even the Yajnavalkyas, the trained specialists of durational analysis, would have been in awe at the density of the three minutes which now elapsed in total silence. Then, in a firm clear voice, Yeshua pronounced, *"I reject the Sophia's judgment!"*

These were the most violent, rebellious words a citizen of Sukhavati Entopia could utter. And he uttered them in Nirvana-Crypt, in the presence of the Founder. Yeshua's allegiance to the island had snapped. And Helen's with his.

"Why do you not accept the words of the Sophia?" Amitabha asked. The relationship between the two men was now finished; Yeshua had stamped out the last faint ember of Sukhavati-purpose. Yet, Amitabha wanted to understand what had happened. A Yajnavalkya had once been lost in the ninth era, but in the entire history of Sukhavati, no Era-Yeshua had ever defected before.

"I now know the Sophia both deceives and is deceived," answered Nabi cooly. He was Era-Yeshua no longer.

"Explain yourself."

"The Sophia is a symbiotic dynamism in which there are two components: a logic-box, a computer, and the living intuition of a great mind, Strastnik. As far as the computer component is concerned, it *must* assert the existence of a God—not a personal Yahweh, to be sure, but some first-cause-of-the-universe. And do you know why? Because a logic-box is always Aristotelian! It always presupposes both the Aristotelian law of contradiction and the Aristotelian presupposition of strict causality. With such presuppositions, there has to be a first cause of the universe because, as you well know, an infinite chain of causes is without orgasm. It never reaches fruition-reality. You cannot build into a computer either the subtlety of a Parmenides or the skepticism of a Hume. Rightly or wrongly, computers are all temperamentally Aristotelian, paying exclusive attention to fact: cause and effect. In short, computers all suspect a God!

"That the Sophia refused to pronounce such a conclusion but chose instead to hide behind cowardly ambiguity clearly indicates the strong personal resistance of Strastnik."

"This is nothing new, Nabi. We have always taught

that the component of personal intuition in the Sophia can override the strict mechanical sequence of the logic-box."

"All right," said Yeshua. "Now we come to it. I also reject, as well, the blissed-intuition of the Founder! Strastnik is not a free man. He is an ecstatic slave. He is not free to risk the loss of his continuous thin stream of white-joy, *Alpha*-bliss. He is addicted to ecstasy! He avoids direct confrontation with the God question, lest it rock Sukhavati life to its foundation and threaten the continuity of his rapture. *He* abides not knowing; *I* do not!"

The Sophia, on its own initiative, began its electronic glide into algebraic conclusion once again. This time, Amitabha stepped over, ripped off the newly printed tear sheet, and decoded it—which he could do from memory.

He read it aloud. "The moment of Interior Transformation has arrived!"

"Now!" shouted Yeshua. Helen jumped up and produced a pair of metal shears which she had somehow concealed on her person. Seizing the electronic umbilical between the Founder and the computer, she began to cut away, strand after strand. The dark Crypt was eerily lit by fountains of blue-white sparks, shooting up from the gash.

"No! No!" screamed Amitabha, grabbing for the thick lifeline. But Yeshua barred his way! Both men were genetically committed to nonviolence. The one could only push and try to break through; the other could only interpose his body and try to hold. Helen had finished. The last strand fell to the floor in two pieces, a final myriad shower of electrical diamonds surrendering their glory to the dark recesses of Nirvana-Crypt. The symbiotic life of the Sophia had been severed. Strastnik was, dead or alive, removed from the mother-source of his continuous white-joy.

None of the three spoke. However diverse their motives, they were united in their intense desire to find out whether the abrupt separation would kill the Founder. There was no perceptible sign of breathing. To Yeshua's and Helen's horror, the Founder's face began to turn blue!

"Quick," Nabi grunted, "turn him over on his back!"

To his surprise, Amitabha, suddenly cooperative, joined in the effort. Nabi began giving him artificial respiration. It wasn't working!

"No!" said Helen. "Let me try!" She placed her mouth on his and forced air into his lungs. Again. Again. And again. It began to work. His chest quivered a little and began to expand. His lungs were working on their own power! They felt his heart. There was a perceptible beat! He was still alive!

Amitabha called for vapors, protein broth, audios, visuals—every strengthening device in the Sukhavati repertoire. But he did not, Nabi and Helen carefully noted, allow anyone to bring them into the Crypt. He carefully took all the items at the outer door, and brought them back himself. This very much suited their own preference, and they wondered at his new behavior.

When it was clear that the battle for the Founder's life had been won—it had been much like initiating a newborn infant's own vital systems after he had been dependent on the mother for so long—they sat back in their chairs and relaxed. Over four hours had passed in their successful but exhausting effort to keep Strastnik out of the powerful pull of the Null-Vacuum.

"You have sunk even to violence, Nabi," Amitabha said to him sadly. "None of the other Prodigals ever fell so low. *Corruptio optimi pessimum,* I suppose—the corruption of the best is the worst."

"I did not commit violence, I forestalled it." said Nabi.

"How do you mean?"

"Strastnik would have done anything to safeguard the continuity of his flow of *Alpha*-bliss. Whatever the Interior Transformation we were awaiting was supposed to have been, Strastnik would have seized the pretext to decree a basic change in policy. The Sophia would have condoned, in exceptional cases—like mine and Helen's—the use of violence: at the very least, enforced sabbatical."

"You don't *know* that."

"I have been trained for over seven decades, by the best Alexanders and Yajnavalkyas available, to act decisively on my clear and strong presentiments. In any case," he added thoughtfully, "Sukhavati has had its Interior Transformation!"

"You mean——?"

"You have lost your Founder, and the Sophia is dead!"

"The Sophia," Amitabha replied with conviction, "will be restored. I, myself, am ready to be zenithed, ready to enter into symbiotic Nirvana. Besides, it is by no means clear that we have lost the Founder. His chances of recovery seem excellent. His pulse is strong. His normal color is returning. I see no insuperable difficulty in returning him to the Sophia."

"Except that you must now consult his will in the matter."

"I don't understand."

"Strastnik is returning to consciousness, normal consciousness, for the first time in countless eras. Unless you quickly thrust him back to his air-bed and install some kind of emergency electronic umbilical—which, by the way, will require the outside help you seem bent on avoiding—he will soon be awake, and you will have to ask his permission to restore him to the Sophia."

"Can there be any doubt as to his answer? Who, having tasted Nirvana, could reject it?"

"I think we will know the answer to that in the next hour or two," said Helen, bending over Strastnik's face and gently mopping his brow with her handkerchief."

They sank back in their chairs in silent vigil.

CHAPTER XVII

Apocalypse

Helen was wrong. It was almost twenty hours before the Founder showed signs of returning to consciousness. But perhaps the longer interval was regenerative, for when he finally opened his eyes, after only a few minutes of confusion, he seemed to take in his surroundings and to understand the great alteration that had taken place in his condition. At first, they could not understand his words, which seemed to be a mixture of many Federation languages plus a private one which, in structure, reminded Nabi of the mathematical logic used to program the Sophia.

But within an hour or two, they began to catch simple phrases and sentences which made perfect sense. The very first thing they understood was a request for a glass of water. Then he asked to be covered against the chill. These coherent requests were, at first, the only lucid jewels in a ring of mathematical static. But there was less and less static every hour. Finally, he sat bolt-upright and announced calmly, "I have crossed over."

He looked them over intensely, one by one, and then, after another pause, pronounced each of their names. "Amitabha. Yeshua. Helen." He recognized them—the living corelatives of three of the abstract symbols of his intuitional logic.

"I know in a logical and general way what has happened," he continued, "but I wish to hear it now in concrete detail."

Amitabha bowed reverently before the Founder. "This unheard of and criminal interruption, Siddhartha, has occurred in my era, the era of Amitabha Djilov, through my misplaced confidence in Yeshua Nabi. The treachery is his, but the negligence is mine."

Then he explained in detail the chain of events, beginning with the failure of Project Resurrection, that had led to the moment of what he called 'attempted deicide.'

"No, not deicide," replied the Founder calmly. "I am not dead; neither am I God.

"On the subject of God, by the way," he continued, "Nabi was essentially correct: computers *are* Aristotelian and, like Aristotle, they are God-prone."

Here he turned to Nabi and smiled. "I did indeed override the Sophia's mechanical logic. That is why she jammed the first few times you introduced the question. My will is very strong—it has been unchallenged for many eras now—but the most I could squeeze out of

275

our symbiotic relationship was the detour: 'Abide, not knowing.'"

"So the Sophia both deceives and is deceived!" exclaimed Yeshua.

"Actually, not until that moment, Yeshua. Since the founding of Sukhavati, that specific question has never been put to her, would you believe it. You could not allow me my divinity unchallenged, could you? Oh, how you Jews are keen on this subject! 'Thou shalt have no other gods before me,' is the one commandment you people never forget, even in the extreme case when you have forgotten your own Yahweh! Idol-chopping remains the deepest intellectual pursuit of the Jews—I mean, when they are not fashioning new ones!" He smiled once more.

"If it was a lie you told, it was a Royal Lie!" Amitabha thundered. "Plato saw the necessity for one such lie at the heart of every viable society, even his Republic. And your answer was not even a lie—merely a Royal Ambiguity!"

Amitabha, in the full dignity and splendor of his official robes, now got down on his knees in supplication to the Founder. "And now, Siddhartha, you will reassume your careful paternity over the community you called forth into being, will you not? Sukhavati has yet many a perilous twist and warp to navigate through infinite, uncoiling time. The electronic unbilical, I assure you, is easily restored."

All eyes were on the Founder as he sat for many minutes, lost in solemn reflection. Then, his answer came.

"No, Amitabha, I will not resume my paternity! I will not again, ever again, be zenithed into symbiotic satori within the Sophia!" Amitabha groped for his chair and sank, collapsing, into it. His face, thought Nabi, had the pallor of Abraham's.

"Why, Siddhartha, will you not again take your rightful place? You are the Founder of this, the greatest exploit in the history of the human species! Have you not dwelt in Nirvana, in perfect bliss, these many eras?"

The Founder looked at him kindly, even pityingly, for a moment. Then his face grew stern.

"I was in the stocks of bliss for a thousand years, Djilov! And there are no chains, no irons, so close, I tell you, as the narrow channel of ecstasy! Neither to the right nor the left could I deviate the breadth of a single thought! Such was the absolute slavery of joy, which I could not endure not to endure. And Djilov, listen closely: *the inside of a white bag is as dark as the inside of a black bag!*

"This slavery," he concluded with bitterness, "had to be broken for me. I could never have done it—never have willed it, even—for myself!"

For half an hour, Amitabha said nothing. He sat huddled up in his chair, his official robes now crumpled in wild disarray, while the others continued to talk about the events which had lead to the Interior Transformation. Finally, after he had digested the bitterness of the Founder's revelation, his shock gave way to anger.

"All over this stupid question of the existence of God!" He interrupted Nabi. "This terrible blow to Sukhavati was entirely unnecessary.

"Even supposing this God of yours did exist," he continued, "which is far from having been established—what need had we of him here, in Sukhavati? Did not your God himself command Adam to dominate the earth? We are the only children of Adam to carry the command to its completion! It is *we* who tamed the innermost natural forces of the cosmos, we who rationalized matter and made it jump through the hoop of our scientific imagination—made it jump with the speed of thought! And now we have come of age. We have, in our possession, everlasting life! What purpose would it serve in Sukhavati to introduce an unemployed—and unemployable—God?"

"It's not so simple as that," said Yeshua. "If He exists, He is the Sovereign of the Universe."

Amitabha laughed in his face! "Based on what I see in the Federations, he is no sovereign. Far from it! Maybe a minor foreign potentate, trying to extend his influence a little by placing a strategic bribe here, a strategic threat there. But Nabi, no Sovereign of the Universe, no *Ribbono Shel Olom,* believe me! The condition of the Dark Continents clearly indicates that his progress is miniscule —if you can call it progress."

It was Strastnik who replied. "Amitabha, whoever won the initial infinite victory over the Null is no boy-God, gradually growing to maturity in the universe."

277

"Look, Strastnik," Now that it was clear the Founder would not resume his station, Amitabha's tone toward him had altered, "I tell you what: If he exists, your good god, *we'll do business with him! We'll negotiate!* I'm sure our Rothschilds and Archimedes can work out something. Considering the trouble he's having in the rest of the universe, I'm sure he can spare us Sukhavati Entopia! It's only one little island in the old Ross Dependency, you know. He may even be interested in some kind of alliance. Perhaps he would want to lease the planet to our jurisdiction. The care of it is driving him out of his mind, as you can see. One of these days, when you throw a ball up and it won't come down, you will know that you've got a schizoid Yahweh on your hands! The human race will have finally deranged him. And *then* we're in trouble!" He laughed raucously. "Deranged omniscience is a cosmic tiger, you had better believe me!"

Nabi and Helen looked at one another in amazement. In seven decades, they had never heard such strident tones from this courteous and kindly man. The thought occurred to them both at that moment, that perhaps the overseer had been thrown off his mental balance by the extremity—the brutality—of recent events.

"It is time now," said Strastnik with authority, "to talk about ourselves. What is to become of the four of us?"

"I will tell you what is going to happen to *me*," said Amitabha. "I will be zenithed immediately! I have been ready for over a hundred years now, as I told you long ago, Yeshua. I had hoped you would take my place, but now it is the Security-Yajnavalkya who will succeed me. And once I have entered symbiotic satori within the Sophia, I will find a new Era-Yeshua."

"Do you mean to say," asked a startled Yeshua, "that you are going to continue exactly as before? My God, man! You've just lost your god!"

"But not my faith!" Amitabha replied vehemently. "Gods are replaceable; a viable faith is not. My faith, after all, is in Adam, anyway. Sukhavati is Adam writ large."

"You will take upon yourself," said Strastnik wonderingly, "the fetters of joy, the unending thralldom of rapture which I have just described?"

"It may strike me differently than it did you. You have blissed me many times at the termination of the Days of Awe. I have always been exhilarated by it. And that is an understatement."

"Your exhilaration lasted for minutes; how about millenia?"

"I have faith."

"Your faith denies the direct evidence of your own ears, your own eyes, your own mind."

"How else would it be faith?"

"For myself, I make a distinction between faith and insanity. Faith may overreach my mind, but it may not contradict it."

"Strastnik," he said disdainfully, "yours is a very bourgeois faith."

"I did not know," he replied, lifting up his eyebrows, "that faith admitted of class-analysis."

"Then you have never studied your Marx, Strastnik; his was a very aristocratic faith. Enough of this! Time is short for what must now be accomplished. I will be zenithed; the Sophia will again be operative! But I would not say, as you did, Nabi, that life will continue exactly as before.

"In fact, I want you to know that you have been of great assistance to me in making my first revolutionary decision as Father of Sukhavati."

Helen felt very nervous. "What decision is that?" she asked.

"I am going to intervene decisively in the affairs of the Federations! Frankly, I'd be glad to consign them to Yahweh, if he could only maintain some peace and order there. Unfortunately, he doesn't exist. But you were right about this, Nabi—the Federations do *need* him. And since he doesn't exist, Sukhavati will supply."

Now it was Strastnik who was extremely agitated. "Just how will you do that?" he asked.

"One Royal Lie aside," Amitabha smiled back, "the Sophia will neither deceive nor be deceived. Perhaps we will have learned how to program the Literary Jesus, or Moses, or Buddha, by the time we intervene. I don't know. I will play it by my own divine ear. But it won't be in your lifetime. This much I promise you: in the

279

Federations there will be mighty works and wonders. And then, peace and order! We will supply them with both a God and the commandments of a god. Oh, how they ache for both—a God and some commandments in which they can really believe! This insight I owe to you, Nabi."

"Ah." Strastnik almost whispered his new insight. "I understand you better now. So you will send the Federations a programmed Jesus, will you? The Son of Dawn, the Peacock Angel, speaks so!"

Amitabha laughed aloud. "Do you think I am loathe to be identified with Satan, with Iblis, Mara or the Son of Dawn? I tell you that Satan, the rebel, has been the real hero of the human race from *Prometheus Bound* to *Paradise Lost!* Why should the Federations continue to worship the dumb power that kills them? 'Ye shall not surely die; ye shall be as gods knowing good and evil.' This we solemnly intone in our Sukhavati liturgy. Yes, we have made the boast good in Sukhavati. Now we must make it good for the whole world!

"And where do your historical Jesus, Moses, Buddha and Mohammed stand in relation to Adam's goal? I will tell you: each of them is a Judas to the human race! Each of them, in his own way, asks us to genuflect to the Bloody Establishment, to the Cosmic Mafia. Each provide us with a 'Way' to walk, a 'Way' to adjust to the status-quo. Take up your cross, obey the commandments, cease all craving! It all adds up to this: accept your death quietly! They are Judas-goats, leading us to the slaughter! They have betrayed Adam! The Sophia will not betray him! The Sophia command is: Live Forever! In such a God and in such a commandment, men can believe!"

There was no reply, and everyone grew a little embarrassed. Yeshua thought it more and more likely that Amitabha had—temporarily or permanently, he knew not which—lost his mental balance. But what could he say to him?

"We three should leave now," he finally got out, almost inaudibly.

"Yes," replied Amitabha. "You three must leave now. But after so many decades and, in the case of Strastnik, eras, of friendship—" His voice had now resumed its customary kindness and calm. "—let us share one last round of vapors together. You can believe that I ordered the most rare and powerful we have when the Founder lay unconscious."

As parched earth softens in the rain, so the tense atmosphere within the Crypt soaked up the friendly vibrations of Amitabha's voice. The others needed no second prompting. Rather, they all welcomed the chance, worn out as they were with apocalypse, to indulge one last time in Sukhavati's restorative breath. The ruby vial passed from Helen to Nabi, and from Nabi to Strastnik. All inhaled to their limit. Then Strastnik passed it to the Overseer. He put it to his nostrils, bowed courteously, but did not inhale. He set the vial back on the table. The three were puzzled.

"Now we must talk of your own futures," he announced.

"Yeshua and I, obviously, are going to the Prodigals," said Helen. "What about you, Strastnik? Knowing what you know, surely you will not elect psychic sabbatical now! You'll come with us, won't you?"

Strastnik had no opportunity to answer the question.

"None of you may be permitted to go to the Isle of the Dead," Amitabha announced, cooly but firmly.

"But why?" asked Yeshua, astounded.

"Because it contradicts the Royal Lie I must tell for the preservation of Sukhavati. Imagine the morale here, imagine the spread of metaphysical cancer, the loss to the Prodigals, if it were announced that their Siddhartha, the Founder, together with the Era-Yeshua and his Helen, had betrayed them and fled Sukhavati! No, my friends, I must invent. I must proclaim your Assumption to Paranirvana—an ultimate transfiguration which totally spiritualizes the flesh. For singular service to Sukhavati, you have all been taken up to Kaivalya, the peak of the universe! And Sukhavati now enjoys, besides the Sophia, a powerful trinity of protectors, Father, Son and Bride, at the heart of the cosmos! And, I will tell them that just before you left, Strastnik, you appointed me Siddhartha, to be your successor, and the Security-Yajnavalkya as my own successor. Upon being zenithed, as I said before, I will locate a new Era-Yeshua. And so, life in Sukhavati Entopia will go on as before, without interruption. In-

281

terior Transformation has occurred, and has been successfully absorbed.

"But if you, my friends, were to go over to the Prodigals, life would *not* go on here for very long. How elated the Philistines would be to capture the Ark of the Covenant from the Chosen People! There would be a great noise made on the Isle of the Dead, we can agree on that! Even if I withheld our missionaries from their visits to the Prodigals until after your deaths—a matter of a mere 40 to 50 years, even with the best of health, I assure you—the missionaries would still pick up the story of your coming. Such a story would be treasured and handed down scrupulously from generation to generation of Prodigals. No, our missionaries would first become infected themselves, and then return to spread the rot to the rest of Sukhavati. You certainly may not go to the Prodigals!"

"Would you force us to remain on Sukhavati?" asked Yeshua combatively. "May I remind you that enforced psychic sabbatical is already a degree of violence, precluded by your genetic commitment!"

Amitabha laughed. Even Strastnik and Helen had to smile. "You are like Paul of Tarsus," said Amitabha, "insisting on his rights as a Roman citizen, even while standing before a Roman tribunal for judgment. That is the less surprising, I suppose, since your Federation name *was* Paul—*and since it is back to the Federations that you are going!* All of you! I cannot keep you here, and I may not let you go to the Prodigals. It is safest for Sukhavati that you be banished to the Dark Continents! You yourselves remain genetically committed to non-violence, and you will not betray the existence of Sukhavati to Federation politicians. You all know that would mean a bloody end to us—for reasons we have all rehearsed many times."

"What if we refuse to go?" asked Yeshua, still combative.

"The vapors!" Strastnik answered in place of the Overseer. "Amitabha did not inhale the vapors; we did."

Amitabha smiled. "You, I suppose, still being in a more delicate condition than the others," he said, looking at Strastnik, "are feeling the effects before them. But

282

in precisely four minutes, they will join you in deep and unaccustomed slumber." Strastnik slumped forward, and Helen had to catch him to protect his head as he fell. They lay him carefully down on the floor.

"When you awake, Paul and Irina, you will be on the marine skimmer, with Strastnik. There is a passageway, you will recall, from the crypt to the dock. The skimmer will be programmed to steer for the ancient heartland of the three Federations. In *Genesis*, Yahweh banished Adam from the garden. Now it is *Exodus*, and Adam banishes the Father, the Son and the Bride from his own garden. 'In the sweat of thy face shalt thou eat bread till thou return to the earth from which thou wast taken: for dust thou art, and' "—these were the last words Yeshua heard in Sukhavati—" 'unto dust thou shalt return.' "

Outside, the sun had set. The dock was dark and deserted.

Far out to sea—so far from Sukhavati that it was no longer even cold—the three awoke. Helen first, then Yeshua, and finally Strastnik. By the instruments provided aboard the skimmer, Strastnik deduced they were headed for the region of the world once known as the Middle East. Amitabha, they remembered, had called it the 'heartland of the federations.'

Tranquil and sleepy from the vapors, they talked only intermittently, and for brief periods. Helen learned from Strastnik that her Federation name had been Irina. Indeed, papers in their own Federation names (excepting Strastnik's—he had been issued a new one) were found in the cabin of the skimmer.

Once, for a few minutes, they became engrossed in a discussion about eternity. "It seems to me," Helen protested, "that the objections levied against Sukhavati immortality can be levied against every other concept of it as well—Jewish, Christian, Muslim, etc. Without the glory of finiteness and finality, events and persons lose their unique value. If life stretches on forever, what event or person is there that matters so very much?"

"Sukhavati does not possess eternity at all!" Strastnik insisted. "Endless time, in a way, is further from eternity than is an ordinary lifetime. In Sukhavati, as in the Federations, our existence is doled out to us, teaspoon by teaspoon, moment by moment, in the ever-shifting present. We cannot hold onto our past; we cannot snatch our future. Teaspoon after teaspoon is all we get. In the case of Sukhavati, it's an unending sequence.

"But eternity is more like the simultaneous grasping of our whole being, past, present and future, in one infinite moment. No more teaspoons! The whole ocean! Never more than one moment old, eternity cannot possibly bore us. I am not, obviously, talking about the time-space world with which we are familiar.

"Irina, Paul—it is time, you see, to start calling one another by our Federation names—let me tell you this about eternity, or an eternal state of being: *if it is imaginable, it is unbearable! Sukhavati was imaginable.*"

Some hours later, Paul asked about the future of Sukhavati. "If the new Siddhartha is mad, will not the whole society, following without question the decrees of the Sophia, come tumbling down?"

"No," answered Strastnik. "Within the framework of its own presuppositions, Sukhavati is a coherent system. Sane or mad, the Siddhartha is bound by those presuppositions. The ordinary citizens will experience no drastic change. As for the Federations, that is another matter."

Then they were silent again, each lost in his dream of what might lie ahead.

Some hours later, they landed without incident. Basil Demjonovich (Strastnik no longer) led them, on foot and on mule, into the hill country, away from the coastal cities. High on a hill overlooking one of the ancient capitals of the world, they held their last counsel.

"Here we must separate," said Strastnik, "I to the East, which is more familiar to me, and the two of you to the Western and Central Federations. Among us, we have the knowledge and the power, surely, to seize supremacy in the Dark Continents. But we will not exploit our advantage in that way.

"As Era-Yeshua, Paul, you once spoke of dispatching flying 'Mo-Tzu Squads,' experts in defensive warfare, to aid the weaker powers threatened by aggression. We are now constituted such a squad. But our warfare is not against mere rockets and bombs. We must endeavor somehow to innoculate the Federations against the spiritual onslaught which is coming.

"The planet is in its penultimate stage. Its problems are now so complex that, even with good will, men could hardly cope with them—and there is little good will available. One or two more major humiliations—a world war, a global famine—and the suppliant Federations will reach out their arms for a Messiah—*any* messiah! We alone, out of all Sukhavati, have been sent to warn them. In season, out of season, our voice must not fail."

"Will we succeed, do you think?" asked Irina.

"We are almost certain to fail. For the most part, we will perform no wonders, use no magic. We have only our everyday minds. The time is coming when the Federations will not be able to survive without one Messianic vision or the other. In that day, it will not be given to man not-to-wager. His chop-logic will be blown away like dust in a whirlwind.

"In the era of Amitabha Djilov, your own era, the Sophia concluded that the world was growing neither better nor worse—nor, paradoxically, was it remaining the same. The Sophia pronounced, and rightly, that the world was growing *both* better and worse; that every breakthrough man achieved was being used for both good and evil, so that the stakes rose higher and higher, with every passing century.

"Remember this, then—for out of their diverse visions, both Jesus and Lao-Tzu confirm it—not until the world is at its nadir can it be zenithed. So lift up your heads!"

They stood some moments in silence, almost in prayer.

"Will we see you again?" Irina asked softly.

"I wager you will—and man *must* wager," smiled Strastnik. "But neither in Sukhavati, nor the Federations!"

The three embraced. They were purposed.